"But I am a man!" shouted Davis.

"If he's a Man," cried a voice in the crowd, "where's his comb and wattles?"

Another girl trod forth. "Please, ma'am, I have an idea."

The Old Udall smiled at her. "Yes, Elinor?"

"It says it is a Man," Elinor waggled her lashes at Davis. "Let it prove it."

"How?" demanded Davis eagerly.

"Fertilize the corporal."

Barbara stepped back, white-faced. "No!" she gasped.

"Why, think of the honor, dear Babs," purred Elinor. "The first woman in three hundred years to have a child by a living Man. Or are you afraid?"

Davis saw Barbara flush red. She knotted her fists and closed her eyes. After a very long moment, she opened them again and looked squarely at him with an air of having but one life to give for her country.

"Yes," she said defiantly. "You may fertilize me, Davis—if you can!"

BAEN BOOKS by POUL ANDERSON

Virgin Planet
Fire Time
Inconstant Star
Three Hearts & Three Lions
Hoka! Hoka! Hoka!
(with Gordon R. Dickson)
Hokas Pokas!
(with Gordon R. Dickson)

VIRGIN PLANET

PLANET

AND STAR WAYS

POUL ANDERSON

A Baen Book Omnibus

Baen Publishing Enterprises
P.O. Box 1403
Riverdale, NY 10471
www.baen.com

ISBN: 0-671-31944-2

Cover art by Clyde Caldwell

First Baen printing in this edition, September 2000

Distributed by Simon & Schuster
1230 Avenue of the Americas
New York, NY 10020

Production by Windhaven Press, Auburn, NH
Printed in the United States of America

contents

VIRGIN
PLANET
AND STAR WAYS

VIRGIN PLANET

CHAPTER I

Corporal Maiden Barbara Whitley of Freetoon, hereditary huntress, wing leader of the crossbow cavalry and novice in the Mysteries, halted her orsper and peered through a screen of brush. Breath sucked sharply between her teeth.

She had come down the wooded mountain slope by a route circling south of town. The forest ended before her, as cleanly as if an axe had cut it, and the hills rolled away in a blaze of green and of red firestalk blossoms, down to the wide valley floor. Behind her and on either side the Ridge lifted, bending toward the north to form a remote blue wall; she could just see the snow on those peaks and the thin smoke of a volcano. Ahead, nearly on the horizon, was a line of trees and a metallic flash beneath low suns, telling where the Holy River poured into the sea.

Tall white clouds walked in a windy sky. At this

3

time of day and year, when midsummer approached, both suns were visible. The first, Ay, was a spark so bright it hurt the eyes, sinking down the western heaven; the second, Bee, was a great gold blaze ahead of Ay, close to the edge of her world. Minos was waxing, huge and banded, in its eternal station a little south of the zenith. The moon Ariadne was a pale half-disc, shuttling swiftly away from the planet. By daylight the inmost moon Aegeus, tiny hurried starpoint, was not visible . . . but the six hours of night to come would be light.

It was on the thing in the valley, five kilometers away where the foothills ended, that Barbara Whitley focused her gaze.

The thing stood upright, aflash with steel pride, like a lean war-dart, though it lacked fins. As a huntress and arbalester, the corporal was necessarily a good judge of spatial relationships, and she estimated its height as forty meters.

That was much smaller than the Ship of Father. But it was nearly the same shape if the hints dropped by initiates were truthful. And it *must* have come from the sky.

A chill went along her nerves. She was not especially pious: none of the Whitleys were, and keeping them out of trouble had been one reason or making them all huntresses in peacetime. But this was Mystery. They had always said it; they sang it in the rituals, and they told it to children on rainy nights when the fires leaped high on the barrack hearths . . .

Some day the Men will come to claim us.

The orsper shifted clawed feet and gurgled impatiently. The creak of leather and jingle of iron seemed thunder-loud to Barbara Whitley. "Father damn you, hold still!" she muttered, and realized with a shudder that her habit of careless profanity might call down wrath from the Men.

If this was the Men.

She could not see any movement about the dart thing. It rested quiet in the valley, and the stillness of it was somehow the most unnerving of all. When a gust of wind rustled the leaves above her, Barbara started and felt sweat cold under the leather cuirass.

Her hand strayed to the horn slung at her waist.

She could call the others. When the shining object had been seen descending this morning, with none who could tell what it was or just where it had landed, Claudia, the Old Udall, had sent out the whole army to search. She, Barbara, had chanced to be the one who found it. (Or was there such a thing as chance where the Men were concerned? Or was this a ship of the Men at all?) There must be others within earshot, perhaps already watching.

The Old Udall had given no specific orders. That was unlike her, but this was too unprecedented. There was, to be sure, an implication that the first scout to locate the unknown should report back immediately, but . . .

This might be a vessel of the Monsters. The Monsters were half folk-tale; it was said that they lived on the stars, and Men had dealings with them— sometimes friendly, sometimes otherwise.

A stray lock of rusty-red hair blew out from under Barbara's helmet and tickled her nose. She sneezed. It seemed to crystallize something in her.

Now that she thought about it, there must be Monsters in that ship, if it was a ship. The Men would arrive much more portentously, landing first at the Ship of Father and then at the various towns. And there would be haloes and such-like about them and creatures of metal in attendance . . . well, there ought to be. And prodigies—didn't the Song of Barbara One-Eye, in speaking of her own ancestress and the raid on Highbridge, say: "And Minos shall dance in the sky when the Men pass by?"

It wasn't a canonical epic, but it dealt with a Whitley, so it must hold more truth than the Udalls and the Doctors would admit. They were a lot of old hags anyway.

Corporal Barbara Whitley was rather frightened at the idea of Monsters—she felt her heart thump beneath the iron breastshields—but they *were* less awesome than Men. If she went meekly back to town, she knew exactly how Claudia Udall would take charge in her own important way. The army would be gathered and move according to tactics which were, well, simply *rotten*, like the time when it had been led directly into a Greendale ambush. And a mere corporal, even a wing leader, would be just nobody.

Barbara had never needed much time to reach her own decisions. She checked her equipment with rapid, professional care. The cuirass was on tight and the kilt-strips covered her thighs to the knee; below them, boots protected the calves and feet. Her morion was secure on her head, and the blue cloak firmly pinned. The axe at her saddle had been sharpened only yesterday; her dagger was keen and her lasso oiled. She cocked the repeating crossbow and tucked it in the crook of her left arm. Her right hand lifted the reins, and she clucked to the orsper.

It trotted forward, out of the woods and into the open, down the hill at the swift rocking pace of its breed. The blue-and-white feathers lay sleek and the great head, beaked and crested, with fierce yellow eyes, was sternly lifted. Barbara hoped she wouldn't have trouble—the orspers were brave enough when they understood conditions, but apt to squawk and run when something new appeared.

"Well, my girl," she said to herself, "here we go and Father knows what'll happen. I do hope it's only a crew of friendly Monsters." The Whitleys all had a way of speaking their thoughts aloud, another reason why they belonged to the noncom caste. A town chief or officer had to be more discreet.

The wind blew in her face, murmuring of the sea and the Ship whence it came. The sun Bee was almost in her eyes, so she began a circling movement to approach the dart-thing from the west. She imagined a hundred scouts watching her in admiration from the forest. But her fellow Whitley couldn't be among them—obviously—otherwise she'd be riding right along with her. A good thing, too! That little bitch Valeria already had too much unearned credit.

Still no motion from the object—not a sound, not a stirring. Barbara grew quite convinced that there were Monsters aboard. Men would have come out long ago. And she could talk to a Monster—or fight it—at the worst, be killed by a thunderbolt, or whatever they used for weapons. Monsters had unknown powers, but they were still of this universe. Whereas Men . . .

Barbara had never thought a great deal about the Men. The songs and sayings she had had to learn had gone smoothly across her tongue without really penetrating her brain. "The Men are the males of the human race. We were coming to join the Men, but the Ship went astray because of our sins. The Men are taller and stronger than we, infinitely wiser and more virtuous, and they have hair on their chins and no breasts. . . ." She realized now that she had always vaguely thought of a Man as being like a very big woman, in fact, like her dimly remembered mother.

Once, when they were all little girls, Elinor Dyckman had tried to draw a picture of a Man, breastless and with hair on his face. The Dyckmans drew well, but the picture had been so silly that Barbara had broken into giggles.

Now, as she rode toward the ship, the memory

returned and another unholy fit of humor came on
her. She was laughing aloud, above all the tension
and wariness, as she reached the vessel.

"Hoy, there!"

She cried it forth, and heard her voice faintly
shivered back from polished metal. No answer. A flock
of gray rangers went overhead, calling to each other,
incredibly unconcerned.

"Hoy! Corporal Maiden Barbara Whitley of Freetoon
speaking! I come in peace. Let me in!"

The ship remained smugly silent. Barbara rode
around it several times. There was a circular door in
the hull, out of her reach and smoothly closed. She
yelled herself hoarse, but there was not a word of
reply, not a face in any of the blank ports.

Really, it was too much to bear!

She whipped the crossbow to her shoulder and
fired a bolt at the door. The missile clanged off; it
left no mark. The orsper skittered nervously, fluttering
useless wings. For a moment Barbara was afraid of
death in reply, but nothing happened.

"Let me in!" she screamed.

Now she was in a fuming temper. She loosed
another futile bolt and blew her horn as loud as she
could. A runner started from the long grass and
dashed toward the river, its tail feathers wagging
ridiculously. Barbara shot at it—a miss, and at such
a range.

No wonder the stories said never trust a Monster!

Bee was very low now, the western clouds turning saffron and shadows marching across the valley.
Ay was still high, but Ariadne had moved and Minos
grown noticeably fuller. Streaks of mist floated above
the forests of the eastern mountains.

The startled screech of the orsper jerked Barbara
back to reality. There was someone running from the
west.

Barbara could not see the person very well . . . yes,

it had human form, it was not a Monster. On the other hand, it was not dressed like any townswoman she had ever heard of. It wore some kind of tunic; the legs were sheathed in cloth; there was a small packsack on the shoulders, and . . .

She spurred the orsper forward. "Hoy-aaah!" she called. "What in the name of ruin are *you* doing here?"

The stranger stopped. Barbara got near enough to see that it was a remarkably ugly person. The broad shoulders were not unpleasing, but the hips were grotesquely narrow. There was yellow hair cropped short, and a lean face with too much nose and chin, altogether too much bone and too little flesh.

Father! Maybe it *was* a Monster!

Thoughts runneled through her head as she dashed toward the being. It was certainly no member of any town, any family—she knew what all the five hundred families looked like, and while some were homely enough, none were so bad. Nor did any townsfolk on this side of Smoky Pass dress in that fashion. And it was approaching the ship . . . must have been looking around outside when she came, yes, that copse would have hidden it from her—and it was *deformed!*

She remembered from the old stories that Monsters had many shapes but some of them looked like deformed humans.

A single Monster!

Squinting into the sun-glare, Barbara saw that it had drawn something from a holster. A small tube, clutched in one hand and aimed at her . . . She whirled around to get the sun out of her eyes and saw that the crimson tunic was open at the neck, the chest was flat and hairy and there was thick hair on the arms . . .

Then she hardly had time to think. The Monster might or might not be peaceful. She couldn't simply down it with a crossbow bolt. At the same time, she wasn't going to be shot down herself like a sillyhead on its nest.

She released her grip on the bow and let it swing free from its shoulder strap. Her knees guided the leaping orsper and her hands whirled up the lariat.

The Monster stood there gaping. Its weapon tried to follow her skilled movements, the jumps and dashes meant to throw off an enemy aim. It took a deep breath and she heard words of her own language, but distorted, alien: "Cosmos in All, what's going on here?"

Then the lasso snaked out and fell around its body. The orsper sprang away, rope whirred through the hondo and the noose pinned arms to side.

Corporal Maiden Barbara Whitley galloped in triumph toward Freetoon, dragging the Monster behind her.

CHAPTER II

The episode had begun a couple of weeks earlier, and nearly two hundred light-years away.

All aglisten in fashionable tunic and culottes, boots polished to bedazzlement, Davis Bertram vaulted up the steps of the Coordination Service building. The morning sparkled around him and the raw ugliness of a new city on a new planet seemed only a boisterous good cheer. The door opened for him; he patted it kindly and strode into the lobby. His soles clashed on the floor and his whistling resounded in the corridors.

Smith Hilary was making feeble attempts to get information from the desk robot. He gave Davis a bloodshot look and said something about mutants with lead-lined stomachs and no soul at all.

"Merely virtuous living, and high thinking," said Davis Bertram. "Have you tried aneurine?"

"I've tried every pain killer known to human and

11

nonhuman science," groaned Smith. "But after last night—*what* were we drinking?"

Davis warbled a popular song in reply.

"I hope the gobblies get you," said Smith. With a bleary malice: "Are you sure you can stand a month in space all by yourself?"

"No," admitted Davis blandly. "But then, I don't expect to. I expect to discover a planet full of beautiful women and stay for years. Is the Cosmic All at home?"

"The office opened an hour ago," said Smith. "If he didn't arrive on the dot, there must have been a supernova to stop him. Go away. I hope he eats you."

Davis threw him his beret and went on down the hall. A thousand light-years from Sol, on the edge of the known and settled by humans for barely two generations, Nerthus was the local Cordy headquarters, and you had to get clearance from them. A stellagraphic voyage meant the chief's personal okay.

The door identified him and opened. Coordinator Yamagata Tetsuo occupied a large office, with a full-wall transparency to show him the spires of Stellamont and the plains beyond. He nodded curtly, a man grown bleak in a lifetime's war against the universe. "Sit down, Citizen," he invited. "You're two days overdue."

"I was in bed all the time. Quite a high temperature."

Yamagata gave him a sharp look. There was always the danger of a new disease on a new planet. "What diagnosis?" he snapped.

"Nothing reportable, sir," said Davis meekly. As a matter of fact, the organism responsible was 1.6 meters tall, with blue eyes and a high center of gravity, but he saw no reason to mention that.

"Well . . ." The gaunt face remained expressionless. Yamagata pressed a stud and asked the info-master for the Davis file. The machine grumbled to itself and spat the papers up onto the desk. The Coordinator riffled them with thin fingers while Davis fidgeted.

"Yes, I remember now. You were educated on Earth." The old man's eyes went outward, toward the sky, as if he would pierce its blinding blue and look across a thousand light-years to an unforgotten home. "Moved to Thunderhouse for astronautical training. Why?"

A flush crossed Davis' lean, somewhat too sharp features. He was a tall blond young man—a rare sight these days—with an athletic slenderness of which he was well aware. "I wanted to, uh, see a different planet. I'd only been in two systems, Sigma Hominis Volantis where I was born and then Sol. Variety— stimulus . . ."

"Hm. The Earth academy is the strictest in the known Galaxy, and Thunderhouse's is notoriously slack. Well, I'm afraid that's technically none of my business. You have just been licensed for independent operation and you want to make a survey based on Nerthus. Your own spaceship, I see."

Davis shrugged. Even nowadays, a personal fortune meant something. A chap whose father had made a good thing of it wasn't necessarily a wastrel, was he? Davis had never liked Earth much; he considered it a stodgy planet. Too bad Earth dominated the Union.

"I have no right to stop you," said Yamagata in a sour voice. "Not on the basis of this file. But a one-man expedition into deep space—one man with almost no practical experience— Look, there's a stellagraphic survey planned for the Fishbowl Cluster. Leaves in three weeks. Excellent crew, and the skipper is Hamilton himself. I could probably get you a berth."

"No, thanks," said Davis.

"But why do you want to go to Delta Wolf's Head?

Of all the lunatic . . . You *know* there's a vortex in that area. That's precisely why it's never been visited."

The eagerness burst from Davis: "Then anything might be in there!"

"Including your own death. We can't send rescue parties, you know. Space is too big—they'd never find you. Nor do we have personnel to throw away."

"I've got a Mark XX cruiser, sir. Armed, robotic, it does everything but think."

"That's supposed to be your function."

"I know why you're worried, sir," said Davis. "You don't like these unsupervised expeditions because they're apt to be bad for any natives. If you look at my psychograph, you will see a high goodwill quotient. *I'm* not going to rob or murder anybody."

Yamagata shook his head impatiently. "All right, all right. Let's discuss your orbital plan."

It was simple. The vortex, an unusually big one, had made a region fifty light-years across unsafe for as long as men had been around here: almost six decades now. It was finally withdrawing from the area of the star Delta Capitis Lupi. The Service intended to explore that double sun in another two or three decades, when there would be no chance of disaster. They ran enough risks in the ordinary line of work without taking on even the smallest additional hazard. But as of this moment, the star could *probably* be reached. Davis planned to go there, make the standard preliminary survey of its planets, and return.

If there were intelligent natives, or an uninhabited world suitable for colonization, Davis' Star would become a very proud blazon in the Pilot's Manual. If not, he had only lost a few weeks.

Looking at the young man across the desk, Yamagata sighed and wondered if Columbus had been such a headlong idiot.

"Very well," he snapped. "If you do not return,

Citizen Davis, we'll have to assume the vortex got you after all."

"Or the natives."

"Doubtful. We know very well there is no race with atomic energy in that system. Our neutrino detectors would have spotted it long ago if there were. I presume you can handle primitives, and know the rules against getting too rough with them."

Davis nodded, a little sulkily. He had had vague notions about being the great white god to a grateful folk with tails and antennae . . . adolescent daydreams, of course; culture patterns deserved protection, could not be upset overnight without grave damage.

It would be enough to make the trip. If he did find an important planet—there was that girl over in the Jupiter Valley, and the glamor of a discoverer . . .

Yamagata stood up. "Good luck, Citizen," he said formally.

Davis bowed and went out. Yamagata heard him whistling as soon as he was in the corridor.

Presently Smith entered, to make a routine inquiry. He was a strictly interplanetary freightman, dealing with Hertha, the next world sunward. Yamagata stopped him. "You know that fellow Davis," he said. It was not a question.

"Yes. Uh, matter of fact, Coordinator, I was out on the town with him last night."

"Rich man's son." Yamagata stared through the wall. "Odd how things happen all over again on the frontier, isn't it? Phenomena like cities and private ostentation, that Earth outgrew a long time ago. Sometimes I wish only Solarians could be licensed to pilot spacecraft. The people who emigrated were those who didn't like the restraints of being civilized."

Smith waited, awkwardly.

"What do you think the boy's chances are?" asked Yamagata.

"Eh? Oh . . . pretty fair, I'd say. He's a natural-born

pilot, has a good mind when he cares to use it. And he's got a fireball of a ship."

"He'll have to have a lot knocked out of him," said Yamagata. "I hope the process isn't fatal."

CHAPTER III

The *At Venture* lifted noiselessly on gravity beams, and the sky darkened and Nerthus became a great cloudy shield in a cold magnificence of stars. Davis Bertram let the autopilot do the work, plotting a course and steering it, and didn't bother to check the data. The robots were always right—almost always. He sat watching Carsten's Star dwindle and felt the loneliness close in.

At the appropriate distance, the ship went into hyperdrive and outpaced light, reaching for the Wolf's Head constellation. It would be about ten days to his goal.

He had intended to study advanced astrogational theory on the way. The tapes were there, and nothing to distract him; he couldn't even tune in a radio any more. But there was also a supply of stereofilms, and he might as well relax.

One of them looked interesting: *Murder Strikes*

Twice. But it was from Earth, and turned out to be a symbolic verse drama in the ancient, rigidly stylized form of the Retribution. Davis swore and opened another spool.

On the third day he started his textbook work, and wrestled with the first problem given him for a good two hours. It was fun to start, but when he couldn't solve it he knocked off for a beer and somehow never got back to it. After all, he had a hundred and fifty years ahead of him, if the vortex didn't grab him off.

Conscientiously every watch, he set the internal field at two gravities and went through a routine of calisthenics. It bored him stiff, it always had, but a body in good trim was an asset.

Who had ever begun the idea that spacefaring was one long wild adventure?

Davis had spent enough time in flight, including the cruises of cadet days, to know how empty the hours could become. But he had always vaguely assumed that on *his* ship it would be different.

He broke out his paints and brushes, set up a canvas, and started a portrait of Doris from memory. The art courses in the Earth schools had been among the few he really enjoyed. The academy on Thunderhouse had a mural of his in the messhall, a view from the inner moon.

It took him only a few hours to discover that painting a portrait of Doris from memory was a mistake. She had an interesting face, but the rest of her had been still more interesting. Davis suddenly realized he had spent nearly a whole watch period in reminiscences. He looked at the charcoal sketch he had made almost without thinking, blushed, and wiped his canvas clean. Too bad Doris wasn't here to pose. Only then he wouldn't be getting much painting done either. He recalled various psychopedagogues in his boyhood who had told him he must always be firm and upright, and brought his mind to heel. When

he got back, rich and famous, there would be time
enough for gynecological studies. Meanwhile, he'd
better do something neutral, like a landscape.

Space itself, with no planets in view, nothing but
a million unwinking stars and the great curdled rush
of the Milky Way and the far cold coils of the
galaxies . . . could not be painted. He was honest
enough with himself to realize that.

On the eighth Earth-day, a frantic buzzing and a
seasick quiver brought him out of his bunk, blind with
panic. He had touched the vortex.

It wasn't close enough to matter. The thing was
behind him in seconds. But he needed a depressor
pill to stop shaking.

Uneasily, he looked up trepidation vortices in the
Manual. It taught him nothing he didn't already know.
For some little understood reason, there were traveling sections where the geometry of the continuum
was distorted. The primary effect was that of violently
shifting gravitational fields, and a big one could dis-
turb a planet sufficiently to make the rotation period
fluctuate by a few seconds. A spaceship on hyperdrive,
its discontinuous psi functions meshing with those of
the vortex, could be ripped to pieces—or flung a
thousand 'light-years off course.

Space was unthinkably enormous. Even the largest vortex was not likely to encounter a ship by
chance. But there had been vessels in the past, before
the storms were known to exist, which had simply
disappeared. There were suns and clusters today,
interdicted because a vortex was in the neighborhood.

Well . . . this one hadn't hurt him. And it had saved
Delta Capitis Lupi for his personal exploration!

CHAPTER IV

Minos was full, drenching Freetoon with cold amber
light, and the air had grown chill. Barbara Whitley
walked through silent streets, between darkened
buildings, to the cavalry barrack. It formed one side
of a square around a courtyard, the stables and arsenal
completing the ring. Her boots thudded on the
cobbles as she led her orsper to its stall.

A stone lamp on a shelf gave dim light, and the
snoring grooms—all Nicholsons, a stupid family used
only for menial work—stirred uneasily on the straw
when she tramped in. She nudged one of the stocky,
tangle-haired women awake with her toe. "Food," she
demanded. "And water for the bird. Beer for me."

"At this hour?" grumbled the Nicholson. "I know
my rights, I do. You soldiers think you can barge in
at all hours, when honest folk is asleep after a hard
day's work, and—" Barbara smiled, drew her dagger,
and felt its edge in an absent-minded way—"oh, very
well, very well, ma'am."

Afterward Barbara undressed and washed herself in the courtyard trough. Not all the girls were so finicky, but she was a Whitley and had appearances to keep up. She regarded her face complacently in the water. The Minos-light distorted colors, ruddy hair and long green eyes became something else, but the freckled snub nose and the wide mouth and the small square chin were more pleasing than . . . oh, than that Dyckman build, supposed to be so female. The Dyckmans were just *sloppy*. Barbara hugged her own wide shoulders, ran hands over firm young breasts, down supple flanks and legs. She wasn't too thin, she reassured herself a little anxiously. Except around the high cheekbones, she hadn't an angle which wasn't properly rounded off. She shivered as the wind dried her skin, picked up her clothes and departed.

The dying hearthfire within the barrack led her to her place. She threaded a way between long-limbed forms sprawled on straw ticks, hung her harness on its peg and stowed her weapons in their chest, trying to be quiet. But Whitleys were light sleepers, and her cousin Valeria woke up.

"Oh, it's you. Two left feet as always," snarled Valeria, "and each one bigger than the other. Where did you park your fat rump all day?"

Barbara looked at the face which mirrored her own. They were the only Whitleys in Freetoon, their mothers and aunts died in the Greendale ambush fifteen years ago, and they should have been as close as cousins normally were. But theirs was a trigger-tempered breed, and when a new wing leader corporal was required, the sacred dice had chosen Barbara. Valeria could not forgive that.

"I took my two left feet and my fat rump—if you *must* describe yourself that way—into the valley and captured a Monster in a star ship," said Barbara sweetly. "Good night." She lay down on her pallet and closed her eyes.

But not long. Bee had not even risen when there was a clank of metal in the doorway and Ginny Latvala of the Udall bodyguard shouted: "Up, Corporal Maiden Barbara Whitley! You're wanted at the Big House."

"Do you have to wake everyone else on that account?" snapped Valeria, but not very loud. The entire company had been roused, and Captain Kim Trevor was a martinet.

Barbara got to her feet, feeling her heart knock. Yesterday seemed somehow unreal, like a wild dream . . .

Ginny leaned on her spear, waiting. "The Old Udall is pretty mad at you, dear," she confided. "We may have all sorts of trouble coming because you roped that Monster. Suppose it gets angry? Suppose it has friends?" The Latvalas were slim blonde girls, handy with a javelin and so made hereditary guards in most towns. They were pleasant enough, but inclined to snobbishness.

"I have my rights," said Barbara huffily. "All the scouts got their orders before witnesses, and I was never ordered *not* to lasso a Monster."

She let the barrack buzz around her while she dressed for the occasion: a short white skirt, an embroidered green cloak, sandals, and dagger. Nobody outside the Big House, except the few troopers she had met who helped her bring the Monster home, knew what had happened. Yet! Barbara and Ginny agreed silently that it would be good for their souls to wonder a while.

The air was still cold and the fields below the town white with mist when she came out. A pale rosy light lifted above the eastern Ridge, and Minos was waning. The moon Theseus was a wan red sickle caught in the sunrise.

There were not many people up. A patrol tramped past Barbara and Ginny in full harness, all of them

husky Macklins, and the farmhand caste yawned out
of their barracks on the way to a day's hoeing. The
street climbed steeply upward from the cavalry house,
and Barbara took it with a mountaineer's long slow
stride, too worried to heed Ginny's chatter. They went
past the weavery; she glimpsed looms and spinning
wheels within the door, but it didn't register on her
mind—low-caste work. The smithy, a highly respected
shop, lay beyond, also empty; the Holloways still slept
in their adjoining home.

Sickbay was not on this street, but the maternity
hospital was, on the other side of the broad plaza.
Hard by it were the nurseries. Both stood just under
the walls of the Big House, so the children could be
moved into its shelter first in case of attack.

Passing the shuttered window of one of the rooms
into which the nurseries were divided, Barbara heard
a small wail. It grew, angrily, and then stopped.

The sound broke through her worry with an odd
little tug at her soul. In another year or so, she would
be an initiate, and make the journey to the Ship. And
when she came back, no longer called Maiden, there
would be another redhaired Whitley beneath her
heart. Babies were a nuisance, in a way; she'd have
to stay within town till hers was weaned, and—and—
it was hard to wait.

The stockade bulked above her, great sharp stakes
lashed together and six Latvalas on guard at the gate.
They dipped their spears and Barbara went through.

Inside, there was a broad cobbled yard with several
buildings neatly arrayed: barracks, stables, storehouses,
emergency shelters, the Father chapel. All were in the
normal Freetoon style, long log houses with peaked
sod roofs and a fireplace at one end. The hall, in the
middle, was much the same, but immensely bigger, its
beam ends carved into birds of prey.

Henrietta Udall stood at its door. She was the
oldest of Claudia's three daughters: big and blocky,

with harsh black hair, small pale eyes under tufted brows. The finery of embroidered skirt and feather cloak was wasted on her, Barbara thought, and the axe she carried didn't help matters much. None of the Udalls could ever be handsome. But they could lead!

"Halt!"

Barbara came to a stop, spread her hands and lowered her head.

"Your hair is a mess," said Henrietta. "Do those braids over."

"But your mother wants to see me now," protested Barbara.

Henrietta hefted her axe. Ginny looked uneasy. "You heard me."

Barbara bit her lip and began uncoiling the bronze mane. It was hacked off just below her shoulders.

Spiteful blowhard, she thought. *Wants to get me in trouble. Come the day, Henrietta, and you won't find me on your side.*

The death of an Udall was always the signal for turmoil. Theoretically, the power went to her oldest daughter. In practice, the sisters were as likely as not to fight it out between themselves; a defeated survivor fled into the wilderness with her followers and tried to start a new settlement. Freetoon was old, almost a hundred years, and had already begotten Newburh. Now the population was up again to nearly eight thousand, about as many as the arable land within a safe distance could support.

Daydreams of heading into unknown country for a fresh start drove the sulkiness from Barbara. If, say, she rose high in the favor of Gertrude or Anne ... she might become more than a noncom, and her daughters would inherit the higher caste, and . . .

"Hurry it up! The Old Udall is waiting."

Barbara used some choice cavalry language under her breath. The chance of reaching her dream was

very little, after all. Whitleys just weren't politicians.
It wasn't worth it.

"All right," said Henrietta as Bee rose. She led the
way inside. Barbara followed, her face still hot.

The main room of the Big House was long, and
despite the fire and the opened windows and the
bright tapestries it was gloomy. Sconced torches
guttered above the Old Udall's seat, and the conifer
boughs strewn on the dirt floor rustled as Barbara
walked over them. Servants scurried around, ignored
by the middle-aged, high-caste women seated on the
bench below the throne. They were having breakfast,
gnawing the drumsticks of runners and tossing the
bones to the aquils which swooped from the rafters.

"Well!" said Claudia. "It took you long enough."

Barbara had learned the hard way never to blame
an Udall for anything. "I'm sorry, ma'am," she muttered. It was an effort to get the words out and to
bend the knee.

The Old Udall finished a bone and snapped her
fingers. While an adolescent Craig ran up with a
wooden plate of choice pieces, she leaned back and
let her chambermaid comb the stiff gray hair.

Elinor Dyckman had gotten that job. The Dyckmans
were good at flattery. There weren't many of them in
any town; they had small mother instinct and neglected
their children, so that the youngsters often died. But
they were said to be shrewd advisers. Certainly they
did well enough for themselves. A Dyckman nearly
always became the lover of someone influential; Elinor
had latched onto Claudia herself. Barbara's scornful
reflection, *I wouldn't be a parasite like that,* was tinged
with wistfulness. No Whitley ever had a sweetheart.
Their breed was too independent and uncompromising—or too huffy, if you wanted a more common
description of them.

Elinor was in her middle twenties; her own baby
was dead and she hadn't asked for another. She was

medium tall, with a soft curving body and soft bluish-black hair. Her small heart-shaped face smiled sweetly on the chief, and she combed with long slow strokes.

"You'll have to be punished for that," said the Old Udall. "Suggestions, Elinor dear?" She laughed.

Elinor blinked incredible lashes over melting dark eyes and said: "Not too severe, ma'am. Babs means well. A little KP ought to . . ."

Barbara's hand fell to her dagger. "I'm in the army, you milk-livered trull!"

"Watch your language," said the Counselor Marian Burke, white-haired and rheumatic.

Barbara stamped her foot. Since she wasn't wearing boots, it hurt, and tears stung her eyes. "Ma'am, you know the law," she said thickly. "If I'm to be so disgraced—*dishwashing*, by Father!—I demand a courtmartial."

"You'll demand nothing!" snapped Claudia.

Elinor smiled and went on combing. "It was only a joke," she murmured. "Hadn't we better get down to business?"

The Old Udall gazed at Barbara. *Trying to stare me down, are you?* thought the girl savagely. She would not look away. There was a silence that stretched.

Then an aquil stooped, to snatch a piece of meat off the table, and the serving girls screamed indignantly. Claudia chuckled. "Enough," she said. "Yes, Elinor, you're right as usual, we can't stop to quarrel now."

She leaned ponderously forward. "I've heard reports from the scouts," she went on. "Most of them, of course, saw nothing, and returned by nightfall. There were about half a dozen in your vicinity who saw you and helped you bring the Monster back. Their ranking officer has told me what you did."

Barbara remained silent, not trusting her tongue. Captain Janet Lundgard had emerged from the woods and taken charge: set a guard on the ship, slung the unconscious Monster on a spare orsper, and ridden to town with the rest of them for escort. She had reported directly to the Big House while the others went back to barracks. But what had she told?

"Apparently you attacked the Monster unprovoked," said Claudia Udall coldly. "Father knows what revenge it may take."

"It had drawn a weapon on me, Ma'am," answered Barbara. "If I hadn't lassoed it, maybe it would have destroyed all Freetoon. As it is, we have the thing a prisoner now, don't we?"

"It may have friends," whispered Elinor, her eyes very large. A shiver went through the hall.

"Then we have a hostage," snapped Barbara.

The Old Udall nodded. "Yes . . . there is that. I've had relays of guards sent to its ship. None of them report any sign of life. It, the Monster, must have been alone."

"How many other ships have landed, all over Atlantis?" wondered Henrietta.

"That's what we have to find out," said Claudia. You had to admit the Udalls were brave enough; they faced a situation and made a swift decision and stuck by it. "I'm sending a party to the Ship—the Ship of Father—to ask the Doctors about this. We'll also have to send scouts to the nearest other towns, find out if they've been visited too."

Both missions would be dangerous enough. Barbara thought with a tingling what her punishment would be. As a non-initiate, she couldn't go to the Ship, but she would be sent on a mission toward Greendale, Highbridge, or Blockhouse, to spy. *But that's terrific! When do we start?*

The Udall smiled grimly. "And meanwhile, for weeks perhaps, we'll have the Monster to deal with . . . and our own people. This can't be hushed up. The whole town must already be getting into a panic.

"We have to learn the truth about the Monster . . . yes,

and all the people had better know the facts. We'll do it this way. The carpenters will set up a cage for the Monster, right in the plaza, and while everybody not on duty watches, someone will go into that cage and we'll see what happens."

Barbara felt sweat on her skin, and there was a brief darkness before her eyes.

"Who's going to volunteer for *that* job?" grumbled Marian Burke.

Elinor smiled. "Why, who but our brave Corporal Whitley?" she answered.

CHAPTER V

Davis Bertram kept waking up. Then some new jolt
would throw him back into blankness. A few times
he tried to talk, but only a hoarse gobble came out.
Finally everything passed over in a heavy sleep.

He came back to half consciousness in a night as
thick as the taste in his mouth. A while he lay existing,
a mere collection of assorted pains. Eventually it
occurred to him that he might open one eye.

Straw rustled beneath him. His arms didn't respond
to his will, something held them, but he got to a kneel-
ing position. Now he could sense he was between
walls. A door was vaguely outlined, yellowish light
seeping past its edges. Davis stumped forward, pro-
pelled more by instinct than any decision, until he
knelt against the door. He retched. Leaning his forehead against rough wood, he had an eye close to a
hole. Out of some forgotten past experience, words
trickled: *Hole for a latchstring.* He bleared a glance
through it.

A courtyard lay under flooding amber radiance. He could see how each individual cobblestone humped up from a puddle of darkness, into that glow. On the farther side, another building was silhouetted against a purple black sky where stars twinkled. In front of this was a, what, oh, yes, a stone trough.

He wondered dully where he was and what had happened. Then the dullness vanished.

A girl walked out of the opposite place. She was tall and lithe, clad in a rigid upper garment, short skirt, and high boots. She carried a helmet under one arm; the light seemed to strike sparks from her hair. He associated her, incoherently, with a terrible curve-beaked bird, with panic and pain. But he didn't cringe. Whatever had occurred, she made up for it now.

Stopping by the trough, she laid down her iron hat, put one foot on the edge, unlaced a boot and removed it. Then the other. Her legs were terrific. She jerked at straps and buckles, took off her corselet, wriggled from the undershirt.

Davis gasped. Her breasts stood forth from shadow, gleaming in the light, like the cobblestones: but there the resemblance ended. *Fifth order function, isn't it?* said his mathematical reflexes. *Five points of inflection, counting the central cusp as three.* He checked again to make sure. Yes, five. Of course, his mind mumbled, that was thinking in terms of plane geometry, whereas the view here was decidedly three-dimensional. . . . The girl stretched herself, muscle by muscle, standing on tiptoe and arching her back. *Four-dimensional! Mustn't forget the time variable!*

She undid her belt, stepped out of kilt and undergarment. *Yow!* thought Davis. He would have spoken it if his mouth hadn't been so puffy; he was stiff and swollen in a number of places.

The girl scooped handfuls of water from the trough and washed herself. The clear splashings were the only sound in all the night. Afterward she unbraided her hair and shook it loose down her back. A small breeze played with her locks and slid about her body. Davis wished he were a small breeze. Drops of water sparkled on her skin, wherever shadows did not edge roundedness. She leaned over the trough, stared into it, touched herself and smiled. It made her look very young. Not too young, though. She shivered, which was also a sight worth watching, gathered her stuff and walked out of sight.

Davis lay down on the straw again. His battered self was still not functioning very well. The vision felt like a dream, already fading in his mind. But a most consolatory dream. . . . *Delirium,* he decided as the hormones stopped moaning. *All quite impossible. Too bad.* He plunged back into unconsciousness.

He woke when the door was opened and lay there for a minute, trying to remember where he was and what had happened and why his flesh ached in a hundred places. After two short-lived attempts, he got his eyes to function.

There was a spurred boot in front of his nose. He rolled over, cautiously, letting his gaze travel upward. The boot, a laced affair of reddish leather, ended at a shapely knee. Above was a kilt of leather strips with iron bands clinched on as reinforcement. There was a wide belt supporting a sheathed knife on one side and a small pouch on the other. The belt went over a laminated cuirass of hardened leather, breastplate and backplate laced around a slender torso; a bust bucket of thin iron jutted from the front. Then there was a slim neck, a lot of yellow hair braided under a flat helmet with plumes, and a rather attractive sun-tanned face.

Davis sat up, remembering. Cosmos! That girl on the nightmare bird, the lariat and . . .

"What's going on?" he croaked. "Who are you?"

"F-Father!" stammered one of the girls. "It talks!"

She spoke Basic—a slurred, archaic form, but it was the Basic of Earth and all human planets. She must be human, thought Davis weakly; no alien was that humanoid.

A handsome wench, too, though a bit muscular for his taste. Davis began to smile through bruised lips at all ten of them.

"Gak!" he said.

The ten were identical.

Well, not quite . . . some leaned on spears and some bore light, wicked-looking axes, and some had a beltful of needle-nosed darts. That was not an enjoyable way of distinguishing girls.

He shuddered and grew aware that he had been stripped. He scrambled to his feet. Now Davis' home planet was a trifle on the cold side, and its customs had developed accordingly. They didn't exactly include a nudity taboo, but he had certainly found summer days on Earth—with too intellectualized a culture for taboos of any sort—more than a little distracting. "Sunblaze!" he gulped, under the interested eyes of decuplet girls. A jerk at the wrists told him his hands were tied behind his back. He sat down again, lifting his knees and glaring across them.

"I imagine Monsters would have learned the Men language, Ginny," said one of his visitors. On closer observation, Davis saw that she was older—in fact, the ages seemed to range from twenty to forty—and had a scar on one cheek. Some kind of insigne was painted on her breastplate—sunblaze, it was the six-pointed star of an astrogator's mate!

"It *looks* harmless," said one of the younger women doubtfully.

"Let's get it out, then," decided the officer. "You, Monster!" She shouted at him, as if to help him understand. "We friends. We not hurt-um you. You obey-um. Or else you get-um spear in-um guts."

"But *I'm* a friend too!" wailed Davis.

"Up!" said the officer, raising her battle-axe. She was tense as a drawn wire—they all were, all more than half afraid of him and doubly dangerous on that account. Davis rose.

They formed a circle and marched him out of the shed. He saw a courtyard, rudely paved with stones, a number of primitive buildings, and a high palisade around all. There was a catwalk beneath the stakes, and warriors posted on it with some kind of cross-bow.

When he came out of the gate, Davis saw quite a small army alert for whatever he might try. Some were on foot, some mounted on birds like the one he'd seen before: larger and stouter than ostriches, with feathers of blue-tipped white and cruel hawk heads. He decided not to try anything.

A rutted unpaved street snaked downhill between big, clumsy houses. Beyond the town, it became a road of sorts, wandering through cultivated grainfields; he could just see the forms of laborers out there, guarded by a few girls on birdback. The fields covered a sloping, boulder-strewn plateau, which dipped off into the forest and ran down toward the remote river valley. Behind the castle, the mountains rose steep and wooded.

Ignoring botanical details, this might also have been Earth of some older age. But not when you looked at the sky. It was a terrestrial heaven, yes, blue and clear, with towering white cumulus masses in the west. Overhead, though, were two crescent moons, dim by daylight, one almost twice the apparent size of Earth's, the other half again as big as Luna seen from home. And there was the emperor planet, the world of which *this* was only another satellite. When full, it would sprawl across fourteen times as much sky as Luna. Just now it was a narrow sickle, pale amber. The morning sun was approaching it. That is, the smaller, Sol-type sun, Delta Capitis Lupi B in standard

astrographic language, about which the giant planet
moved. The primary sun, bluish-white A, had not yet
risen; it would never seem more than the brightest
of the stars.

Davis shook an aching head and wrenched his
attention back to the ground. Be damned if this was
like Earth, after all, even with the women and children clustered around and chattering. Not just their
dress—the civilians wore little, the kids nothing. Their
likeness. Women and children—all female, the children—seemed to be cast from a few hundred molds.
Take two from the same mold, like those gawping
dairymaid types over there, and the only difference
was age and scars.

Cosmos, but he was thirsty!

The procession debouched on a wide open space.
At its farther end were some thousands of civilians,
jammed together, craning their necks, held back by
a line of guards. Their high-pitched, excited voices
sawed on his nerves. In the middle of the square was
a tall old tree, not unlike an elm if you didn't look
too closely, and beneath this was a large wooden cage.

"In there," said the blonde captain. She drew her
knife and cut his bonds.

Davis shuffled through the cage door. "Is this a
zoo?" he asked. "Where are all the men, anyway?"

"Don't *you* know?" The captain almost dropped her
knife.

"Look here—I—oh, never mind!"

"Very well, Babs, let's see how you get out of this
one!"

It was a new voice, quite low and attractive. Davis
looked through the bars and saw a red-haired girl
among the cavalry—the same one who'd roped him
yesterday!

Or was she? Her twin, also in armor, came walking slowly forth across the square, carrying a tray.
Davis stepped warily back as the newcomer entered

his prison. The blonde officer shut the door on them, clicked down the latch, and stood aside with a struggle between dignity and relief.

The girl put down her tray and touched her dagger. She was cute, thought Davis; he could have gone for her in better circumstances. Her greenish eyes widened, and she breathed hard.

"Will you eat, Monster?" she whispered.

Davis saw food on the tray, a roast fowl, and some kind of tuber, a bowl of yellow liquid, a dish of fruit. He hesitated, thinking about poison. Terrestroid worlds were tricky that way.

But his biotic analyzers had told him the life here was both harmless and nourishing; nor had they found any microorganisms which would regard him as a free lunch. Of course, he had only sampled one small area . . .

But *she* was human. They all were. If they could live on this stuff, so could he.

He gulped down the drink, a thin sour beer which made him wolfish for the food. He squatted down and ripped it between his teeth.

Four women came near the cage, all of the same unprepossessing genotype. The oldest wore a headdress of plumes. "Well, Corporal," she snapped, "question it."

"Yes—yes, ma'am," said the girl in a small voice. She stood as far from Davis as she could get. "I— I am Corporal Maiden Barbara Whitley, Monster."

"The one who captured you," said one of the elders.

"Be quiet, Henrietta," said the oldest. With a certain fearless price: "I am Claudia, the Udall of Freetoon."

"Honored, Citizen," said Davis between bites. "My name is Davis Bertram T." She didn't ask him about the initial, and he saw no reason to explain it stood for Terwilliger.

"Why . . . that could be a human name," said
Barbara shyly.

"It is," said Davis. He was beginning to feel better, almost kindly. "What else should it be?"

"Oh—oh, yes, the stories did say you Monsters
learned the arts from the Men." She smiled, the least
little bit.

"But I—" Davis stood up. "Who said I was a
monster?" He was not, he told himself, vain; but more
than one woman had informed she liked his face.

"But you are! *Look* at you!"

"Damn it, I'm not! I'm as human as you are!"

"With all that hair?" snapped Henrietta Udall.

"Let the corporal do the talking," said Claudia.

Davis fingered his chin. He'd never had a strong
growth of beard, and the stubble was scarcely visible even now. He gave the Udalls an unfriendly
glance. "You've got more mustache than I do," he
growled.

"Look here," said Barbara reasonably. "We're not
blind. I admit you're not unlike a person. You have
two legs and five fingers and no feathers. But you're
bigger than any of us, and haven't got any more
breasts than a ten-year-old."

"I should hope not!" said Davis.

"In fact—" Barbara scratched her neck, puzzledly,
and pointed. "Just what *is* that? Do you fight with
it?"

"It doesn't look prehensile," said the blond captain.

If he hadn't still had a headache, Davis would
have been tempted to beat his skull against the bars.
He told himself wildly that he had not gone insane,
that he was not delirious, that he really was here
on the Earth-sized third satellite of Delta Capitis
Lupi B I. But somehow it seemed to slip through
his fingers.

He put his face in his palms and shuddered.

"Poor Monster." The girl trod impulsively forward

and laid a hand on his arm. "You haven't been very well treated, have you?"

He looked up. She paled a little with fright, under the smooth brown skin, and made half a step back. Then her lips stiffened—unfairly attractive lips—and she stayed where she was.

"We had no way of knowing," she said. "The stories are so old and so vague. Some Monsters are friendly with the Men and some aren't. We couldn't take chances."

"But I am a man!" shouted Davis.

A groan went through the crowd. Somebody screamed.

Barbara clenched her fists. "Why did you say that?" she asked in a wobbly voice.

"Can't you *see*, girl?"

"But the Men . . . the Men are powerful, and beautiful, and—"

"Oh, Evil!" Davis took her fingers, they felt cold in his, and laid them against his cheek. "Feel that? I haven't got much yet in the way of whiskers, but . . ."

Barbara turned faintly toward the Udall. "It's true, ma' am," she whispered. "There's hair starting to grow out of his face."

"But you lassoed him!" said the blonde captain. "We fetched him back on an orsper like a sack of meal!"

"Yeh," cried a voice in the crowd. "If he's a Man, where's his comb and wattles?"

Davis took hold of his sanity with both hands. "Look," he began between clenched teeth. "Look, let's be reasonable about this. Just what the jumping blue blazes do you think a man is?"

"A Man is . . . is . . . a human male." He could barely hear the Barbara girl's reply.

"Good. And what is a male?"

"Don't you *know?*"

Davis drew several long breaths before answering: "Yes. I do know. I want to find out if you do."

"A male is . . . well . . . there are male animals and female animals. A male fertilizes the female and she brings forth the eggs . . . or the living young, in the case of some fish and snakes . . ."

"All right. I just wanted to get that settled. Now— have you ever seen a human male before?"

"Certainly not." Her courage was returning. "You must indeed be from far away, Monster. There are no Men on all Atlantis."

"Oh . . . is that what you've called this world? But how do you manage—how long since . . ."

"Humans came here some three hundred years ago," she said. "That is, by a year I mean the time Minos needs to go once around the sun Bee."

Minos . . . the big planet, of course. Davis had measured from space that it was about one Astronomical Unit from B, which had nearly the same mass as Sol. So one Minos year was approximately one Earth year. Three centuries—why, they were barely starting to colonize then! The hyperdrive was newly invented and . . .

"But you have children!" said Davis feebly.

"Oh, yes. By the grace of Father, the Doctors at His Ship can— I don't know any more. I've never been there."

Davis took a while to swallow that one.

At least these barbarians had preserved something: a little elementary astronomy, the Basic language, the idea of farming and metallurgy. A shipwreck three hundred years ago, and an incredible hoax played by some gang known as the Doctors . . .

"Very well," he said at length. "Thanks, Barbara. Now we're getting somewhere. You see, I *am* a man, a human male."

"Nonsense!" snorted the old battle-axe in the war-bonnet.

Davis felt trapped. It was worse than being asked to prove by rigorous logic that he existed.

Something came back to him. In the few hours he'd been on Atlantis, before this Barbara wench caught him, he had seen plenty of animal life. Lizard-like forms, fish in a brook, flying birds and flightless birds. Some of the earthbound avians had been the size of buffalo.

But no mammals. In all those herds and flocks, not a mammal. And the girl had said . . .

Excitement gripped him. "Wait a minute!" he cried. "Are there any . . . well, I mean, does Atlantis harbor any warm-blooded animals with hair that give live birth and suckle their young?"

"Why, no," said Barbara. "None but us, and our folk came from the stars."

"Ahhh-ha. Mammals never evolved here, then. No wonder you didn't recognize—I mean, uh . . ."

"What do you mean?" asked Barbara innocently.

Davis' tongue knotted up on him. Since the mammal is the only terrestroid life form whose males—apart from all secondary characteristics—are conspicuously male, it was understandable that a certain confusion existed on Atlantis. But he didn't feel up to explaining such matters. He didn't feel up to much of anything. They probably wouldn't believe him in all events.

"This is ridiculous," barked the Old Udall. "It's well understood that the Men will come in all their power and glory. This wretch is a Monster, and the only question is what to do about it."

Another girl trod forth. Even now, Davis felt his eyes bug out. She was dark, throaty-voiced, with gold bangles on slender arms and red flowers in her long black hair, high in the prow and walking like a sine wave. "Please, ma'am," she said. "I have an idea."

The Old Udall smiled at her. "Yes, Elinor?"

"It says it is a Man." Elinor waggled her lashes at Davis. "Let it prove it."

"How?" demanded Davis eagerly.

"Barbara," said Elinor with scientific detachment.

"What?"

"Certainly," said Elinor. "Just fertilize the corporal."

Barbara stepped back, white-faced. "No!" she gasped.

"Why, think of the honor, dear Babs," purred Elinor. "The first woman in three hundred years to have a child by a living Man. I think . . . don't you think, ma'am, anyone getting such an honor should be upgraded?"

"Indeed I do," said Claudia earnestly. "Corporal Whitley, we've had our little differences, but now the future of Freetoon may depend on you. You won't fail your duty."

"My duty isn't . . ."

"Or are you afraid?" murmured Elinor.

Davis saw Barbara flush red. She knotted her fists and closed her eyes. After a very long minute, she opened them again and looked squarely at him with an air of having but one life to give for her country.

"Yes," she said defiantly. "You may fertilize me, Davis—if you can!"

Davis looked at several thousand interested faces. He wished he could disappear.

How did you explain the effect of social conditioning to a tribe which had never heard of such matters?

"Not now," he begged hoarsely. "Give me time . . . privacy . . . I can't do anything here . . ."

The Old Udall lifted a skeptical brow.

"Oh, never mind," said Davis. "Have it your way. I'm a monster."

CHAPTER VI

Barbara was not happy.

That sorry business in the plaza had returned her to Claudia's favor and won her a good deal of respect elsewhere. After all, nobody knew if the Monster had poison fangs. Thinking back, though, she could only remember how bruised and beaten the poor creature had been. Evil or not, someone who rode proudly between the stars shouldn't be questioned before a crowd of lunkheads.

In the four days since, she had been out hunting. The great grazing birds could not be domesticated— hard enough to tame the carnivorous orspers—and the small fowl at home furnished no steaks. Her peacetime duty was to keep up Freetoon's meat and leather supply. Usually the huntresses went in groups, for help and safety: the local game, grown timid, often had to be tracked for days. This trip Barbara elected to make alone. She found it ever harder to get along with anyone.

We Whitleys are a crotchery lot, she admitted. For once, the reflection was less arrogant than gloomy. Perhaps the sight of the lonely captive Monster had changed her viewpoint. If there were more of her family in Freetoon, it might have been different; she couldn't have quarreled with all of them, and her mother she remembered as a tall kindliness.

Childhood friends grew apart. That was the curse of the Whitleys. They had good enough minds and a proud enough tradition to be the equals of Latvalas, Trevors, Lundgards . . . but they were too short-tempered, too impolitic to belong to so high a caste. After the rites of becoming acolyte, when serious training began, a barrier grew up. In early adolescence, a Whitley nearly always got a crush on an older Trevor. But it was never reciprocated, and after a few years it died away leaving its scar, and the Whitley made her own lonesome road through life.

But that Monster! Ever since she had been in the cage with it, there had been this moodiness. Had the Monster psyched her?

The vagueness of the concept was frightening. They whispered about it on winter nights, psyching, that was something the ancestresses had done, undefined, dark, and powerful. The lower castes had charms against being psyched by the Critters and the Gobblies and other unseen mountain dwellers.

To escape herself, therefore, Barbara got Kim Trevor's permission to hunt, saddled one orsper and took another to pack home her kill, and headed northward into the Ridge.

She spoored a stamper herd on the second day and caught up to it on the third. After dark, in a light rain, she shot one of them and stampeded the rest. Otherwise the old male would try to kill her. Then she had to stand guard against the jacklins that coughed and boomed in the forest, drawn by the smell of blood. Toward morning the rain stopped and the sky cleared; she set to work cutting up the bird and finished quickly.

And now the night was suddenly cool, a bright mystery where wet leaves sparkled gold beneath Minos, a scent of young blossoms, the High Gaunt rearing its stern stone peak like a lance among the stars. An irrational happiness filled her. There was a tingle all through her.

And this was not to be understood either. After a while she grew scared of it, and by dawn she was back in the blackest depression.

"I wonder what's happening to the Monster?" she said. Her voice seemed unnaturally loud in the mists. It was high time she got home. The trail had arced, so that she could be in Freetoon tonight if she cut across the Geyser Flats and rode hard. Suddenly she wanted very much the harsh sweaty comfort of the barracks.

Sleep was no problem. Normally you slept about four hours out of the twelve between a sunset and a sunset, but huntresses could go for days on birdnaps. Barbara fed her orspers, loaded the pack bird, and started back at a trot. She ate in the saddle, not stopping even for the holy time of eclipse, when Bee went behind Minos and the stars came out. Ay and Ariadne gave light enough for those ten-plus minutes, and a muttered prayer to Father met minimum requirements.

Shortly afterward she struck the Ironhill road. It was wider and more rutted than most. "All roads lead to Ironhill"—its folk supplied metals from their mines, trading for the timber of the forest people, the grain and jerked meat of the valley settlements, the salt and fish of the seadwellers. You could buy anything in Ironhill.

Otherwise there was not much trade between towns. They were too scattered and too hostile.

Jogging along in her own gloom, Barbara forgot

all caution. She rounded a bend and could have been
shot by the Greendalers before realizing they were
there.

A dozen of them, in full armor, riding toward
Freetoon . . . the standard bearer had their flag on
a tall shaft, the double sun emblem, but there was
the white cloth of truce a-flutter beneath it. Barbara
reined in, gasping, and stared at the crossbows as they
swiveled around. She wore only the doublet and kilt
of the pot-hunter.

The Greendale leader laughed. "We won't harm
you today, darling, if you behave yourself," she said.
She was a middle-aged Macklin with a broken nose
and some missing teeth. "Freetooner yourself, aren't
you? We're going your way."

Barbara nodded distantly and joined their party.
She didn't hate them, but war was as normal a part
of life as the harvest festival. She had been in several raids and skirmishes since gaining her growth,
and her kin were dead at Greendale hands.

There was a Whitley sergeant in the band, about
fifty years old. Barbara rode beside her. "I'm Gail,"
she introduced herself. "I see you had luck. There
hasn't been a stamper herd in our territory for fifteen years."

"What's your mission?" asked Barbara, rather snap-
pishly.

"What do you think?" answered Gail. "You people
ought to know better than to send spies our way when
I'm on patrol duty."

"Oh. You bushwhacked them, then." Barbara felt
a cold stabbing along her spine.

"Every one. Caught three of them alive. One . . . Avis
Damon, yes, that's her name . . . got pretty much cut
up in the fracas, and rather than bleed to death she
told us what she knew."

It was bad news—very bad—but Barbara's first
reaction was scorn. "I always claimed those Damons

aren't fit for combat." Then, slowly: "So what do you think you learned?"

"A star ship landed in your country." Gail said it with care, and a ghost of fear flickered in her eyes. "There was a Man aboard."

"A Monster," corrected Barbara. "We made it admit that."

"Mmmm . . . yes . . . I thought so myself. You couldn't have captured a Man against his will."

A thin, dark-haired Burke interrupted, above the plopping feet and creaking leather: "Are you sure it was against his will?"

That was the trouble with the Burkes. They thought too much, they disquieted everybody. Barbara's hands felt clammy. "Yes." she answered. "I myself dragged the Monster at a lasso's end."

"If it is a test of faith, though . . ." The Burke shook her head dubiously.

"Shut up!" There was a harsh, strained note in the Macklin captain's voice. She turned around and said to Barbara: "What plans do you have now?"

"I don't know. I've been gone ever since— We've sent to the Doctors, of course, to ask what we ought to do."

"And meanwhile you have the Monster. The ship can fly, and the Monster knows how to make it fly." Anger writhed across the leathery face. "Do you think we're going to stand by and let you make an ally of the Monster?"

"What do you want?" replied Barbara.

"We're bringing an ultimatum," said Gail Whitley. "Your Udall has to turn the Monster over to a joint guard till we get word from the Ship of Father That'll take many days, and we're not going to let you have that power all to yourselves in the meantime."

"And if we don't?" asked Barbara unnecessarily.

"War," said Gail, equally redundant.

Barbara thought about it for a while. She ought

to make a break for it, try to reach Freetoon ahead
of this gang . . . no, that would earn her nothing more
than a bolt in the back. There was going to be war;
no Udall would cough up a prize like the Monster.
The two towns were pretty evenly matched. Freetoon
could not be taken by the Greendalers and the crops
were too young to burn—*anyway, who says we can't
defend our own fields? We'll toss them out on their
rumps, and chase them all the way home.*

The battle would probably start tomorrow, the
ultimatum being refused tonight. It was about thirty
hours' ride to Greendale—less by the roads, but an
army didn't want to be too conspicuous en route. The
enemy soldiers must already have left and be biv-
ouacked somewhere in the Ridge.

So be it! Barbara felt a welcome tension, almost
an eagerness. It was a pleasant change from her mood
of the past days.

The Burke girl took a small harp from her saddle-
bag, and the band broke into song, one of the good
old stirring cavalry songs said to go back to the Men
themselves . . .

Barbara chimed in, the orspers broke into a brisk
jog, and they all enjoyed the rest of the trip.

Bee and Ay were under the horizon when they clattered up to Freetoon, but Minos, Ariadne, Theseus,
and the two tiny moons Aegeus and Pirithous gave
plenty of light. The outer patrols stopped them on
the edge of the grainfields and then, not daring to
leave the post when an army might be near, sent them
on in Barbara's charge.

The embassy had dismounted in the courtyard and
stamped into the Big House when Barbara realized
her usefulness was over. She turned her kill over to
the servants and put the two orspers in the castle
barn. Poor birds, they were so tired. Then she wondered what to do. Go back to barracks, where the
girls sat around the hearth talking, drinking, playing

games . . . go back and tell them what to expect? She
ought to, but didn't feel like it; they'd get the word
soon enough. And if there was to be combat tomorrow, she ought to have a good night's sleep, but she
was too nervous.

"Where's the Monster being kept?" she asked,
before thinking.

"In the shed under the north wall, ma'am," said
the Nicholson groom. "Didn't dare have him anywhere
but in a sep'rate building, they didn't, so we fixed
the shed up nice and we brings him his meals and
clean straw and water and all while the guards
watches, and he ain't done no harm but . . ."

"*He!*" said Barbara. "Why do you call it he?"

"Why, he says he's male, ma'am, and, uh, well, he
says . . ."

Barbara turned her back and walked out into the
yard. No reason why the Monster shouldn't be male.
They were Man and woman, the wise happy people
of the stars, and doubtless Monsters, too . . . But why
should the thought of this Davis creature's maleness
be so odd to her, half frightening and thus resented?

She remembered that final ludicrous scene in the
cage. Her ears burned with . . . and why was that? If
Davis had been a Man, it would have been an honor
so great that . . . as it was, only Davis had been
humiliated, trapped in his own pathetic lie. She had
been afraid, indignant, bewildered, all at once, and
yet . . .

Damn Davis!

Barbara grew aware that she had walked around
the Big House and was in its multiple shadow looking toward the Monster's prison.

A door of wooden bars had been erected for the
shed. It . . . he . . . Davis stood against the bars,
flooded with cool Minos-light and moonlight. He
showed sharp and clear in the radiance, but it hazed
him somehow with its own witchery; the hollow

cheeks and flat hairy breast and bulging muscles were no longer ugly. They had given him clothes, kilt, cloak, and sandals; his hair was combed and a yellow beard was growing out on his face.

He was holding hands between the bars with a girl in a long feather cloak. Their voices drifted to Barbara—Elinor Dyckman, of all pests! Where did she get the right to talk alone with Davis?

"Oh, I really must be going, Bertie," she said. "Those awful Greendalers . . . didn't you see them come in? Claudia will be just *furious*."

"Stick around, beautiful." The Monster's low chuckle was somehow paralyzing, Barbara could not have moved after hearing it. "It's worth being lassoed, and kicked around and caged and goggled at, just to get you here alone at last."

"Really . . . Bertie, let go of me—you scare me," Elinor tittered.

"Aw, now, I'm not going to eat you. Let me only feast on your silken hair, your starry eyes, your Cupid's-bow mouth, your swan-like throat, your . . ."

"You say *such* things." Elinor leaned closer against the door. "Nobody says such things here."

"Ah, nobody is able to appreciate you, my little one. To think I crossed the stars and found you. It was such a small deed. I ought to have moved planets, juggled suns, fought dragons to deserve a word with you. Come here . . . lend me that adorable mouth . . ."

"Bert! I . . . I . . . mmmmmm . . ."

The night blurred before Barbara. She wondered why, gulped, realized it was tears, and cursed herself.

"I *mustn't*, Bertie, dear! Claudia will be so angry. You're a . . ."

"A man. And you're a woman."

"But you said . . ."

"I had no choice then."

"Oh, I can't, Bertie, I just can't! You're locked in, and . . ."

"You can swipe the key, can't you? Of course you can. Here, give me another kiss."

It was too much. And a Whitley was no sneaking spy like a, a, a Dyckman. Barbara strode across the yard, jingling her spurs as noisily as possible. "What's going on here?" she yelled.

"Oh!" Elinor squealed. "Oh . . . Babs, is it? Babs, dear, I was only . . ."

"I know what you were only. Get out, you bitch, before I knock your teeth down your throat!"

Elinor wailed and fled.

Barbara turned furiously on Davis. "What were you plotting?"

The Monster sighed, shrugged, and gave her a rueful grin. "Nothing very evil," he said. "You again, eh? It seems you always interrupt me when things are getting interesting."

Heat and cold chased each other across Barbara's face. "Maybe Father did pick me for that job," she spat. "Somebody has to keep Atlantis for the Men . . . not for your sort!"

"You know," answered Davis, "this is the kind of thing I used to daydream about in my teens. A brand new world, like Earth but more beautiful, and I the only man among a million women. Well . . . I've found it now and I want out!"

Barbara raised a fist. "Yes, so you can go home and call your friends to come raiding."

"We intend no such thing," said Davis earnestly. "We want to help you—blast it all, we're not your kind of bloodthirsty pirate. And I *am* a man, as human as you are. If you'd not come along, Elinor Dyckman would have found that out."

"Elinor!" sneered Barbara.

"All right," said Davis blandly. His smile grew altogether insolent. "Maybe you'd like to give me another chance? Honestly, you're one of the best-looking girls I've seen anywhere."

"Blast if I do!" Barbara turned her back.

"Don't go away," begged Davis. "It's lonesome as space here. All I've done is argue with that barrel-shaped queen of yours."

Barbara couldn't help it. The epithet was too good. She began to laugh and was unable to stop for a full minute.

"That's better," said Davis. "Shall we be friends?" He stuck his hand through the bars. Barbara stared at it, looked at him, he raised a mocking brow, and she gave the hand a quick clasp. She'd show him she wasn't afraid!

"Why do you claim to be a Man?" she asked. "You've already admitted that you aren't."

"I told you I had no choice then. I tell Siz Claudia that I'm a benevolent Monster and if they'll let me at my ship—under guard, if they want—I'll go home and bring the Men. I mean it, too."

"But she doesn't dare," said Barbara slowly.

"Well, not so far. Can't say I blame her. How can she know what powers I might get, once aboard my boat, and what I might do? Say, have you found my blaster?"

"Your what?"

"My weapon. I had it in a hip holster, dropped it when you . . . No? I suppose it must be lying out in the grass somewhere. You won't find anything very useful in my pack. Medical kit, lighter, camera, a few such gadgets. I've offered to demonstrate them, but the old sow won't let me. How long am I supposed to rot here anyway?" finished Davis on a querulous note.

"What were you doing when I . . . found you?" asked Barbara.

"Just looking around. I analyzed basic surface conditions from space, then came down to let my robots check on the biochemistry and ecology. That looked safe too, so I violated all doctrine and went

for a stroll. I was just coming back to the boat when—
Oh, Evil, I don't imagine you understand a word."
Davis smiled. "Poor kid. Poor little amazon."

"I can take care of myself!" she flared.

"No doubt. But come over here. I won't hurt you."

Barbara went to the door. He held her hands and
pressed his face against the bars. "I want to show you
something," he said gravely. "Maybe that way . . . one
kiss, Barbara."

She couldn't help it, she felt bonelessly weak and
leaned toward him.

The main door of the Big House crashed open.
Torchlight flared, spilling on the cobbles, Minos became
suddenly wan. Iron clanked, and the Greendale Macklin
strode forth, tall and angry, her women bristling about
her.

The voice jerked Barbara to awareness. She sprang
from the Monster and grabbed for the crossbow at
her shoulder.

"This means war!"

CHAPTER VII

Civilians and movable goods were brought inside the stockade that night, and armed females streamed forth. But the fighting didn't start till well after sunrise.

Davis could just hear the horns and shouts and clash of metal. There was a good-sized battle on the edge of the forest, he guessed. He looked across a courtyard littered with women, children, and assorted dry goods and wondered what the desolation to do.

Claudia Udall tramped over to his jail in full armor and toting a battle-axe. Elinor Dyckman undulated in her wake, thinly clad and scared. Davis would rather have looked at her, but thought it more tactful to meet the queen's eyes.

"Well, Monster, now a war has started on your account," said Claudia grimly.

Davis gave her a weak smile. "It wasn't my idea . . . uh, ma'am. What do they want me for, anyway?"

"The power, of course! Any town which had you and your ship could conquer the rest in days." After an embarrassing silence: "Well?"

"Well," stuttered Davis, "I offered to . . . it's too late now, isn't it? I mean, with an army between us and the boat?"

Claudia snorted. "Oh, that! We'll have those Greendale pests chased away by eclipse. But then will you help us?"

Davis hesitated. Union law was unreasonably strict about one's relationship with primitives. You could fight in self-defense, but using atomic guns to help a local aggression meant a stiff sentence.

"Let me aboard my ship . . ." he began.

"Of course," beamed Claudia. "Under guard."

"Hm, yeh, that's what I was afraid of." Davis had intended only to light out for Nerthus and never come back. Let the Service disentangle this Atlantean mess; they got paid for it. He gulped and shook his head. "Sorry, I can't. You see, uh, well, I have to be alone to make the ship work. There are rites and, uh . . ."

"Bertie!" Elinor wobbled toward him. Her white indoor face was beaded with sweat. "Bertie, darling, you've got to help us. It's death for me if the Greendalers take this place."

"Hm?"

"Yes," she chattered frantically. "Don't you understand? The Greendale Udall already has two Dyckman attendants. They won't want a third . . . they'll see to it . . . *Ber-r-rtie!*"

Davis licked his lips. It was understandable. A queen's favorite dropped the word, and in the course of the fracas Elinor would accidentally get her throat cut. The fact that, on the winning side, she would do identically the same, was no comfort.

"Nonsense, child." Claudia glared jealously at them both. "They can't take Freetoon. There are no more of them than there are of us, and we're on home ground."

"But . . ."

"Shut up! Monster, right now the Greendalers do hold the area where your ship is. Can they get in?"

Davis laughed nervously. "Axes and crowbars against inert steel? I'd like to see them try!"

Short of atomic tools, there was only one way to open that airlock. He had set it to respond to himself whistling a few bars of a certain ballad.

"You won't help us after we've driven them away?" Claudia narrowed her eyes.

Davis began a long speech about friends who would avenge any harm done to him. He was just getting to the section on gunboats when Claudia snorted and walked off. Elinor followed, throwing imploring looks across her shoulder.

Davis sat down on the straw and groaned. As if he didn't have troubles enough, that minx had to slither around in a thin skirt and a few beads . . . just out of reach.

Then he found himself wondering about Barbara Whitley. He hoped very much she wouldn't be hurt.

Eclipse came. It happened daily, at noon in this longitude, when Atlantis, eternally facing her primary, got Minos between B and herself. An impressive sight: the planet, dimly lit by the remote companion sun, fourteen times as wide as Earth's moon, brimmed with fiery light refracted through the dense atmosphere . . . dusk on the ground and night in the sky. Davis looked hungrily at the stars. Civilized, urbane, *pleasant* stars.

The Old Udall's estimate had not been far wrong. An hour later, the battle had ended and the Freetoon girls came back to the castle. Davis noticed that the warriors were divided into about thirty genotypes, no more. When everyone in a single line of descent was genetically identical, a caste system was a natural development. And, yes, he could see why the Atlanteans had reverted to the old custom of putting surnames last. Family in the normal sense just wasn't very important here; it couldn't be.

The armored girls, foot and orsper (horse bird?) troops, clamored for lunch and beer. They had a number of prisoners; Davis saw one angry woman who was an older version of Barbara. She went haughtily toward the detention shed, ignoring a slash on her leg. Very nice looking in spite of those gray streaks in her hair; Barbara, then, would always be a handsome lass. If she was still alive. Davis watched the Freetoon casualties. There weren't many dead or seriously wounded—couldn't be, with these clumsy weapons powered by female muscles. But there had been some killed, by axe, knife, dart, bolt . . .

"Barbara!" Davis whooped it forth.

The tall redhead looked his way and strolled through the crowd. Her left hand was wrapped in a wet crimson bandage. "Barbara! Cosmos, I'm glad you're . . ."

She gave him an unfriendly grin. "Mistake, Monster. I'm her cousin Valeria."

"Oh. Well, how is she?"

The girl shrugged. "All right. No damage. She's helping mount guard on your ship."

"Oh, then you did win."

"For now. We beat them back into the woods, but they haven't quit." Valeria gave him a hard green stare. "Now I know you're a Monster. The Men would fight."

"Big fat chance you've given me," said Davis. "Anyway, I didn't ask for this to happen. Why can't you tribes compromise?"

"Who ever heard of an Udall compromising?" laughed Valeria.

"Then why do you obey them?"

"Why? Why, they're . . . they're the *Udalls!*" Valeria was shocked. "When I took arms, I swore . . ."

"Why did you swear? My people have learned better than to allow absolute rulers. You've got a whole world here. What is there to fight about?"

"Land, hunting grounds, honor, loot . . ."

"There's plenty of land if you wanted to move somewhere else."

"A gutless Monster *would* say that." Valeria walked away.

Davis slumped. After all, he reflected, the human race was not famous for reasonableness, and the least-effort law was hard to beat. Once the towns had gotten into the habit of obeying these Udalls . . .

The day dragged. The civilians avoided him, superstitiously, and the soldiers appeared to have other business on hand, resting, reorganizing, changing the guard. He was fed, otherwise ignored. Night came, and he tried to sleep, but there was too much noise.

Toward morning he fell into a doze, huddled under his feather quilts against the upland chill. A racket of trumpets and hurrying feet woke him.

Another battle! He strained against the bars, into darkness, wondering why this one should be so much louder. And wasn't it getting close? The sentries on the catwalk were shooting and . . .

Elinor screamed her way across the courtyard. The multiple shadows thrown by Minos and the moons rippled weirdly before her. "Bertie, you've got to help! They're driving us back!"

He reached out and patted her in a not very brotherly fashion. "There, there. There, there." When it made her hysterics worse, he shouted. After a struggle, he got some facts.

The Greendalers had returned with allies. Outnumbered three to one, the Freetooners were driven back through their own streets.

Newburh, Blockhouse, and Highbridge banners

flew beyond the walls. It was clear enough to Davis. Having learned about the spaceship, and well aware she couldn't take it alone, the Greendale Udall had sent off for help—days ago, probably. And the prize looked great enough to unite even these factions for a little while.

"But now Claudia will have to make terms," he blurted.

"It's too late!" sobbed Elinor. "Can't you see, now that they finally have gotten together, they'll finish us off, divide our land between them . . . Bertie, help! Help! Uhhhhh . . ."

"Let me out of here first," snapped Davis. He rattled the awkward padlock. "I can't . . . ulp!"

"What?"

"Skip it." Davis had suddenly realized there was no point in exposing himself to those crossbow quarrels which fell so nastily in the yard. The victorious allies wouldn't kill *him* if he kept safely neutral. He might even make a better deal with them.

Elinor moaned and ran toward the Big House. Only Warriors were to be seen, the others had retreated into their long shed.

The fighting didn't halt even for eclipse. At midafternoon the gates opened and Freetoon's surviving soldiers poured into the court.

Step by step, the rearguard followed. Davis saw Barbara at the end of the line. She had a round wooden shield on one arm and swung a light longshafted axe. A red lock fell from under the battered morion and plastered itself to a small, drawn face.

A burly warrior pushed against her. Barbara lifted her shield and caught the descending axe-blow on it. Her own weapon rang on the enemy's helmet, chopped for the neck, missed, and bit at the leather cuirass. It didn't go through; low-carbon steel got blunted fast. The enemy grinned and began hailing blows. Barbara sprang back. The other woman followed. Barbara threw her axe between the enemy's legs. Down went the woman. Barbara's dagger jumped into her hand; she fell on top of the other and made a deft slicing motion.

Davis' stomach groaned; he turned from the sight.

When he came back to the door, there was a lull in the battle. The Freetooners had been pumping bolts and javelins from the catwalk, discouraging the allies' advance long enough for the gates to be closed. There was a kind of ordered chaos, the dead and wounded dragged off, the hale springing up on the wall, fires kindled and kettles of water set over them. Davis could hear angry feminine screeches.

Presently Barbara herself came to him. She was a-shiver with weariness, and the eyes regarding him had dark rims beneath. There was blood splashed on her breastplate and arms.

"How is it for you?" she asked hoarsely.

"I'm all right." With more anxiety than a neutral party ought to feel: "Are you hurt?"

"No. But I'm afraid this is the end. We can't stand a long siege. It's early in the year, our stores are low."

"What . . . what do you think will happen? To you, I mean?"

"I'll get away at the last if I can." Her voice was numb.

Davis told himself sternly that this mess wasn't his fault. He had come to bring the gift of Union civilization. The last thing he wanted was . . .

The *first thing* he wanted, he thought, had been the glory of finding a new inhabited planet. And the money prizes, and the lucrative survey commissions, and the adoring women.

But it wasn't his doing that the woman stood mute, with red hands and bent neck, waiting to be killed.

"Cosmos curse it," he shouted, "I can't help your stupidity!"

Barbara gave him a blind, dazed look and wandered off.

The battle resumed. The invaders had cut down young trees to make scaling ladders, and there was brisk fighting on the wall. Fires roared beneath the great kettles, but that particular form of pest repellant was slow to heat up.

By Bee-set the enemy had given up the attempt, and there was a respite for eating and napping. Davis, who had always cherished a certain romantic affection for the old barbarian days on Earth, decided that if this was a fair sample there had been nothing glamorous about them—just people who hacked and shot at each other.

Claudia Udall passed as Ay went under the horizon. She stopped to give him a bleak word. "Are you ready to help us now?"

"How can I fight?" asked Davis reasonably. "I haven't got any of my weapons here. But if you'll let me out and give me the stuff from my packsack, I could do something for the wounded."

The queen cursed him, expertly, and added: "If *we* can't have you, Monster . . . I might decide not to let anybody have you."

"Yipe!" said Davis, backing away.

"Just a minute while I get a crossbow," said the Udall, and left him.

"Eek!" yelped Davis. "Hey! Come back! I'll help you!"

A fresh ruckus broke loose beyond the walls. Trumpets howled, and the resting soldiers leaped from the ground. By Minos-light Davis saw Claudia hurry toward the gate.

Thunder crashed, and the wood groaned. The ladies from Greendale must be using a battering ram. They could have cut down a big tree, put some kind of roof over it, attacked with ladders at other points to draw off the defenders . . .

Fire kindled outside; flame ran up and splashed the sky. Somehow a house must have been touched off. The top of the stockade loomed black across the blaze, like a row of teeth; the warriors on the catwalk were silhouetted devils. Davis wondered crazily which of them was Barbara, if Barbara was still alive.

The main gate shuddered and a hinge pulled loose. Freetooners jumped off the wall to make a forlorn line. There was a boilershop din of axes where the enemy came up their ladders. The fire roared, higher and higher till red light wavered over the yard.

Someone galloped toward him on a frantic orsper. She was leading two others. She jumped from the saddle and stood before the shed with an axe in her hand.

"Barbara!" he whispered.

"Valeria again." The girl laughed with scant humor. "Stand aside, I'm going to get you out."

Her axe thudded against the bolt.

"But what—why . . ."

"We're finished," snapped Valeria. "For now, anyway. For always, unless you can help us. I'm going to get you out, Monster. We'll escape if we can, and see what you can do to remedy matters."

"But I'm neutral!"

Valeria grinned unpleasantly. "I have an axe and a knife, my dear, and nothing to lose. Are you still neutral?"

"No, not if you feel that way about it."

Valeria hewed. Behind her, the gate came down and the invaders threw themselves at the defensive line.

Another orsper ran from the stables, with a rider who had a spare mount. Valeria turned, lifted her axe, lowered it again. "Oh, you."

"Same idea, I see," answered Barbara. *Of course,* thought Davis, *genetic twins normally think alike.*

"Put on your cloak, Monster," ordered Valeria between blows. "Pull the hood up. They won't bother with three people trying to get away . . . unless they know what you are!"

There was confused battle around the gate. A band of invaders had cleared a space on the catwalk; now they were leaping down to attack the Freetooners from behind.

The bolt gave way. Valeria wrenched off the lock and threw the door open. Davis stumbled out.

"Up in the saddle, you!" Valeria waved her axe at his head.

Davis got a foot in a stirrup and swung himself aboard. Valeria mounted another bird at his side; Barbara took the lead. They jogged toward the broken gate, where Claudia and a few guards still smote ferociously at a ring of enemies. The orsper's pace was not so smooth as a horse's, and Davis was painfully reminded that a mounted man does well to wear tight pants. This silly kilt was no help. He swore and stood up in the stirrups.

Someone ran from the Big House, her scream trailing. "Help Ohhhh . . ." Davis glimpsed Elinor's face, wild with terror. He leaned over, caught her wrist, whirled her toward a spare orsper.

"Get that sissy out of here!" yelled Valeria.

Elinor scrambled up. Barbara freed her axe and broke into a gallop. Willy-nilly, Davis followed.

A band of women stood before them. A bolt hummed maliciously past his ear. Barbara's orsper kicked with a gruesomely clawed foot. Valeria leaned over and swung expertly at a shadowy form; sparks showered.

Then they were past the melee, out in the street, into the fields and the forest beyond.

CHAPTER VIII

By morning they were so far into the mountains that it looked safe to rest. Davis almost fell off his orsper into the grass.

He woke up after eclipse. For a moment he knew only one pulsing ache, all over, then memory came back and he gasped.

"Are you all right?" asked Barbara.

"I'm not sure. Oof!" Davis sat up. Someone had opened a bedroll for him and gotten his snoring body into it. His legs were so sore from standing as he rode that he didn't think he would ever walk again.

"Where are we?" he inquired blearily.

"We headed north through the Ridge." Barbara pointed to a great thin peak, misty across a forested gulch. "That's the High Gaunt, so we must have come about forty kilometers. We'll eat soon."

The saddlebags held a pretty complete camping outfit. She had made a little smokeless fire and was

toasting strips of dried meat. A loaf of coarse black
bread and a hunk of lard lay nearby. There was a
spring that burbled from rocks green with pseudo-
moss; Davis crawled to it and drank deep.

Then he felt well enough to look around. This was
tall country, ancient woods on steep hillsides. Northward it became higher still; he could see snow on not-
so-distant ranges and the ashen slopes of a volcano.
The day was clear and windy; sunlight spilled across
green flowery slopes and Minos brooded remotely
overhead, topped by a crescent moon. Ay was a
searing spark to the east, daily overtaking the closer
star.

Now if only those gossiping birds would respect
a man's headache . . . !

"Bertie!"

Davis lurched to his feet as Elinor came from the
woods. She had woven herself a flower garland, a big
thick one which teased him with glimpses, and sleeked
back her long hair. She fell into his arms and kissed
him.

"Bertie, you saved my life. Oh, I'm *so* grateful . . . do
you know, Bertie, *I* believe you're a Man . . ."

"You might come slice your Man some bread," said
Barbara acidly.

Elinor stepped back, flushing. "Have you forgotten I'm an Udall attendant?" she shrilled.

"Aren't any more Freetoon Udalls, unless one of
'em broke away like us," snapped Barbara. "Why
Davis dragged as useless a hunk of fat along as you,
I'll never understand. Now come help or I'll fry you
for breakfast!"

Elinor turned to Davis. "Bertie, are you going to
let this low-caste bitch . . ."

"I'm out of this," he said prudently.

She burst into tears. Barbara got up, cuffed her,
and frogmarched her toward the fire. "You work if
you want to eat."

Elinor pouted and began awkwardly sawing at the loaf. Barbara looked at Davis; "Why did you bring her?" she asked slowly.

"Holy Cosmos," he protested, "she'd have been killed if . . ."

"Better women than her are dead today. Kim, Ginny, Gretchen—I don't know if they're even alive, and you have to . . . Oh, be quiet!" Barbara went back to her work.

Valeria came into sight, crossbow on her shoulder and a plump bird in one hand. "It's easily settled," she drawled. "The Dyckman beast doesn't have to come along. Leave her here."

"*No!*" Elinor stood up with a shriek.

"You can ride back," sneered Valeria. "Be good for you. And I daresay you'll grease somebody into giving you a safe job."

"I'll die!" screamed Elinor. "There are jacklins in these woods! I'll be killed! You can't—*Bertie!*"

"She'd better stay with us," said Davis.

"You keep out of this," snorted Valeria.

Davis blew up. "I'll be damned to Evil if I will!" he roared. "I've been pushed around long enough!"

Valeria drew her knife. Davis cocked his fists. He'd been taught the science of self-defense and the art of boxing—which are not identical. In his present mood, he'd welcome an excuse to clip that copper-topped hellion on the jaw.

Barbara pulled down her cousin's arm. "That's enough," she said coldly. "Enough out of all of you. We have to stick together. Davis, if you insist, we'll let this . . . Elinor come along till we reach some town. Now sit down and eat!"

"Yes, ma'am," said Davis meekly.

They had their brunch in a sullen silence. But the food was strengthening; it seemed to give Davis back his manhood. After all . . . well, it was a bad situation, but he was out of that filthy jail and he was the biggest, strongest human on this planet. It was time for him to start exercising some choice.

The Whitleys calmed down as fast as they'd flared up, and Elinor showed tact enough to remain inconspicuous. Davis wished very much for a cup of coffee and a cigaret, but neither being available, he opened the council. "What are your plans?" he asked.

"I don't know," said Valeria. "Last night I only thought about getting away. Now, what do you think we can do?"

"Depends." Davis tugged at his beard. It itched, but there probably wasn't a razor on all Atlantis. "Just what will happen to Freetoon? Will the invaders kill everybody?"

"Oh, no," said Barbara. "Towns have been conquered, now and then, and the winning Udall makes herself their chief. All the civilians have to do is obey a new boss and pay her their tax and labor dues. The soldier children are brought up like the winning town's . . . yes, they usually mingle the populations."

"It's the older members of the military caste who can't be trusted," added Valeria. "People like us, who've sworn service to one Udall line. Some of them will take a fresh oath . . ."

"Damons," snorted Barbara. "Burkes. Hausers."

" . . . but the rest either have to be killed or driven out. Most of our girls managed to escape, I suppose. They'll live as outlaws in the woods, or drift elsewhere to take service. Some distant town which was never an enemy . . . you know."

"Why are you still loyal to your Udalls?" asked Davis. "I can't see where you ever got much benefit from them."

"We just are!" barked the Whitleys, almost simultaneously.

"All right, all right. But look—Claudia and her daughters are most likely dead now. You haven't got any chief. You're on your own."

The cousins stared at him and at each other. They had known it intellectually, but only now did the fact penetrate.

"Maybe one of them escaped," said Barbara faintly.

"Maybe. But what do you want to *do?*"

"I don't know." Valeria scowled. "Except that the powers of your ship aren't going to be used for Bess Udall of Greendale! Not after she killed barracks mates of mine."

"I thought . . ." Barbara looked at Davis. He found it hard to meet her eyes, though he didn't know why. "I thought maybe we could sneak back, get you to your ship . . ."

"Big chance of that!" he said bitterly.

"The allies are sure to fall out over the spoils," said Valeria. "If we waited a while— No, somebody's bound to win, and that ship is going to stay guarded."

"Maybe we can find allies of our own." Barbara looked at the northern ranges. "They say there are some strange peoples living beyond Smoky Pass. Nobody's been that far for, oh, generations. If we could get help . . . promise them the loot from the enemy . . ."

"Wait a minute!" Davis broke into a new sweat. He wasn't sure how Union law would judge a case like his. A surveyor caught in a violent situation was permitted to use violence himself if it would save his life or help rectify an obviously bad run of affairs; but he didn't think a Coordinator board would see eye to eye with Barbara on what constituted rectification.

"Wait!" he said quickly. "Maybe we can do it, maybe we can't." His brain whirred at a gear-jamming speed. "But-but-but . . . look here . . . wasn't there a message already sent to, uh, this holy Ship of yours?"

"To the Doctors? Yes," said Valeria.

"And do *you* know what the Doctors would decide?"

"No . . . no, nothing like this has ever . . ."

Regulations said: when in doubt, the surveyor

should cooperate with whatever local authority existed.
And these mysterious Doctors were as close to a
central government as the planet had. Furthermore,
they lived in this Ship . . . the original spaceship in
which the ancestresses had arrived? . . . and they
knew enough science to operate a parthenogenesis
machine. He'd have a better chance of convincing
them of the truth than anyone else.

"So since the final disposal is up to the Doctors
in all events, why don't we go there?" he proposed.
"We can explain it to them and get redress for
Freetoon too."

"We can't!" said Valeria, quite aghast. "Barbara and
I aren't full initiates. And *you*—the Ship is sacred to
Father!"

Davis was still thinking rapidly. "But I'm a man,"
he said, "or a monster, if you insist. The law doesn't
apply to me." He glanced at Elinor. "You've been
there already, haven't you?" She nodded eagerly. "All
right. When we reach the taboo area, you can escort
me the rest of the way."

It took a great deal of wrangling. Once Davis had
to roar. Being shouted down out of bigger lungs was
a new and salutary experience for the Whitleys.
Eventually they agreed.

"But we can't go through the valley," said Barbara.
"The Holy River highway will be guarded. You realize,
Davis, there's a hunt on for you already, through the
whole Ridge."

Davis gulped.

"We'll swing north," decided Valeria. "Over Smoky
Pass and down through the valleys on the other side
to the coast. Then we can perhaps get passage with
one of the seadweller ships." Her eyes gleamed.
"Quite likely the Doctors will order your boat
returned to you. But as for Freetoon, they never mix
in wars or politics. So if, on the way, we can make
a deal with someone . . ."

"Hey!" croaked Davis.

Valeria took a whetstone from her pouch and began honing her axe. It didn't seem worthwhile to argue further. Not just now.

"*Are* there people beyond the mountains?" asked Elinor timidly.

Davis nodded. "There must be. I could see from space, through the telescopes, that there was cultivation all over this part of the continent."

How many amazon towns were there in all—how many people? He could only guess. Let's see, about five hundred prototypes, and three hundred years in which to increase their numbers . . . less the attrition of war, wild animals, and other hazards . . . a quarter million total was a fair estimate. And they couldn't all have formed societies on the pattern of this region.

That was hopeful. He could scarcely imagine a less comfortable culture than Freetoon and Greendale.

"How long will it take us, do you think?" he inquired.

Valeria shrugged. "A few weeks, if we don't meet enemies or a late blizzard."

Atlantis, riding nearly upright in the equatorial plane of her primary, did not have seasons of Earth's kind. But the orbit of Minos was highly eccentric, as you'd expect of a planet in a double-star system. This was early summer, they were still approaching Bee, but in six months the sun would be getting farther away and there would be snow on the uplands. At these latitudes, about twenty degrees north, and at this height, Davis guessed the climate would answer to, oh, say Switzerland.

There was a permanent tidal bulge, frozen rock; the gravitation of Minos, with five thousand Earth masses, had deformed the great satellite. Most of the land was therefore on the inner hemisphere, and this central continent was a labyrinth of mountains. It was going to be a rough trip.

Davis looked at the tethered orspers, ripping up their rations with hooked beaks. "Do you have any sewing equipment?"

"Of course," said Barbara. "That's right, Davis, you'll need warmer clothes to cross the mountains."

"So will I," piped Elinor. The Whitleys paid no attention.

"This is a, uh, special garment I need," said Davis.

"I'll make it for you," said Barbara eagerly. "Just let me get the measurements."

Davis' ears glowed cadmium red. "No, thanks! You wouldn't understand."

Elinor seemed to have regained a little self-confidence. "If it's going to take us that long," she said, "the Freetoon couriers will have reached the Ship well ahead of us. The Doctors will send word back . . ."

"That's all right," said Valeria. "Just so we don't fall into Greendale hands." She drew a finger across her throat.

"Must you?" said Elinor faintly.

"And you, Davis Bertie," went on Valeria. "I don't know if the Greendalers would kill you or not. Probably not. But there are ways to make you do anything Bess Udall wants."

"Would she dare?" inquired Davis.

"Since you failed to do anything yesterday but run away . . . yes. Claudia was talking about red-hot pincers. I heard her."

Davis didn't think she was lying.

He glanced up at Minos. The big planet was almost half full. It wasn't as bright by day, but he could see clearly . . . the amber face blurred by a crushingly thick atmosphere, hydrogen with the vapors of water, methane, ammonia; cloudy bands across the face, dull green, blue, brown; dark blots which were storms big enough to swallow Earth whole; the shadow of an outer moon. He shivered. It was a long and lonesome way home. Light would need two centuries to reach the nearest civilization; the Service didn't plan to visit Delta for another generation.

He didn't think he could survive that long. He *had* to get his boat back, through the Doctors or through the Whitley scheme of finding allies. He knew that Bess Udall of Greendale—or her opposite number in the allied towns, whichever of them beat out the rest in the inevitable war—wouldn't give him a chance to escape.

In short, I have no choice. I'm on the Whitley team.

He looked at the cousins and then at Elinor; she smiled back at him. It could be a lot worse, he thought complacently.

CHAPTER IX

During the first two weeks—or one week, if you counted by Earth days—they traveled hard. Once they heard horns blowing, and hid in a cave for a day; Elinor whimpered her terrified way into Davis' arms, but he was too worried to enjoy it.

Otherwise it was steady riding, by sunlight and Minos-light, with three or four hours of rest in the twelve. Davis was in fairly good condition, but keeping the saddle aboard an orsper required muscles he had never heard of, and said muscles objected strenuously. Elinor was too numb even to complain much.

They lived off the country. It was not the season for nuts or berries; game was plentiful, but Davis wearied of the carnivorous diet. Ordinarily he and Elinor would keep the trail with one Whitley, while the other went off to bag the day's rations. A feeling of uselessness oppressed him.

He did try out the arbalest that was part of the
equipment at his saddlebow. It was a cleverly engi-
neered piece of work; the original design must be due
to some early castaway who had given up trying to find
the ingredients of gunpowder. (Presumably the Ship
had carried no firearms; a colony shuttle wouldn't
normally.) A chamber holding six short iron-tipped
quarrels fed them automatically into the slot; a tightly
wound spring furnished energy enough to recock the
bow several times. It was a hard-hitting, accurate
weapon with a high rate of fire, and Davis knew enough
gunnery to become good with it.

But Valeria told him coldly that he made entirely
too much noise to help stalk game.

Freetoon lay in mere foothills compared to the
range which now lifted before them. It rose steep
and terrific, with a long barren stretch above timberline, deep in snow and scoured by glaciers. There
were no paths, and the Whitleys had to guess at a
route toward the pass, of which they knew only by
hearsay.

Slowly his frame adapted, and he began to feel
some surplus energy. On the last night below timberline he offered to stand a watch. They intended to
rest through the whole darkness, gathering strength
for the push over the range.

"Well . . ." Valeria looked doubtful. "No, we don't
need that. Anything could sneak up on you."

Barbara frowned. "That's not fair, Val," she said.
"Davis may not be used to this land, but he's stronger than we are. I could use a little extra sleep."

"Oh, very well." Her cousin laughed. "No jacklins
or wolfers around, so let him have his fun."

Davis felt grateful to Barbara. He wasn't sure
whether she really meant what she said. Maybe it had
been only to spite Valeria; maybe she felt his ego
needed a shot. But it did, that was the fact, and she
had spoken gently.

The women rolled up in their blankets and went to sleep. Davis pulled on the crude jerkin Barbara had stitched together for him, drew his cloak over that, and stretched numb feet toward the fire. His sandals were falling apart, and there were no boots for him.

It was a cloudy night. Davis had a glimpse of Theseus, nearly full above Minos, a ruddy moon hazed by its own thin atmosphere, seeming to fly between great wind-driven darknesses. His telescope had spotted signs of intelligent life there, too, he thought wistfully, but of course he had landed on Atlantis before visiting an ocherous Mars-like pill.

He poked up the small fire for what little comfort it could give. A few dry snow-flakes gusted across his vision. The scrubby growth crowded around him, demonic with thorns, branches twisted and creaking. Something far away made an idiot laughter noise.

The dim ember-glow picked out Barbara's face . . . or was it Valeria's? No, the left hand was out of the blankets and lacked a healing scar. Barbara, then. She looked curiously innocent as she slept. Elinor looked voluptuous even through the bedroll, but Elinor snored.

No coffee and no tobacco closer than his ship, and it was ringed with spears. Davis commiserated his own poor lonely harried self. He began to nod, jerked back awake, swore, and indulged thoughts of champagne, baby shrimp mayonnaise, mutant oysters, boeuf tartar—oops! He discovered that he had lost all taste for boeuf tartare.

"Peep," said a voice.

"Yipe!" said Davis. He grabbed for his bow.

The peeper stepped daintily into view. It was a fluffy little bird, round as a butterball, with a parrot bill and large pathetic eyes. Davis thought of potting it—no, they had meat enough already and the bird was settling happily down beside him. It liked the fire, he guessed. He ventured to pat it, and the peeper wriggled with pleasure.

"Sure, make yourself at home," whispered Davis. "There's a nice bird. I need someone to talk to. I feel lonesome."

"Peep," said the peeper sympathetically.

Davis chatted to it till he began to grow uncontrollably sleepy. Better let Valeria take over. He reached his toes across the firecoals and nudged her with a certain malicious pleasure.

"Oh . . . oh, yes." The girl yawned and rolled out of her blanket. "Nothing much—*Hoy!*" She froze where she stood.

"Oh, this?" Davis stroked the peeper, which had cuddled on his lap. "Meet Trespassers W. Came in, and . . ."

Valeria was quite pale. "Don't move," she breathed through stiffened lips. "Don't move for your life."

Her hand stole to her belt; very very slowly, she withdrew a dart. "When I kill it, roll away. Understand? *Now!*"

The missile leaped from her hand and skewered the peeper. Davis scrambled to get free of its death throes. "What the . . ." he shouted.

Barbara and Elinor sat up. Elinor screamed.

Valeria let out a rattling laugh. "That thing has a bite with enough poison to kill ten people."

Davis made no reply.

"You're relieved from further watch duty," snapped Valeria. "Get to sleep now—if you can!"

"That's all right," said Barbara as he slunk to his bedroll. "You couldn't know, could you?"

"And the more fools us, for not realizing it," snorted Valeria. "Him a Man? Hah!"

In the morning they saddled up and started over the pass. The tongue of a glacier had to be crossed, and the orspers registered a protest which landed Davis and Elinor in the snow. The Whitleys beat the birds into submission, deftly avoiding kicks which might have disemboweled them.

Davis couldn't really blame the orspers. They had such large bare feet. After a few hours, it seemed like forever since he had been warm.

They were still under the pass when they made a miserable camp, huddled together for warmth. The next day was spent crossing, hard-packed snow underfoot and bleak blue-gray walls on either side and wind hooting in their faces. The acrid smoke of a nearby volcano stung their eyes. Barbara worried aloud about the condition of the mounts. "Jaded, chilblained, limping, half-starved. We'll have to give them a rest when we're down in the woods again."

The range dropped even more steeply on the north side. From the pass, Davis looked across a downward-rolling immensity of green, veined by rivers, here and there the flash of a lake. He wished for his paints, to capture the scene. He could make out no signs of cultivation, but there must be some; his telescopic cameras had registered small clearings and dots which might be houses.

"Haven't you any idea what the people down there are like?" he asked. "Seems like you'd all meet at the Ship."

"No," said Elinor. "You see, Bertie, each town sends its own parties to be fertilized, by their own route. It's seldom that two groups are at the Ship at the same time, and even if they are, they don't talk to anyone but— Oh, I mustn't say more."

"Hm. What about an escort? Couldn't such a party be attacked?"

"Oh, no. Everybody knows that a procession bound for the Ship, with their flags and their tribute and gifts and everything . . . well, we're holy. Going or coming on such an errand, we mustn't be hurt. If somebody did attack us, why, the Doctors would refuse to fertilize that whole town forever after."

Which would be one form of excommunication that really worked, thought Davis. He gave Elinor a sidelong glance. Her nose was frostbitten and peeling. She had lost weight, but she was still an interesting lesson in solid geometry. And he wanted a lot more information from her, whether it was taboo to non-initiates or not. He was going to enjoy persuading her.

Meanwhile, though, they had to get down where it was warm.

Later he remembered the next two days only as a nightmare of struggle. He could hardly believe it when they reached timberline and the nearly vertical descent began to flatten.

This was a conifer forest, widely spaced trees looking not unlike jack pines, though the smell was different, sweeter and headier. The ground was thick with brown needles, tall trunks and lichenous boulders thrusting out of it, the orsper footfalls a muted *pad-pad*. They saw only small, noisy birds, darting red and gold between bluish-green branches, but there was spoor of big game.

Even Davis could see how worn the orspers were. There was no choice; they had to rest.

At the end of the day, they reached a king-sized lake. It blinked amiably in the low sunshine, reeds rustled on the banks and fish leaped in the water. "We couldn't find a better campsite, I think," said Barbara.

"Skeeterbugs," said Valeria.

"Not this early in the year."

"Yeh? Look here, rockhead, I've seen skeeterbugs when . . ."

While the cousins argued, Davis dismounted. Elinor looked down at him. "Oh, I'm so tired," she said.

"Allons! Leap, my pretty one." Davis held out his arms. She giggled and jumped into them.

Either she was more hefty or he was weaker than he'd thought. They went over together, rolling down the slope. The position in which they ended was rather compromising.

Elinor wriggled. "I'm all dizzee-ee," she said. "Let me up."

"Not just yet," grinned Davis.

"Oh . . . Bertie, stop! Oh! Oh, you're so . . ."

Valeria stormed into view. She tossed her axe. It thunked in the ground among Elinor's tresses. "We camp here," she yelled. "Get up, you lazy frump, and give us a hand!"

Davis reached a final decision. He did not like Valeria.

There were no skeeterbugs. This did not improve Valeria's temper.

The orspers needed plenty of food to recover their health. In the morning, both Whitleys went out afoot after game, planning to be gone most of the day. Davis and Elinor were to watch the camp and try for fish: there were hooks and lines in the saddlebags, floats and poles were easily cut though Valeria fumed at putting her axe to such menial use.

Davis watched the twins leave, Barbara headed east and Valeria west. It was a cool, sun-drenched day and a flock of birds with particularly good voices were tuning up nearby. Davis' grin spread.

"What are you so happy about?" Elinor looked rather grimly up from the utensils she had been scouring.

"At having you all to myself." He knew her type.

"Oh, now . . . Bertie! There may be the most awful things around . . ."

"For you I would gladly face dragons," said Davis, "though of course I'd rather face you. Let's take a stroll." He jerked his thumb at the tethered orspers. "I never saw anything stare the way those overgrown chickens do."

"Bertie!" Elinor pouted. "I'm so tired. I just want to sleep."

"As you wish." He sauntered off. In a moment she pattered after him. He took her hand, squeezing it rather more than necessary.

"Bertie! Bertie, be careful, you're so *strong* . . ."

Davis wandered eastward along the lakeshore, eyes alert for a secluded spot. He was in no hurry; all day before him, and he was going to enjoy the fishing, too. Hadn't fished for years.

"You're a brave little girl, Elinor," he said. "Coming all this way and . . ." he paused, took a deep breath, and prepared the Big Lie . . . "never a complaint from you."

"I could complain," she said bitterly. "Those awful Whitleys. Skin and bones and nasty red hair and tongues like files. They're just jealous."

It would have been profitable to agree, but for some reason Davis couldn't backbite Barbara. "It's a long way to go yet," he said, "but I hope the worst is over. You ought to tell me what to expect when we reach the Ship."

"I can't, Bertie. I mustn't. Nobody who's been there is allowed to talk about it to anyone who hasn't. It's too holy for children."

"But I'm not a child," he argued. "I am, in fact, a Man. You do believe that, don't you?"

"Yes . . . you must be . . . even if your whiskers *tickle.*"

Davis stroked his short yellow beard patriarchally. It had become gratifyingly thick. "Well, then," he said, "the Doctors are only, uh, filling in for Men . . . I mean . . . Sunblaze!" He backed up and started over. "What are they like, the Doctors?"

"I can't . . ." Davis stopped for some agreeable physical persuasion . . . "I mustn't—mmmmm—Bertie!" After a while: "I really *can't* say. They have this big beautiful town, with the Ship in the very middle. There's a causeway over the swamps. But I never saw a Doctor. They're always veiled."

Davis was struck by a ghastly suspicion. "But they *are* women, aren't they?" he barked.

"Oh, yes. Yes, I could see that much. Bertie, please! I *mustn't* tell you anything."

"I can guess. The, uh, fertilizing rite—it involves a machine, doesn't it? A lot of tubes and wires and things?"

"If you know that much," said Elinor, "yes." She made a wry face. "I didn't like that part. It hurt a little, and it was so scary. But the other rites are beautiful."

Davis nodded absently. The picture was taking shape.

Three hundred years ago, the hyperdrive was new and Colonization more art than science. You couldn't trust an apparently Earthlike planet; chances were its biochemistry would be lethal to man. It was rare good luck to find a world like Atlantis.

Even apparently habitable planets might harbor some unsuspected germ to which man had no immunity. First a planet was thoroughly surveyed. Then an all-male party landed, spent two or three years building, analyzing, testing. Finally the women came.

He didn't know the history of Atlantis' Ship. Somewhere in the Service archives lay a record of a female transport with a female crew—you didn't mix the sexes on such a journey unless you wanted trouble. Judging from the names and the fragments of Christian belief, its complement had been purely North American; regional distinctions had still been considered important in those days. The Ship was bound for a new colony, but it vanished. A trepidation vortex, of course—perhaps the same one he had so narrowly missed. That was back before anyone knew of such a thing.

The Ship had not been destroyed. It had been tossed at an unthinkable pseudovelocity across two hundred or more light-years. The hyperdrive must have been ruined, since it didn't return home. But it must have emerged quite near Delta Capitis Lupi.

Pure good fortune that Atlantis was habitable. Doubtless the humans landed without preliminary tests they were not equipped to make . . . nothing to lose. Probably the Ship had been wrecked; they were cut off, no way to call for help and no way to get back.

They had little machinery, no weapons, scant technical knowledge. The crew must have done what they could, but you can't reproduce blasters and nuclear converters without certain machines. They discovered what the edible grains and the domesticable fowl were, set up a primitive agriculture, located iron and copper mines and established crude smelters, named the planet and moons in classical tradition . . . but that was all, and their knowledge slipped from them in a few illiterate lifetimes.

But in the first generation there had been a biochemist. There must have been. The thought of growing old and dying, one by one, with nobody to help the last feeble survivors, was unwelcome. Human parthenogenesis was an ancient technique. The biochemist had taken what equipment was in the Ship to make such a machine.

The right chemicals under the right conditions would cause a single ovum to divide. Once that process was initiated, it followed the normal course, and in nine months a child was born, genetically identical with the mother.

"It's an appalling situation," said Davis. "It will have to be remedied."

"What are you talking about?"

"You'll find out," he grinned.

They had come to a little bay, with soft grass down to the water's edge, rustling shade trees, the mountains looming titanic above. Flowers blossomed fiery underfoot and small waves chuckled against the shore.

There must be a sheer drop-off here to unknown depths, the water was so dark. But its surface glinted silver.

It was, in short, an ideal spot for romance.

Davis planted his fishing pole in a forked twig, the hook baited with a strip of jerky. He laid aside his bow and the axe Barbara had lent him, sat down, and extended an invitational arm.

Elinor sighed and snuggled up to him.

"Just think," she whispered. "The first Man in three hundred years!"

"High time, isn't it?" Davis gathered her in. She closed her eyes, breathing hard.

Davis laid a hand on her knee. She didn't object, so he slipped it upward. Elinor moaned a little. Her own hands moved along his back and hips, and around again. "Oh!" she exclaimed. "Your kilt—what's happening?"

"If you want a demonstration—" he leered.

"I do, I do." She wriggled. "I'm so *interested!*"

He let her glide downward in his embrace, until she lay on the grass. She clasped his neck, pulling his head toward hers. "Hold me close," she whispered.

"Just a minute and I will." He fumbled with her belt buckle.

Something roared behind him.

Davis leaped a meter in the air. Elinor shrieked. The thing looked like a saw-beaked, penguin-feathered seal, but bigger. It had swallowed his hook and was quite indignant. The flippers shot it up on the shore and over the grass at express speed.

Elinor tried to get to her feet. The fluke-like legs batted out. She went rolling and lay still. Davis clawed for his axe. The beak closed on his left ankle. He chopped wildly, saw blood run, but the soft iron wouldn't bite on that thick skull . . .

The seal-bird knocked him down, held him with one flipper and snapped at his face. Jaws closed on

the axe haft and crunched it across. Davis got a hand
on the upper and lower mandibles. Somehow he
struggled free, threw a leg over the long sleek back
and heaved. The brute roared and writhed. He felt
his strength pour out of him, the teeth were closing
on his fingers.

A crossbow bolt hummed and buried itself in the
wet flank. Another and another—Barbara ran over the
grass, shooting as she went. The monster turned its
head and Davis yanked his hands free.

"Get away!" yelled Barbara.

Her bow was empty now. She crouched, drawing
her knife, and plunged toward the creature. It reared
up, roaring. She jammed her left arm under its beak,
forced the head back, and slashed.

The flippers churned, and the seal-bird bowled her
over. Davis glimpsed a slim leg beneath the belly. He
picked up his own bow and fired pointblank, hardly
aware of what he did. Blood gurgled in the monster's
voice.

Then it slumped, and the arterial spurting was only
a red flow across slippery grass.

"Barbara . . ." Davis tugged at the weight, feeble
and futile. His own throat rattled.

The leg stirred. Barbara forced her way out from
under.

She stood up, gasping, and stared at him. Blood
ran from her face and breast and arms, dripped to
the ground, she stood in a puddle of blood. Davis'
knees gave way.

"Are you all right?" she whispered. "Bert, darling,
are you all right?" She stumbled toward him.

"Yeh . . ." He had a nasty gash in the ankle, and
his palms were lacerated, but it was nothing serious.
"You?"

"Oh, th-th-this isn't my blood." She laughed shortly,
sank to her knees before him, and burst into tears.

"There, there." He patted the bronze head,

clumsy and unsure of himself. "It's all over, Barbara, it's finished now ... Sunblaze, we've got meat for the pot . . ."

She shook herself, wiped her eyes, and gave him an angry stare. "You *fool!*" she snuffled. "If I hadn't h-h-happened to be near . . . heard the noise . . . oh, you blind gruntbrain!"

"Guess I've got that coming," said Davis. "Why do you drag me along, anyway?"

"I don't know," said Barbara, rising. "Get up!"

Elinor stirred, looked around, and started to cry. Since she wasn't much hurt, she got no attention. "Well!" she muttered.

Barbara swallowed her rage. "I never saw a thing like this before," she admitted. "I suppose you couldn't have known, Bert. You were giving it a good fight."

"Thanks," he said uncomfortably.

"And as you said . . . plenty of meat." She squared her shoulders. "I'll stand guard. You take Elinor back to camp, and when Valeria returns we can all drag it back."

"Yes," said Davis weakly. "I guess that's best."

CHAPTER X

When Valeria had blown off enough pressure by a magnificent description of Davis' intelligence, education, and personality, she offered news. There were clear signs of nearby settlement to the west: recent campsites, a beaten trail, smoke rising over the treetops. "They'll be sure to find us," she said, "and it mightn't look so well that we didn't go directly to them."

"Oh, yes!" babbled Elinor. "We can't stay here, those *things* in the lake . . ." Valeria glared her into silence.

Barbara's eyes gleamed. "And maybe we can make a deal with them. By the time we get home with help, the allies will have fallen apart, and our own messmates in the woods will join us. Let's go!"

"In the morning, child," said Valeria.

"Don't call me a child!" shouted Barbara. "I'm only three days younger than you, and my brain is twenty years older!"

"Girls, girls," began Davis. Then he apparently thought better of it and sat back to listen.

His injuries throbbed abominably, but sheer exhaustion put him to sleep. At Bee-rise he was able to limp around and help Barbara re-haft her axe.

She regarded him with concern. He had seemed such a big coward, she reflected . . . and yet he didn't try to run from the lake bird, but saved Elinor's life— Damn Elinor, anyway! If Davis had died on her account— And he had crossed an unimaginable chill gulf of distance, to a world hidden from all his people. Maybe it was only that he had never been trained as she had been. The concept of cultural difference was a new one; she knotted her brows over it. How would a Man, surrounded by robots, fire-shooting weapons, orsperless wagons, buildings as high as mountains, how would he think?

But it was heresy to admit this creature, barely two meters tall, who could sweat and bleed and be afraid, was a Man!

Then the Men were a thing colder and more remote than she had realized. Davis was *here*, warm and breathing. She could smell the faint pungency of his skin; his beard was like spun gold in the early sunlight and his eyes were blue with the most fascinating crinkles when he laughed. Yes, he sang her a bouncy little song as they worked, and laughed with her, which was beneath the dignity of the stony Men.

His hand brushed her knee, accidentally, and for a moment it seemed to burn and the world wobbled. What was wrong with her? She wanted to laugh and cry at the same time. She had cried yesterday, something no Whitley did past the age of twelve.

"Damn!" said Barbara.

"What's the matter?" asked Davis.

"Oh, nothing. Leave me alone, will you?" Then: "No, I didn't mean that!"

Davis gave her a very long look. She couldn't meet

it, she wanted to squirm. Savagely, she finished whittling the handle and put it through the axhead. Davis held it while she drove in the wedge with a stone, concentrating furiously on the work.

Valeria, somewhat handicapped by Elinor's assistance, had butchered the lake bird. Its hide might be a valuable gift to the Udall where they were bound. She loaded the orspers evenly and said the party had better walk to spare them.

"Except Davis," said Barbara.

"Never mind Davis!" said Valeria.

Barbara swung her axe so it whistled. The new shaft was carved from a seasoned branch and felt strong enough. "We started out to snatch him away from the enemy," she answered stiffly. "Now he's got a hurt leg. What's the point of having him along at all, you clothead, if we don't take care of him?"

"Have it your way," shrugged her cousin.

They went slowly along the shore. Davis swapped mounts from time to time. Toward evening they found a hard-packed path through a meadow, and could see a curl of smoke against sinking Theseus.

Barbara glanced uneasily into the shadowed forest and hefted her crossbow. She had a sense of being watched . . . yes, the songbirds were too quiet. Well . . . "This road seems headed for the town," she said. "We can follow it."

Whoever paced them between the trees was a skilled tracker. Barbara grew certain there was somebody.

And this silent following was not the way of the folk who dwelt near Holy River. Barbara shuddered, remembering dark stories mumbled by the helots, Critters and Gobblies. She found herself edging closer to Davis.

They rounded a bend, where a growth of canebrake hid what lay beyond, and met the strangers.

There were half a dozen, mounted, their shadows

long and black ahead of them. They were all Burkes:
tall slender women with dark, close-cropped hair and
blue eyes; the faces were a bit too long, but the wide
brows and pert noses would have been pretty if the
lips were not so thin. At home Burkes were soldiers,
artists and artisans in peacetime—not very popular,
because of their habit of coming up with unconven-
tional ideas, but often made Udall counselors.

These bore arbalests, javelins, and a weapon at the
belt new to Barbara, a curved knife a meter long,
obviously meant for slashing from orsperback. They
were peculiarly dressed, in cloth trousers, puff-sleeved
shirts, leather doublets with some distinguishing mark
branded on each.

There was a noise behind Barbara. She whirled and
saw another dozen coming from the woods, ringing
in her party. More Burkes!

Valeria lifted empty hands. "We're from Freetoon
over the mountains," she said. "We come in peace."

The oldest woman, about fifty but still lithe, rode
a way ahead of her troop. "Over Smoky Pass?" She
spoke with a clipped accent, hard to follow. "Why?
What's this with you?"

Davis nodded genially. "I am a Man," he said.

"Hm?" The Burkes looked hard at him. They did
not break into chatter among themselves, as Freetooners would have done.

"Man?" snapped the oldest one. "Where from?"

Davis pointed to the sky. "Up there, the stars." He
beamed at them. "I'm the genuine article. Beware of
imitations."

There was a long silence. It was disconcerting.

"What d'you want?" asked somebody.

"We'll discuss that with your Udall," said Valeria
haughtily.

"Our . . . oh. No Udall. Talk to Council. Come."

No Udall! Barbara was too stunned to do more
than follow meekly as the riders urged her forward.

"But this is awful," whispered Elinor. She trembled.

Davis narrowed his eyes. "Wait a minute," he said. "Is there anyone but your sort around here?"

The leader smiled. "No. Burkes of Burkeville. I'm Gwen, army chief."

"Not much of an army," said Valeria brashly.

She received a scornful look. "Don't need much. War's stupid. If we're attacked, ev'ry Burke fights."

Nothing more was said. Barbara felt bewildered. *Of course,* she thought numbly, *of course if they are all Burkes they can all bear arms. But no Udall? How do they decide what to do?* Then, after wrestling with the matter: *I suppose they must all want much the same thing, so it can't be a great problem for them.*

Both suns were down and Minos well into the second quarter when they reached Burkeville. There was light enough to see by. The town was built on piles in a narrow bay of the lake, some fifty long buildings of planed lumber and shingled roofs, in a graceful, airy, riotously carved and painted style. Slim boats were moored to the piles, with masts and furled sails—not that Barbara recognized that item. There was a drawbridge for crossing ten meters of open water, it thudded beneath the orsper feet.

Word must have gone ahead. Burkes of all ages stood in front of their barracks. They spoke little to each other, which seemed unnatural to Barbara. Here and there, above the plank deck of the town, rose tall wooden statues. They seemed to be stylized representations of humans and animals in violent action. A smell of fish told her that Burkeville got most of its food from the lake, probably had only a few small fields on shore. . . yes, they could barter . . .

About two thousand adults, she estimated through the blue night, and as many children. All were scantily clad and had their hair cut short.

The party stopped before a house in the middle

of town. They entered without formality, leaving the doors open so the rest of the women could look in. A line of red pillars carved with vines and birds marched down the hall. There was a fireplace, but most of the light came from bracketed candles—the room was positively brilliant. And beautiful, thought Barbara, looking at the chairs and tables, the feather tapestries and copper plaques.

Indoors there was an even more casual attitude toward clothes than at Freetoon. Most of the women wore little more than a few beads. Davis' eyes shuttled. Barbara felt a thick anger. She could show these snake-hipped, flat-chested creatures a thing or two!

Several mature women sprawled in the big chairs near the hearth. They rose and stared at Davis. He grew uncomfortable after a minute. "Hello," he said.

"Greetings." The one who spoke was a trifle more ornamented than the rest, with a feather skirt and a plume in her hair. She was in her thirties. "Kathleen the Second. I speak for Council. Sit."

Davis lowered himself, shaking a dazed head. "What goes on here? I don't understand. Are you nothing but, uh, Burkes?"

"Right. Live as we want to. Ever'body else stupid." Kathleen gave the Whitleys a challenging glance; both of them flushed but decided not to make an issue of it. "Began hun'erd years 'go, Flormead overrun an' sev'ral Burkes got away t'gether."

"I see. Well . . ."

"'Bout y'selves. Oh, y'll wan' food, drink." Kathleen nodded to a few adolescents who stood nearby. They went out, silently. "Glad see you. Only rumors 'bout other side of the mountains."

Valeria cleared her throat. "We come as refugees, ma'am," she said with the proper blend of pride and deference "But not as beggars. Our arms are at our hostess' service and if you will accept a

small gift, the hide of a great bird we killed
yesterday . . ."

The hall rang with laughter. Valeria jumped to her
feet.

"'Scuse." Kathleen wiped her eyes. "Not our custom. Story goes y' have chiefs an' such silliness.
Correct? Like certain folk on this side, s'pose."

"What else would we have?" asked Barbara,
bridling.

"*We* all think same way. Natural. Council makes
routine decisions. It don' make Councilors any
better'n anyone else. Ah!"

The girls were returning with laden trays. Davis,
Barbara, and Valeria attacked the food hungrily. Elinor
minded her manners. The drink was merely unfer-
mented berry juice; Barbara recalled that *her* Burkes
didn't like beer. Kathleen and the others watched
them.

"Now, then," said the Speaker when they had finished. "Who're you?" She looked at Davis.

"Davis Bertram," he smiled. "A Man . . . a human
male."

There was a rushing of whispers, but only from the
children.

So he says! thought Barbara. She was about to blurt
how he lied, but shut her lips. Valeria's snapped closed
at the same time. It would be helpful if the Burkes
were convinced.

"Story?" said Kathleen at last. Her face was impassive.

Davis sketched it for her.

There was another stillness. Heads shook, slowly,
and the slim bodies shifted. A few spears were raised
beyond the door.

"Wait," said Kathleen. "This is new . . . have t'
think . . . Can y' prove it?"

"Of course," said Davis smugly. Barbara wanted to
slap him.

"Hmmm . . . we never thought highly o' stories, handed out from Ship. If Men're human males, means they're human—like us—no more." Kathleen traded looks with her twins.

"'Stonishing. Hard t' swallow, but—" Abruptly: "What y' plans?"

"We were seeking to help to win back Freetoon," said Barbara.

There was another rain of laughter.

"Not int'rested," said Kathleen. "What's a mixed town t' us?"

"We're going to the Ship," added Davis.

"Hm . . . yes. I see." Kathleen rose. "Y're tired now. Welcome here. Talk t'morrow."

It was a dismissal.

CHAPTER XI

The Burkes lived in barracks like the Freetooners, but there was no caste distinction. Barbara was led to a house as ornamented as the Council room. The decorations lacked a master plan; each woman had her own stretch of wall above a low bed and did what she wished to it, but the overall effect was of harmonious repetition. There were a few vacant bunks, luxurious after the straw ticks of Freetoon and the bedrolls of the march.

The morning bustle woke her. She joined the rest in a chow line, where cooks were dishing up bread and fried fish. It could almost have been home, save that the KP's were Burkes also.

"How do they settle who does the cooking?" she wondered aloud.

"All take turns at menial work," said a townswoman. "Otherwise carry on our sep'rate trades."

The fishing fleet had already set forth. Elsewhere

Burkes carved, painted, wove, and there was one who
sat with a harp composing a song. Barbara shook her
head. "They can't do all that!"

"Any gifted person can do a lot of things," Davis
told her. "I know two brothers, identical twins, on
Earth. One is a psycho-technician and one a spaceship captain. And both of them play second fiddle
in an amateur orchestra. I myself am a painter of
sorts."

"Oh, an *artist!*" squealed Elinor.

Davis seemed less interested in her today. At least
he had taste enough to go for the Burkes, thought
Barbara resentfully . . . not that that was saying much.
There were some children swimming gaily between
the piles; the lake monsters must have learned this
bay was unsafe for them. Davis looked at cool, glistening water, stripped, and plunged. After a moment,
the Whitleys followed suit.

Davis was a good swimmer. He shouted, dove
under, and got a grip on Barbara's ankle. She came
up again sputtering. He appeared beside her, grinned,
and planted a kiss on her lips.

"Don't!" she gasped.

"Why not? Confidentially, you and Val are the best-
built wenches on Atlantis."

"Stop that!" said Valeria. "We're on trial here. I
don't like this situation one tiny bit."

She swam off with long smooth strokes. Davis
eyed her sullenly. Barbara used the chance to
escape . . . *escape from what?* she wondered. There
was still a cold damp tingle on her mouth.

Afterward they sat on the deck, drying, while Burkes
clustered around. There were eager questions, and
their own queries were answered freely enough. But
Barbara noticed a sort of relay, her words being passed
through the crowd toward the Council hall. It gave her
an uneasy feeling.

The Burkes talked little among themselves, she

noticed; no reason for conversation, ordinarily. There was something psychic about this place, she decided—she had never feared any woman, not even the Old Udall, but these Burkes were too alien for comfort.

"An' y're really a Man?" asked a young girl. The children here were a brash lot, above a curious inward restraint.

Davis nodded. "I am. But as Kathleen put it, I'm only human."

Valeria and Barbara looked at each other. Chattering like a baby! The blind chickwit! If he would only act as a Man should, they would have had a chance to overawe all Burkeville.

An older woman frowned. "We ne'er gave much heed t' old tales," she said. "Burkes think f'r 'emselves. Must'a been shipwreck, f' natural reasons, in old days . . ."

"That's right," said Davis.

"Doctors have power because only Doctors can fertilize. We tried t' build fertilizing machine. No luck. So we have t' pay tribute an' go through their silly rites like ever'body else."

"Oh!" whispered Elinor. "Talking about it in front of . . . of *children!*"

"So y've initiations on y'r side mountains? Big secret. Jus' like swampfolk. We all grow up knowing truth."

Barbara's universe, already somewhat battered, quivered and lost a few more bricks. These Burkes broke every law in the canon and throve. Could it be that Father was not behind the Doctors?

She waited for a thunderbolt. None came. Defiantly, she repeated the thought. Glancing over her own tanned form, she saw no shriveling.

But then, she thought wildly, then everything Davis claimed made sense! Then he might actually *be* a Man!

Vaguely, through a clamorous heartbeat, she heard

the dry Burke voice: "'Course, we don' tell Doctors
what we think. Raise our kids t' keep mouth shut
when legates arrive."

"Sensible girls," said Davis.

He was dry now, and resumed his kilt and cloak.
The Whitleys wound up their wet hair and did like-
wise. They were all guided around town, shown the
sights; the peace and plenty of Burkeville were
bragged up for them, and Barbara had to admit there
was truth in the boasts.

"But the life must be dull," she murmured to
Valeria. The cousins had found an excuse to wander
off by themselves; interest was all centered on Davis.
"The same person, over and over."

"A pretty many-sided person, though."

"Yes . . Val, I was just thinking . . . we, our way of
living, it may have shrunk us somehow. Everybody
knowing just one thing, one skill—any of these Burkes
can talk about anything."

"You may be right," nodded Valeria. "I've had much
the same notions today, and Father didn't kill me for
having them. But I don't think the Burkes are any
better than us, not really."

"Mmmm . . . yes. I see what you mean. They make
all these pretty carvings and things, but one piece of
art is so much like another. And they miss all the fun
of talking to somebody different. Remember how we
used to argue with Kim and Ginny?"

Sudden tears stung her eyes. Sharp before her rose
Freetoon—but it was done, finished, dead. Even if
she returned in triumph, drove out the enemy and
found all her friends still alive for her it could not
be the same, it was too narrow and lonesome.

She could never go home.

She wanted to find Davis and blurt her woe to
him.

"It would be better if the Men came," said Valeria
softly. "We've never lived as Father—or whoever made

the stars—meant us to live. We've just hung on, hoping, for three hundred years."

Barbara felt a smile tug at her mouth. "It would be fun to have a Man-child," she mused. Then, in stabbing realization: "But Val! Bert *is* a Man!"

"Rotten specimen of one," snapped Valeria.

Barbara felt puzzled. They thought so much alike that it was hard to see why Val despised Davis.

Her mind wandered back to the Man, and she forgot the question.

"Better get back," said Valeria. "I don't trust that Davis out of my sight."

Elinor was seated outside their barrack. She looked small and scared. No one else was around; the Burkes had again clustered by the Council hall.

"Where's Davis?" asked Barbara. Her throat felt tight.

"In there." Elinor pointed to the house. "They sent for him . . . that Kathleen!" She looked up, her eyes wide. "When are we getting out of this awful place?"

"As soon as possible," said Valeria grimly. "Whenever that may be. No help here, and I wouldn't put anything past them."

Elinor began to cry, noisily wishing herself back with darling Claudia. The Whitleys glared at her and moved away.

"I'd give a lot to hear what's being said," whispered Valeria. "If we weren't asked to join . . . it doesn't look so good for us."

"Maybe they didn't think of it." Barbara ran across booming planks to the edge of the crowd. "Let me in, please."

"Sorry, no." An armed Burke waved a saber. "Private discussion."

"What's private *here?*" flared Barbara.

Other trousered warriors moved closer. The sunlight was hot on their spearheads. Barbara cursed and returned to the barrack.

"I think we could make a break for it," said Valeria. "That bridge is still down, and there are fresh orspers just across the street. Nobody's looking."

"What good would that do?" countered Barbara. "Without Davis, we're nothing but outlaws. But if I could listen . . ."

The close-packed Burkes were whispering, relaying to each other what was said within the hall. The younger ones kept glancing furtively at the Freetooners.

"Come inside," said Barbara. "I have an idea."

The emptiness of the barrack was welcome after all those eyes. There was a trapdoor on the floor, opening on the lake; the Burkes sometimes liked to fish through it, or you could throw stones down on enemy boats. "I think I can get at the hall this way," said Barbara. "Nobody's on the other side of it."

"I'll go," said Valeria.

"You will *not!* I thought of it first!"

"Yeh . . . and somebody has to watch this." Valeria gave Elinor an unfriendly stare. "Go, then. If they set on me, I've got my axe, and I can stand them off for a while."

Barbara removed her clothes and opened the trap. She hung by her fingers . . . the water was three meters below. Valeria grinned tightly and handed her a lasso from her kit. Barbara went down it cautiously and began to swim.

Sunlight and shadow streamed between the piles. Through clear water, she could see a weedy bottom and fish sliding over stones. The sails of the fleet shone red and blue across five kilometers, the forest was green beyond and the sky brilliant overhead. It was very near eclipse.

She waited until Bee went behind Minos. Ay still threw feeble light, the planet glowed ghostly and banded, but a dense dusk flowed across the world. Barbara swarmed up the ladder at the far end of the deck. She could barely see the crowd on the opposite side of the hall. Their light cloaks glimmered. Her own sun-darkened form must be invisible at this distance.

Business did not halt for eclipse . . . had those bitches no respect for anything? Barbara ran across the planks, dodging from house to house. The hall was before her. She glided to one of its large windows and peered carefully in.

There were only a few Burkes speaking directly to Davis. All but Kathleen were old: their most experienced Councilors. Candles had been lit against the eclipse, and Davis towered splendidly in the glow.

He spoke, and Barbara thought—even now—what a fine thing a deep voice was. Whitleys were contraltos, but these Burkes were all yattering sopranos, and . . .

"All right, Kate, so I've convinced you I am a Man."

"Not entirely. Still need final proof." She didn't even blush!

"Sure! Whenever we can get some privacy."

"Oh, y' wish t' be alone? Very well."

"Who will . . . er . . ."

"I—if all goes well, if I'm not hurt—"

"You won't be." Davis was grinning like a foolfish. "Good."

Kathleen slipped off her mantle and let it fall at her feet. She wasn't wearing anything beneath. She stood up straight, throwing her shoulders back and bosom forward. *Well, she's got to make the most of what she has!* thought Barbara. But then, driven by a stubborn realism: *What she has isn't so bad. Not really. She's too thin, but nothing haggard about her. She has the muscles to bounce around as readily as anyone.*

She thought: *Davis sees that also,* and wondered why tears blurred her vision.

Kathleen caught the Man's hands between her own and looked up at him. "B'lieve kissing cust'mary 'mong mixed-fam'ly tribes," she said.

Davis glanced at the impassive audience, shrugged a little, grinned one-sided, and pulled Kathleen against him. She placed his palms on her flanks and hugged his neck. As their lips met, Barbara told herself with an oath that she would *not* bawl.

"Pleas'rable," said Kathleen. "See potential'ties of an elab'rated technique in this. What methods d'y' rec'mmend?"

"Well, uh, you might try moving around a little," choked Davis.

She writhed. Her fingers stroked him experimentally, sensitive to his own response. As he came up for air, Davis gasped: "Great Cosmos! I n-n-never expected—an intellectual like you—would—"

"All arts best when an'lyzed." Kathleen was as flushed as he, starting to breathe hard. "Once I get a background o' 'sperience, I might . . . yes . . . originate new styles in this art."

"For all things' sake," exploded Davis, "Let's go accumulate some background!"

"Yes. At once. F'r sake of all Burkeville, anyhow, best we get this project org'nized fast. Come." She seized his wrist and urged him toward the inner building.

A hesitation came upon Davis. His gaze flickered back to the Councillors. They had taken on avid expressions, but the atmosphere was, somehow, disturbingly unbiological. He cleared his throat.

"But wait a minute, sweetheart. I can understand your, uh, natural curiosity. But have you any plans beyond that?"

"'Course." Kathleen smiled at him. "We know well enough, we need Men. Watched birds in springtime. Y' give new experience, healthy life, t' whole town."

"Mmmm . . . ye-e-es . . . in the course of time!"

"An' children!" Kathleen's tone grew fierce. "Y'

think we like having Doctors boss us? Y'll make us free o' Doctors. We'll have t' hide y', first, play waiting game. But when y'r sons begin t' grow up—un'erstand? *We'll* own Atlantis!"

Davis' jaw dropped. He backed away. "Wait!" he exclaimed. "Wait just a minute. I thought you'd help me get my own ship back—I could bring all the Men you want . . ."

"An' Burkeville b'comes nothing? No, no, Davis. Here y' stay."

"But . . ."

Kathleen made no signal. None was needed. A dozen warriors stepped from the crowd, into the hall, and leveled their spears.

Davis looked about him, wildly. "But my friends!" he stammered.

"Fishbait."

A cold wind sprang up, ruffling the dark lake waters. Barbara wrenched herself from the window. No one was looking her way—they *mustn't* be! She found the ladder and returned to the lake. Swimming slowly for quietness was strain enough to break her.

She swarmed up the rope into the barrack gloom. "Well?" said Valeria.

"Father, Val! Those bitches . . . going to keep him here . . . kill us . . . where's my armor?"

Elinor screamed. Barbara cuffed her. "Shut up! Shut up or die!"

The Whitleys began helping each other, lacing corselets above the iron kilts, tugging on boots, strapping down helmets. "Quick!" choked Barbara. "Eclipse is almost over. Elinor, you see that stable across the way? Fetch out four orspers—fresh ones—and . . . yes!" She snatched a brand from the small hearthfire. "Shove this into the straw."

"I, I, I . . ."

Valeria helped her on her way with a lusty kick. "Either that or get your throat slit, my dear," she said.

The westward rim of Minos was turning incandescent when the Whitleys were dressed. They hurried into the street as Elinor shooed four birds through the barn door. No time for saddle or bedroll—but you needed reins, and the fishhead had forgotten that, of course. Barbara darted into the stables. A fire was leaping up in a pile of dry straw. She snatched harness off the wall and ran out.

A Burke child saw them and screamed. The crowd faced slowly around, hampered by its own mass. Barbara slapped a bit into an orsper beak, heard it click home in the notch, threw the crownpiece and front around the stiff blue crest, made the bird crouch, and mounted, tightening the buckle as she did. Elinor wailed. Valeria leaned over. "Harness one for Davis!" she shouted.

Then the Whitleys charged the Burkes.

Father be praised, orspers were stupid enough to turn on their own mistresses, and these had been trained like Freetoon birds. Barbara let beak and claws cut a way for her while she leaned to right and left plying her axe. She didn't know if anyone got killed, didn't care. "Bert! Bert, come out!"

A thrown spear glanced off her cuirass. A saber hewed at her leg, slashing the boot. She cut back and nearly fell off. There was a seething of Burkes; they screamed and tried to run and tripped over each other. The armed women would have held steady, but the mob swirled them away.

Davis appeared. He swung the remnant of a chair and whooped. Part of Barbara's mind said there had never in all the starry universe been so gallant a sight.

Bee drew clear of Minos, full day flooded across the lake. Somehow the Whitleys and Davis were back at the stable. Fire wavered pale in the door, the orspers within screeched. Barbara felt sorry for them, poor birds; she hoped they could be freed, she wished it hadn't been necessary to make them too frantic to ride for a while.

Davis pulled at the crest of a free orsper. It bent down for him and he mounted, a precarious seat without stirrups. Barbara noticed in faint surprise that Elinor was on her own steed—she'd expected the Dyckman to wring her hands till the Burkes chopped her up.

The drawbridge thundered beneath them. There was a road which led from it, westward on the long downgrade to the sea. Dust whirled up from clawed feet and Barbara gave herself to the rocking rhythm of a full-speed run.

The Burkes would put out the fire, she thought bleakly, calm their orspers, and pursue with saddles and spare mounts. She hoped her party had enough of a head start.

CHAPTER XII

Several kilometers from the lake town, Valeria's orsper coughed blood and sank on its breast. "Wounded in the fight," she said bitterly. "I'll double up with Elinor."

"That'll wear her bird out pretty quick," panted Barbara.

"We can switch around," said Valeria.

They resumed at an easier pace. The road was wide and deeply rutted; it must be a trade highway. Forest crowded tall on either side. Already the air was warmer. The trees were hardwood species; midge-like insects glinted in the sun. This land was a steep decline into some great river valley.

"We'd better leave the road as soon as possible," said Barbara.

Davis nodded. "I never . . . I won't say you saved me from a fate worse than death, kid, but I am grateful."

"Maybe now you'll behave yourself," snapped the girl.

Davis shrugged. It almost cost him his seat on the slippery orsper back. He concentrated on staying mounted.

But sunder it! he thought resentfully, it wasn't fair to put him on a planet aswarm with pretty girls and interrupt him every time things began to get interesting. He felt much abused.

His mind turned to the abandoned orsper, dying on a hot dusty road . . . to Burkes, Freetooners, Greendalers maimed and slain, to Barbara and Valeria driven from their home and hunted across high mountains. The situation was unfair to everybody. And Davis Bertram had brought it on.

No court of law would call it his fault. But still, he *had* catalyzed cruelty and murder, and his own blundering had made it worse. Strength, education, a good if somewhat rusty mind gave him the power, and hence the responsibility, to make the crucial decisions. So far he had failed that job.

He got into such a glow of good resolutions that he almost fell off again. It was an effort to ride these birds without a saddle.

Down and down the road wound, snaking about one tumbled vine-grown cliff after another. The low suns blazed in their faces. Now and then they stopped to switch the double weight; otherwise, they continued with the memory of spears at their back. Davis thought that the Burkes would kill him if they couldn't have the exclusive franchise. They were too jealous of their little ingrown society. That was one culture the Service was bound to decide should not be protected.

Meanwhile, though, the orspers neared exhaustion.

Valeria broke a lengthy silence. "It won't do us any good to ride these brutes much longer. It wears us and them out, and the enemy will have spare birds."

"They'll have saddles, too," added Barbara. "We can't fight saddle-mounted riders."

"Better strike out on foot," finished Valeria. "If we can't lose them in these woods they have my permission to barbecue us for breakfast."

"Don't!" Elinor turned slightly green.

"Yeh," said Davis. "I do wish you wouldn't mention food. It's been all day since I ate."

Bee smoldered in coppery sunset clouds. Faintly to their right could be heard the noise of a waterfall. Barbara rubbed her snub nose thoughtfully. "Didn't we pass a trail a kilometer or so back?" she asked.

"Yes . . . little weed-grown bush trail," nodded Davis.

"Well, that means people, and I don't think any people could be very friendly with the Burkes. Especially if you keep your mouth shut, Bert, and act the way a Man ought to."

Ouch!

They rode their orspers off the road, dismounted carefully, and shooed the birds on down the highway. Valeria glided into the forest; Barbara brought up the rear, smoothing out all trace. Thereafter it was a struggle through murky thickets to reach the path.

Minos-light spattered cold between dense leaves. The trail was a tiny one, obviously seldom used, plunging downhill between boulder outcrops and subtropical canebrakes. There was a heavy smell of green life, growing and rotting; luminous fungi speckled trees nearly choked with vines; the waterfall sound grew louder.

It was a good two hours before they reached the source. Then they emerged on wet stones to see a great river, gunmetal under Minos, leap a full kilometer off a sheer precipice. The king planet grew hazy in a chill mist where dim rainbows danced. The crashing of the waters drowned all voice; human heads rang with it.

The trail, barren and slippery, went down the brink

into a canyon. Valeria pointed in that direction.
Through the cold foggy light, Davis saw her raise
questioning brows and nodded. She took the lead
again, feeling a careful way while rainbowed death
roared beside her.

Davis stole a glance at Barbara. The girl was
watching the torrent, eyes wide and lips parted.
Droplets of mist glimmered like jewels in her hair.
His heart gave a thump.

Past midnight, they reached the bottom of the cliff.
For a while they rested, watching the whirlpool and
the white column of the fall. Then, with a little sigh,
Barbara stood up and trudged on.

The trail followed the riverbank. In the brilliant
unreal planet glow, Davis saw that the canyon walls
spread out ahead of him until they were several kilometers across. But the river widened too, until a sheet
of water broad as a lake flowed smoothly between
scarps and crags. It occupied nearly the whole canyon floor; this river was as big as the Colorado.

Across a broken shimmer of Minos-light, they could
see small rocky islands dotting the surface. Now that
they were away from the fall, the air grew warm
again. But there wasn't room for forest down here,
or even for grass. Poor hunting, if any.

Davis counted up their assets. The girls had their
fighting equipment: armor, axes, bows, dirks, lassos
looped around the shoulder, hooks and line in their
pouches. No bedrolls or frying pan . . . oh, well, they
were in a mild climate now.

He and Elinor had nothing but the tattered kilts
and the disintegrating sandals they stood up in.

And my strength, of course. Davis looked complacently at the muscles of his arm. Given the initial
distraction of the Whitley attack, he'd had small
trouble fighting his way clear of Burke Hall. Kathleen
the Second would have a lump on her head to
remember him by. *And my education.*

Trouble was, crossbow bolts had small respect for muscle power, and it was no good knowing how to pilot a spaceship and fire a blaster if spaceships and blasters weren't available.

Toward morning, under a rosy eastern sky, Davis made out a really big island ahead of him. It was nearly circular, ten kilometers or so across and thickly overgrown with forest. It came within a few meters of shore, and he thought of swimming out.

Then the dawn-glow showed him that the place was inaccessible: a giant basaltic outcrop, black cliffs rising ten vertical meters with the woods growing on top. Short of antigrav equipment or magnetronic boots, nobody could . . .

"Hoy!" Valeria came to a halt; stones rattled beneath her feet.

After a moment, Davis saw it too: a slender suspension bridge from the clifftop to the shore. It was anchored by cables of woven vine to a rusty crag on this side, to fronded trees on the island.

Barbara's crossbow clanked into position. "So somebody does live here," she whispered.

"This is where the trail ends," agreed Valeria. "The question is who, and what can we talk them out of?"

Davis felt it incumbent on him to lead the way, though his guts crawled at the thought of a shot. He spoke rapidly, through a dry mouth: "Whoever it is doesn't have to take any nonsense from the Burkes, or anybody except the Doctors. That island must be self-sufficient, and it can't be taken."

"No?" growled Valeria. "I'd beat my way across that bridge alone."

"All they have to do is shoot from the shelter of the woods. And meanwhile they cut those cables. Down comes the bridge. How do you build a new one with the islanders potshotting your engineers?"

"How did they get there in the first place?"

"Ladders, I suppose. Which won't work against any proper defense."

"Mmmm . . . yes. I see." She spoke slowly, as if reluctant to admit he was correct.

Davis halted at the foot of the bridge. There must be someone watching at the other end, in the twilight beneath the trees. He cupped hands around his mouth and bawled: "Hello, up there! We come in peace!"

Echoes clamored between the river and the talus slopes up the canyon wall. There was a brief wait.

Then a slender girl clad in long brown hair and a few flowers stepped to the head of the bridge. She had a crossbow, but didn't aim it at them. "Who are you?" she called timidly.

"She's a Craig," whispered Barbara to Davis. "At home they're all poets and weavers. Now why would a Craig be on sentry-go?"

He paused, drawing himself up impressively. "Know that I am Davis, a Man come from Earth to redeem the old promise," he intoned, feeling rather silly. Barbara smothered a giggle.

"Oh!" The Craig dropped her bow and broke into a tremble. "A Man—*Ohhhh!*"

"I come as the vanguard of all the Men, that they may return to their loyal women and drive evil from the world Atlantis," boomed Davis. "Let me cross your bridge that I may, uh, claim your help in my, er, crusade. Yes, that's it, crusade."

The Craig squeaked and fell on her face. Davis started over the bridge. It was too steep a climb for an impressive march, but the timing was perfect— B just rising in a golden blaze over the waterfall. Barbara and Valeria tramped boldly behind him; even Elinor seemed to regain enough strength to smooth back her tangled hair.

Past the bridge, there was a downward path; the island was cup-shaped. Only the rim of the cup held true forest; elsewhere, the trees grew in orderly groves. The grass beneath them was clipped and there were hedgerows and brilliant flowerbeds.

A few other women emerged from the woods, laying down their bows and axes. They were as sleek, suntanned, and informally dressed as the first one. And their reactions were just as satisfactory, a spectrum from abasement to awed gaping.

"More Craigs, couple of Salmons, a Holloway, an O'Brien," murmured Valeria. "Artist, artisan, entertainer and poet classes at home—that sort."

Davis stooped over the first girl and raised her. "You may look on me, my dear," he said unctuously. She herself was worth looking at, too. "I come as your friend."

She dug her toes in the dirt and blushed in various places.

A Holloway, rather big and corpulent, cleared her throat shyly. "We never thought there would be so great an honor for *us*," she whispered. "We thought when the Men came, they'd, er . . ."

Davis puffed himself up. "Do you doubt I am a Man?" he roared.

"Oh, no, ma'am!" The Holloway wrung her hands, cringing from possible thunderbolts. "You're exactly as the songs say, big and beautiful, with a voice like the Leaping Water."

She herself, like the other islanders, had a very pleasing voice. The local accent was a curious blend of exact pronunciation and melodious overtones; they must all have had first-class vocal training. Looking more closely beyond her, Davis saw that the hedges and gardens were arranged with elaborate tastefulness.

But he'd better get his theology straight. "There has been much evil done," he declared, "and to right it, I, the Man, must go as . . . well, as any woman, with only these few loyal attendants. I'm here to summon all women of good will to my cause. The Men help those who help themselves."

"Will you come to our homes, ma'am?"

"The proper form of address is 'sir.' Yes, we will come take rest and refreshment with you, and after that confer with your leaders." Davis beamed and clapped his hands. "Don't . . . I mean, be not afraid. Rejoice!"

"You big chatterbird," hissed Barbara in his ear.

"Shut up," muttered Davis. "I'm having trouble enough keeping a straight face."

The guards needed no more than his consent to start rejoicing. Some dashed ahead, crying out the news, while others ran to pluck flowers and strew them in his path. When he had walked through two kilometers of parkscape, smiling like a politician in a representative-government culture, the whole population came to meet him.

There were about twenty genotypes, he saw, all of the artist-artisan variety. Altogether they numbered about a thousand, including children. They had put on their best clothes, woven dresses, lacy scarfs, feather bonnets, draped leis—the total effect stunned him, a riot of carefully chosen color, flame red and cobalt blue, forest green and hot gold and burnished copper. All bore plain signs of good, easy living; the older women were tremendously fat, the young ones slim and full of grace, with faces and bodies intricately painted.

They danced around him, sang in a choir, reed pipes skirled and a great drum thundered through the woods. Flowers rained on his path and tangled in his hair. Mothers pressed their babies toward him for the touch of his hands. Tame birds with tails like rushing fire strutted on cool grass; whole trees pruned into living statuary rustled overhead; the morning wind went like a benediction across the land.

The village nestled at the bottom of the cup,

surprisingly large. But each of the simple grass huts could only have held a few people . . . by Cosmos, here was one place on Atlantis where you had a right to privacy! One long house in the middle of town was of split bamboo-like material, probably used on public occasions. It faced on a green plaza rimmed with cooking pits.

About this time, the past twelve hours caught up with Davis. He managed somehow to inject sufficient pomp into his demand for breakfast and bed. They brought him eggs, fruits, small sweet cakes, and berry wine. Then they conducted him to the chief's house and tucked him into feather bolsters and sang him a lullaby.

Nobody spoke above a whisper all the time he slept.

CHAPTER XIII

Davis awoke near sunset. A girl posted at his bed waved her arm through the curtained door. Others who must have been waiting entered, to kneel with towels and basins of hot water, or stand playing the harp.

"Well, well." Davis yawned enormously. "This is more like it. When do we eat?"

"A feast has been prepared, our unworthy best, if the Man will deign to taste it."

"The Man will deign to make a pig of himself." Davis got out of bed. The floor had been covered with flower petals. The girls were plainly expecting to bathe him, but he chased them out.

An embroidered kilt, a plumed headdress, golden bangles, and a dirk in a tooled-leather scabbard were laid forth for him. He dressed and brushed through the door.

Bee was low between the trees on the island rim;

shadows lapped the great bowl, but the air was mild. Women scurried about the roasting pits. When Davis emerged, a crowd of musicians struck up and another band of girls chosen for youth and beauty went out on the green to dance before him.

Valeria stood waiting. She had loosened her red hair, put armor aside in favor of a simple kilt and lei, but the scarred left hand rested on her knife. "Well," she said, "it took you long enough. Nobody would eat before you, and I'm ravenous."

"We seem to have found the kind of place we deserve," said Davis. He started around the plaza toward a dais richly draped with feather cloaks. Barbara lounged by it, in conversation with a Craig who wore the ornaments of leadership and held a carved staff.

"I don't know," said Valeria. "They're friendly enough, but gutless. This place is so easy to defend, they don't even need a warrior caste—never had one."

"What's it called?"

"Lysum. It's another offshoot of the same conquered town those Burkes ran from. In this case, only a certain class of people got together. They can fish in the river, they have tame fowl, fruits and nuts the year 'round, all the wood and metal they want already stored—they never go anywhere!" Valeria looked disgusted.

Davis felt she was being unjust. Her own rather repulsive virtues, hardihood and fearlessness, would be as redundant here as fangs on a turtle. "How do they spend their time, then?" he asked.

"Oh, they do what little work there is, and the rest of it goes to arts, poetry, craft, music, flowers . . . Yah!"

Glancing at the delicately carved wood, subtly designed ornament, intricate figure dances, listening to choral music which was genuinely excellent, Davis got fed up with Valeria. Nobody had a right to be so narrow-minded. Here on Lysum they seemed as free as in Burkeville—no, infinitely more so; there wasn't the deadening monotony of a single genotype. Eventually, no doubt, this culture would stagnate if left to itself—but today it was young, creative, and happy.

The Craig on the dais stood up for him. She was not old enough to be fat; given a stronger chin she would have been quite pretty . . . though Barbara, in kilt and lei, was unfair competition. "Be welcome among us, Man." Now that the first shock had worn off, the Craig spoke with confidence. "Atlantis has never known a happier day than this—oh, we're so *thrilled!* All Lysum is yours."

"Thanks." Davis sat down, and she lowered herself to the ground before him. "You are the leader here?"

"Yes, sir. Yvonne Craig, Prezden of Lysum, your servant."

Davis looked around. "Where's Elinor?"

"Still pounding her ear, of course," snorted Barbara. "Want to wait for her?"

"Cosmos, no! When do we—I mean, Prezden Yvonne, let the banquet begin!"

Horns blew, the dance ended, the women of Lysum hurried to their places. Rank seemed strictly according to age, the oldest seated on the ground nearest Davis—which was a pity, in a way, though it was pleasant to see a casteless society. The children began serving at once, and that was a relief.

The food was delicious; the first cuisine he had encountered on Atlantis. And the courses went on and on, and the wooden winebowls were kept filled.

Sundown smoldered across the sky. Theseus, half full, came from behind Minos to add his ruddy light; stars powdered a velvety heaven and a warm breeze flowed down from the island rim with a smell of spices. Davis ate onward.

Music was played, but nobody spoke. He leaned

toward Yvonne. "I am pleased with what I have seen here," he told her.

"You are *so* sweet . . . I mean, gracious," she thrilled happily.

"Elsewhere there's devilment on the loose. The will of the Men is for peace among all, but first the wrongdoers must be punished."

"Your serving woman"—that got a scowl from Barbara and a snicker from Valeria—"told me that the Burkes had dared set on you with force."

"Ah, yes. You know the Burkes of Burkeville, then?"

"Slightly, sir. Nasty folk! Really, I don't know what the world is coming to. Why can't people leave each other in peace?" Yvonne had drunk a bit more than was wise—so had everybody—and spoke fast. "*Honestly,* sir, you wouldn't *believe* what some of those towns are like! Thank Father we don't have to have much to do with them. They're just *vile!*"

The Whitleys flanked Davis on the seat. Valeria leaned over and whispered: "See what I mean? No help here. I told this featherbelly we'd want some spears to follow us, and she near fainted."

"Mmmm . . . yes." Davis felt a moment's grimness. He couldn't look for armed assistance from Lysum— if offered, it would be rather less than no good—and he couldn't stay holed up here forever. No wonder Val was so down on the islanders; she was more disappointed than intolerant. Not a bad girl, Val, in her waspish way. Davis tilted his winebowl. His free arm stole about Barbara's waist. She regarded him mistily.

"Strong, this drink," she said. "Wha's it called?"

"A jug of wine, and thou," smiled Davis.

"Bubbles in my head . . ." Barbara leaned against him.

"Oh, here comes dessert," said Yvonne.

Davis could barely wrap himself around the elaborate confection.

The Prezden gave him a large-eyed look. Minos-light streamed over sprawling feminine forms. "Will you require us all tonight, sir?" she asked interestedly.

"Yipe!" said Davis.

"Go ahead." Valeria's low tone was surly. "I don't suppose it'll hurt matters here."

"Like hell you will!" Barbara opened her eyes, sat straight up, and glared at him.

Yvonne looked bewildered. Barbara was quite tight enough to start an argument, and that would never do. Davis donned a somewhat boozy benevolence.

"I thank you," he said. "It would not be fitting, though. Tonight I must, urp, think on weighty problems. I would be alone."

Yvonne bent her long-tressed head. "As the Man wishes. My house is his." Her dignity collapsed in a titter. "I am his too, if he changes his mind. Or any of us would be so *thrilled*—"

Sunblaze! thought Davis. This was too good a chance to miss. What had gotten into Barbara, anyhow? She sat brooding at Minos, nearly on the point of tears. Too much wine, no doubt.

Yvonne stood up and clapped her hands. "The Man wishes to be alone tonight," she called. "All you girls scat!"

In five minutes the door curtains had closed on the last islander. Davis gaped. It was not what he had meant.

Valeria got to her feet, put an arm under Barbara's shoulders. "I'll see her to bed," she said coldly. "Goodnight."

"Oh, no, you don't," said Davis. "Run along yourself. Babs and I have a little matter to discuss of who's boss here."

Valeria grinned. "Care to stop me . . . Man?"

Davis watched them disappear into one of the huts. "Death and destruction!" he said gloomily, and poured himself another drink.

He was tipsy, but there was no sleep in him. Presently he wandered off across a sward glistening with dew, under the light-spattered shade of high trees.

The fact is, and we might as well face it with our usual modesty, Barbara is in love with me. Maybe she doesn't quite realize it yet, but I know the symptoms. Well?

Davis realized he was a little scared . . . not of her, he decided after cogitating for a while, but of the consequences to himself. From time to time, there had been such girls, and he'd run like a jackrabbit. He didn't want to be tied down yet!

He climbed the long slope until he stood on the island rim and looked across the swirling darkness of the river. It murmured and chuckled beneath him, around him, the light of Minos and two moons and the few stars not drowned out shivered and broke on the surface; he saw foam where a rock jutted upward.

He stood for a time, watching. After all, he wasn't important; nobody was, in this broken wilderness of stone and water and moonlight. He couldn't just walk away from Barbara; he needed her for a guide if nothing else. But he wasn't so almighty wonderful that she couldn't forget him as soon as some other spacemen arrived.

If she got mad at him, he thought woozily, it would help her over the infatuation. And what would make her mad at him? Why, jealousy would do it. A Man had every right to change his mind; it wouldn't disillusion Lysum if he . . . Yes, they were disappointed in him already; he'd better remedy that situation at once.

He started quickly back toward the village. Let's see, now, protocol doubtless made Yvonne the candidate for tonight . . . uh, which hut was she using now?

He came out of a grove, with the valley open

before him down to the darkened houses, and stopped. There was a tall form approaching. "Barbara," he said numbly.

She came to him, smiling and shaking the loose red hair down over her back, but her eyes were big, solemn, a little afraid. "Bert," she whispered. "I wanted to talk to you."

She had no right to be so beautiful. Davis choked. She halted and stood with hands clasped behind her back, like a child. It was the only childlike thing about her, as Minos made abundantly clear.

"Um . . . sure . . . you got rid of that spitcat cousin of yours, I see," he began feebly.

"She's asleep. I wanted this to be between us two."

"Oh, yes, of course. Can't settle anything with Valeria sticking her nose into the business. Ask her a civil question and you get a civil war."

"Val . . . oh." The girl looked away. Light and shadow flowed across her. Suddenly she swung her head back to him. "What do you have against Valeria?"

"What does she have against me?" he shrugged. "She's a natural born shrew, I suppose."

"She means well. It's just that she . . . never quite knows what to say . . . and she's afraid of you."

"Afraid!" Davis laughed.

"I know her. We *are* of the same blood. Can't you . . ."

"Scuttle Valeria!" said Davis thickly. "Come here, you."

She crept into his arms, her hands stole from behind her back and closed around his neck. He kissed her, taking his time and savoring it . . . Her response had an endearing clumsiness.

She laid her face against his breast. "I couldn't stand it, Bertie," she confessed. "You and all those other women . . ."

"When you put it that way, every other woman in the Galaxy goes out of existence for me," said Davis.

She looked up again; the cool gold light glimmered off tears. "Do you mean that?"

"Of course I do," said Davis, concluding that he was sincere after all. At least, he was ready to forego everybody in Lysum if . . .

"I was so afraid," she said brokenly. "I didn't know what was happening to me, I thought I was psyched."

"Poor little Babs." He stroked her hair. "Sit down."

They spent a while without words. He was delighted to see how fast she learned.

"I was always alone," she said at last. "I had to be, don't you understand? It was hard for me to admit to myself . . . that I could belong to anyone else . . ."

Touched, he kissed her more gently. They were in the shadow of a frondtree; he could scarcely see her save as a warm breathing shape next to him.

She waited a little, as if gathering courage, then said: "Do whatever you want to, Bert."

Davis reached for her—and pulled up cold.

It was one thing to make love to an Elinor, a Kathleen, an Yvonne. Barbara was a different case entirely. He couldn't just run off and leave *her;* he had to live with himself. He wasn't that kind of scoundrel; she was too whole-hearted, it would hurt her too much when he finally left.

At the same time, he wasn't going to humiliate her into storming off. That had been the plan, half an hour ago, but conditions were changed. He needed time to decide what he really wanted.

"Well?" she asked.

"Well, this is a serious matter," said Davis. "You'd better think it over for a while."

"I've thought it over for days, darling."

"Yes, but . . ."

"But nothing! Come here." Small calloused hands closed on his wrists.

Davis talked. And talked. And talked. He wasn't sure what he said, but it included words like sanctity.

At the end, with sweat running down his ribs, he asked if she understood.

"No," she sighed. "But I suppose you know best."

"I wonder—never mind! Of course I do."

"It's really been enough, to be here with you. There'll be other times. Whenever you want to . . ."

"Cut that out!" groaned Davis. "Give me a kiss and go to bed."

She gave him a long one. Then, rising: "There is one thing, my beloved. The others in our party . . ."

"Mmmm, yes. I can handle Elinor, but I hate to think what Val would say."

"Don't let on to anyone. Not to me or . . . only when we're alone."

"All right. That does make it easier. Run along, sweetheart. I want to think."

"With the Craig?" she asked coldly.

"Cosmos, no!"

"I'll kill you if you do. I mean it."

"Yes," he muttered, "I'll take your word for that."

"Goodnight, Bertie. I care for you."

"The word," he said, "is love."

"I love you, then." She laughed, with a little sob, and sped down the hill.

Davis rose to his feet, not unpleasantly stunned. She ran like a deer, he thought—why couldn't she be trained for spatial survey? Married teams were common enough . . .

The girl stumbled. She spread her hands, regained balance, and continued.

Davis felt the wind go out of him. There had been a scar on her left hand.

CHAPTER XIV

Barbara woke up and wished she hadn't.

There were hammers behind her eyes, and she was abominably thirsty. A jug of water stood by her bed. She poured herself a long draught. At once the planet waltzed around her.

She grabbed her head and reeled off a string of cavalry oaths. The young O'Brien who peered in blushed. "Does my lady want anything?" she asked shyly.

"Don't shout at me!" snarled Barbara. "What the fire and thunder did you feed me last night?"

"Only the banquet, my lady, and the wine— Oh. I see. If my lady will permit . . ." The O'Brien scuttled out again.

Barbara rolled over on her stomach and buried her face in her hands. Foggy recollections came back; yes, Val had helped to bed and then she passed out . . . Davis making eyes at that Yvonne trollop . . . Father!

The O'Brien came back with a bowl of herb tea. It helped. Breakfast followed, and life was merely desolate. Barbara tottered out into the open.

It was a little past eclipse. The islanders were going about their usual business in their usual leisurely fashion. Prezden Yvonne ran warbling to greet her, received a bloodshot glare, and backed off. Barbara smoldered her way toward a fruit grove.

Valeria came into sight, wringing out her hair and glistening with wetness. "Oh, hello, small one," she grinned. "I recommend a swim. The water's wonderful."

"What have you got to be so happy about?"

Valeria did a few steps of the soldier's axe dance. "Beautiful, beautiful, beautiful day," she caroled. "I *love* this place!"

"Then it's too bad we're getting out of here."

"Whatever for?"

"What reason is there to stay? So that Davis can make up to all the women on Lysum?" Barbara kicked miserably at the turf. "I imagine he's still sleeping it off."

"Well, he did get to bed quite late, poor dear," said her twin. "But he was just walking around, thinking."

Barbara started. "How do you know?"

Valeria flushed. "I couldn't sleep. I sat up and watched till nearly Bee-rise."

"Then you ought to be snoring yet."

"Don't need sleep." Valeria jumped after a red fruit, seized it, and crunched it between small white teeth. "Look, Babs, we're not in your kind of hurry. We need a rest, and this is the place to take it. Also, we'll have to get orspers . . . negotiate with some other town; they don't have 'em here . . ."

"I thought you knew. One of the local yuts told me yesterday. This river runs straight down to the sea, and that waterfall behind us is the last one. They have boats here. We'll commandeer one and make the trip twice as fast. That's how the Lysumites go to the Ship. They buy passage from the seafolk and . . ."

"Oh, hell, Babs." Valeria laid a hand on her shoulder. "We have a fair chance of getting killed somewhere along the way, and life's too good to waste. Let's take a few days off, at least."

"What's got into you, anyway?" Barbara narrowed her eyes.

Valeria didn't answer, but strolled down the slope toward the village.

Barbara drifted glumly in the opposite direction. Her cousin's advice was hard to refute, but she didn't like it. This place was just sickly sweet. That Yvonne— ugh!

She passed the guards at the bridge, ignoring their respects, and walked across to the shore. The water did look clean and cool. She peeled off her clothes and waded moodily out.

The swim helped. Seated again on the rocky bank, she found her head clear enough to hold the problem. Which was that she wanted Davis for herself.

Just what that would mean, she wasn't sure, but the thought made heat and cold chase each other through her skin. There was his funny slow smile, and his songs, and his gentleness . . .

Then the thing to do was tell Davis. Tonight, when everybody was asleep, she'd sneak out and find him and . . . Somehow, the thought made her giddy. But to know where she stood and what she meant to do about it was like a fresh cup of that what-you-call-it drink. And maybe just as treacherous, but you couldn't stay alive without taking risks.

She put her kilt back on and returned almost merrily.

Elinor was in front of the Big House chatting to a Holloway. "Oh, my dear, you wouldn't believe it, it is simply *awful* up on the pass, I honestly thought I would freeze to death, and you know I was used to *much* better things in Freetoon, I was really quite impor— Oh, Barbara."

The Whitley felt such an all-embracing benevolence that it even included Dyckmans. "Hello, dear," she smiled, and stroked the other girl's hair. "You're looking lovely." She nodded and drifted on.

"Well!" said Elinor. "Well, I never! After the way she treated me, to come greasing up like . . . Prudence, darling, let me tell you . . ."

Davis emerged from the Prezden's hut. He looked wretched. Barbara's heart turned over with pity. She ran toward him calling his dear name and wondered why he jerked.

"Bert, what's the matter? It's such a beautiful day. Don't you feel well?"

"No," said Davis hollowly.

Valeria joined them. Barbara had never seen her cousin walk in that undulant fashion—why, she might almost have been a Dyckman. Was everybody falling sick?

Davis started. "Lemme out of here," he muttered.

Valeria's cheeks flamed. "Hello," she said. Her tone was not quite as cool as usual.

"Gwmpf," said Davis, backing away.

Barbara took his arm and looked reproachfully at Valeria. "It's such a shame you two don't get along," she said. "We've been through so much together."

Valeria drew her knife and tested its edge with her thumb. Davis turned green and disengaged himself from Barbara.

"I don't feel so good," he said in a ramshackle voice. "Let me alone for a while, you two, please."

As he wobbled away, Barbara turned on her twin in a rage. "Will you keep your paws off my business?"

"What business?" Valeria tossed the knife up and caught it.

"When I have private matters to talk over with him, I don't want you around!"

"Oh . . . so that's it?" Valeria stood for a while in thought. "I'd hoped you would have enough decency to stay in your hut at night."

"Just because you're a dull fish with a clinker for a heart . . ."

"In fact," began Valeria, "I must insist, Babs, that . . ."

The musical winding of a horn interrupted her.

Both Whitleys felt their sinews tauten. "From the bridge," said Barbara through stiff lips. "Somebody's coming."

"It may not mean anything," answered Valeria. "But let's not take chances. We'd better keep out of sight. You collect Elinor, I'll fetch Bert. Meet you in that tanglewood stand up on the rim."

Barbara nodded and ran off. Elinor, stretching langorously before the burly Holloway, was suddenly yanked off her feet. "Come along," said Barbara.

"What do you mean, you . . . you *creature?*"

"Jump." A drawn dagger gleamed across the sky. Elinor jumped.

Valeria guided Davis after them. Oddly, he seemed almost relieved by the prospect of action. They entered the copse and looked from its concealment toward the bridge path.

"Everybody's seen us come up here," said Davis. "If it's an enemy . . ."

" . . . we can jump off the cliff and swim to the boat dock," said Barbara. Her veins pulsed.

Elinor closed her eyes and swooned toward Davis. He stepped aside and she hit the ground with an outraged squawk.

There was a bustle down in the village; its people leaped to form ceremonial ranks. A troop of guards emerged from the park. A veiled woman on orsperback, leading four other birds, jogged solemnly after.

"Father!" whispered Valeria. "It's a legate!"

"A what?" asked Davis.

"Messenger from the Doctors. What does she want?"

Barbara peered between the branches, and the awe of eight years ago rose within her. That had been the last time a legate was in Freetoon. There had been a crop failure, and she had come to adjust the payment of annual tribute.

She was tall, unidentifiable under the long travel-stained gown of white, hooded blue cloak, trousers and gold-chased boots, heavy veil. One of the extra orspers bore a pack, the others were merely saddled. As the legate dismounted, Yvonne prostrated herself.

Valeria snapped her fingers. "I think I have it," she said excitedly. "Remember, we sent our fastest couriers from Freetoon to the Ship when Bert first arrived. They must have gotten there a couple of weeks ago. Now the Doctors are sending to every town . . . word about the Man . . ."

"Wait a minute," said Davis. "The Ship is a long way off. Nobody could get here so soon."

"A legate could," Barbara told him. "They can requisition anything they want—food, orspers, guides—and they're trained to ride for days and nights at a stretch."

"Well," said Davis. "Well, this is terrific! Our troubles are over, girls. Let's go see her."

"Not just yet," muttered Barbara. "She'll send for us when we're wanted."

"Yeh?" Davis bristled. "Who does she think she is?"

"I know, I know," said Valeria. "But why give offense?"

Davis shrugged. "As you will."

The veiled woman entered the Big House. Her baggage was removed and brought in after her, then she was alone. A party of girls ran up the slope.

"Man! Man, you're wanted—the legate wants to see you!"

Davis smiled importantly and stepped out of the

thicket. The Whitleys followed, ignoring the chatter of everyone else.

They came down to the plaza. Yvonne, throwing on her best feather bonnet, laid a finger across her lips. "Shhhh!"

"I want to see the legate," said Davis.

"Yes, sir, yes . . . she'll come when she's ready . . . just wait here."

Davis went to the dais.

"Oh, you mustn't sit, sir!" Yvonne tugged at his arm. "Not when the legate is here!"

Davis gave her a frosty stare. "For your information," he said, "a Man ranks a legate by six places."

Yvonne looked unhappy.

Stillness lay thick over the island. The Lysumites huddled together, watching Davis and the Big House with frightened eyes. Barbara and Valeria joined him, but dared not be seated. Elinor squeezed next to the Prezden and shivered.

There was a half hour's wait. Davis yawned, stretched, scratched himself, and looked increasingly mutinous. Barbara grew afraid of what the legate might think.

She stiffened herself. He was her Man, and she would fight the whole Ship for him if she had to!

Father did not strike her dead. She felt a sense of triumph, as if the fact were a personal victory.

Nevertheless, when the legate emerged her knees bumped together.

The woman had changed into full ceremonials. A robe of green fell sheer to her feet, a gloved hand gripped a long staff of some unknown shimmery metal, a plumed mask in the shape of an orsper head covered her own and made it coldly unhuman.

Davis got up. "Hello, ma'am," he smiled.

The tall woman did not stir. She stood a few meters away from him, alien in the long sunbeams, and waited. Sweat glistened on Valeria's forehead;

Barbara felt it on her own. She stood rigid, as if on parade.

Davis said, "I am the Man. You, uh, you know about me?"

"Yes," said the legate. She had a low voice, curiously distorted by the mask, and a stiff accent.

"You've, ahem, come about me?"

"Yes. The Ship and all Atlantis have awaited the Men for three hundred years. How many of you are there?"

"I came by myself. Otherwise no one would have done so for a long time yet."

"Will others follow you?"

"Sure. If I go back and tell them about this place, there'll be Men all over it."

"But otherwise not?"

"I don't know how much you know of the situation . . ." Davis stepped toward her.

"Word came from Freetoon that a ship had landed with someone aboard who might be a Man. Legates have been sent everywhere to inquire if there were others. How did you get here, so far from Freetoon . . . did you fly?"

"Well, no." Davis cleared his throat. "You see, there was a, a misunderstanding. Four other towns allied themselves against Freetoon to capture me and my ship. They overcame us. Being weaponless, I got away with three friends. We were going to the Doctors, to request their assistance in getting my ship back."

The voice remained altogether emotionless; it wasn't *human*, thought Barbara with a chill, to greet this news that way. "But the allied towns cannot use your ship, can they?"

"Oh, no. Can't even get into it. Not without me." Davis came closer, smiling all over his face. "They'll give it up again, on your orders, and I'll go fetch all the Men you want."

"It was a risk," said the legate calmly. "If you had

died on this journey, there would be no Men coming after you."

"True," said Davis. "I'm an explorer, you see, and the Galaxy is so big . . ." He preened himself. Barbara thought he looked much too smug, but it was lovable just the same.

"Have you any weapons?" asked the legate.

"No, I told you. Only this dirk here . . . but . . ."

"I understand."

The legate strode from him, toward the bridge guards who stood holding their bows in what Barbara considered a miserable approximation of dress parade. Her voice rang out:

"This is no Man, it's a Monster. Kill it!"

CHAPTER XV

For a moment nobody stirred.

The legate whirled on Yvoune. "I order you in the name of Father," she yelled. "Kill the filthy thing!"

Davis spread his hands, stunned into helplessness. The women of Lysum wailed; a baby burst into tears; Elinor Dyckman shrieked.

Barbara had no time to think. She jumped, snatched a bow from a half paralyzed guard, and lifted it to her shoulder. "The first one of you to move gets a bolt through the belly," she announced.

Valeria's dagger flared directly before the legate. "And this bitch gets a slit throat," she added. "Hold still, you!"

In Freetoon the arbalests would have been snapping already. But these were a timid folk who had not known battle for generations. "Drop your weapons," said Barbara. She swiveled her own from guard

139

to guard as she backed toward the house. "Quick! No, you don't!" She fired, and the Salmon who had raised a bow dropped it, stared stupidly at a skewered hand, and fainted. "Next time I aim for the heart," said Barbara.

Weapons clattered to the grass. There went a moan through the densely packed crowd.

Davis shook a benumbed head. "What's the matter?" he croaked. "I *am* a Man. Give me a chance to prove it . . ."

"You have proved it," shouted the legate. "Proved yourself a Monster when you assaulted the Ship's own envoy. Prezden, do your duty!"

Yvonne Craig shuddered her way backward, lifting helpless hands. "You mustn't," she whimpered. "You can't . . ."

"Can't we just?" leered Valeria. She flourished her dagger across the long green robe. "Behave yourself, or Lysum becomes the first town in the world where a legate was stabbed."

To the masked woman: "What's the meaning of this?"

"Barren will you be," said the legate, "and outlaw on Atlantis."

Barbara looked through a haze of terror at Davis. Surely the Man could override such a curse!

He shook himself, and spoke swiftly: "Unless you want to die, lady, you'd better tell these people to obey us."

Valeria emphasized the request with another flourish. Malevolence answered Davis: "So be it, then . . . for now! Don't think you'll escape Father."

Davis turned to the Whitleys. He was pale and breathed hard, but the words rattled from him: "We have to get out of here. Keep these people covered. I'll take charge. You, you, you, you . . ." His fingers chose young, horror smitten girls. "Fetch out all our stuff. And the legate's pack. You over there, I want food, plenty of it. Bread, fruits, fowl, dried fish. Bundle it up!"

Yvonne sank to her knees, and covered her face. "Excuse us, lady," she whimpered. "We'll do what you say . . . anything . . ."

"Let them have their way for now," said the legate coolly. "Father isn't ready yet to strike them down."

"Pick up some bows, Elinor," said Davis.

"No . . . no, you Monster . . ." she gasped.

"Suit yourself," he laughed harshly. "Stay here if you want to be torn to pieces as soon as we're gone."

Shaking, she collected an armful of weapons.

The girls came out with their bundles. "Here, give me an axe," said Davis. "We're going. Babs, Val, cover our rear . . . make everybody follow at a distance so we can't be shot from the woods. I'll watch the dear legate."

Barbara obeyed in a mechanical fashion. Her mind was still gluey; she didn't know if she could move any more without him to think for her.

They went up the path, a scared and sullen village trailing them several meters behind and staring into the Whitley bowsights. Davis told the women to stop at the bridgehead, took his own party across, then cut the cables with a few hard axe strokes. The bridge collapsed into the water and broke up.

"How do we get back?" cried a young Holloway.

"Are you going to eat us?" shivered a Craig.

"Not if you behave yourselves," Davis told her. "As for getting back, you can swim out and let 'em lower ropes for you. I just don't want word of this to get out for a while, and it'll take a couple of weeks at least to rebuild a bridge that orspers can cross. Now, take us to those boats I heard somebody mention."

The burdened women led the way along the shale bank. Yvonne stood on the cliffs and howled loyal curses. Valeria faced around when they were out of bowshot and said slowly, "Bert, I never thought you would be so . . ."

"*This* kind of situation I can handle," he said.

Barbara's tautness melted as she looked at him. Physical courage was cheap enough, especially when you were desperate, she thought, but he was being as swift with decision as an Udall . . . and ever so much nicer.

A bluff jutted into the river ahead of them, screening a small inlet where the Lysumites had built their dock. A score of long slim bark canoes with carved stemposts were drawn up on the land. Davis told his prisoners to load one. "And set the others afire," he added to Barbara. "Too bad, but we've got to bottle up the word of this till we can get clear."

She nodded, and took forth tinder and fire piston from her pouch. Flame licked across the hulls, and the girls of Lysum wept.

"All right," Davis selected paddles and patching materials. "Now we tie up our guest and get started. Scram, you females. Boo!" He waved his arms, and the youngsters fled a flurry of screams.

Barbara took a certain satisfaction in binding the legate's wrists and ankles and tossing her among the supplies. Elinor huddled near the captive; big help she'd be unless they could extract her knowledge of the Ship . . . but a rattlepate like her wouldn't have noticed anything useful . . . They shoved the canoe into deeper water and climbed aboard.

"Ever used a boat like this?" asked Davis. "No? Well, you'll get the trick soon enough. We'd better paddle two at a time . . . Val, you get in the bow, Babs take the stern. Elinor and I will spell you; I can make up for her, I suppose. Now, then, you kneel, hold your paddle like so . . ."

The current was fast in midstream. Barbara fell quickly into the rhythm of paddling; it wasn't such hard work, though you had to beware of rocks.

Ariadne rose above Ay-set, and Theseus was already up. It would be a bright night. Barbara could have wished for clouds, she felt so exposed under the naked sky; there was a blotch on Minos like a great bloodshot eye glaring down at her.

No, she told herself, Father was a lie ... at least, the stiff lightning-tossing Father of the Ship did not exist; or if he did, then Bert with his long legs and blue eyes and tawny beard was a stronger god. Merely looking at him made her want to cry.

He grinned into her gaze and wiped sweat off his face. "I don't want to go through that again!" he said. "It'll take a week for me to uncoil."

Valeria looked over her shoulder. "But we got away," she whispered. "Thanks to you, we got away."

"To me? Thunderation! If you two hadn't ... Well, the problem now is, what do we do next?"

What indeed? thought Barbara. A Man and three women ... two and a half women ... with every hand on Atlantis against them ... But he would think of something. She just knew he would.

Davis regarded the legate thoughtfully where she lay. "I wonder what's beneath that fancy helmet," he murmured. "Let's see."

"You'll fry for this!" she spat.

"Don't," wailed Elinor.

"Shut up." Davis leaned over and lifted the gilt orsper head. Barbara, who had half expected haloes or some such item, was almost disappointed when the ash-blonde hair, cut short, and coldly regular features of a Trevor appeared.

Elinor covered her eyes and crouched shuddering. "I d-d-didn't want to see, ma'am," she pleaded.

"You've fallen into bad company, child," said the Trevor. Then, to Davis: "Are you satisfied, Monster?"

"No." He ran a hand through unkempt yellow hair. "What have you got against me? Don't you know I'm a Man? You must have *some* biological knowledge to operate that parthenogenetic wingding."

"You aren't a Man. You can't be. It isn't possible." The Trevor lay back, scowling in the light that spilled from the sky. "There is a certain sign by which the Men shall be known . . ."

"What sign? Quick!"

"It's a holy secret," she snapped.

"You mean you can't think of anything," said Davis. "And even at Freetoon, where they also doubted I was a Man, they didn't want me murdered out of hand."

After a moment, he went on, almost to himself: "It's a common enough pattern in history. You Doctors have had it soft for three hundred years—two hundred, anyway, once these people had gotten scattered and ignorant enough for the present system to grow up. You must always have dreaded the day when the Men would finally arrive and upset your little wagon. When I told you—foolish of me, but how was I to know?—when I told you I'm alone and there won't be any others for a long time if I don't return— well, your bosses at the Ship must already have told you what to do if that was the case."

"You're a Monster!" said the Trevor. Dogmatic as ever.

"Even if you honestly thought I was, you wouldn't have told them to cut me down. Even a Monster could go home and call the true Men. No, no, my friend, you're a pretty sophisticated lot at the Ship, and you've already decided to rub out the competition."

"Be still before Father strikes you dead!"

Davis grinned. He let her squirm for a while. "Not quite so much twisting, if you please," he said. "A canoe is easy to upset. We can all swim ashore, but you're hogtied."

The Trevor grew rigid.

Davis nodded and looked at Barbara. "Legates sent to every town on this continent," he said. "Orders to learn what the facts are. You'll dicker with the Men if there really are a lot of them or if they can call for help—otherwise kill them and deny everything."

"I'd like to kill *her*," said Barbara between her teeth.

"You Whitleys always were a Fatherless lot," said the Trevor.

"How do you know?" snapped Davis. "Babs, have you any idea who the Doctors are . . . how many, what families?"

"I'm not sure." She frowned, trying to remember. A child always picked up scraps of information meant only for initiates . . . she overheard this, was blabbed that by a garrulous helot—"There are a few thousand of them, I believe. And they're said to be of the best families."

"Uh-huh. I thought so. Inferior types couldn't maintain this system. Even with that tremendous advantage of theirs—that the next generation depends on them—there'd have been more conflict between Church and States unless . . . Yeh, Trevors, Whitleys, Burkes, that sort—the high castes of Freetoon, with the wits and courage and personality to override any local chief—Well."

Barbara shoved her paddle through murmurous waters. The boat moved swiftly. The canyon walls were already lower on either side, a Minos-drenched desolation.

"But what are we going to do?" she asked in helplessness.

"I think—yes. I really think we can get away with it. How long'll it take us to reach a place where they have warriors?"

"That girl I spoke to on the island said it was about ten days by canoe to the sea, and the sea people have a base there."

"Good! Nobody will be off Lysum by that time."

"*I* would skin down a rope and hike after help," said Valeria.

"*They* won't. You know what they're like. Or even if they do, the word will still be far behind us when we get to the coast." Davis took a long breath. "Now, then. Either of you two is about the size of this dame. You can pass for a legate yourself . . ."

Barbara choked. After a moment, Valeria shook her head. "No, Bert. It can't be done. Every child in the soldier families gets that idea as soon as she can talk . . . why not pass a Freetoon Whitley off as a Greendaler? There are countersigns and passwords to prevent just that."

"I'm not surprised," said Davis. "But it isn't what I meant. Look here. We won't try to get into the Ship, but one of you will wear this robe and mask. How are the sea people to know you're not a genuine legate, bringing back a genuine Man? Only, on his behalf, you requisition an escort and a lot of fast orspers. We ride back to Freetoon, demand my own boat—oh, yes, our tame legate can also order your town set free. Then we all hop into my spaceship and ride to Nerthus—and return with a thousand armed Men!"

Barbara thought dazedly that only he could have forged such a plan.

CHAPTER XVI

Eight Atlantean days later, the canoe nosed into Shield Skerry harbor.

The tides on this world varied with the position of the other moons, but they were always enormous—up to seven times the corresponding rise on Earth. A tidal bore here amounted to a virtual tsunami. Except for the frequent case of sheer cliffs, the continents had no definite shorelines, only salt marshes that faded into the ocean. Two hundred kilometers away, the river grew brackish; another hundred kilometers and its estuary was lost in the swamps.

That was a weird gray land, shifting hourly between flood and drenched muckflats, seabirds filling the air with wings and harsh screams as they looked for stranded fish, and always a damp wind out of the west, smelling of kelpish decay. The local life had adapted. Trees lifted gloomily above high tide; ebb

showed amphibious grass in queasy hummocks;
flippered relatives of the lake monster cawed from
their rookeries. It would have been a thirsty trip,
blundering lost through a brine-drenched wilderness,
had the swampfolk not met them.

There were a few women who lived here, building
their miserable huts on whatever high ground
existed, gliding in pirogues to hunt and fish, catching
rainwater in crude cisterns. They were the weaker
and duller families, the servile class of Freetoon,
who had colonized a country no one else wanted,
and they had fallen to a naked neolithic stage of
tomtom rites and bones through the nose. But they
were inoffensive enough, specialists in guiding parties
between the sea-dweller base and the upper valley.
It earned them a few trade goods.

Valeria, impressive in veil and robe, simply com-
mandeered help. A few husky Nicholsons at the
paddles made the canoe move like greased lightning.
Meanwhile Barbara sat next to the Trevor with a knife
in her hand and a sweet smile on her face.

Several days earlier, Valeria had suggested cutting
their prisoner's throat, but Davis wouldn't have it.

"Why not?" asked Valeria. "Perfectly normal pre-
caution. She's only a dangerous nuisance."

"Well, it just isn't done. Cosmos! It'll take the
psychotechs a hundred years to fit you hellcats into
civilization." Davis searched for a reason she would
understand. "We may find some use for her yet . . .
information, hostage . . ."

Valeria shrugged doubtfully. But neither of the
cousins was disposed to argue with their Man.

The lack of privacy and the weariness of inces-
sant paddling, watch and watch, was a blessing,
thought Davis. It staved off his own problem. The
notion that someday he'd face it again—maybe alone
in space with two jealous Whitleys, because he
couldn't leave them defenseless against the Doctors'

revenge—made his nerves curl up and quiver at the
ends.

Not that it had seemed such a bad idea at first.
He had even toyed with thoughts of bigamy. Now that
he had gained some insight about Valeria, he found
her no different from her twin. They were both
spitcats, yes, but a man could soon learn to handle
them. He couldn't think of two girls he would rather
learn to handle. As far as civilized law was concerned,
and even custom on most planets, his sex life was his
own business. . . .

Inspired by the beautiful logical simplicity of it all,
he decided one afternoon to lead up to the suggestion. He was off duty, resting near the bow while the
canoe glided between forested riverbanks. Elinor and
the Trevor were asleep; Valeria knelt in the stern,
driving her paddle in the same powerful rhythm as
her sister.

Davis looked from one Whitley to another. Sunlight spilled over ruddy hair. Their bare brown skins
glistened with sweat. Each time the paddles bit
water, muscles stood forth on Barbara's back and
Valeria's belly, and their breasts rose and fell. He
got to his own knees, just behind Barbara, and
leaned close. The warm sweet smell of her was a
drunkenness; his temples pounded. "Babs," he
husked.

She turned her face just enough for him to see how
smooth her cheek was. "Yes?" Her answer was low
and not entirely steady.

"I wanted to say . . . I'm sorry I got you into all
this—"

"You didn't," she breathed. "And even if you did,
I'm not sorry. Not as long as you're in the same mess."

"After this is all over . . . could we maybe—the
three of us—keep on messing around?"

He realized later she must not have noticed that
detail of 'three.' She murmured, "I'd adore to." He

cupped her breasts in his hands. She leaned back against him, shivering.

A knife thunked into the wood beside them. Valeria's hurled paddle bounced off Davis' head. "Get away from him, you goldbricking slime worm!" she yelled.

Barbara whipped about, drawing her own knife. "Who do you think you are, telling me what to do?"

The canoe had nearly capsized before Davis restored peace. Thereafter he abandoned all notion of a *menage à trois,* postponed the unsolvable problem of choosing one of them, and concentrated on immediate matters.

He tried to quiz the legate. Beyond the information that her name was Joyce, and that he was a Monster destined for hell's hottest griddle, she would tell him nothing. Barbara remarked practically that Trevors never gave in to torture, and anyway an unstable canoe was no place to apply thumbscrews. Davis shuddered.

Elinor had been very quiet on the trip. She made herself useful to Joyce, probably too scared of both sides to reach a decision. Davis felt sorry for her.

And then finally they were out of the marsh.

The chief Nicholson told him in her barely intelligible argot that this was a great bay . . . yes, she had heard there was a string of islands closing it off from the mighty waves of the open sea . . . many, many seafolk on many, many islands, all kinds people, Shield Skerry was only a port where coastwise traders dropped off women bound inland, or picked them up; that was all she knew. She wasn't even very curious about the Man.

The rock was a long one, awash at high tide. It was nearly hidden by the stone walls erected on its back: expert work, massive blocks cut square, a primitive lighthouse where oil fires behind glass burned in front of polished copper reflectors, two long jetties

enclosing a small harbor. The canoe buried its nose
in a wave, sheeted foam, climbed, rolled, and
snuggled down again. Elinor leaned over the side,
wished herself dead, and made feeble remarks about
the wrath of Father.

Davis looked back. The swamps were a vaporous
gray, low in the sea; a storm of shrieking birds made
a white wing-cloud under Minos and the two suns,
otherwise there were only the great foam-flanked
waves that marched out of the west. The water was
a chill steely bluish-gray, the wind shrill in his ears.

The surface grew calm between the jetties. Davis
saw that a good-sized ship—by Atlantean standards—
was in. A counter-weighted wooden crane powered
by a capstan wheel was unloading baled cargo, presumably for the upland trade. There was a bustle of
strong sun-tanned women, barefoot and clad in wide
trousers and halters, their hair cut off just below the
ears. Beyond the dock was a small collection of
warehouses and dwelling units. They were of stone,
with shingle roofs, in the same uncompromising
square style as the town wall and the pharos.

The ship was carvel-built, rather broad in the beam,
with a high poop and a corroded bronze figurehead—
a winged fish. Davis guessed it had a rather deep
draught and a centerboard, to maintain freeway in
these tricky waters. There was no sign of a mast, but
a wooden frame lifted skeletal amidships with a great
windmill arrangement turning idly at the peak.

Otherwise the harbor held only a few boats, swift-
looking, more or less conventionally yawl-rigged.

"Highest technology I've ever seen here," he remarked.

"What? Oh, you mean their skills," said Barbara.
"Yes, they say the seafolk are the best smiths in the
world. It's even said a few of their captains can read
writing."

"I hope *I* won't have to do that," muttered Valeria
behind her veil. "I thought only Doctors knew how."

Davis assumed that the pelagic colonies were old, founded perhaps before the final breakdown of castaway civilization. The sea held abundant food if you knew how to get it. And they must be in closer contact with the Ship than any other tribe. That would doubtless be valuable to them; they would get hints when they sailed past the Holy River estuary and saw the colony of the Doctors.

"What kind of people are they?" he asked.

"We don't know much about them in the uplands," said Barbara. "I've heard they're a violent sort, hard to get along with, even if they do do a lot of trading and ferrying."

And if she thought so . . . !

"Well," said Davis, "we'll find out pretty quick." His stomach was a cold knot within him. "Let me do most of the talking, Val. They won't be so suspicious of my mistakes."

Work at the dock was grinding to a halt. A horn blew brazenly, and women swarmed from the buildings and hurried down tortuous cobbled streets. *"A legate, another legate, and who's that with her?"*

The Nicholson steerswoman brought the canoe expertly to the wharf. The four other swampdwellers laid down their paddles and caught the rope tossed to them. The chief Nicholson bent her head. "We gotcher here, ma'am," she said humbly.

Valeria did not thank her; it wouldn't have been in character. She accepted the hand of a brawny Macklin and stepped up onto the quay. Davis followed. Barbara nudged the wrist-bound Trevor with a knife and urged her after. Elinor slunk behind.

There was a crowd now, pushing and shoving. A few must be police or guards; they wore conical, visored helmets and scaly corselets above their pants. The rest were unarmed. Davis noticed flamboyant tattoos, earrings, thick gold bracelets . . . and on all classes. A Nicholson stood arm in arm with a Latvala;

a Craig pushed between a Whitley and a Burke to
get a better view; a Holloway carrying a blacksmith's
hammer gave amiable blackchat to a Trevor with spear
and armor. What . . . ?

Valeria raised her staff. "Quiet!" she shouted.

The babble died away, bit by bit. A gray-haired
woman, stocky and ugly, with an official-looking copper brassard on one arm, added a roar: "Shut up, you!
It's a legate!"

"Yes, ma' am," piped a voice, "but what's that with
her?"

The gray woman—an Udall, Davis recognized
uneasily—turned to Valeria and bobbed her head.
"Begging your pardon, ma'am, we just put in from
a rough trip and some of the girls been boozing."

"Are you in charge?" asked Valeria.

"Reckon I am, ma'am, being the skipper of this
tub . . . *Fishbird* out o' Farewell Island, she is. Nelly
Udall, ma'am, at your service."

Joyce Trevor opened her mouth. She was white
with anger. Barbara nudged her and she closed it
again.

Valeria stood solemnly for a moment. It grew quiet
enough to hear the waves bursting on the breakwater.
Then she raised her veiled face and shouted: "Rejoice!
The sins of the mothers are washed away and the
Men are coming!"

It had the desired effect, though a somewhat
explosive one. Davis was afraid his admirers would
trample him to death. Nelly Udall stood before him
to cuff back the most enthusiastic and bellow at
them. "Stand aside! Hold there! Show some respect,
you—" What followed brought a maidenly blush to
Barbara herself, and she was a cavalry girl.

When the racket had quieted somewhat, Davis
decided to take charge. "I am a Man," he said in his
deepest voice. "The legate found me in the hills and
brought me here. She knows you are a pious people."

"Bless you, dearie," said the Udall through sudden tears. "Sure, we're pious as hell. Any Father-damned thing you want, ma'am, just say so."

"But there is evil afoot," boomed Davis. "I am only the vanguard of the Men. Unless you show yourselves worthy by aiding me to destroy the evil in Atlantis, no others will come."

A certain awe began to penetrate those hard skulls. The show was rolling, and Davis mellowed toward the seafolk.

"I would speak with you and your counselors in private," he said. "I must let you know my will."

Nelly Udall looked confused. "Sure . . . sure, ma'am. Yes, your manship, anything you say. Only—you mean my first mate, maybe?"

"Oh . . . no authority here, is there? Well, where does the Udall of the sea-dwellers live?"

"What Udall?" The woman looked around as if expecting one to pop out of some valley. "There's a cousin of mine who's landskipper at Angry Fjord, but that's just a little town."

Davis shook his head. "Who is your ruler—queen, chief, president, whatever you call it? Who makes the decisions?"

"Why, why, Laura Macklin is the preemer, ma'am, if she ain't been voted out," stuttered Nelly. "She's at New Terra, that's the capital. But did you want everybody to come there and vote, ma'am?"

A republic was about the last thing Davis had expected to find. But it was plausible, now that he thought about it. Even on this planet, where the infinite variability of humankind had been unnaturally frozen, it would be hard to establish despotism among a race of sailors. The cheapest catboat with a few disgruntled slaves aboard could sail as fast as the biggest warship.

"I don't get it," said Barbara in a small voice.

"Never mind," said Davis majestically. "I'm afraid

you misunderstood me, Captain Udall. Take us to a place where we can talk alone with you."

"Yes, ma'am!" Nelly's eyes came to light on Joyce Trevor's sullen face. She jerked a horny thumb toward the prisoner. "Enemy of yours, ma'am? I'll chop her up personally."

"That will not be required," said Davis. "Bring her along."

Nelly rolled over to Elinor and chucked her under the chip. "Poor dear," she said. "All skin and bones, ain't you? Never mind, chick, we'll fatten you up."

Elinor cringed back and looked at the Udall from terrified eyes.

"Awright, awright, clear a way!" roared Nelly. "Way for the Man! Stand aside there, you! You'll all get a look at him later. Make way!" Her fist emphasized the request, bruisingly, but nobody seemed to mind. Tough lot.

Davis led his party after her, through a narrow street to a smoky kennel with an anchor painted on the gable. "We'll use this tavern," said Nelly. "Break open a keg of . . . no, fishbrains! This is private! We'll roll out a barrel for you when the Man is finished. Git!" She slammed the door in their faces.

Davis coughed. When his eyes were through watering, he saw a room under sooty rafters, filled with benches and tables. A noble collection of casks lined one wall; otherwise, the inn was hung with scrimshaw work and stuffed fish. A whole sealbird roasted in the fireplace.

They parked Joyce in a corner. Elinor crept over beside her. The rest gathered at a table conveniently near one of the barrels while Nelly fetched heroic goblets and tapped the cask.

"Why don't you take off that veil, ma'am?" she asked Valeria. "Even a legate gets thirsty."

"Thanks, I will." The girl did so, grabbed for a beaker, and buried her nose in it. "Whoooo!"

"Oh . . . so sorry, dearie . . . I mean, ma'am. D'you think it was wine? Brandy."

Davis sipped with warned caution. Raw stuff, but it glowed pleasantly inside him. So the sea-dwellers knew about distillation . . . excellent people!

"Now, then, your maleship, say away." Nelly leaned back and sprawled columnar legs across the floor. "Death and corruption! A Man after all these years!"

Formality was wasted on her, Davis decided. If the sea women didn't go in for it, it wouldn't impress them much. He told her the censored tale he had given at Lysum.

"Heard of those wenches." Nelly snorted. "Well, ma'am . . . sorry, you said it was 'sir,' didn't you? what happened next?"

"This Trevor showed up," said Davis. "She was one of the agents of evil, the same who had whipped Greendale and the other towns into attacking Free-toon. She tried to stir up all Lysum against me. I made her captive, as you see, and we went on down the river till we came here."

"Why didn't you see her gizzard, sir?"

"The Men are merciful," said Davis. "Do you have a place where she can be held incommunicado?"

"A what? We've got a brig."

"That'll do." Davis continued with the rest of his demands: passage to the Holy River mouth and an escort to Freetoon, where the lady legate would give the orders of the Ship.

Nelly nodded. "Can do, sir. We don't need to go by way of New Terra, even, if you're in a hurry. There are twenty good crewgirls on the *Fishbird,* and a causeway from the Ship over the swamps . . ."

"We needn't stop at the Ship," said Valeria quickly. "In fact, I'm commanded not to come near it till the Man is on his way back to fetch the rest of the Men.

And this has to be kept secret, or we may have more trouble with the, uh, agents of hell."

"Awright, ma'am. We'll just leave the ship at Bow Island and get orspers and ride straight inland. There's a ridge we can follow through the marshes."

Davis frowned. Whatever legate had gone to Freetoon might have planted a story that he really was a Monster, to be killed on sight. Or no, probably not . . . *that* legate had no way of knowing he was the only male human on Atlantis; she'd have to ride back for orders . . .

"The faster the better," he said.

"We'll warp out at Bee-rise tomorrow, sir," said Nelly Udall. She shook her head and stared into her goblet. "A Man! A real live Man! Father damn it, I'm too old . . . but I've seen you, sir. That's enough for me, I reckon."

CHAPTER XVII

The Shield Skerry brig was a verminous den, but it was solidly built. Davis watched Nelly commute the sentence of its inmates to a few good-natured kicks, toss Joyce within, lock the door, and post a guard to assure that the prisoner saw no one but an attendant who brought meals—and didn't speak even to that person.

Then she led his party down to the dock, where he had supper and delivered a short but telling speech to the assembled women. The inquiries of the preceding legate—whether a Man had been seen—had paved the way for his arrival; there was no one who disbelieved him. He doubted if his injunction to strict secrecy would be respected for many days: it wasn't humanly possible. But the *Fishbird* could head south and be at Holy River in three or four revolutions of Atlantis. Thereafter, given hard riding on relays of orspers, he would be ahead of the news . . . Cosmos!

In two Atlantean weeks—a single Earth week—he could be back in space!

Cloud masses piled blackly out of the west, and a smoky-gray overcast hid Ay-set. Wind rose shrill in rigging and streets, surf roared on the breakwater, scud stung his face. He felt the weariness of being hunted. How long had it been already?

"I would retire," he said. "You'll be ready to sail at dawn?"

"Yes, sir, if the girls aren't still too drunk." Nelly gave him a wistful look. "Sure you won't come down to the Anchor with us and . . ."

"Quite sure!" said Barbara and Valeria together.

The crowd trailed them to a long house which Nelly said was reserved for ships' officers. "Best we can do, sir. It's not much but anything we can do for you . . . this way in, sir, my ladies."

There was a sort of common room, with a hall leading off lined by small bedchambers. Elinor slipped into the first; they heard the door bolted behind her. Valeria took the next, then Davis, then Barbara . . . he closed the shutters, turned off the oil lantern, and crept through a sudden heavy darkness into bed. Ahhhh!

Now that he was stretched out and the gale no more than a lullaby, it wasn't easy to fall asleep. Too much to think about, too many memories of home . . .

He was half unconscious when the door opened. As he heard it close again, sleep spilled from him and he sat up. Bare feet groped across the floor.

"Who's that?" Davis fumbled after his dirk, tossed away with the other clothes. His scalp prickled.

"Shhh!" The husky voice was almost in his ear. He reached up and felt a warm roundedness. "Bertie . . . I couldn't stand it any longer, I had to be with you . . ."

Davis made weak fending motions. The girl laughed

shyly and slipped under his blankets. He fumbled away, but two strong arms closed about his neck.

"You must know, Bert," she whispered. "You know so much else."

Davis' morality rose in indignation, slipped, and slid. You can only try a man so far. "C'mere!" he said hoarsely.

Her lips closed against his, still inexpert, but she'd learn.

"Bert . . . Bert, darling. I don't know what . . . what this is, to be with a Man . . . but I care for you so much . . ."

"I told you the word was 'love'," he chuckled.

"Did you? When was that?"

"You remember, Val, sweetheart . . . you didn't fool me that night in . . ."

"Val!"

She sat bolt upright and screeched the name into darkness.

"What?" Davis turned cold. "I mean . . . you . . ."

"*Val?* What's been going on here?"

"Oh, no!" groaned Davis. "Barbara, listen, I can explain . . ."

"I'll explain you!" she yelled. A fist whistled past his cheek. It would have been a rough blow if it had connected.

Davis scrambled to get free. The blankets trapped him. Barbara cursed and got her hands on his throat. "Awk!" said Davis. He tore her loose, but she closed in again with ideas of mayhem.

The door opened, and light spilled into the room. The tall red-haired girl carried an axe in her right hand, and the left which held the lantern was scarred.

"What's happening?" barked Valeria.

To the untrained eye, a wrestling match is superficially not unlike certain other sports. Valeria cursed, set down the lantern, and strode forward with lifted axe. Barbara let go, sprang out of bed, snatched up Davis' knife, and confronted her twin.

"So *you've* been fooling around!" she shouted.

"I wouldn't talk if I were you," answered Valeria from clenched jaws. "The minute my back is turned you come oozing in and . . ."

They whirled on Davis. He got out of bed one jump ahead of the axe and backed into a corner. "Now, girls," he stammered. "Ladies, ladies, please!"

Something intimated to him that this was not just the correct approach. The cousins stalked closer.

"Look," begged Davis, "this wasn't my idea, I swear it wasn't, honest!"

Valeria threw her axe to the floor. It stuck there, quivering. "I wouldn't befoul a good weapon with your blood," she said.

Barbara drove his knife into the wall so the blade snapped. "I wouldn't bury him in a fowlcoop," was her contribution.

Their attitude was distinctly more reassuring than it had been, thought Davis. But it still left something to be desired.

"It's all a mistake!" he gibbered.

"The mistake was ever bringing you along," said Valeria. She whirled on Barbara. "And you!"

"You moulting corvoid," replied her cousin. "Get out of here before I kill you!"

They neared each other, stiff and claw-fingered. Davis cowered into his corner.

The wind hooted and banged the shutters. Above it suddenly, he heard a roar. It swept closer, boots racketing on cobblestones, clattering iron, a mob howl.

The Whitleys heard it too. Valeria wrenched her axe from the floor. Barbara darted back to her own room and returned with a bow. The vague light threw their shadows monstrous across the walls.

"What's going on?" said Davis. "What is it . . . ?" He went to open the shutters and look out. A crossbow bolt thudded through the wood. He decided not to open the shutters.

Feet pounded down the hall. Nelly Udall burst into the chamber. There were gashes on her squat body, and the axe in her hand dripped. "Hell and sulfur, Man!" she bawled. "Grab your weapons! They're coming to kill you!"

A Macklin and a youthful Lundgard followed her. They were also wounded, hastily armed, and they were crying.

"What happened?" rattled Davis.

"I bolted the outer door," said Nelly between hoarse breaths. "They'll break it down in a minute." A groan of abused wood chorused her. She turned to Davis, blinking back her own tears. "Are you a Man, dearie, or were you just handing me a line of snakker?"

"I . . . of course I'm a Man," said Davis.

The gray head shook. "Reckon I'll have to take your word for that. I did . . . that's how I got these cuts . . . wreck and plagues! The legate says you aren't. Why didn't you have the sense to kill that shark, child?"

"The legate . . ." Valeria straightened. "I am the legate."

"Yeh? That Trevor says otherwise. And she proved it pretty well."

"Trevor!" Davis grabbed the Udall's shoulders and shook her. "What's happened? Is she loose?"

"Yeh," said Nelly in a flat voice. "We was all down at the Anchor, drinking your health, and this Trevor walks in with that Dyckman of yours—says she's the legate and you're a Monster—proved it by running through the rites every mother knows are said at the Ship—challenges your Whitley to do the same . . ." Nelly shook her head again. "It was quite a fight. We three here beat our way out o' the tavern and got here ahead of 'em."

"Elinor!" Barbara's voice seethed.

"She must have sneaked out," said Davis hollowly. "Gone to the brig, told the guard she had new orders from me, set Joyce free . . . what're we going to do now?"

"Fight," answered Nelly. She spat on her hands, waved her axe, and planted herself firmly in the doorway.

There was a final crash, and the mob came down the hall. A Salmon leaped yelling, with drawn knife. Nelly's axe thundered down, the body rolled at her feet. A Hauser jabbed at her with a spear. Barbara shot the Hauser.

It dampened them. The few women who could be seen milled in the narrow corridor. The noise quieted to a tigerish grumble.

Davis took a long breath, summoned all the psychophysiological training they had hammered into him at school, and stepped forward. "Who has been lying about me?" he shouted.

A scarred elderly Damon faced him, bold under the menace of Nelly's axe. "Will you call a truce?" she asked.

"Yes," said Davis. "Hold your fire, Babs. Maybe we can settle this."

Joyce Trevor pushed her way through the crowd. Ragged skirt and matted hair took away none of her frozen dignity. "I say you are a liar and a Monster," she declared.

"Elinor," said Davis, very quietly, still not believing it. "Elinor, why did you do this?"

He glimpsed her near the front of the mob, thin, shaking, and enormous-eyed. Her lips were pale and stiff. "You are," she whispered. "You attacked a legate. The legate says you're a Monster."

Davis smiled wryly. It was too late to be afraid. "I was alone, and there were a lot of Doctors. That's the answer, isn't it? You'll sing a different tune if the Men ever come."

"Shut up, you Monster!" screamed Elinor. "You and those Whitleys kicked me around once too often!"

"I'm not blaming you," said Davis. "It was my fault, asking you to do what nature never intended you for."

"Someday I'll bash your sludgy brains in, Dyckman," promised Valeria.

Elinor whimpered her way back into the crowd.

"This is a waste of time," snapped Joyce. "If that Whitley is a true legatee let her prove it by reciting the rites."

"Never mind," said Davis. "She isn't."

"You should'a told the truth from the beginning, dearie," said Captain Udall. Her tone reproached him. Paradox: you have to trust people to accomplish your ends, but not all people can be trusted.

"I know . . . now," said Davis. "But it's too late. I *am* a Man. I can bring all the Men here. The legate lies about me because the Doctors don't want them. It would mean the end of Doctor power."

"I sort of thought that," muttered the Lundgard girl in the room. "That's why I came along."

"Get me to my spaceship," said Davis. "That's all I ask."

"Of course it is," said Joyce. "Women of the sea, once the Monster is aloft how long do you think any of you will live?" She whirled on the crowd. "I lay the eternal curse of Father on anyone who helps this thing!"

Davis cleared his throat and roared back: "Father is another lie! If he exists, let him strike me dead! If he doesn't, you can see for yourselves how the Doctors have lied!"

"*We* are Father's instruments," shouted Joyce. "Kill it!"

Nelly hefted her axe, grinning. "Who's next?" she inquired.

"The Men are coming," said Davis smoothly. "Whatever happens to me, the Men will come in another generation. And they'll punish or reward according to how the first Man on Atlantis was treated."

That was a forty-carat whopper. The Service never took revenge on a society, or on any member thereof who acted in terms of its structure. But Davis was in no mood to explain Union law.

He heard feet shuffle in the corridor, voices buzz and break, spears drag on the floor. And there was the sound of new arrivals, a few pro-Davis women stamping in and one pronouncing the lovely, eloquent, rational words: "Whoever touches the Man gets hung!"

The bulk of Shield Skerry didn't know what to think; they inclined to believe the legate, but they had cooled off just a little. Women have slightly less tendency to act in mobs than men do. Davis straightened, licked his lips, and walked forward.

"I'm going out," he said. "Make way."

Barbara, Valeria, Nelly and her two companions, followed at his heels. A handful of determined roughnecks shoved through the paralyzed crowd, toward him, to join him.

"Kill them!" yelled Joyce. "Kill them or Father curse you!"

Barbara whirled around, her crossbow raised. "If you try anything," she said bleakly, "the legate dies first."

Davis brushed past Elinor. She hid her eyes from him. He felt no anger; it was useless. What he had to do now was clear out before somebody got heated up enough to break this explosive quiet.

As gently as possible, he went through the packed hall and the jammed common room. There were a score of armed women with him now, to form a comforting circle. They started for the quay.

The wind raved in coalsack streets. Davis

shuddered and forced himself to forget the cold and the heavy waves beating beyond the harbor. He heard the crowd follow, but it was too dark for him to see them.

Barbara—he felt the hard stock of her arbalest— whispered venomously: "Don't think I'm coming along for your sake, you slimy double-face. I haven't any choice."

Davis stumbled on a cobblestone and swore. The wind whipped his oath from him. These few dozen meters were the longest walk he had ever taken.

When they emerged from canyon-like walls, onto the wharf, enough light to see by trickled down from the pharos. Nelly led the way toward her ship. "I'm staking one hell of a lot on your really being a Man," she cried into the wind.

"Thanks," said Davis inadequately.

"I don't dare believe anything else," she said in an empty voice.

A gangplank was thrown from quay to hull. Davis could just make out the crowd, where it swirled in the shadows. It would be no trick for them to shoot at him. But praise all kindly fates, they were used to thinking for themselves in a rough tarry-thumbed fashion; they were still chewing on the unknown.

Joyce would talk them around soon enough, but by then he would be gone.

Valeria edged close to him and hissed: "Yes, I'll believe you're a Man too . . . and the hell with all Men! I'm only coming because I haven't any other choice."

Nelly tramped over the gangplank. When she had a deck beneath her feet, she seemed to draw strength from it. "All aboard, you scuts! Man the capstan! Look lively or I'll beat your ears off!"

She went aft, up on the poop to a nighted helm. The other women scurried about, doing incomprehensible things with ropes and pulleys. The great windmill, sweeping within a meter of the main deck, jerked, whined, and resumed more slowly. There was a white threshing at the stern, and the *Firebird* moved out of the harbor.

CHAPTER XVIII

Morning was gray over an ice-gray sea, where waves snorted from horizon to horizon. A dim streak in the east was land. The ship wallowed and yawed.

Davis emerged from one of the little cabins under the poop to find the fo'c'sle drawn up before a small galley for breakfast. He joined the line, hugging a cloak he had found close to his skin. Valeria was ahead of him, Barbara already eating in the lee of the bulwarks. Both ignored him. The sailors—mostly young women of the more warlike families, he noticed—chattered happily, but he was in no mood for their conversation.

His eyes went over the decks. Aft was the wheelhouse and a sort of binnacle—yes, they undoubtedly had some kind of compass. The main dock held the galley and the cargo hatches. Up by the prow, immediately behind the figurehead, was a harpoon-gun catapult.

The windmill faced into the stiff northwesterly wind. It squealed less than he would have expected— must be well oiled. From the gear housing at the peak an ironbound shaft went down through the derrick, into the hold, turning.

Neat arrangement, thought Davis. There must be a set of universal gears at the windmill head, so it could swig directly into any breeze. Its rotation was transmitted by shafts and other gears to a screw propeller. The *Fishbird* could sail straight against the wind if the skipper chose. Of course, the gears would have to be ground with precision, and being of rather soft steel would need frequent replacement; but if you didn't know how to build a steam engine, it was a good idea.

Nelly Udall waddled down from the poop as he got his tray. "'Morning, dearie," she boomed. "Sea bother you?"

"No," said Davis. A spaceman, trained to all gravities from zero on up, didn't mind a little rolling.

"Good. Kind of hard to believe in a seasick Man, eh? Haw, haw, haw!" Nelly slapped his back so he staggered. "I like you, chick, damn if I don't."

"Thanks," said Davis weakly.

"Come into my cabin. We'd better talk this over."

It was a very small room. They sat on her bunk and Davis said: "I'm not sure what to do next. Go on to Holy River?"

"Wouldn't recommend it," said Nelly. She took out a pipe and began stuffing it with greenish flakes from a jar. Davis' eyes lit up. It wasn't tobacco, but it could be smoked. Her words brought him up cold. "Not unless you want a dart in your liver."

"Huh?"

"Think a bit, dearie. That Father-damned legate has preached hellfire to 'em back at Shield. By now, the boats must be headed for the Ship to bring the glad tidings. They can sail rings around one of these propeller buckets, if the wind is right . . . and it is, for tacking, anyway. Time we get to Bow Island, all that country will be up in arms."

"Glutch!" strangled Davis.

Nelly ignited a punk stick with her fire piston, got the pipe going, and blew nauseous clouds. "Sure you aren't seasick, duck?" she asked. "All of a sudden you don't look so good."

"What're we going to *do?*" mumbled Davis.

"Right now," Nelly told him, "I'm bound for my home port, Farewell. Got friends there, and nobody'll think to bring them the news for a while. Won't be nobody to conterdick whatever you want to say. And what'll that be?"

She watched him with expectant little eyes. Davis stared through the rippled glass of the port. A wave smacked against it, water streamed down and the ship lurched.

"Think they'll still support us when they do hear?"

"I know a lot who will, dearie. I did, didn't I? Eighteen of us, besides your two Whitleys, and *that* was with the legate hooting in our faces. We've gotten almighty sick of the Doctors, I can tell you. We see more of 'em than the uplanders do, the . . ." Nelly devoted a few minutes to a rich catalogue of the greed, arrogance, and general snottiness of the Doctors.

They couldn't be quite such villains. Very likely, a number of them honestly thought he must be a Monster; his advent hadn't fitted in with the elaborate eschatology they seemed to have evolved. Others were doubtless more cynical about it, but Davis could not regard that as a crime.

However—he knew enough Union law to be sure that just about anything he did to the Doctors would be all right with the Coordination Service. This was not a matter of passing anthropomorphic judgments on some nonhuman civilization; Homo sapiens values were rigorously established, and they included a normal family life.

The idea grew slowly. He scarcely heard the Udall rumble on: "I reckon we can raise a few shiploads. We can go far up the coast, then strike inland to get at your boat from the rear . . ."

"No!" said Davis. "Too risky. It'll be guarded as heavily as they can manage. The Doctors aren't going to give up till they've seen my pickled head. And they may have tools enough left in the Ship to take to Freetoon and demolish my boat. We've got to act fast."

"So . . ." Nelly waited, her pipe smoldering in stumpy fingers.

"So we get a fleet together at Farewell . . . yes. If you really believe your girls are ready to hazard their lives to be free— Do you?"

Nelly smiled. "Chick, with that beard and that voice you can talk 'em into storming hell gate."

"It won't be quite that bad," said Davis. "I hope. What we're going to do is storm the Ship."

CHAPTER XIX

High tide on battle day was just after Bee-rise. As the morning fog broke up into ragged gray streamers, the rebel fleet lay to at Ship city.

Davis stood on the *Fishbird's* deck and watched his forces move in. There were twenty other propeller craft, and about as many fishing schooners and smaller boats. Their windmills and white sails were like gull wings across waters muddy-blue, rippled and streaked by an early breeze. At their sterns flew the new flag he had designed. His girls were quite in love with the Jolly Roger.

The rebels numbered some two thousand women from the Farewell archipelago. It had been estimated that there were half again as many at the Ship— but less tough, less experienced in fighting (the seafolk were not above occasional piracy), a number of them children or aged. The odds didn't look so bad.

Valeria stamped her feet so the deck thudded. "I'm going ashore," she said mutinously.

"No, you don't, chickabiddy." Nelly Udall twirled a belaying pin. "Got to keep some guard over the Man. What's the use of it all if he gets himself skewered?"

Barbara nodded coldly. "She's right, as anybody but a gruntbrain like you could see," she added. "Not that I wouldn't rather guard a muckbird! But if our friends are stupid enough to *want* the Men, I'll play along."

Davis sighed. In the three Atlantean weeks since they left Shield Skerry, neither of the cousins had spoken to him, or to each other without a curse. After the hundredth rebuff, he had given up trying to reconcile them.

Yet somehow he couldn't just say to Evil with them and console himself elsewhere. He remembered strolling alone on the cliffs of Farewell one day. It was chill and cloudy, the surf ramped below him, and wind flung scud far up into his face and hissed in harsh grass. Suddenly a girl appeared from a thicket. She was a Lundgard, young and pretty. More than the weather had flushed her face and brightened her eyes. As she approached him, he saw with unease that she wore under her cloak only the briefest of tunics.

"Hail to ye," she said.

"Uh, hello," he faltered.

She stood hands on hips, looking him up and down. At last she smiled. "It'll be more fun than awesome, I think," she said.

"What will?" he gaped.

She took off her cloak and spread it on the ground. Three deft motions dropped the tunic beside it. She opened her arms wide. Her blush crept astonishingly far downward, but her tone was calm. "If you're in truth the Man, here I am for your use."

"Ulp!" said Davis. He backed away. "But, but, but—"

"Please," she begged. "I made a bet you would."

"Oh, no!" groaned Davis.

It seemed most ungentlemanly to cost her her wager. But that morning he had spied Barbara and Valeria on the street. He had called to them, and they turned their faces away. It was the reason he had come on this walk. He wished he could rid himself of the ridiculous obsession that made all other women nearly meaningless. But it wasn't possible.

"I'm sorry." He hurried on past the girl.

She looked after him a moment, smiled wryly and picked up her clothes again. "Well," she said, "win one, lose one."

Davis was positively glad that now all such chances were behind him. He had hated himself for wasting them.

Nelly picked up a megaphone and bawled at a vessel maneuvering toward the wharf. "Sheer off! Sheer off or you'll pile up!"

The Ship must have been badly crippled, thought Davis, to land here; probably it had come down where it could, on the last gasp of broken engines. The walls which now enclosed it had been built on a hill that just barely stuck out over high tide. Eastward lay the marshes, a dreary land where a broad stone causeway slashed through toward the distance-blued peaks of the Ridge.

There must have been heavy earth-moving equipment and construction robots in the Ship's cargo. A few thousand women could not have raised this place by hand. Now the machines were long ago worn out, but their work remained.

The city was ringed by white concrete walls five meters high, with a square watchtower at each corner. The walls fell straight into the water of high tide or the mud of ebb: inaccessible save by the causeway entering the eastern gate or the wide quay built out from the west side. Against this dock the nearest

rebel boats were lying to. Gangplanks shot forth and
armored women stormed onto the wharf. The ships
beyond nudged the inner ones, forming a bridge for
the rest of the crews. The *Fishbird* lay just outside
the little fleet.

Davis let his eyes wander back to the city. He
could see the tops of buildings above the walls, the
dome-roofed Carolinian architecture of three centuries
ago. And he could see the great whaleback of the
Ship itself, three hundred meters long from north wall
to south wall, metal still bright but a buckled spot
at the waist to show how hard it had landed.

Barbara looked at the yelling seafolk. She was clad
like them: visored helmet on her ruddy hair, tunic
of steely scaled orcfish hide, trousers, spike-toed boots.
The accessories included axe, knife, crossbow and
quiver—she had become a walking meat grinder. She
and Valeria still kept their lassos around their
shoulders.

Davis, equipped like them, felt the same sense of
uselessness. Not that he *wanted* to face edged metal;
but when women were ready to die for his sake . . .

Bee struck long rays into his eyes. Ay was so close
as to be hidden by the glare of the nearer sun. Minos
brooded overhead in the gigantic last quarter. There
was a storm on the king planet, he could almost see
how the bands and blotches writhed.

Horns blew on the walls, under the Red Cross flag
of the city. Women, lithe tough legates and acolytes,
were appearing in cuirass, greaves, and masking
helmet, all of burnished metal. Crossbows began to
shoot.

There was no attempt to batter down the double
door at the end of the quay; it was of solid iron, the
hinges buried in concrete. A howling mass of sailors
raised ladders and swarmed skyward.

"Cosmos!" murmured Davis.

A Doctor shoved at one of the ladders, but there

was a good nautical grapnel on its end; it could not easily be thrown. Davis saw her unlimber a long rapier. The first rebel up got it through the throat and tumbled knocking off the woman below her.

"Let me go!" yelled Valeria.

"Hold still," rapped Nelly. Her worried eyes went to Davis. "I didn't think they'd have so good a defense, chick. They've never had to fight, but it seems they were always prepared. We'd better get them licked fast."

He nodded. They had only a couple of hours before the tide dropped so far that any ship which remained would be stranded till the next high. There were locks to take care of ordinary visitors, but a vessel in such a basin would be trapped as effectively as one sitting in the mud.

"So we stay," growled Barbara. "Isn't that the idea?"

"Yeh," said Davis. He drew hard on a borrowed pipe. "Only the Doctors must have raised a local army from the upland towns, to keep us from getting to Freetoon. Now they'll send for its help. If things go badly, I'd like a way to retreat."

"*You* would," she agreed, and turned her back on him.

Axes, spears, swords clashed up on the wall, bolts and darts gleamed in the cool early light. The Doctor fighters were rapidly being outnumbered. One of them, in a red cloak of leadership, winded a horn. Her women fought their way toward her.

Nelly Udall jumped up and down, cackling. "We win!" she cried, and pounded Davis on the back. "We've got the walls already!"

He staggered, caught the rail. It couldn't be that simple! No, the Doctor forces had rallied and were streaming down a stairway into their town. A slim young Burke cried triumph; he could hear the hawk-shriek above all the racket and see how her dark hair flew as she planted the Jolly Roger on the city wall.

The women on the dock poured antlike up the
ladders. It grew thick with rebels above the Ship.

Something moved between the crenels of the two
flanking towers. Big wooden flywheels spun on the
parapets. Davis could see Doctors manning an intricate machine. A ratcheted belt fed to grooves in each
wheel, a rain of darts gushed out.

Primitive machine gun, he thought wildly. *But it
works!*

Slaughter raged along the wall. The young Burke
who carried the flag dropped it, clawed at her breast,
and toppled off. A Tottino fell, dripping blood on the
concrete.

"Get this damned bilgebucket in!" howled Valeria.
She fired wildly at the nearest tower, tears whipping
down her face.

"No," groaned Nelly. "The Man . . ."

Barbara lifted her axe. "Hell rot the Man! They're
being butchered up there! Land us!"

A party of sea women reached the stairway and
started down into the city. The Doctors defended it
with sword and spear and bow; it was too narrow a
passage to force in a minute. Murder glittered and
whistled from the parapets.

Someone cried out, picked up the fallen flag, and
raced for a tower. A hundred girls streamed after her.
They couldn't all be cut down. They got into the cone
of safety, below which the machine could not be
depressed, and shook their spears at the wall before
them.

Nelly roared into her megaphone: "Another ladder! Another ladder, two others, you witless ninny-
hammers!"

A troop of older women, held in reserve, ran
ashore with the ladders. They planted them against
the city walls, next to the towers. The rebels above
dragged them up and laid them against the battlements.

Up and over! There was a red flash of axes. The dart throwers whirred on, spewing no more . . . until somebody grabbed one, pulled down the feeding lever, and raked the stairway.

Nelly grabbed Davis and whirled him a wild stomp around the deck. "We got 'em, we got 'em, we got 'em!" she caroled. Planks shuddered beneath her.

The storming party went down the stairs. Others followed, an armored wave up the ladders and into the city. The Red Cross was pulled down from its tower and the Jolly Roger flapped in its place, skull grinning over a hundred corpses and two hundred wounded.

Davis felt sick. His whole culture was conditioned against war; it remembered too well how cities had gone up in radioactive smoke and barrenness crept stealthily over green hills.

"Scared?" jeered Barbara. "You're safe enough."

"Sure," said Valeria. "If it looks like you might get hurt after all, we'll take you away."

"I'm not going to retreat!" said Davis in a raw voice.

"Yes, you will, duck, if we got to," said Nelly. "If you get killed, what's for us?" Her seamed face turned grimly inland. "We've got to win . . . no choice . . . if the Doctors win, there'll never be another baby on the islands."

That was what drove them, thought Davis. And an even deeper need, which made political grudges the merest excuse given to the conscious mind. Instinct said that a machine was too unsafe a way of bringing new life into the universe.

Except for the casualties and a few guards, nearly the whole rebel force was now out of sight within the city. He could just hear the noise of battle. It seemed to be receding . . . that meant his side was driving the Doctors back.

So what if he won? A victory where you yourself did nothing was no victory for a man.

Damn! His pipe had gone out.

The iron doors were flung open. He could not see through them from where the *Fishbird* lay, but it showed that the west end of town was firmly held by his side.

"I think we'll have the place before ebb," said Nelly. "But then what do we do?"

"We'll have the parthenogenetic apparatus," Davis reminded her. "Not to mention the prestige of victory. We'll own the planet."

"Oh . . . yeah, that's right. Keep forgetting. I'm growing old, dearie," Nelly waved her axe. "But I'd still like to part the hair on a few Doctors!"

There was a shriek through the doorway.

Sailors poured out of it, falling over each other, hurling their weapons from them in blind panic. A couple of hundred women made for the ships.

"What's happened?" bawled Nelly. "Avast, you hootinannies! Stop that!" She went into a weeping tirade of profanity.

Barbara snatched the megaphone from her. "Pull in!" she cried. "We're going ashore!"

The helmswoman looked ill, but yanked a signal cord. Down in the hold, the engineers shoved levers to engage the windmill. It caught with a metal howl and the *Fishbird* swung around. The forward watch went to the capstan, the anchor rose and the ship wallowed across a narrow stretch of open water.

Nelly Udall waited mutely. Her vessel bumped against one of the docked schooners. Two girls at the bulwarks flung out grapples.

"Let's go," snapped Valeria. She leaped onto the schooner deck, axe aloft.

Barbara saw Davis follow. "No!" she yelled.

"Yes," he answered harshly. "I've stood enough."

She grabbed his arm. He shook her off, blind with fury, and dashed across to the wharf.

The mob was still coming out of the door and over the quay to mill around on the ships. One anchor was already weighed. Davis grabbed a Craig and whirled her around.

"What's the matter?" he shouted.

She gave him an unseeing look. "The fire," she whimpered. "Oh, the fire!"

He slapped her. "Talk sense! What happened in there?"

"We . . . street fighting . . . Doctor troop . . . flame, white flame and it *burned* our forward line . . ." The Craig collapsed.

Davis felt something sink within him. He turned slowly to the *Fishbird* crew. "Did you ever hear of a fire weapon?" he asked.

"No," said Nelly. "No, never."

"It's Father himself!" gasped a Macklin.

"Shut up!" rapped Davis. "I know what it is. They must have found my blaster up by Freetoon and the legate took it back here. Maybe records in the Ship describe blasters." He shook his head numbly. "Chilluns, this is not a good thing."

"What are we going to do?" whispered Barbara.

"We're going to get that blaster," he said. "It's only a weapon. There's nothing supernatural about an ion stream. And there's only one of them."

"You'll be killed," said Valeria. "No, wait here, Bert . . ."

"Follow me," he said. "If you dare!"

They trotted after him, a dozen from the *Fishbird* and as many more from the retreat whose morale had picked up.

He went through the doorway and saw an ordered gridiron of paved streets between tall concrete houses. The Ship rose huge at the end of all avenues. This close, he could even read the name

etched on the bows, *New Hope*. It seemed a cruel
sort of name.

From two other streets came the noise of fighting. The battle had spread out, and most of its groups
had not yet seen the fire gun. They would, though,
if he didn't hurry; and that would be the end of all
rebellion.

"We went down this way," pointed a Latvala from
the original party. "Three streets down, and then we
met this band of enemies at our left."

Davis jogged between closed doors and broad glass
windows. Looking in, he saw that the Doctors did
themselves well; no such luxury existed elsewhere on
Atlantis. He could understand their reluctance to
abandon such a way of life.

He skidded to a halt. The Doctors were coming
around the corner ahead of him.

There were about twenty. A party of young legates,
their helmets facelessly blank, spread from wall to wall
with interlocked shields. Behind them lifted swords
and halberds.

"Get them!" shouted Nelly.

Three girls sprang ahead of Davis. One of them
was a Whitley; he thought for a moment she was one
of *his* Whitleys and then saw Barbara and Valeria still
flanking him.

Over the shield tops lifted a Burke face. It was an
old face, toothless and wrinkled under a tall bejew-
eled crown, and the body was stooped beneath white
robes. But his blaster gleamed in a skinny hand.

Davis flung out his arms and dove to the ground,
carrying Barbara and Valeria with him. Blue-white fire
sizzled overhead.

The three young girls fell, blasted through. It could
have been Val or Barbara lying there, thought Davis
wildly. He remembered how he loved them.

He rolled over, into a doorway. "Get out!" he
screamed.

His gang were already stampeded. Nelly stood firm, and Barbara and Valeria were beside him. Nelly threw her axe; it glanced off a shield, and the legate stumbled against the old Doctor. Her next shot missed, and Nelly pumped thick legs across the street.

She hit the door with one massive shoulder. It went down in splinters. Davis sprang into a sybarite's parlor.

"Quick!" he said. "Out the back way!"

Two legates appeared in the doorframe. Barbara's crossbow snapped twice. Valeria and Nelly were already out of the parlor.

Davis followed and saw a stair. "Give me your lasso, Babs," he said. "I have an idea."

"We're all coming." She uncoiled the rope as they pounded after him.

A bedroom overlooked the street. Davis shoved up the window. The blaster party was just underneath. He threw his axe down, missed the old bitch, and cursed. Her gun swiveled toward him.

Barbara shoved him aside, leaned out the window, and sent her lariat soaring. It closed around the chief Doctor; Barbara grinned and drew the noose taut.

"Help!" screamed the Burke. "I've been roped!"

Davis sprang into the street. Almost, he skewered himself on one of the halberds. He landed on an armored legate and both went down with a rattle and a gong.

She didn't move. Davis jumped up and landed a left hook to the nearest jaw. Valeria's lasso snaked from the window, fastened to something. She came sliding down it with her axe busy. Nelly followed. Barbara took a few judicious shots before joining them.

The old one snarled. She fought free and reached for the blaster. "Oh, no, you don't!" Davis put his foot on it. A rapier struck his scaly coat and bent upward, raking his cheek. He kicked, and the woman reeled off to trip somebody else. A slender form closed with

him; a dagger felt for his throat. He got his hands
on the waist, lifted her up, and tossed her into the
melee.

Nelly had picked up an axe. "Whoopee!" she
bellowed, and started chopping. Barbara and Valeria
stood back to back, their weapons a blur in front of
them. Davis was still too inhibited to use whetted steel
on women, but every blow he dealt shocked loose
some of his guiltiness.

The fight was over in a few minutes. Davis stooped
for the blaster and spent another minute incinerat-
ing the Doctors' dropped weapons. "Let's go," he
panted.

"Are you just going to leave these scuts here?"
Nelly pointed at the enemy casualties.

"Sure. We've pulled their teeth." Davis stuck the
gun in his belt. "Can't you get it through your thick
head, this fight is for everybody on Atlantis—Doctors
included?"

"No," she grunted. "Oh, well."

They went on down the street. There was a narrow
passage between the Ship's ruined gravity cones and
the wall. On the other side lay a broad square, lined
with impressive temples, a few dead and wounded
women strewn across it.

But no more sound of fighting . . . odd!

A sailor troop emerged from behind one of the col-
umned sanctuaries. "It's the Man!" squealed somebody. They ran toward him and drew up, flushed. The
leader gave a sketchy salute.

"I think we just about have the town, sir," she
puffed. "I was patrolling on the east end. Didn't see
anyone."

"Good!" Davis shuddered his relief. He *could* not
have used a blaster on women; the memory of the
dead Whitley girl was burned too deeply in him.

"Get our people together here," he said. "Mount
guards on the towers and at the gates. Round up

all the Doctors left, herd 'em into one of these chapels . . . and don't use them for target practice! Set up a sickbay for the wounded—and that means enemy wounded, too. Nelly, you take charge. I want a look around."

He walked through empty streets. Behind him he could hear cheers and trumpets, the tramp of feet and triumphal clang of arms, but he was in no mood for it.

Minos was a thin sliver, with Bee sliding close. Nearly eclipse time . . . had all this really taken three hours? It seemed like a nightmare century.

The Whitleys trailed him. He heard one of them speak: "I take a lot back, Val. You fought pretty good."

"Hell, Babs, you're no slouch yourself. After all darling, you are identical with me."

The street opened on another plaza, a narrow one that ran the length of the east wall. There was a doorway in the middle, with wrought-iron gates. Davis looked through the bars to the causeway and the marshes. Mud gleamed on the ridge which the road followed, birds screamed down after flopping fish. The tide was ebbing, the ships stranded . . . but what the Evil, they had won, hadn't they?

Hold on there!

The highway bent around a clump of saltwater trees three kilometers from the city. Davis saw what approached from the other side and grabbed the bars with both hands.

"An army!" he croaked.

Rank after rank poured into view. He thought he could hear the slap of orsper feet and the war-cries lifted among haughty banners. Now he saw leather corselets, iron morions, boots and spurs and streaming cloaks. They were the hill people and they were riding to the relief of the Doctors.

"A couple of thousand, at least," muttered Barbara. "The legates must have gone after them as soon as we attacked . . . They've been waiting around to kill you, my dearest . . ." She whirled on him, her visored face pressed against his side. "And it's too late to retreat—we're boxed in!"

"Not too late to fight!" Valeria dashed toward the inner town, shouting. Sea women on the walls lifted horns to lips and wailed an alarm.

Davis looked at the gate. It was locked, but it could be broken apart. His hand went to the blaster. Before Cosmos! That would stop them—it was the least he could do for these girls who trusted him.

No!

The rebel army pelted into the plaza. Right and left, arbalesters swarmed up the staircases to the walls. The dart throwers swiveled about on their turrets. *Cosmos,* thought Davis, *hasn't there been enough killing?*

Behind him, Nelly Udall scurried along the ranks of the women, pushing them into a semblance of order. Davis regarded them. Tired faces, hurt faces, lips that tried to be firm and failed; they would fight bravely, but they hadn't a chance against fresh troops.

The pirate flag fluttered defiantly up on a staff over the gate. The nearing cavalry whooped. Bolts whistled to make a rag of it.

"Shoot!" screamed Barbara. "Burn them down, Bert!"

The blaster was in his hand. He looked at it, dazedly.

Up on the parapets, the dart throwers began to clatter. Orspers reared, squawked, went off the road into the mud and flapped atrophied wings. The charge came to a clanging halt, broke up, fought its way back along the road . . . it stopped. Leaders trotted between panicked riders, haranguing them.

Hill women dismounted. Their axes bit at a road-side tree. It wouldn't take them long to make a battering ram. They would slog forward under the dart fire; they would be slaughtered and others would take their place. The ram would get into the cone of safety and the gates come down.

"When they're in range," leered Nelly, "let 'em have it!"

Bee slipped behind Minos. The planet became a circle of blackness ringed with red flame. Of all the moons, only firefly Aegeus was visible. Stars glittered coldly forth. A wind sighed across the draining marshes, dusk lay heavy on the world.

"Let me try something," said Davis.

He fired into the air. Livid lightning burned across heaven, a small thunder cracked in its wake. Screams came from the shadow army on the road; he fired again and waited for them to flee.

"Hold fast! Stay where you are, Father damn you!" The voices drifted hoarse through the gloom. "If we let the Monster keep the Ship, you'll die with never another child in your arms!"

Davis shook his head. He might have known it.

Someone clattered up the road. Four short trumpet blasts sent the sea birds mewing into the sudden night. "Truce call," muttered Valeria. "Let 'em come talk. Answer the signal."

"Might as well," said Nelly. "I don't *want* to see 'em fried alive." She took a horn from the girl beside her and winded it.

The mounted woman approached. She was an Udall herself. Barbara squinted through the murk at the painted insignia. "Bess of Greendale!" she hissed. "Kill her!"

Davis could only think that the Doctors' desperation had been measured by their sending clear up to Greendale for help. The swamp and the upper valley must be aswarm with armies intent on keeping him from his boat.

"No," he said. "It's a parley, remember?"

The Udall rode scornfully up under the walls. "Is the Monster here?"

"The Man is here," said Barbara.

Davis stepped into view, peering through iron bars and thick twilight. "What do you want?"

"Your head, and the Ship back before you ruin the life machine."

"I can kill you," said Davis. "I can kill your whole army. Watch!" He blasted at the road. Stone bubbled and ran molten.

Bess Udall fought her lunging orsper to a halt. "Do you think that matters?" she panted. "We're fighting for every unborn kid on Atlantis. Without the machine we might as well die."

"But I'm not going to harm the damned machine!"

"So *you* say. You've struck down the Doctors. I wouldn't trust you dead without a stake through your heart."

"Oh, hell," snarled Valeria. "Why bother? Let 'em come and find out you mean business."

Davis stared at the blaster. "No—there are decent limits."

He shook himself and looked out at the vague form of the woman. "I'll make terms," he said.

"What?" yelled Barbara and Valeria together.

"Shut up. Bess, here's my offer. You can enter the town. The sea people will return to their ships and sail away at next high tide. In return, they'll have access to the life machine just as they always did."

"And you?" grated the Udall. "We won't stop fighting till you're dead."

"I'll come out," said Davis. "Agreed?"

"*No!*" Barbara leaped at him. He swung his arm and knocked her to the ground.

"Stand back!" His voice rattled. "I'm a Man."

Bess Udall stared at him. "Agreed," she said. "Open the gates and come out. I swear to your terms by Father."

The rebels shuffled forward, shadow mass in a shadow world. Davis could barely make out his Whitleys. Valeria was helping Barbara up.

"Don't move," he said. "It isn't worth it . . . my life . . . The Men will be here in another generation anyway."

His blaster boomed, eating through the lock on the gates. He pushed them open, the hot iron burning his hands, and trod through. With a convulsive gesture, he tossed the blaster into a mudpool.

"All right," he said. "Let's go."

Bess edged her orsper close to him. "Move!" she barked. A few women surged from the gateway. She brandished her spear. "Stand back, or the Monster gets this right now!"

Minos was a ring of hellfire in the sky.

"Wait!"

It was a Whitley voice. Davis turned. He felt only an infinite weariness; let them kill him and be done with it.

He couldn't see whether it was Barbara or Valeria who spoke: "Hold on there! It's us who make the terms."

"Yes?" growled the rider. Her spear poised over Davis.

"We have the life machine. Turn him back to us or we'll smash it and kill every Doctor in town before you can stop us!"

A sighing went through the rebels. Nelly cursed them into stillness. "That's right, dearie," she cried. "What the blazes is a bloody machine worth when we could have the Men?"

Davis waited, frozenly.

The Whitley walked closer, cat-gaited. "These are *our* terms," she said flatly. "Lay down your arms. We won't hurt you. By Father, I never knew what it means to be a Man till now! You can keep the town and the machine—yes, the Doctors—if you want. Just let us bring the Man to his ship and bring the Men back for us!"

Bess Udall's spear dropped to the ground.

"You don't know he's a Man," she stammered.

"I sure do, sister. Do you think we'd have stormed the Holy Ship for a Monster?"

Night and silence lay thick across the land. A salt wind whined around red-stained battlements.

"Almighty Father," choked Bess. "I think you're right."

She whirled her orsper about and dashed down the road.

Davis stood there, hoping he wouldn't collapse.

He heard them talking in the orsper host. It seemed to come from very far away. His knees were stiff as he walked slowly back toward the gate.

Several riders hurried after him. They pulled up and jumped to the ground and laid their weapons at his feet.

"Welcome," said a voice. "Welcome, Man."

The sun swung from behind Minos and day burned across watery wastes and the far eastern mountains.

Davis let them cheer around him. Barbara knelt at his feet, hugging his knees. Valeria pushed her way close to lay her lips on his. "Bert," she whispered. He tasted tears on her mouth. "Bert, darling."

"Take either of us," sobbed Barbara. "Take us both if you want."

"Well, hooray for the Man!" said Nelly. "Three chee—whoops! Catch him! I think he's fainted!"

CHAPTER XX

It had been a slow trip through the valley. They had to stop and be feasted at every town along the way.

Davis Bertram stood in tall grass, under a morning wind, and looked up the beloved length of his spaceship. He whistled, and the airlock opened and the ladder descended for him.

"I'll be back," he said clumsily. "It'll take me a little longer to reach Nerthus—I want to be sure I don't hit that vortex—but inside a hundred of your days the Men will be here."

And what would they say when he walked into Stellamont wearing this garb of kilt, feather cloak, and war-bonnet? He grinned at the idea.

The Freetoon army was drawn up in dress parade a few meters off. Sunlight flamed on polished metal and oiled leather, plumes nodded and cloaks fluttered in the breeze. More of their warriors had survived

191

the invasion than he expected. They came out of the woods to worship him as their deliverer when he ordered the town set free. A cheap enough deed; local sovereignty would soon be obsolete here.

Gaping civilians trampled the meadows behind them. Davis wondered how many of their babies he had touched, for good luck. Well, it beat kissing the little apes . . . not that it wouldn't be nice to have a few of his own someday.

Barbara and Valeria stood before him. Under the burnished helmets their faces were drawn tight, waiting for his word.

His cheeks felt hot. He looked away from their steady green eyes and dug at the ground with his sandals.

"You're in charge here," he mumbled. "If you really want to make Freetoon a republic . . . and it'd be a big help—you folk have a difficult period of adjustment ahead . . . at least one of you has to stay and see the job is done right."

"I know," said Valeria. Her tone grew wistful. "You'll bring that psych machine you spoke of to . . . make her forget you?"

"Not forget," said Davis. "Only to feel differently about it. I'll do better than that, though. I'll bring a hundred young men, and you can take your pick!"

"All right," said Valeria. "I pick you."

"Hoy, there!" said Barbara.

Davis wiped sweat off his brow. What was a chap to do, anyway? He felt trapped. "It'd be better if you both stayed," he stuttered. "You'll have a . . . a rough time . . . fitting into civilization."

"Do you really want that?" asked Barbara coolly.

"No," said Davis. "Good Cosmos, no!"

After all, he was a survey man. He wouldn't be close to civilization for very long at a time, ever. Even a barbarian woman, given spirit and intelligence, could be trained into a spacehand.

And a few gaucheries wouldn't matter. A Whitley in formal dress would be too stunning.

"Well, then," said Valeria. Her knuckles tightened around her spearshaft. "Take your choice."

"I can't," said Davis. "I just can't."

The cousins looked at each other. They nodded. One of them took a pair of dice from her pouch.

"One roll," said Barbara.

"High girl gets him," said Valeria.

Davis Bertram stood aside and waited. He had the grace to blush.

AUTHOR'S NOTE

Science fiction readers are interested in science, and it's a pity they get so little of it. With a few honorable exceptions, writers are all too prone to create either rank impossibilities or minor variations on the Earth and the Western civilization we already know. So far, to my knowledge, only Hal Clement has actually set forth his calculations, and his *"Mission of Gravity"* is therefore a fascinating logical exercise. The present story makes no claim to such intellectual stature, but a few background details which could not get into the narrative may be of interest.

A fantastic yarn is properly allowed only one assumption contrary to fact. In the present case, I have made the postulate—which may be true, for all anyone knows—that relativity gives only a partial picture of the structure of the universe, and that someday new discoveries will be made which will force us to modify our physical theory.

I assume, in short, that faster-than-light travel is possible. This is not supposed to be through simple acceleration; that idea has been ruled out both theoretically and experimentally. But while the group velocity of a particle-wave train is limited by that of light, the phase velocity is not. Accordingly, in this "future history" the invention of a device for handling discontinuous psi functions permits a spaceship to assume a pseudo-velocity (*not* a true speed in the mechanical sense) limited only by the frequency of the engine's oscillators.

On the basis of this postulated physics, it seems reasonable to suppose that gravity control, both to generate an internal field and as a propulsive mechanism for sub-light travel, is attainable, and that a phenomenon like the "trepidation vortex" may actually exist. Neither assumption is necessary to the plot, but they help it along.

Everything else is strictly within the realm of present science. A blaster gun could be built today, though it would be a large, clumsy machine. (The gun in the story depends on a nearly perfect dielectric, something on which the Bell Laboratories are now working.) Electronic readjustment of an emotional pattern is foreshadowed by such therapeutic techniques as electric shock and tranquilizing drugs. Our present computers and automata are embryonic robots. Parthenogenesis has already been induced in mammals, and there is no known reason why further research should not make it applicable to man.

Given interstellar travel, there are certain logical social consequences. Men would emigrate to new worlds for one reason or another; in this story, there is no economic motive for leaving Earth, but there is a psychological drive analogous to the wholesale migration of European liberals to America after 1848, in that the majority of men do not find the mechanized, highly intellectualized culture of Earth congenial.

Interstellar war and interstellar government are both improbable: space is too big, an entire planet too self-sufficient. But a loose alliance of the civilized worlds (the Union) and a joint patrol to protect individuals and backward societies from the grosser forms of exploitation (the Coordination Service) are quite likely to be organized. Other features of my future civilization, such as the basic language and the philosophical pantheism of Cosmos—neither one replacing all its older counterparts—are necessarily guesswork; we can only be sure that the future *will* be different from the present. In fact, a story laid some centuries hence must be thought of as a translation, not merely of language but of personalities and concepts corresponding only approximately to anything we know.

Like all new technology, interstellar travel will pose more problems than it solves. Of these, cartography is not the least. Not that anyone in his right mind would bother with three-dimensional maps of the Galaxy; a catalogue of astronomical data is so much hardier. But the Galaxy is so big that numbering each individual star would be a system too clumsy and too prone to error.

I assume instead, that large regions are taken more or less arbitrarily, and that the constellations as they appear from some base planet within each region are named. Thereafter all other stars of the region can be referred to this system of constellations in the usual manner of 20th-century astronomy.

Thus, the Pilot's Manual will catalogue these base planets, or rather their suns, and every such entry will refer you to an entire region. Naturally the larger stars, e.g., Canopus, visible through many regions, will have a different designation in each, but this is a simple matter of cross-reference.

The terrestroid planet Nerthus is such a base. It

is about one thousand light-years from Sol in the direction of Argus. The Wolf's Head is a conspicuous constellation in its skies. The proper designation of Atlantis' double sun, translated from Basic to the Latin we use today, is therefore (Ar 293) Delta Capitis Lupi. As in 20th-century astronomical practice, the "Delta" indicates that this star is the fourth brightest in Caput Lupi as seen from Nerthus.

The members of a double star system revolve around their common center of gravity. In practice, the more massive star is chosen as central and called A, its companion B. (Of course, popular names are often given.) The planets of a star are numbered outward, I, II, III, etc., and similarly the moons of any planet.

(I have not *assumed* that nearly every star—of Population I, at least—has planets. This is pretty well-established fact.)

The names of bodies within a given system, as opposed to the numbers, are customarily chosen to fit a consistent pattern. The volcanoes and watery outer hemisphere of our world suggested the name Atlantis; mythical Cretan and Greek motifs followed logically for the other bodies, since the Atlantis of legend may well be a dim recollection of the Minoan empire.

Delta Capitis Lupi A (later called Daedalus) is of type AO, a hot bluish star with a mass of four Sols and a luminosity of eighty-one Sols (taken from the mass-luminosity diagram). Its companion B (Icarus) is of type GO, almost identical with Sol. If we regard A as the center, which we may legitimately do, then B revolves about A at an average distance of ninety-eight Astronomical Units with a period of four hundred eighty-five years. From the vicinity of B, A has an apparent luminosity of 0.00085 times that of Sol seen from Earth. This is comparable to Sol at eleven A.U., a way beyond Saturn, but the angular diameter of A at B is much less. To the naked eye at B, A is little more than a super-brilliant star.

A has three planets of its own, none habitable to man. B has two, of which Minos is the first. Otherwise, because of stellar gravitational effects, there are only asteroids.

Minos has an average distance from B of one A.U. Therefore it gets on an average nearly the same amount of heat and light as Earth. However, the gravitational pull of A has elongated this orbit toward itself, so that the ellipse has an eccentricity of 0.2. Hence the seasons on Atlantis, winter coming when Minos is farthest from B and closest to A, summer when these conditions are reversed.

Minos is of the general type of 61 Cygni C, the extrasolar planet discovered by Strand in 1944. Its mass is about five thousand times that of Earth, its equatorial diameter fifty-one thousand two hundred kilometers, its rotation period some ten hours. Like all giant planets, it has a dense atmosphere, mostly hydrogen.

It also has eighteen satellites. Most are so small and far out as to be insignificant, but the inner ones are conspicuous from Atlantis, which is the Earth-sized third moon of Minos.

In the table on page 200, Column 1 gives the equatorial diameter of each of the first five satellites, in kilometers. (Their density is about the same as Earth's, 5.5 g/cc.) Column 2 lists the average orbital radius about Minos in kilometers, Column 3 the period of each orbit in hours. Column 4 shows the angular diameter as seen from Atlantis at closest approach, in degrees of arc. (For comparison, Luna seen from Earth is about 0.5 degree across.) Column 5 lists the time between successive oppositions to Atlantis, in hours. Finally, Column 6 shows the respective names.

All these orbits are ellipses of small eccentricity,

approximately in the Minoan equatorial plane though
slightly skewed with respect to each other.

Moon	1	2	3	4	5	6
I	162	161,000	2.45	Point	3.1	Aegeus
II	3218	272,000	5.2	0.9	9.05	Ariadne
III	12,502	483,000	12.2	—	—	Atlantis
IV	4793	720,000	22.2	0.7	26.9	Theseus
V	1610	1,920,000	97.0	0.07	14.0	Pirithous

The drag of the major planet has given these
satellites a period of rotation equal to that of revo-
lution, so that they always turn the same face to their
primary. For the same reason, this inner hemisphere
is bulged toward Minos and there is little axial tilt,
though considerable precession.

In the case of Atlantis especially, this permanent
deformation has concentrated most of the land in the
inner hemisphere and made the main continent, on
and about which the action of the story takes place,
extremely mountainous. (Later this continent was
named Labyrinth.)

The inner hemisphere of Atlantis has a spectacular sky. Minos shows an angular diameter of about
seven degrees and, having an albedo of forty-five
percent, is brilliantly luminous, equivalent in full
phase to roughly twelve hundred full moons of Earth.
In addition, Ariadne and Theseus each give several
times as much light as Luna. Aegeus and Ariadne
never set, but are seen to move across Minos from
west to east, then back again behind Minos in the
opposite direction. As Column Five shows, to an
observer accustomed to Earth's moon, these satellites
would appear almost to hurtle. Aegeus is seen to
complete its path through the sky in 3.1 hours and
to go through a full cycle of phases in about thirty
hours; the apparent path is some eighteen degrees
across. This moon, however, shows merely as a small,

rapid star of fluctuating brightness. Ariadne completes its apparent path, ca. thirty-two degrees wide, in 9.05 hours and a cycle of phases in about sixty-three and one-half hours or some five Atlantean days. Because of orbital inclination, all the moons are usually "above" or "below" Minos when they pass it. An occasional sight is the full Ariadne transiting the full Minos at midnight and turning a dull coppery hue as it enters the Atlantean shadow cone. The large outer moon Theseus rises and sets in a normal manner, moving a trifle more slowly than Luna, and completes a cycle of phases in about one hundred thirty-five hours or eleven Atlantean days.

The outer hemisphere never sees Minos, sees the inner moons rise and set low in the sky only near the hemispheric boundary, and sees less of Theseus.

The system Ariadne-Atlantis-Theseus begins a new cycle of motions about every three hundred fifty hours.

During the winter half of the Minoan year, which is about as long as Earth's, the companion sun A illuminates Atlantis after B has set. In summer the two stars seem gradually to approach each other, until at mid-summer A is occulted by B.

The inner hemisphere of Atlantis sees a total eclipse of B every day, when the satellite gets Minos between itself and the star. The precise time depends on longitude; it is nearly at noon in the locale of this story. The theoretical duration of this eclipse is about eleven minutes, actually somewhat less because of the refracting effect of the Minoan atmosphere. A is eclipsed sometime during the day in summer and sometime during the night in winter. There are also occasional eclipses of either sun by the other moons.

Ariadne and Theseus have strong tidal effects on the oceans of Atlantis, the first raising tides about equal to those of Earth, the second, tides almost six times as high. In addition, there is the more or less steady influence of Minos and the shifting, weaker effects of B and the smaller moons. This leads to turbulent oceans with fantastically complicated patterns of waves, ebb, and flow. Low shores are turned to salt marshes, high shores whipped by a murderous surf. Tidal bores are very common along the uneven continental shelves. Only inland seas approach terrestrial conditions.

The same gravitational forces make Atlantean diastrophism more rapid than Earth's. The satellite has extensive volcanic regions and few areas are free of earthquakes. The release of carbon dioxide through vulcanism in tectonic eras, followed by its equally rapid consumption in the exposed rock of newly risen mountains, makes the geological history one of sudden climatic shifts. Because of the higher Coriolis force, cyclonic storms on Atlantis are both more frequent and more violent than those of Earth.

At the time of this story, however, there is a mild interglacial climate and the life, whose biochemistry is quite terrestroid—as one would expect on a world so similar to Earth—is flourishing. There are no polar icecaps, but the highest mountains retain a few glaciers and the uplands have snow in winter.

It might seem inevitable that mammals would develop under such changeable conditions, but there is nothing inevitable about evolution. The progress of Atlantean life has, indeed, been retarded by the undependable weather and cataclysmic geology, which tend to kill off new land forms before they can become well-established. Only the birds are equipped to escape changes more sudden and powerful than anything Earth has ever known—and 20th-century geologists are coming to believe that the climatic revolutions of our own planet took place more rapidly than was once thought. Whenever conditions have again become favorable, the Atlantean birds have exploded into a new multiplicity of species, including giant flightless types.

As a matter of fact, there are a few primitive mammals on Atlantis, on the outer hemisphere, where the greater water surface makes the weather a bit more stable. But they have not yet reached the inner section, and the human castaways, unable to sail far on those tricky seas, never see them.

And this is the scientific background of the story. The reader is invited to make his own calculations on the basis of my assumed data, and challenge me if he thinks I've gone wrong anywhere. That's one of the things which makes science fiction fun.

STAR WAYS

CHAPTER I

There is a planet beyond the edge of the known, and its name is Rendezvous.

Few worlds are more lovely to the eyes of men. As the weary ships come in from space and loneliness, they see a yellow star against the great cold constellations; and nearing, they see its crowded glory swell to incandescence. The planet grows as the ships strain closer; it becomes a sapphire shield banded with clouds, blurred with rain and wind and mountain mists. The ships sweep around the planet, mooring themselves to an orbit between the moons, and it is not long before the boats spring from them and rush down out of the sky to land. And then, for a little while, the planet comes alive with noise and movement as human life spills free.

This might have been Earth, in some forgotten age before the glaciers went south. Here, there is the broad green swell of land, reaching out to a remote horizon. Far away, mountains begin; on the other side is the sea. The sky is big here, lifting above the world to blue immensity.

But the difference is what haunts you. There are trees, but they are not the oak and pine and elm— or palm, baobab, sequoia—of Earth, and the wind blows through their leaves with an alien sound. The fruits of the trees are sweet, pungent, luscious to eat, but always there is the hint of a taste men never knew before. The birds are not yours; the animals of plain and forest have six legs and a greenish shimmer to their fur. At night, the constellations bear the look of strangers, and there may be four moons in the sky.

No, it is not Earth, and the knowledge becomes a hunger in you and will not let you stay. But you have never seen Earth; and by now, the hunger has become so much a part of you that you could not find a home there, either. For you are a Nomad.

And only you have learned where to find this quiet place. To all others, Rendezvous lies beyond the edge of the known.

CHAPTER II

There was nobody else on the boat. They had all swarmed off to pitch their booths and mingle with the rest, to frolic and fight and transact hardheaded business. Peregrine Joachim Henry's footsteps echoed hollow between the bare metal walls as he entered the airlock. The boat was a forty-meter column of steely comfortlessness, standing among its fellows at the end of Nomad Valley. The temporary village had mushroomed a good two kilometers from the boats.

Ordinarily, Joachim would have been down there, relaxed and genial; but he was a captain, and the Captains' Council was meeting. And this was no assembly to miss, he thought. Not with the news he had to give them.

He took the gravity shaft, floating along the upward beam to the top bunkroom where he had his box. Emerging, he crossed the floor, opened the chest.

Joachim decided that a shave was in order, and ran the depilator quickly over his face.

He didn't usually bother with regalia—like all Nomads, he wore any outfit he cared to, or went nude, on a voyage. Visits to planetary surfaces didn't ordinarily require him to dress formally; but the uniform was expected of him.

"We're a hidebound bunch, really," he reflected aloud as he glanced in the mirror. It showed him a stocky man of medium height, dark-skinned, with grizzled hair and squinted gray eyes in a mesh of crow's-feet. The face was blunt and battered, crossed with deep lines, but it wasn't old. He was in early middle age—sixty-five years—but there was vitality in him.

The kilt, with its red-black-and-green Peregrine tartan, was tight around his waist. Had the damn thing shrunk? No, he was afraid he had expanded. Not much, but Jere would have kidded him about it, and let out the garment for him.

Jere. It was fifteen years now since she had made the Long Trip. And the children were grown and married. Well—He went on dressing. Over his light shirt he slipped an elaborately embroidered vest, with the Joachim coat of arms woven into the pattern. His sleeve bore the insignia of rank—captain—and service—astrogation. Buskins went on the legs; pouch and holstered gun at the waist, and plumed bonnet on the close-cropped head. Because it was hereditary and expected of him, he wore the massive gold necklace and its diamond-crusted pendant. A purple and scarlet cloak flapped over his shoulders, gauntlets on his hands.

Joachim crossed the bunkroom and went down the shaft, out the airlock, and down the retractible gangway ladder again. A dim path wound up from the valley and he took it, moving with a slightly rolling, bearlike gait. The sky was utterly blue overhead;

sunlight spilled on the wide green sweep of land; wind brought him the faint crystal laughter of a bellbird. No doubt of it, man wasn't built to sit in a metal shell and hurry from star to star. It wasn't strange that so many had dropped out of Nomad life. Who had that girl been—Sean's girl, from Nerthus—?

"Salute, Hal," said a voice behind him.

He turned. "Oh Laurie. Haven't seen you for long."

Vagabond MacTeague Laurie, a walking rainbow in his uniform, fell into step beside Joachim. "Just got in yesterday," he explained. "We're the last, I suppose, and we carried word from the *Wayfarer* and the *Pilgrim* that they couldn't make it this year. So this one reckons all the ships are accounted for by now—anyway, Traveler Thorkild said he was calling the meeting for today."

"Must be. We spoke to the *Vagrant* out near Canopus, and they weren't coming. Had some kind of deal on; I suppose a new planet with trading possibilities, and they want to get there before anybody else does."

MacTeague whistled. "They're really going far afield. What were you doing out that way?"

"Just looking around," said Joachim innocently. "Nothing wrong in that. Canopus is still free territory; no ship has a claim on it yet."

"Why go on a Jump when you've got all the trade you could want right in your own territory?"

"I suppose your crew agrees with you?"

"Well, most of them. We've got some, of course, that keep hollering for 'new horizons,' but so far they've been voted down. But—hm." MacTeague's eyes narrowed. "If you've been prowling around Canopus, Hal, then there's money out there."

The Captains' Hall stood near the edge of a bluff. More than two centuries ago, when the Nomads found Rendezvous and chose it for their meeting place, they had raised the Hall. Two hundred years of rain, wind, and sunlight had fled; and still the Hall was there. It might be standing when all the Nomads were gone into darkness.

Man was a small and hurried thing; his spaceships spanned the light-years, and his feverish death-driven energy made the skies of a thousand worlds clangorous with his works—but the old immortal dark reached farther than he could imagine.

The other captains were also arriving, a swirl of color and a rumble of voices. There were only about thirty this rendezvous—four ships had reported they wouldn't be coming, and then there were the missing ones. The captains were all past their youth, some of them quite old.

Each Nomad ship was actually a clan—an exogamous group claiming a common descent. There were, on the average, some fifteen hundred people of all ages belonging to each vessel, with women marrying into their husbands' ships. The captaincy was hereditary, each successor being elected from the men in that family, if any were qualified.

But names cut across ships. There had only been sixteen families in the *Traveler I*, which had started the whole Nomad culture, and adoption had not added a great many more. Periodically, when the vessels grew overcrowded, the younger people would get together and found a new one, with all the Nomads helping to build them a ship. That was the way the fleet had expanded. But the presidency of the Council was hereditary with the Captain of the *Traveler*—third of that name in the three hundred years since the undying voyage began—and he was always a Thorkild.

Wanderer, Gypsy, Hobo, Voyageur, Bedouin, Swagman, Trekker, Explorer, Troubadour, Adventurer, Sundowner, Migrant—Joachim watched the captains go in, and wondered at the back of his mind what the next ship would do for a name. There was a tradition which forbade using a name not taken from some human language.

When everyone else had entered, Joachim mounted the porch himself and walked into the Hall. It was a big and goodly place, its pillars and paneling carved with intricate care, hung with tapestries and polished metal reliefs. Whatever you could say against the Nomads, you had to admit they were good at handicrafts.

Joachim sank into his chair at the table, crossed his legs, and fumbled for his pipe. By the time he had lit up and was emitting cheerful blue clouds, Traveler Thorkild Helmuth was calling the meeting to order. Thorkild was a tall, gaunt, and stern-faced man, white of hair and beard, stiffly erect in his carved darkwood seat.

"In the name of Cosmos, rendezvous," he began formally. Joachim didn't pay much attention to the ritual that followed.

"All ships except five are now present or accounted for," concluded Thorkild, "and therefore I call this meeting to discuss facts, determine policy, and make proposals to lay before the voters. Has anyone a matter to present?"

There was, as usual, quite a bit, none of it very important. The *Romany* wanted a territory extending fifty light-years about Thossa to be recognized as her own—no other Nomad ship to trade, exploit, build, organize, or otherwise make use of said region without permission of the assignee. This was on grounds of the *Romany's* having done most of the exploration thereabouts. After some discussion, that was granted.

The *Adventurer* wished to report that the Shan of Barjaz-Kaui on Davenigo, otherwise known as Ettalume IV, had laid a new tax on traders. The planet being known to the Coordination Service, it wasn't possible for Nomads to overthrow the Shar by violence, but with some help it might be possible to subvert his government and get a friendlier prince. Was anyone interested? Well, the *Bedouin* might be; they could talk it over later.

The *Stroller* had had more direct difficulties with the Cordys. It seemed the ship had been selling guns to a race who weren't supposed to be ready for such technology, and Coordination Service had found out about it. All Nomads had better watch their step for a while.

The *Fiddlefoot* was going to Spica, where she intended to barter for Solarian products, and wanted to know if anyone cared to buy a share in her enterprise. Goods hauled clear from Sol were expensive.

It went on—proposal, debate, argument, report, ultimate decision. Joachim yawned and scratched himself. His chance came finally, and he flicked a finger upward. "Captain Peregrine Joachim," acknowledged Thorkild. "Do you speak for your ship?"

"For myself and a few others," said Joachim, "but my ship will follow me in this. I've got a report to make."

"Proceed."

Then eyes turned on him, down the length of the Council table.

Joachim began recharging his pipe. "This one has been sort of curious for the last few years," he said, "and he's been keeping his eyes open. You might think I was a Cordy, the way I've been reconstructing the crime. And I think it is a crime, or maybe a war. A quiet but very thorough war." He paused calculatingly to light his tobacco. "In the past ten years or so, we've lost five ships. They never reported back to anyone. What does that mean? It could happen once or twice by sheer accident, but you know how careful we are in dealing with the unknown. Five ships is just too many to lose. Especially when we lose them all in the same region."

"Now hold on, Captain Peregrine," said Thorkild. "That isn't so. Those ships disappeared in the direction of Sagittarius—but that includes a hell of a lot of space. Their courses wouldn't have come within many parsecs of each other."

"No-o-o. Maybe not. Still, the Union covers even more territory than this volume of space where our people vanished."

"Are you implying—No, that's ridiculous. Many other ships have been through that region without coming to harm, and they report that it's completely uncivilized. Such planets as we touched at have been thoroughly backward. Not a mechanical culture on even one of them."

"Uh-huh." Joachim nodded. "Isn't that an odd fact? In so big a chunk of space, there should be some race which has at least gotten as far as steam engines."

"Well, we've touched on—hm." Thorkild stroked his beard.

Romany Ortega Pedro, who had a photographic memory, spoke up. "The volume within which those ships disappeared is, let us say, twenty or thirty million cubic light-years. It contains perhaps four million suns, of which virtually all are bound to have planets. It's an unpromising region precisely because it is so backward, and few ships have gone there. To my knowledge, Nomads have stopped at less than a thousand stars in that volume. Now really, Joachim, you consider that a fair sample?"

"No. I just mention it as a little—indication, shall we say? I repeat, this one denies that five ships in ten years could have been lost because of unknown diseases, treacherous natives, trepidation vortices, or the like. Their captains weren't that stupid.

"I've talked with Nomads who've been there, and also with outsiders—explorers, traders, scouts looking for colony sites, anyone. Or any thing, since I also got hold of some otherlings"—he meant nonhuman spacemen—"who had passed through or stopped by. I even talked my way into the Cordy office on Nerthus, and got a look at their Galactic Survey records.

"Space is too big. Even this little splinter of the Galaxy that man has traversed is larger than we can think—and we've spent our lives in the void. It's thirty thousand light-years to Galactic center. There are some *hundred billion* suns in the Galaxy! Man will never be able to think concretely in such terms. It just can't be done.

"So a lot of information lies around in the shape of isolated facts, and nobody coordinates it and sees what the facts mean. Even the Service can't do it—they have troubles enough running the Union without worrying about the frontiers and the beyond-frontiers. When I started investigating, I found I was the first being who'd even thought of this."

"And what," asked Thorkild quietly, "have you found out?"

"Not too much, but it's damned indicative. There have been otherling ships which vanished in that region, too. But Coordination and Survey never had any trouble. If something had happened to one of *their* vessels, they'd have spyboats out there so fast they'd meet themselves coming back. You see what it means? *Somebody* knows a lot about our civilization—enough to know who it's safe to molest.

"Then there are any number of E-planets—which is what you'd expect—and not too many of them seem to have natives—which is what you wouldn't expect. They—well, there are at least a dozen which remind you of Rendezvous, beautiful green worlds with not a building or a road in sight."

"Maybe they're shy, like the ones on this planet," said Vagabond MacTeague. "We'd been here for fifty years before we knew there were natives. And a similar case happened on Nerthus, you remember."

"The Nerthusians have an unusual sort of culture," said Romany Ortega thoughtfully. "No, most likely those worlds you speak of are really inhabited."

"All right," said Joachim. "There's more to tell. In a few cases, there were E-planets with what we'd considered a normal culture: houses, farming, and so on. Contact was made rather easily in all those instances, and in general the natives seemed not unfamiliar with the sight of spaceships. But when I checked the reports against each other, I found that none of those planets had been visited before by anyone from *our* civilization."

"Now hold on," began Thorkild. "You aren't suggesting—"

"There's more yet." Joachim interrupted. "Unfortunately, few scientifically minded expeditions have been in the—the X region, so I couldn't get an accurate description of flora and fauna. However, a couple of those I talked to had been struck by what seemed remarkably similar plants and trees on some of these supposedly uninhabited E-planets. Galactic Survey had some helpful information there. They had noted more than similarity—they had found *identity* of a good dozen plant species on six uninhabited worlds. Explain that away!"

"How did Survey explain it?" asked Fiddlefoot Kogama.

"They didn't. Too much else to do. Their robotfile had integrated a reasonable probability that the similarity was due to transplantation, maybe accidental, by a Tiunran expedition."

"Tiunra? I don't think I've heard—"

"Probably you wouldn't have. They're the natives of an M-planet on the other side of Vega. Strange culture—they had space travel a good five hundred years before man left Sol, but they never were

interested in colonization. Even today, I understand
they don't have much to do with the Union. They're
just uninterested.

"Anyway, I took the trouble to write to Tiunra. Sent
the letter off on Nerthus a good two years ago. I
asked whoever was in charge of their survey records
about the X region. What had they found out? What
had been done by them, or to them, out here?

"I got my answer six months ago, when we stopped
back at Nerthus. Very polite; they'd even written in
human Basic. Yes, their ships had gone through the
X region about four centuries ago. But they hadn't
noticed the things I mentioned, and were sure they
hadn't done any transplanting, accidentally or otherwise. And *they* had lost four ships.

"All right." Joachim leaned back, sprawling his legs
under the table, and blew a series of smoke rings.
"There you have it, lads. Make what you will of it."

Silence, then. The wind blowing in through the
open door stirred the tapestries. A light metal plaque
rang like a tiny gong.

Finally Ortega spoke, as if with an effort: "What
about the Tiunrans? Didn't they do anything about
their missing ships?"

"No, except leave this part of space alone," said
Joachim.

"And they haven't informed Coordination?"

"Not as far as I know. But then, Coordination never
asked them."

Thorkild looked bleak. "This is a serious matter."

"Now there's an understatement," drawled Joachim.

"You haven't absolutely proved your case."

"Maybe not. But it sure ought to be looked into."

"Very well, then. Let's accept your guess. The X
region, perhaps the entire Great Cross, is under the
rule of a secretive and hostile civilization technologi-
cally equal to ours—or superior, for all we know. I
still can't imagine how you'd conceal the kind of

technology involved. Just consider the neutrino emission of a large atomic power plant, for instance. You can find your way across many light-years to a planet where they're using atomic energy, just by the help of a neutrino detector. Well, maybe they have some kind of screen." Thorkild tapped the table with a lean forefinger. "So, they don't like us and they've spied us out a bit. What does that imply?"

"Conquest—they figure to invade the Union?" asked MacTeague.

Trekker Petroff said, "They may just want to be left alone."

"What could they hope to gain by war?" protested Ortega.

"I'm not guessing about motives," said Joachim. "Those creatures aren't human. I say we'd better assume they're hostile."

"All right," said Thorkild. "You've given most thought to this business. What follows?"

"Why, look at the map," said Joachim mildly. "The Union, both as a cultural and a semipolitical unit, is expanding inward toward Galactic center, Sagittarius. The X empire lies squarely across the Union's path. X, however peaceful, may feel that countermeasures are called for.

"And where are *we?* On the Sagittarius-ward frontier of the Union, and spreading into the unmapped regions beyond. Right smack between the Union and X. The Coordination Service of the Union doesn't like Nomads, and X has already shown what he thinks of us. We're the barbarians—right between the upper and nether millstones!"

Another pause. Death they could face, but extinction of their entire tribe was a numbing concept; and the whole Nomad history had been one long flight from cultural absorption.

Thirty-odd ships, with some fifty thousand humans—*what can be done?*

Joachim answered the unspoken cry with a few slow words:

"I've been thinking about this for some little while, friends, and have some sort of an answer. The first requirement of any operation is intelligence, and we don't even know if X *is* a menace.

"Here's what this one proposes. Let's just keep the matter quiet for the time being. Naturally, no ship will enter the Great Cross, but otherwise we can go on as usual. But I'll make a scout of the *Peregrine,* and we'll spy out the unknowns."

"Eh?" Thorkild blinked at him.

"Sure. I'll tell most of my crew, at first, that it's an exploratory venture. We'll snoop around as we ordinarily do, and I'll direct the snooping the way I think'll be most useful. We can fight if we must, and once we go into hyperdrive we can't be followed or shot at."

"Well, that sounds—very good," said Thorkild.

"Of course," smiled the Peregrine, "we can't be hampered in our work. I'll want a formal action-in-council authorizing me or my crew to break, bend, or even obey any law of the Nomads, the Union, or anybody else that may seem convenient."

"Hmmm—I think I see where this could lead," said MacTeague.

"Also," said Joachim blandly, "the *Peregrine* will be in a primitive region—and hostile where it's not primitive—and won't have the normal chance to turn an honest credit. We'll want a—say a twenty percent share in all profits made between now and next rendezvous."

"*Twenty percent!*" choked Ortega.

"Sure. We're risking our whole ship, aren't we?"

CHAPTER III

Peregrine Thorkild Sean could not forget the girl who had stayed behind on Nerthus. She had gone alone into the city, Stellamont, and had not come back. After a while, he had taken a flier and gone the twelve hundred kilometers to her father's home. There was no hope—she couldn't endure the Nomad life.

Two years can be a long time, and memories blur. Thorkild Sean walked through the Nomad camp under the heaven of Rendezvous and knew how far away Nerthus was.

Darkness had come to the valley—not the still shadow of Nerthus, which was almost another Earth, but the living, shining night of Rendezvous. Fires burned high, and the camp was one babel. The trading had gone on till it was done. The Captains' Council had met, and its proposals had been voted on by the men of the ships—now the time of rendezvous was ready to culminate in the Mutiny. Unmarried women

were not allowed to attend that three-day saturnalia—
the Nomads were strict with their maidens—but for
everyone else it would be a colorful memory to take
skyward.

Except for me, thought Sean.

He passed a bonfire, crossing the restless circle of
its light—a tall slender young man, fair-skinned,
brown-haired, blue-eyed, his face thin and mobile,
his movements angular and loose-jointed.

Somebody hailed him, but he ignored it and went
on his way. Not tonight, not tonight. Presently the
camp was behind him. He found the trail he was
looking for and followed it steeply upward out of the
dale. The night of Rendezvous closed in on him.

This was not Earth, nor was it Nerthus, or any
other planet where men had built their homes. He
could walk free here, and no hidden menace of germ
or mold or poisoned tooth waited for him; yet somehow Sean felt that he had never been on so foreign
a world.

Three moons were up. One was a far white shield,
cold in the velvet sky; the second a glowing amber
crescent, and the third almost full and hurtling
between the stars so that he could see it moving.
Three shadows followed him over the long, whispering
grass, and one of them moved by itself. The light was
so bright that the shadows were not black; they were
a dusky blue on the moon-frosted ground.

Overhead were the stars, constellations unknown
to the home of humanity. The Milky Way was still
there, a bridge of light, and he could see the cold
brilliance of Spica and Canopus, but most of heaven
was strange.

The hills into which he went stirred with moonlight and shadow. Forest lifted on one side of his path,
high feathery-leaved trees overgrown with blossom-
ing vines. On the other side there was grass and bush
and lonely copse. Now and then he saw one of the

six-legged animals of Rendezvous. None of them were afraid; it was as if they knew he wasn't going to shoot at them.

Light moved here and there. The glowing insects bobbed on frail wings over the phosphorescent glow of lamp-flowers. Sean let the sounds of the night flow into him. The memory of his wife drowned as if in rippling water, and the new eagerness within him was a quiet, steady burning.

She stood where she had told him to come, leaning against a tree and watching him stride across the hills. His footsteps grew swifter until he was running.

The Nomads had looked for an Earthlike planet—E-planet—outside of the ordinary space lanes, a meeting place which no others would be likely to find. They had not explored much beyond the site chosen for their gatherings, but even so it had been a shock, fifty years later, when they learned that Rendezvous had natives after all. The laws on the Union were of small concern, but aborigines could mean trouble.

These dwellers had been a gentle sort, though, remarkably humanoid but possessing a culture unlike any ever created by man. They had sought out the newcomers, had learned the Nomad dialect with ease, and had asked many questions. But they had not told much concerning themselves; nor were the Nomads especially interested, once it became clear that these beings had nothing to trade.

The natives had courteously presented the Nomads with the area they already held, only that they not be molested elsewhere, and this the humans had readily voted into law. Since then, an occasional native had shown up at the assemblies, to watch for a while and disappear again—nothing else, for a good hundred and fifty years.

Blind, thought Sean. *We're blind as man has always been. There was a time when he imagined he was the*

*only intelligent life in the universe—and he hasn't
changed much.*

The thought died in the wonder that stood before
him. He stopped, and the noise of his heart was loud
in his ears. "Ilaloa."

She stood looking at him, not moving or speaking. The loveliness of her caught at his throat.

She could have been human—almost—had she not
been so unhumanly fair. The Lorinyans were what
man might be in a million years of upward evolution.
Their bodies were slim and full of a liquid grace,
marble-white; the hair on their heads was like silk,
floating about the shoulders and down the back, the
color of blued silver. He had first seen Ilaloa when
the *Peregrine* came to Rendezvous and he had wandered off to be alone.

"I came, Ilaloa," he said, feeling the clumsiness of
words. She remained quiet, and he sighed and sat
down at her feet.

He didn't have to talk to her. With men, he was
a lonely being, forever locked into the night of his
own skull, crying to his kindred and never knowing
them or feeling their nearness. Language was a bridge
and a barrier alike, and Sean knew that men talk
because they are afraid to be silent. But with Ilaloa
he could know quiet; there was understanding and
no loneliness.

Let the native females be! It was Nomad law which
needed little enforcement on other planets—who was
attracted by something that looked like a caricature
of man? But no spear had thudded into his flesh
when he met this being who was not less but more
than a woman; and there had, after all, been nothing to disgrace them.

Ilaloa sat down beside him. He looked at her
face—the smooth, lovely planes and curves of it,
arched brows over huge violet eyes, small tilted nose,
delicate mouth.

"When do you leave?" she asked. Her voice was low, richly varied.

"In three days," he answered. "Let's not talk about it."

"But we should," she said gravely. "Where will you go?"

"Out." He waved his hand at the thronging stars. "From sun to sun, I don't know where. It will be into new territory this time, I hear."

"To there?" She pointed at the Great Cross.

"Why—yes. Toward Sagittarius. How did you know?"

She smiled. "We hear talk, even in the forest. Will you come back, Sean?"

"If I live. But it won't be for at least two years— a little more in your reckoning. Maybe four years, or six, I don't know." He tried to grin. "By then, Ilaloa, you will be—whatever your people do, and have children of your own."

"Have you none, Sean?"

It was the most natural thing in the universe to tell her of what had happened. She nodded seriously and laid her fingers across his.

"How lonely you must be." There was no sentimentality in her voice; it was almost matter-of-fact. But she understood.

"I get along," he said. With a sudden rising of bitterness: "But I don't want to speak of going away. That will happen all too soon."

"If you do not want to leave," she said, "then stay."

He shook his head heavily. "No. It's impossible. I couldn't stay, even on a planet of my own kind. For three hundred years the Nomads have been living between the stars. Those who couldn't endure it dropped out, and those from the planets who fitted into our kind of life were taken in. Don't you see, it's more even than habit and culture by now. We've been bred for this."

"I know," she said. "I only wanted to make it clear in your own mind."

"I'm going to miss you," he told her. His words stumbled over each other. "I don't dare think how much I'll miss you, Ilaloa."

"You have only known me for some few days."

"It seems longer—or shorter—I don't know. Never mind. Forget it. I've no right to say some things."

"Maybe you do," she answered.

He turned around, looking at her, and the night was wild with the sudden clamor of his heart.

CHAPTER IV

"You will go to the Sagittarian frontier of the Stellar Union," the machine had said. "The planet Carsten's Star III, otherwise called Nerthus, is recommended as a starting point. Thereafter—"

The directive had been general and left the agent almost complete discretion. Theoretically, he was free to refuse. But if he had been the sort to do that, Trevelyan Micah would not have been a field agent of the Stellar Union Coordination Service in the first place.

The psychology of it was complex. The Cordy agents were in no sense swashbucklers, and they knew the fear of death often enough to realize that there was nothing glamorous about it. They believed their work to be valuable, but were not especially altruistic. Perhaps one could say that they loved the work.

His aircar went on soundless gravity beams over the western half of North America. The land was big and green below him, forest and rivers and grass waving out to the edge of the world. Scattered homes reflected sunlight, upward, isolated houses and small village groupings. Though, in a way, all Earth was a city by now, he thought. When transportation and communication make any spot on the planet practically next door, and the whole is a socioeconomic unity, that world is a city—with half a billion people on it!

The sky was full of aircraft, gleaming ovoids against the high blue. Trevelyan let his autopilot steer him through the fourth-level traffic and sat back smoking a thoughtful cigarette. There was a lot of movement on and over Earth these days. Few were ever really still; you couldn't be, if you had a job in Africa and a—probably temporary—dwelling in South America, and were planning a holiday at Arctic Resort with your Australian and Chinese friends. Even the interstellar colonists, deliberately primitive though they were, tended to scatter themselves across their planets.

There had been no economic reason for the outward surge of man when the hyperdrive was invented; the emigration was a mute revolt of people for whom civilization no longer had any need. They wanted to be of use, wanted something greater than themselves to which they could devote their lives—if it were only providing a living for themselves and their children. Cybernetic society had taken that away from them. If you weren't in the upper ten percent—a scientist, or an artist of more than second-rate talent—there was nothing you could do which a machine couldn't do better.

So they moved out. It had not happened overnight, nor had it fully happened yet. But the balance had shifted, both socially and genetically. And a planet, the bulk of whose population was creative, necessarily controlled the intangibles that in the long run would shape all society. There was scientific research; there was the education that directs men's thoughts, and the art that colors them. There was above all an understanding of the whole huge turbulent process.

Trevelyan's thoughts ended as the autopilot buzzed a signal. He was approaching the Rocky Mountains now, and Diane's home was near.

It was a small unit perched almost on the Continental Divide. Around it, the mountains rose white and colossal, and overhead the sky was pale with cold. When Trevelyan stepped out, the chill struck like a knife through his thin garments. He ran to the door, which scanned him as he neared and opened for him, and shivered once he was inside.

"Diane!" he exclaimed. "You choose the damnedest places to live. Last year it was the Amazon Basin. . . . When are you moving to Mars?"

"When I want to multiplex it," she said. "Hullo, Micah."

Her casual voice was belied by the kiss she gave him. She was a small woman, with something young and wistful about her.

"New project?"

"Yes. Coming along pretty well too. I'll show you." She touched keys on the multiplex and the tape began its playback. Trevelyan sat down to absorb the flow of stimuli-color patterns, music, traces of scent and associated taste. It was abstract, but it called up before him the mountains and all mountains which had ever been.

"It's good," he said. "I felt as if I were ten kilometers up on the edge of a glacier."

"You're too literal," she answered, stroking his hair. "This is supposed to be a generalized impression. I'd like to work in some genuine cold, but that's too distracting. I have to settle for things like ice-blue color and treble notes."

"And you say you never learned the cybernetic theory of art?"

"'Art is a form of communication,'" she quoted in a singsong. "'Communication is the conveyance of information. Information is a pattern in space-time, distinguished by rules of selection from the totality of all possible arrangements of the same constituents, and thus capable of being assigned a meaning. Meaning is the induced state of the percipient and in the case of art is primarily emotional— 'Bother it! You can have your mathematical logic. I know what works and what doesn't, and that's enough."

It was, he realized. Braganza Diane might not grasp the synthesizing world-view of modern philosophy, but it didn't matter. She created.

"You should have let me know you were coming, Micah," she said. "I'd have made arrangements."

"I didn't know it myself until just lately. I've been called back. I came to say goodbye."

She sat quiet for a long moment. When she spoke, it was very low, and she was looking away from him: "It couldn't wait?"

"I'm afraid not. It's rather urgent."

"Where are you going?"

"Sagittarius frontier. After that anything can happen."

"Damn," she said between her teeth. "Damn and triple damn."

"I'll be back," he said.

"Someday," she answered thinly, "you won't come back." Then, getting to her feet: "Well, relax. You can stay tonight, of course? Good, let's have a drink now."

She fetched wine in goblets of Lunar crystal. He clinked glasses with her, listening to the faint clear belling, and raised his to the light before he drank. A ruby flame glowed in its heart.

"Good," he said appreciatively. "What's the news from your end?"

"Nothing. There's never very much, is there? Well, I had an offer from an admirer. He even wanted a contract."

"If he's a right sort," said Trevelyan gravely, "I think you should take him up on it."

She regarded him where he sat, and saw a big, lean man, his body compact and balanced with the training of modern education. His face was dark and hook-nosed, a deep wrinkle between the green eyes, and most people would have called the light of those eyes cold. The hair was straight and black, with a reddish tint where the sun caught it. There was something ageless and impassive about him.

Well—the Coordination Service caught its agents young. They weren't supermen; they were something less understandable.

"No," she said. "I won't."

"It's your life." He didn't press the matter.

Their liaison went back several years. For him, she knew, it was a pleasant convenience, nothing more; he had not offered a contract and she had not asked for one.

"What is your directive this time?" she asked.

"I don't know, really. That's the worst of it."

"You mean the machine wouldn't tell you?"

"The machine didn't know."

"But that's impossible!"

"No, it isn't. It's happened before, and it will happen again with increasing frequency until—" Trevelyan scowled. "The real problem is finding some new principle altogether. It might even be philosophical, for all I know."

"I don't understand."

"Look," he said, "the basis of civilization is communication. In fact, life itself depends on communication and feedback loops between organism and environment, and between parts of the same organism.

"Now consider what we have today. There are approximately a million stars which have been visited by man, and the number grows almost daily. Many of these stars have one or more planets inhabited by beings of intelligence comparable to ours, but often with action-and-thought patterns so different that only long, painstaking study will ever suggest their fundamental motivation. Full empathy remains impossible. Imagine the effects on these of a sudden introduction to an interstellar civilization! We have to reckon with their future as well as our own.

"Remember your history, Diane. Think what happened in Earth's past when there were sovereign states working at unintegrated cross-purposes."

"You needn't strain the obvious," she said, annoyed.

"Sorry. I'm just trying to tie in the general background. It's fantastically complex, and the problem is getting worse. It's a case of transportation outstripping communication. We've *got* to bring all the components of our civilization together. You need only recall what happened on Earth back around the Second Dark Ages. Nowadays it could happen between whole stellar systems!"

She was still for a moment, throwing away one cigarette and lighting another. "Sure," she said, then. "That's what the Union was organized to prevent. That's what Cordy work consists of."

"We've found different types and emphases of intelligence in the Galaxy," he flung at her, "but they can all be given a rating on the same general scale. Ever wondered why there is no species whose average intelligence is appreciably higher than man's?"

"Why—well, aren't all the planets about the same age?"

"Not that close. A million or ten million years should make a real difference to organic life. No, Diane, it's a matter of natural limits. The nervous system, especially the brain, can only become so complex, then the whole thing gets too big to control itself."

"I think I see what you're driving at," she said.

"There are natural limits to the capacities of computing machines, too."

"Uh-huh. Also to systems made up of many machines together. Diane, we can't coordinate as many planets as are included in our civilization-range today. And that range is still expanding."

She nodded. Her face was serious, and there was a foreboding in the eyes that met his. "You're right— but what does this have to do with your new mission?"

"The overworked integrators are years behind in correlating information," he said. "A thing can grow to monstrous proportions before they learn of it. And we, the flesh-and-blood Cordys, are no better off. We perform our missions, but we can't oversee *everything*. The integrator has finally gotten around to considering some reports of disappearing ships, botanical anomalies on supposedly uninhabited planets, and the Nomad clans. The probability indicates something tremendous."

"What is that?" she breathed.

"I don't know," he answered. "The machine suggested that the Nomads might be up to something. I'm going to find out."

"Why do you Cordys have it in for the poor Nomads so much?"

"They're the worst disruptive factor our civilization has," he said grimly. "They go everywhere and do anything, with no thought of the consequences. To Earth, the Nomads are romantic wanderers; to me, they're a pain.

"I doubt that they're behind this business. I suspect something much more significant." He took out a cigarette and put it to his lips. "But the Nomads will make a handy place to start."

CHAPTER V

"No!"

Thorkild Sean looked into his father's eyes. "I don't see what you have to say about it."

"Are you out of your mind?" Thorkild Elof shook his head like an angry bull. The beard and the maned hair of a ship elder swirled white about his shoulders. "I'm your *father*."

Something in Sean stirred then. Ilaloa's fingers closed taut around his. Looking down, he saw fear in the big violet eyes, and remembered how far apart he and Elof had grown in the last four years. He straightened his shoulders. "I'm a free crewman of the Nomads, and I do as I please."

"We'll see about that!" Elof swung about, lifting his voice. "Hal! Hal, come over here, will you?"

Joachim Henry stood watching the people of his ship file into their boats. It was a long straggling line—men still disheveled and hilarious from the

235

Mutiny. The married women proceeded with careful dignity, most of them holding babies; the younger girls and boys looked wistfully back at the valley.

"Sean," whispered Ilaloa. He tightened his arm about her slender waist, feeling her tremble. The long silver hair streamed wildly from her head—with its fine clean molding and white skin and enormous eyes. But he felt the terror deep within her.

Joachim heard Elof's shout. "Now what?" he grumbled. He gave his kilt a hitch and strolled to the argument.

"Hello, Elof, Sean," he nodded. "Who's the—" He caught himself. "The native lady?"

"This is Ilaloa." Sean's voice was strained. Joachim's eyes lingered appreciatively on the female.

"What d'you want?" He gestured with his pipestem at the line of embarkees. "I got enough to do, nursing them back onto the ship. Make it short, will you, lads?"

"It can be," said Elof. "Sean here wants to take this native along. He wants to *marry* her!"

"Eh?" Joachim's eyes narrowed in a mesh of fine wrinkles. "Now Sean, you know the law."

"We're not offending native notions," the boy threw back at him. "Ilaloa is free to come with me if she wants."

"Your father?" Joachim spoke softly to her. "Your tribe? What do they have to say?"

"I am free," she answered. Her tones were the sweetest sound he had heard in a long time. "We have no—tribes. Each of us is free."

"Well—" Joachim rubbed his chin.

"What's going on here?"

It was a woman's voice, low and even, and Joachim turned to the newcomer with a feeling of relief. If he could let them argue it out to a decision of their own, perhaps he could keep clear of the mess.

Besides, he liked Nicki.

She walked up to them with the long swinging stride that was a challenge in itself. She was blonde, as tall as many men, and strongly built; there was a supple flow of muscles under her smooth, pale-gold skin. She walked over to her brother-in-law and looked into his troubled countenance. "What's wrong, Sean?"

A slow smile of greeting lifted his mouth. "It's Ilaloa," he said. "We want to go with the ship—together."

Nicki's blue-eyed gaze locked with the infinite violet of the Lorinyan's. Then she smiled and clapped a hand on the slim white shoulder. "Be welcome, Ilaloa," she said. "Sean's been needing somebody like you."

If proof had been required, Joachim would have considered that sufficient to destroy the malicious gossip about Sean and Nicki. Landlouper MacTeague Nicki had been eighteen, an average Nomad age for marriage, when her father and Elof arranged for her to wed Sean's younger brother Einar. The alliance had been tempestuous; then a landslide on Vixen killed Einar.

His widow was left in an anomalous position, a Peregrine and Thorkild by virtue of marriage, but without children to bind her to the family. Normally, Elof would have acted as her father and arranged another husband for her, but she had rejected the whole idea with an almost physical violence. She lived man-fashion, working for herself as a weaver and potter, and even doing her own trading on planets they visited. And the most irritating part of it, as far as the community was concerned, was that she did very well.

After his own divorce, two years ago, Sean had moved in with Nicki. They had separate rooms and respected each other's privacy. Under Nomad law, marriage was forbidden to them as members of the same ship; and tongues had been wagging ever since.

Elof drew him aside. "The boy's soft in the head, skipper," he said. "Throw the law at him. He'll get over it."

"Hm. I wonder." Joachim looked slantwise at the older Thorkild. "What's the background on this?"

"Well, you know how he tumbled for that Nerthusian wench. I didn't like it, but I didn't want to press him too far, either. She wasn't such a bad sort anyway, for a settler, until she deserted him. But since then—well, you know how Sean's been. Nobody can get along with him except Nicki, and that's bad—don't either of them have any sense of decency? Then the boy disappears this rendezvous, hardly shows himself, and I was all prepared to get him a nice wife from the Trekker Petroffs, too. And now he shows up with *this!*"

"Well," said Joachim mildly, "he's been married once. That makes him legally an adult."

"You know the law, Hal. And you know the biology of it, too. Different species can't interbreed. There'd be no children—only trouble."

Yes, thought Joachim glumly, *there'd be that all right. And what do we really know about this race?*

"There's plenty of room in Sean's and my quarters," said Nicki to Ilaloa. "We'll get along fine."

"A native can't be married, and she can't be adopted," snapped Elof.

Sean's face was white and stiff. "Ilaloa can be useful, Skipper. I think her people are telepaths."

"Eh?" Joachim blinked at him. The word was blown down the wind and a man halted—then moved slowly away.

"Is that so?" the captain asked the Lorinyan.

"I do not know," she answered. The fine hair stirred about her thin-carved face as if it had life of its own. "Sometimes we know things even about you. I have no word for it, but we can—feel?"

"There haven't been any natives around at this rendezvous," said Sean eagerly, "but Ilaloa knew the *Peregrine* was going into the Great Cross. A telepath in any degree can be a big help."

Or a big grief, thought Joachim. He puffed his pipe back into furious life and let his eyes rest on the Thorkilds. Ilaloa interested him. If what she said was true, that her people wouldn't make difficulties over her removal—and he had to assume that much—she might indeed have her uses. Neurosensitivity in any degree was not a gift to be despised.

"Let's be reasonable about this," he said. "We don't want a break in the family, Elof."

"The captain is the judge," answered the older man coldly, "but you've bent the law enough in the past."

"Well, Sean," said Joachim, "of course you can't marry her. The law's quite plain on that. However, there's nothing to forbid you"—he grinned slyly—"keeping a pet."

He had thought Ilaloa would take offense, but she laughed now, a sudden joyous peal, and one arm went about Sean. "Thank you," she said. "Thank you."

Sean looked rattled, but Nicki chuckled.

"Nothing to thank this one for," said Joachim. "I just interpret the law."

"Dad—" Sean spoke timidly. "Dad, when you get to know her—"

"Never mind." Thorkild Elof turned and walked away, his head unnaturally high. Joachim looked after him with a tinge of pity. It was hard on the old man. His wife was dead, his daughters married and out of the family, one son was gone and the other had raised a wall between them. *I know how lonesome a man can get,* Joachim thought.

"I reckon that settles it," said the captain. "Get busy, Sean. We have stuff to load aboard." He sauntered back to the embarkation.

"Nice work," said Nicki. "And welcome again, Ilaloa."

Sean and Ilaloa looked at each other. "You can come with me," said the man wonderingly, not quite believing it yet. "You *will* come."

"Yes," she said.

She looked across the valley; it was as if she listened to the windy roar of trees and the remote shouting of the sea. A shiver went through her and she covered her face briefly. Then she turned again to Sean and her voice seemed to come from very far away: "Let us be going."

He held her close for a moment, then they walked hand in hand toward the boats.

CHAPTER VI

The economy of the frontier planets, and therefore
the physical arrangement of their artifacts, is as different from Earth's as the rest of their culture. Like
most new lands of human history, they show a rever-
sion to older and more primitive types of social
organization; yet it is not a reconstruction of the past
which exists there.

From Sol to the vaguely defined Sagittarius frontier of the Union was a two months' voyage even in
the fastest hyperdrive transport. But the Solarian's own
needs were adequately provided for at home; he had
no particular reason to haul goods out to the stars.
The interstellar colonists had to provide for themselves.

They scattered over the faces of many planets,
those colonists. They weren't isolated, not with their
telescreens and gravity fliers, but they dwelt well
apart. A small but brisk trade went on between the

stars of any given sector, carried by merchant ships
or by such Nomads as weren't heading out into the
depthless yonder. A few goods from Sol itself, or other
highly civilized systems, found their way out to the
frontier, too. That meant spaceports, warehouses,
depots, service and repair establishments, shops—and
with them, local robot factories, entertainment facilities, and administrative centers. The city, a forgotten phenomenon of Solar history, was reborn.

One for a planet, or even a system, was usually
enough. The city on Carsten's Star III, Nerthus, was
called Stellamont. Joachim brought the *Peregrine*
there to get supplies and ammunition.

The trip took about three weeks.

The *Peregrine* contacted Nerthus' robot monitor,
and was assigned an orbit about the world. Her visit
was to be short, so most of the crew were left aboard;
Joachim and a few assistants went "down" in a couple
of fliers to dicker, and a boat took a single liberty
party, chosen by lot. The rest swore philosophically
and carried on with their usual shipboard rounds.
Among other things, the *Peregrine* had a poker and
a dice game in the main recreation room which, with
interruptions, had been going so long—about a century now—that their continuance had become almost
a fetish.

Joachim had based his success in the captaincy on
a number of tricks, among them the fine art of rigging lots. Those of the crew whom he thought needed
the liberty most got it. That included Sean and Ilaloa.
The Lorinyan girl hadn't been well lately. A little blue
sky might help.

When he stood on the ground, Sean drew a lungful
of Nerthusian air and smiled down at Ilaloa.

"Is this better, darling?"

"Yes." Her voice came faint under the clangor of
the spaceport.

Sean shook his head, tasting bitterness. "You'll get

used to it," he said. "You couldn't expect to make a change like that all at once."

"I am happy," she insisted.

The memory of another face and another voice drifted through him. His mouth tightened and he walked from the port with long strides.

They left the concrete prairie of the spaceport behind them and strolled out on a wide avenue. It was a busy scene; humans and nonhumans hurrying on their way, cars and trucks filling the street with a steady roar, aircraft overhead. Ilaloa's hands went up to her ears. She smiled at him ruefully, but her eyes were darkened.

Even in that cosmopolitan crowd, they stood out. Sean wore Nomad costume—kilt, buskins, full shirt and tight jerkin, cape flowing behind him and bonnet slanted across his forehead. Ilaloa, in spite of her professed dislike for clothes, had adopted a loose filmy version of woman's dress. Against its dark blues and reds, the pale beauty of her was spectacular. Both wore side-arms, as crewfolk generally did on any planet except Rendezvous.

"Sean, Sean, let me go."

He drew Ilaloa aside, into a doorway. Her fingers plucked at his sleeve and the eyes turned to his were an unseeing blankness.

"Let me go alone for a little, Sean. It is only for the littlest time, away in the voice of trees. Oh, Sean, I want the sun!"

He stood for a moment, unsure, half-frightened. Then the simple realization came: Ilaloa couldn't take the city. She needed quiet.

"Why—sure," he said. "Of course. We'll go—"

"No, Sean, alone. I want to—think? I will come back."

"Well—well, certainly, if that's what you want." He smiled but his lips felt stiff. "Come on, then."

He guided her to a public aircar station, gave one

of the vehicles some of his scanty Union credit notes, and told Ilaloa how to direct it. She wouldn't have far to go to reach a completely untenanted area, and they would meet again at the station.

She kissed him, laughing aloud, and slipped into the car.

Woods colt, he thought. He didn't dare consider if it would go with Ilaloa as it had gone with his settler wife.

I'm going to get drunk, he thought.

He walked swiftly until he was in the old section of town. Nobody stood on the law in that place. The native quarter was there, a result less of discrimination than of choice. The natives were friendly enough, but didn't feel comfortable in a human district. Tall bipedal beings, green-furred and four-armed, watched Sean out of expressionless golden eyes as he strode under trees and through barriers of flowering vines. Machines were not in evidence, except for a wooden cart drawn by one of the six-legged "ponies" of Nerthus.

The Comet Bar stood on the edge of the quarter, a small low-ceilinged structure where grass and pavement met. Sean walked in. A couple of colonists were drinking beer at a corner table; otherwise the place was deserted. Sean dialed for whiskey surrogate at the bar and sat down. He didn't want silence.

The door opened for a newcomer, admitting a brief sunbeam into the twilight of the room. Sean looked idly at the man. The fact of his being from Sol was plain from his dress: knee breeches and hose, loose tunic, light shoes, featherweight mantle with hood, all in subdued blues and grays. But it was the easy strength of him that stood out most.

He caught Sean's gaze and, after getting a drink from the dispenser, walked over and sat down beside the Nomad. "Hello," he said. The accent was unmistakable. "Don't see many of you fellows around."

"We come in now and then," grunted Sean.

"I've been in Stellamont for a couple of weeks," said the stranger. "Business, of sorts. But it's all wound up and I feel like celebrating. I wonder if you could recommend some good uninhabited places?"

"What business would a Solman have out here?" asked Sean.

"Research," said the Terrestrial. "Yes, you might call it that." He chuckled to himself and held out a pack of cigarettes. "Smoke?"

"Ummm—thanks." Sean took one and inhaled fire into it. Tobacco was expensive on the frontier; only the Earth-grown plant seemed to have the right flavor.

Sean wondered if it was true what they said about the exaggerated Solarian notions of privacy, and decided to find out. "What's your name?" he asked. "Can't just call you Solman."

"Oh, you can if you insist, but the name is Trevelyan Micah. And yours?" His black eyebrows lifted courteously.

"This one is called Peregrine Thorkild Sean. You could read the first two off my outfit if you knew the symbols. Also rank, ensign; and service, flier pilot and gunner."

"I didn't know you Nomads were organized so formally."

"It doesn't mean anything except in a fight." Sean drained his glass, tossed it down the nearest chute, and dialed for another. Trevelyan was still scarcely started on his. "Say we hit hostile natives, or an otherling ship that doesn't like us. That's where the ranks get important."

"I see. Interesting. Ordinarily, though, you're traders?"

"We're anything, friend. We can't make all we use or want—at least it isn't our way—so we float around, buy something cheap here, swap it for something else there, and finally sell what we have for Union credits. Or we might work a mine or something for a while ourselves, though usually we get the natives thereabouts to do it for us."

Trevelyan smiled. "Allow me." He bought the Nomad another drink. "Do go on. I've often wondered why your people choose to lead such a hard and rootless life."

"Why? Because we're Nomads. That's enough."

"Mmmmm-hm." Trevelyan grinned. "That reminds me of one time in the Sirian system—" He told an anecdote, and they started trading stories. Trevelyan drank in moderation; even so, his tongue began slipping a little.

"How about some solid fuel for a change?" he suggested at last.

"You're in your right orbit now," said Sean, speaking with elaborate precision. "But let's go where there's some life."

"Just as you say," responded Trevelyan amiably.

They had dinner in a small and noisy tavern which was beginning to fill up as the sun declined. Trevelyan kept making clumsy passes at the owner, a pneumatic human female. There was almost a fight, and they were frigidly escorted to the door.

"You're a good sort," said Sean, laughing. "A proper fellow, Micah."

"Electron shells," said Trevelyan owlishly. "We're only a pair of little electrons, jumping from shell to shell."

They went down the street, stopping in most of the bars that lined it. They were in a dim and smoky underground room when Trevelyan put his head on his arms, giggled stupidly, and went limp. Sean sat for a moment, blinking across the table at the man, wondering what to do.

"That will be four credits sixty," said a voice from high above. Sean saw a bearded giant with an uncompromising look about him. "That's your score, 'less you want something else."

"Uh—no." Sean felt in his pouch. Empty.

"Four credits sixty," said the giant.

"M' frien's got it." Sean shook the unstirring Solarian. The shoulder was hard under his fingers, but the dark head rolled lax on the folded arms. Sean looked at the blurred form of the denkeeper, considered, and reached the triumphant answer.

He leaned over the table and groped in the Solarian's hip pocket until the leatheroid was in his hand. It was hard to focus. He opened the wallet and looked closer.

The luminescent words on the card within blazed at him:

TREVELYAN MICAH
FIELD AGENT A-1392-zx-843
STELLAR UNION COORDINATION SERVICE
UNATTACHED

And the ringed star that burned over the letters, burned with its own cold fire and seemed to be spinning in dark space—

A Cordy!

Slowly, fighting himself every millimeter of the way, Sean paid the bill and slid the wallet back where it belonged. He couldn't think straight; he had to get a soberpill fast. This might not mean anything, but . . .

"Trevelyan! Trevelyan Micah!" Sean said. "This is the district chief. Whassyer mission on Nerthus? Wake up, Trevelyan! Whassyer mission?"

"Nomads," mumbled the voice. "Catch a Nomad ship, chief. Lemme sleep."

CHAPTER VII

His head ached a little in the smoke and noise of the inn, and Trevelyan had to resist the temptation to steal a glance and see what was happening about him. The landlord had been bribed carefully, and had played his part well.

He could almost feel Sean's eyes on him. The Nomad had bought a soberpill and spent a frantic quarter hour in a communication booth. Now he was sitting with one hand on his gun butt, staring and staring.

The affair had gone off like a robot gun so far.

Recognizing the early symptoms of worry, Trevelyan let his thoughts float free. Civilization was most complex and delicately balanced, but culture was not a physical thing—it was a process. Civilization was not material technology but a thought-pattern and an understanding. Then a voice broke into his thoughts.

"All right, Sean, what'd you get me out of bed for? I warn you, lad, it had better be good."

The voice was a strong resonant bass, speaking with an easy drawl, and the footsteps were heavy. Trevelyan's muscles wanted to leap.

"A C-Cordy, Hal. He's a Cordy. We g-got to drinking together and when he passed out, his wallet—" Trevelyan heard the young Nomad get up and strain across the table. "Here, see for y'self."

"Hm. Since when did Cordys carry this sort of thing? Or get sotted on the job?"

The newcomer was shrewd, thought Trevelyan. Actually his trick had been rather childish. He listened to Sean falter through an account of the evening.

"Ah, so. This one reckons you've been picked up, lad. Now let's see why." A calloused fist grabbed Trevelyan's hair and pulled his face up for inspection. "On purpose, too. This man's no more drunk than I am. All right, friend, you can quit now."

Trevelyan opened his eyes. For a satirical instant he enjoyed Sean's dumbfounded expression, then looked at the other man. This was a stout middle-aged fellow, his hairy body bare except for cloak, kilt, shoes, and gun belt—he must have been roused from sleep and come at once.

Trevelyan stretched luxuriously and sat back in the booth. "Thanks," he said. "I was getting somewhat tired waiting."

"You're a Solman, all right," said the Nomad, "and it wouldn't surprise me a bit to learn you really are a Cordy. Want to talk about it?"

Trevelyan hesitated a moment. "No. I'm sorry you were awakened. Suppose I buy a round of drinks and we call it even."

"You can buy the drinks," said the Nomad, plumping his large bottom onto the seat. "I'm not so sure about the rest of it, though."

Trevelyan signaled the proprietor. "There's been no real harm done," he insisted. "I'm not after you people, if that's what's worrying you. This was a—let's say an experiment."

"I'll need to know more than that."

"If you insist, I'll explain everything. But you wouldn't know whether it's the truth or not, so why bother?"

"There is that," said the Nomad. His face had gone expressionless.

The bearded man took their orders. They sat in silence, waiting.

Sean's voice exploded the quiet. "What to do, Hal?" He pushed the words out of a tautened throat. "What's going on?"

"We'll see." The reply was as wooden as the countenance.

"I'm—" Sean gulped. His face was drawn tight and there was a twitch in the angle of his jaw. "I'm sorry about this, Hal."

"All right, lad. If it hadn't been you, it'd have been somebody else. You at least had the sense to call me." The Nomad's eyes were cold on Trevelyan's, and when he smiled it was catlike. "Just to show we have some manners, I'm Peregrine Joachim Henry—rank, skipper."

Trevelyan nodded. "Hello," he said politely. "I want to warn you, Captain Joachim, against doing anything rash." The phrase was carefully chosen on his guess about the other man's character. The melodramatic flavor should both irritate him and make him underestimate his opponent—very slightly, to be sure, but those things added up.

"I assure you," Trevelyan went on, "that you've nothing to fear." He smiled. "You seem to know that Coordinators don't run around with identification cards, like a fictional hero. So—how do you even know I am one? I could be a practical joker."

"It doesn't smell right, somehow," said Joachim bleakly.

The drinks arrived. They touched glasses and Joachim downed his in three gulps. Decision settled his features into an iron mold. "All right," he said. "You're coming along with us, lad, and at the first wriggle or squeak you get it. Sean will take you up to the *Peregrine*." He turned to the younger Nomad. "I've made all arrangements. The stuff'll be loaded tomorrow and we can leave at about eighteen hundred hours. If this person has friends looking for him, it isn't likely they'll think of us before we get clear of the system."

"Now wait a minute—" began Trevelyan.

"That'll do. We need to find out more about you, and there'll be a nice long voyage to do it in. If you keep clean, you won't get hurt, and we'll let you go eventually."

Trevelyan narrowed his eyes. "I won't say anything about charges of kidnapping," he murmured, "but how do you know I don't *want* to be taken aboard your ship?"

Joachim's grin flashed out, suddenly merry.

"Why, 'twouldn't surprise me at all if you did," he answered. "In which case, I wish you joy of it. All right, friends, let's drink up and get out of here."

Trevelyan walked meekly between the two Nomads. He didn't think of the many days of preparation—research in the Coordination and police files at Stellamont, tediously worked-out equations indicating psychological probabilities, study of the town, and rehearsal of his role. Those were behind him now, and for what followed he had no data, no predictions—

When they came to the spaceport—it must have been a good half-hour's walk and not a word spoken— the gate scanned them and opened. They crossed blank concrete, passing under the dim forms of slumbering spaceships, until they came to a hangar. The door there recognized its lessee and admitted them. There were a couple of small fliers resting here, and Sean opened the airlock of one. Lights came on within the ascetic interior, spilling out into the gloom of the building. Trevelyan saw that the fliers had a heavy retractable rifle in the nose and machine guns and missile tubes in the air fins.

Earth thought it had achieved peace, said his mind grayly, *and now this has bloomed again between the stars.*

He entered and sat obediently down in a recoil chair. Joachim lashed him fast with a few turns of wire. "I'll be going back to my lodgings," he said, yawning. "See that our boy is put under guard at the ship, Sean. Then you can come back here if you want to."

He went out and the airlock sighed shut behind him. Sean's hands moved over the control panel with the deft ease of a skilled pilot. There was a mutter of engines and the panel flashed a clearance from the spaceport robot monitor. The landing cradle moved out of the hangar until it was under open sky. Sean smiled and touched the controls.

Trevelyan relaxed against the thrust of acceleration and looked ahead, out through the forward viewports. In minutes the atmosphere was below them and they were in space.

Trevelyan had seen that vision more times than he could remember, and yet each time it blazed for him with the same cold and undying magnificence. The darkness was like crystal, clear infinite black reaching beyond imagination; and against it, the stars were a bitterly brilliant radiance, white and aflame across the limitless night. *"The heavens declare the glory of God,"* he whispered, *"and the firmament showeth His handiwork."*

Sean gave him a puzzled glance. "What's that?"

"An old Terrestrial book," said Trevelyan. "Very old."

Sean shrugged and punched the computer keys. The flier mumbled to itself and swung about toward the *Peregrine's* calculated position.

The Nomad ship hove into view and Trevelyan studied her. She was a big cylindroid, two hundred and forty meters long from the blunt nose to the gravitic focusing cones at the stern, forty meters in diameter. There were three rings of six boathouses each around her circumference, holding spaceboats as well as fliers, and mounting a gun turret on top. Between each pair of boathouses was, alternately, a heavier rifle turret and a missile tube; and between the rings were the wide airlock doors of cargo-loading shafts. The vessel's flanks gleamed with a dull metallic luster; and as he neared, Trevelyan saw that the hide was worn, patched, pitted and seared in spots.

Sean landed expertly beside one of the boathouses, clamping on, and a tube snaked from its small airlock to fasten over the flier's. Trevelyan felt a normal Earth weight pressing him from the hull.

"All right." Sean freed the prisoner. "Come along."

A bored-looking Nomad on guard duty straightened when he saw the new arrival. "Who is that, Sean?"

"Snooper." Sean's tone was curt. "Hal says to brig him."

The guard thumbed an intercom button and called for help. Trevelyan leaned against the metal wall and folded his arms. "It isn't necessary," he grinned. "I'm not going to make a fight."

"Say—" The guard's eyes grew wider. "You ain't a *Solman?*"

"Yes, of course. What of it?"

"Oh—just never seen a Solman before, that's all. I hope they don't finish you before I get a chance to ask about some things."

Several others arrived with sidearms in hand. They were a rather ordinary-looking bunch, if you excepted the earrings and tattoos of some. Trevelyan made absent, noncommittal replies to their questions and remarks, and was escorted off to his jail.

Under—gravitationally speaking, above—the ship's skin, there was a five-meter space running almost the whole length of the cylindroid. On inquiry, Trevelyan learned that it contained public facilities and enterprises: the food plant and workshops, the recreational and assembly areas. A companionway took the party directly through this ring into the next concentric section, which had a three-meter clearance and was devoted to the residential apartments. The remainder of the ship was given over to control equipment and the great holds for supplies and cargo. Trevelyan was conducted down a hallway in the residential level.

He looked about him with an interested glance. The corridors, which intersected at frequent intervals, were about three meters wide, and lined with the doors of apartments. Underfoot the floor was carpeted with a soft springy material, dark green, most likely the produce of some world unknown to the Union. The walls were elaborately decorated with murals, or with panels of carved wood and plastic. Most of the doors were also wood or molded plastic, with ornamentation of hammered metal. Outside many apartments there were narrow boxes of soil, bearing flowers such as Earth had never seen.

His group accumulated quite a procession of Nomads, men and women and children; many looked highly intelligent. His bemused vision sharpened to sudden focus as one woman stepped from a doorway ahead of him.

She was young, and bigger than most, and there was grace in her movements. The hair that fell past the wide shoulders was a deep-blonde rush of waves, and the blue eyes were frank.

"Hello, who've you got there?" she asked. "Since when are we adopting Solmen?"

A couple of the guards scowled, and Trevelyan

remembered that in Nomad society women had well-defined rights, but were expected to keep in the background. One of the younger men, however, smiled at her. "You ask him, Nicki. Sean brought him up but wouldn't say why, and neither will he."

"Who are you Solman?" inquired the woman, falling into step beside him. He noticed that her hands were smeared with clay, and that she held a shaping tool in one. "Sean's my brother-in-law, you know."

The archaic term reminded him that the Nomads had pretty clear-cut sexual mores—within the ship, at least. He smiled and gave his name. "Your captain has the idea I'm a Coordinator." He added, "So I was brought up here for—investigation."

Her look was slow. "You don't seem very disturbed by it."

Trevelyan shrugged. "What can I do?"

"You're being very cool. I think you *are* a Cordy."

The guards' faces stiffened and gun barrels lifted a trifle.

"Suppose I am?" he challenged.

"I don't know. It's up to Hal. But we don't torture, if that's any comfort to you."

"It is. Though I'd gathered as much from other sources."

The blue eyes were very steady now. "I wondered if you didn't want to be captured."

She was intelligent, maybe too much so. But she was eager to talk, and he might pick up some useful information. "Why don't you come see me at the brig?" he invited. "I'm guaranteed harmless."

"So is a gun until you squeeze the trigger. Sure, I'll come around. You won't be kept there long anyway, I think. After Hal's had a chance to question you, you'll probably be jettisoned or—" She stopped.

"Or killed?" Trevelyan gently.

She didn't answer, but that in itself was answer enough.

CHAPTER VIII

The *Peregrine* slid from Nerthus and its star until she
was in a sufficiently weak gravitational field, then the
alarm bells warned crewmen to their posts. The
indescribable twisting sensation of hyperdrive fields
building up went through human bodies and faded,
and the steady thrum of energy pulses filled the ship.
Her pseudo-velocity grew rapidly toward maximum,
and Carsten's Star dwindled in the rear-view screens
and was lost among the constellations.

From astronaut to engineer, and all jobs between,
the crew settled into a habitual round of ship duties.
There was a relative dearth of automatic and robot
machinery on a Nomad vessel, much being done by
hand that a Solarian craft would have carried out for
herself. This could in part be attributed to the decline
of science among the star-jumpers. But there was also
a genuine need for something to do when a large
group of people, whose most fundamental motivation

was an inbred restlessness, were crowded into a metal
cylinder for weeks or months on end.

Off ship duty, the Nomads had enough occupation.
Workshops hummed around the clock as artists and
artisans produced goods to trade with their fellows
or with outsiders. There were the children to take
care of and educate, a serious task. There were the
various entertainment and service enterprises, including three taverns and a hospital.

When Joachim thought the ship was properly
under way, Trevelyan was escorted to the captain's
cabin. Joachim dismissed the guard and smiled
cheerfully, waving to a chair on the opposite side
of his desk. "If you want a smoke, I have plenty
of extra pipes."

"So you do." Trevelyan's gaze went about the room.
It was laid out with a bachelor fussiness and a
spaceman's compactness—in this corner the desk and
a rack of astrogational instruments and references; in
that corner a bunk and dresser. Doors led off to the
tiny kitchenette and bathroom and to an extra bed-
chamber. A shelf of micro-books held an astonishing
variety of titles in several languages, all seeming well
used. There was a family portrait on the wall; against
another wall was the customary family altar. A large
rack held an unusually good collection of pipes, many
of them intricately carved.

"They're mostly Nomad work. I made some of
them myself," said Joachim. "But here's a curiosity."
He got up and took a long-stemmed hookah from the
rack. "A Narraconan death pipe. Enemies smoke it
together—notice, it has two mouthpieces?—before a
duel."

"Are you inviting me to have a puff?" asked
Trevelyan blandly.

"Well, now, that depends." Joachim sat down on
the edge of his desk, swinging one leg. "Would you
answer some questions?"

"Of course."

Joachim went over to a closet and took out a small instrument. Trevelyan stiffened; he hadn't thought Nomads would have lie detectors.

"I got this one at Spica some years ago," said Joachim. "Comes in handy now and then. You don't mind?"

"No—no, go right ahead." Trevelyan sat back, and took conscious control of his heartbeat, encephalic rhythms, and sweat secretion.

Joachim attached the electrodes to determine encephalic output and cardiac rate. The Damadhva lie detector depended on sensing the abnormal pulsations created by the strain of telling a falsehood; but it had to be adjusted for each subject. As he answered the harmless calibrating questions, Trevelyan's nervous system maintained itself at an artificially high level, a camouflage.

"All right, lad, let's get to business." Joachim relit his pipe and looked up at Trevelyan through tangled brows. "You're a Cordy?"

"Yes, I am. And I did pick Sean up and get myself brought aboard your ship on purpose."

Joachim grinned. "You just pushed the buttons and we danced for you like robot dolls. Well, why?"

"Because it seemed the best way to contact you. If I'm correct, Joachim, the *Peregrine* is acting on a basis of information badly needed by the Stellar Union. I want to go along on your voyage."

"Mmmmmm-hm. And just what do you know?"

Trevelyan detailed what the integrators on Earth had gathered. "I'm pretty sure that there's another civilization in the Great Cross region," he went on, "that it knows of us, and that it is either actively hostile to us or damned suspicious. Why, I have no idea, but you can see that the Coordinators have to take immediate action. I decided that my best chance lay in joining forces with you. But you Nomads are

all so wary of civilization that I had to manipulate
things to get myself abroad."

"Ummm—yes, all right. Only how'd you know
you'd be picked up by the one and only Nomad ship
which is going to investigate this business?"

"I didn't, for sure. But it seemed reasonable that
it would be the *Peregrine*—after all, it was her captain who was doing research in Stellamont."

"I see. And now what?"

"Now I want to go along with you and learn what
you learn. There'll be other Coordinators working on
this problem, of course, but I think my approach is
the fastest. And it's urgent, Joachim!"

The Nomad rubbed his chin. "All right, you're
aboard. I suppose you'll help us out, and I admit a
trained Cordy could be mighty useful at times. Only
suppose we break some Union laws, as could
happen?"

"If it's not too serious, I won't bother about it."

"And suppose, if and when we come back, our
decision on the matter is one you won't like?"

Trevelyan shrugged. "We can argue that out later."

"So we can. What else have you in mind?"

Up to then, Trevelyan had been truthful enough,
as far as he went. Now, when he said, "Nothing in
particular, except to make a full report to the integrators," it wasn't stretching verity too far.

Joachim asked a few more questions, then unclipped
the electrodes and sat back with his feet on the desk
and his hands clasped behind his neck. "Fair enough,"
he said. "All right, consider yourself the guest of the
ship. Now, shall we pool what we know?"

The picture grew as they talked it out. Trevelyan
had been aware of the old Tiunran voyages, but not
of their or the Nomads' losses.

"I suspect that the aliens are colonizing the planets
of G-type suns—or, at least, controlling them in some
manner. They could easily scout around in our

civilization. There are so many space-traveling species today that an intruder can easily pass himself off as a native of some Union planet. But their suspicion of us must be culturally based."

"How so?" asked Joachim.

"It's ridiculous on the face of it that they should want to conquer us for any economic gain, and they must know we have no such intentions toward them. Therefore, in spite of all good intentions, we probably represent a threat to them."

"How's that?"

"Our civilization may be so unlike theirs that contact would be devastating. Imagine, for example, that they have a very conservative aristocratic-religious setup. Interpenetration by our culture would bring social upheavals their ruling class could not afford. That's only one guess, and most likely a wrong one."

"I see." Joachim sat quiet for a while, puffing out smoke. Then: "Well, we've a long trip ahead and lots of time to think."

"Where are you going first?"

Joachim squinted. "Erulan."

Trevelyan searched his memory. "Never heard of it."

"You wouldn't have, and you'll stay aboard ship while we're there."

"Reason?"

"It's illegal," said Joachim tightly. "Let's think about you. You'll get along fairly well, if you aren't too obtrusive. But I'd suggest you get some shipboard garments. Less conspicuous."

"How'll I do it?" Trevelyan didn't push the question of Erulan.

"Well—" Joachim reached in his desk drawer, pulled out a billfold, and tossed it to the other man. "Here's your wallet back. Nice fat chuck o' money there. I picked up some clothes that're about your size. Couple of coveralls, shorts, boots, and so on. Sell you the lot for twenty credits."

"*Twenty credits!* They'll be worth five at the most."

"Well, I could let you have 'em for what they cost me. Fifteen."

"If they cost you seven, I'll eat them—"

They haggled for a while, and finally settled for twelve credits—about one hundred percent profit.

Thereafter Joachim offered the Coordinator the extra bedroom at an only mildly exorbitant rental—along with meals prepared by his housekeeper, for an extra consideration. Trevelyan changed into shorts while Joachim happily counted his take.

"You might as well mooch around and get to know the ship," said the captain. He grinned. "Nicki's place is number two seventy-four."

"Do you know *everything* that goes on?"

"Just about." Joachim chuckled. "Nicki's a good sort, but not like the gossips say, so I wouldn't advise making passes at her."

Trevelyan went down the corridors at an easy pace, hands in pockets and dark face turning from side to side. Nomads stared curiously at him but none did more than nod a greeting. Apparently they were satisfied if their captain was. Trevelyan moved between the muraled walls and the carved doors and wainscots until he found the place he was looking for. No. 274.

The door stood ajar, between two posts graven in the shape of vine-covered trees. Sean's voice floated out: "Come in, Cordy."

Trevelyan entered. There was a bedroom on either side of the door; at the farther side the kitchen and bedroom flanked the exit to the other hall, so that the main body of the apartment was cruciform. One arm of the cross was given over to microbooks, music, tapes, and some rather good murals; the other was a cluttered workshop. Sean sat polishing his spacesuit, and beside him, sitting at his feet, was the Lorinyan girl whom Nicki had mentioned. She was, in truth, the most beautiful creature he had ever seen. Nicki was bent over a table, shaping a clay vase. She looked up and smiled. "You were right, 'Lo," she said.

"She's always right," said Sean. "She knows such things."

"What did she know this time?" asked Trevelyan. Sean was in a good humor apparently bearing no grudge, and Nicki was as friendly as before. Ilaloa— he wasn't sure.

"That you were coming," said Sean. "She senses you. Right, 'Lo?" His hand ruffled the fine silvery hair.

"A telepath?" Trevelyan. He kept his manner casual, but under it his mind was suddenly taut.

She spoke in the voice that was like singing, so low he could barely hear it: "Oh, I cannot—it is not of me to flow the words from the bound-in-darkness self. You are too lonely, all of you locked from each other and from knowingness. Some wills I can tell—the sly little animal-thoughts. But you of humanity, no."

"Then what—oh. Of course." Trevelyan nodded. "You can sense emissions, and each of us has a characteristic pattern."

"Yes, so." She was grave about it. Her look had become troubled now. "And yours is more—other— from mine than the Nomads'. You live more in your head than in your body, and yet it is not an inward sorrow to you, as it is to the men of Stellamont, who do not know what they are. You know, and have accepted it, and are strong in it—but never have I sensed such aloneness as is yours."

She lapsed into silence, as if frightened by her own words, and huddled close to Sean. Trevelyan regarded her for a long moment, not without pleasure. He saw a little shiver go under the lucent skin; there was a deep fright and grief in her, too, and she clutched Sean's knee.

Well, he thought, it's her problem. And Sean's, I suppose. She's too pretty for my taste.

He walked over to Nicki, answering her questions about his present status and intentions. The vase taking shape had the form of two battling dragons. "Nice," he said. "What'll you do with it?"

"Cast it in bronze and sell or swap it," she replied, not looking up. There was an earthiness about her which was at Galaxy's end from Ilaloa, he thought.

"Glad to have you along," she continued. "Maybe. What're your immediate plans?"

"Just to get acquainted and do some thinking. You know, I've been studying the Nomad art, and I'm convinced it's a new idiom. I daresay your literature is unlike ours too."

"We haven't got much, except for the ballads," she said.

"That's enough. Look how different American folk music was from the European—" She glanced at him in some puzzlement, then nodded. "I'd like to hear some when I get the chance."

"Well, I'll give you one right now," said Sean, putting away his spacesuit. He unslung a lorne from the wall and thrummed his fingers across the strings. His voice lifted in a ballad, the immemorial theme of the faithless beloved . . .

"*—She said to me, 'O Nomad, see
I cannot follow you.
The star ways were cold and dree
where all the wild winds blew,
the winds between the stars, my love
the restless wander-call,
blew low, blew high, into the sky,
the withered leaves of fall,
and we were blown, and all alone
we flew from sunlit day
into the waste where stars are sown and
planets have their way—'*"

Sean grimaced. "I shouldn't have picked that one."

"Some other time," said Nicki. She turned to the Solarian, a little too quickly. "I didn't know you concerned yourself with things like that."

"In my work," answered Trevelyan, "everything is significant, and the arts are often the most highly developed symbolic form of a culture—therefore the key to understanding it."

"Are you always thinking of your work?" she asked, bridling.

"Oh, not always," he smiled. "One has to eat and sleep occasionally."

"I'll bet that trained mind of yours never stops," she said.

He didn't answer. In a sense, it was true.

Ilaloa stood up in one rippling movement. "If you will forgive me," she said, "I think I will go to the park."

"I'll come along," said Sean. "Tired of sitting in here. Want to come, you two? We could have a beer down there."

"Not just yet," said Nicki. "I want to finish this vase."

"Then I'll keep you company, if I may," said Trevelyan.

Sean looked as relieved as courtesy allowed. He and Ilaloa went out, hand in hand. Trevelyan draped himself in a chair. "I don't wish to give offense, Nicki," he said. "Just tell me when I'm overstepping your mores."

"You weren't doing anything wrong. That ballad got Sean and Ilaloa to thinking, that's all." Briefly, Nicki explained the details.

"I see," he nodded. "It may not be good. Quite apart from social pressure, there's the fact that they can't have children, and in a family-based society like yours that'll come to mean a good deal in time."

"Well, I don't want to interfere," said the girl. Her

voice was troubled. "Sean's always disliked children anyway. And he needs something now to take his mind off that other wench. Ilaloa—I don't know. She's not happy on board here, but she's shaking down as we travel. A nice kid, I think—shy but nice."

"It's their lives," he agreed, shrugging.

She gave him a long look. "You know, Ilaloa wasn't so far off about you. You're too damned—what's the word?—Olympian."

"Solar civilization is based on the individual as a unit, not the family or clan or state or anything else," he said. "Our psychodevelopment produces a certain attitude which—never mind, it's not important now. I'm not typical, anyway."

She thrust the work aside and ran a hand through her tangled hair. "You have it all figured out, haven't you?" she asked resentfully. "You know how the hidden machinery in you runs and how to push the right buttons in yourself—yes, I can see where you'd get to be lonefarers, all of you, and the Cordys more than everyone."

"Any individualist is isolated," he said, "but in our society he's not at odds with others, or with himself. Solitude comes natural."

She winced. "You've got me charted already, haven't you?"

"Not at all. Nor would I want to if I could."

"Let's have some music," she said, and strode across the room to the tapes. His vision followed her and ran along titles. There was a lot of old Terrestrial music.

Nicki took one out. "You know the *1812 Overture?*"

"Of course," he replied.

The first strains drifted through the room, loneliness and immensity of the winter steppe. Nicki returned to her work, gripping the clay with tight-sinewed force. "Tell me about Earth. What's it like?"

"That's a contract job," he smiled. Within him, his

mind wondered what to say. Could he tell her that Earth was less a planet and a population than it was a dream?

"We're not utopian," he said cautiously. "We have our troubles, even if they aren't the same as yours."

"What do you *do?*" she asked. Stepping back, she looked at the tentative molding of a dragon head, cursed, and wrenched it back into shapelessness. "What do you really want out of life?"

"Life itself," he told her. "And that isn't a paradox. Experience, understanding, adjustment and harmony—but struggle, too, making physical reality over toward a pattern."

He went on, keeping away from abstractions, speaking mostly of the little details of everyday life, of people and events and the land that held them. After a while, Nicki forgot her work and leaned over the table to listen, almost unspeaking.

CHAPTER IX

At full cruising speed, it was about three weeks to
Erulan. The time was put to good use by Joachim,
who had to inform his crew that this was no ordinary voyage of discovery, trade, or exploitation. He
let guided rumors circulate until it was common
knowledge that the *Peregrine* was committed to scouting out a foreign and perhaps hostile domain. Playing down the dangers and building up the idea of
possible huge profits—in addition to the amount
already promised from the other Nomads—belonged
in Joachim's devious tactics.

His public order came when they were close to
their goal: because of delicate negotiations to be
carried out, and the chance of assault from their hosts,
there would be no liberty on the planet.

Trevelyan was a more difficult problem. Joachim
spoke to the Coordinator early in the trip. "You won't

like the truth," he declared, "but we'd better look the situation squarely in the face."

"I've been hearing some things about Erulan."

"Well, I'll begin at the beginning." Joachim stuffed his pipe with elaborate care. "About seventy-five years back, two new ships were founded, the *Hadji* and the *Mountain Man*. Only these were pretty ambitious young folks, who'd figured that regular Nomad life was too bare for them. Still, they couldn't see settling on some colony planet. Well, there was this barbaric world Erulan. With modern weapons, it wasn't hard to take over a warlike nation and help to conquer the rest. Now they sit on Erulan as bosses of a planet."

"Conquest." The word was bitter and obscene in Trevelyan's mouth.

"Oh, it's not so bad, now. They've only done to the natives what the natives were doing to each other. 'Course, all the other Nomads realized this could bring on real trouble with the Union, and passed laws against such capers, but by that time it was too late as far as Erulan goes. We still trade with the place, and they're one of the few cases where it was a Nomad ship that got diddled, instead of the other way around. But you can do pretty good business with 'em if you watch yourself."

Trevelyan's voice was blank: "What do you want with them now?"

"Information, lad. They're well into the Great Cross, and from little things I've picked up, I wonder if Erulan may not be in contact with X." Joachim veiled his face in smoke. "Cheer up, it's really not so awful."

"It's the sort of thing my service was set up to prevent."

"Which is why you're not going with us to the surface, nor are you going to get your hands on any astrogation instruments while we're in that neighborhood." Joachim grinned cheerily.

The ship was close to her destination when Joachim sent for Sean and Ilaloa. "Sean," said Joachim, "you're a good pilot, so I'm letting you take me down to the planet. And there's no reason why Ilaloa can't go."

The younger man inhaled a cigarette. "What's your real motive?"

"You don't rank high enough to be paid much attention to. You might as well take your lady on a stroll through town. Sight-seeing. And if that telepathy or whatever-it-is of hers should just happen to pick up some thoughts—oh, let's suppose thoughts about X aliens on Erulan, or even the thoughts *of* those otherlings—it'd be interesting, wouldn't it?"

"You could have said it in half the words," replied Sean. "All right, Captain, if Ilaloa's willing."

"This is my ship too," she answered.

On the twenty-third day from Nerthus, the *Peregrine* flashed out of hyperdrive and approached the sun of Erulan on gravity beams.

Joachim sat in the bridge, waiting for his communications man to raise the planet. The internal gravity field made the outer hull "down," so that some vision screens were underfoot. The screen buzzed and hummed with cosmic interference, the wordless talking of the stars. There was silence on the bridge, only the patient voice of the operator spoke. "Nomad ship *Peregrine* calling Erulan Station. Come in, Erulan. Come in, Erulan."

A streaked image grew on the screen.

The man that finally looked out was a hard-visaged sort, gorgeous in the furs and jewelry of a noble. His head was shaven, except for a queue, and he spoke with an accent. "What do you want?"

Joachim went over to stand in front of the screen. "Captain Poregrine speaking for his ship," he said easily. "We're coming in toward your planet. Like to pay a call."

"There is no trading just now."

"We weren't going to trade. Only wanted to say salute, me and a few of my officers. All right if we take an orbit and send a boat down?"

"Visitors are not being received."

"You got a new Arkulan?"

"No. Hadji Petroff is still in command. But—"

"Now look, lad," said Joachim, "this one knows your king's sociable. Since when did he give *you* the right to turn down company for him?"

"I speak for His Majesty. And use proper respect, Peregrine!"

"To you?" Joachim grinned nastily. "I'm a peaceful man, but please remember the *Peregrine's* not unarmed. Any time we feel like turning our Long Johns on you, there's nothing you have to say about it. If the Arkulan doesn't want to see us, let him tell me so himself—but ask His Majesty to remember that I'd be most terribly disappointed if he said no. Now give me an orbit and jump to it!"

The proud face stiffened with anger. "That could get you killed."

"Before you try, lad," answered Joachim, "you might think a bit." His tones became a roar. "How long do I have to talk with underlings? If there's any reason for denying us planetfall, let the Arkulan tell me. Now get!" He snapped off the screen.

"Whee-ew!" First Mate Ferenczi's teeth gleamed white in his beard. "That's a long chance, Hal. If you got him really mad—"

"No," said Joachim, relaxing. "That one wouldn't be coming to the 'visor on call if he were a big engine. He's used to bullying his underlings and being bullied by his masters. Since he doesn't know just where I fit in, his natural reaction is to crawl. He'll refer the matter higher up."

"But why should they object?" Ferenczi's gaunt face drew into a scowl. "Erulan's never been hostile to Nomads before."

"It was coming, Karl. They're being absorbed by their conquests. Eventually, they're going to shun all outside contact, because it'd upset their little wagon." Joachim puffed hard. "My guess is, there's something going on behind the Arkulan's back."

"We'd better signal battle stations."

"Yeah. And fliers up, detectors out, everything we've got. Still, I don't expect it'll come to a fight. They'll try to cover up."

A human of top rank was presently on the screen—Mountain Man Thorkild Edward, whom Joachim knew. With him, the Nomad captain was ingratiatingly genial, dropping broad hints of rich gifts, but there was a carefully expressed clash of iron in his voice. It ended with a left-handed apology for the behavior of the subordinate and an invitation for the whole crew to land. Since that would put them all at Erulanian mercy, Joachim pleaded a rush and accepted on behalf of himself and a few officers only.

The *Peregrine* took an orbit close to the planet, but instead of falling free remained directly above Kaukasu. It was an impolite but completely unambiguous gesture. Joachim left Ferenczi in command and chose younger men from astronautics and engineering to accompany him. They'd be a good, harmless-looking front. He winced as he selected presents for his hosts—a small fortune in ornamental objects.

A boat took the festive-clad party down. Sitting near Sean, Joachim saw the planet as a somber disc in the sky, storm-belted, its frigid oceans washing against steep-cragged mountains, the northern hemisphere bleached with snow-fields.

The city of Kaukasu lay in about twenty degrees north latitude, where agriculture was possible. It had been the seat of native warrior-kings, and the new masters hadn't changed it much—the palaces had been air-conditioned and a military base set up.

Joachim saw new buildings on the edge of town, a small shipyard.

"That's a funny one," he murmured. "I'd've sworn the humans here had about given up space travel. What use is it to them?"

The boat landed on the field before the central castle. This was on a terraced hill rising out of the middle of Kaukasu, each terrace ringed by heavy walls of age-blurred stone. Below it, the city sprawled in a chaos of high roofs and bulbous towers, out to the fields and the great forests. On the horizon a rim of mountains lifted white and ragged into the deep purplish heaven. There was traffic in the narrow streets, throngs of natives on foot, mounted, a rare groundcar pushing through turbulent crowds.

Joachim stepped from the airlock and wrapped his mantle around him, shivering. A guard of honor waited, ranked like statues. They lowered spears in salute as a fur-clad human approached.

The Erulani were quite manlike, and were stoutly built, their skins a deep amber-yellow, their faces rather flat and Mongoloid. There were only four fingers to a hand, the ears were large and pointed, the males completely bald. The eyes were the least human feature: under a single straight line of black brow, they were oblique and felinoid—all smoky-red iris, slit-purpled and unwinking. These, the soldiers, wore long blue tunics over legginged breeches and beryllium-copper chain mail, spiked helmets, curved swords at the right side.

Mountain Man Thorkild stopped a couple of meters from the Peregrines and bent his queued head as if it pained him. "Greeting and welcome," he said. The wind shrilled under his words and blew them across the barren flag-stones. "The Arkulan awaits you."

"Thanks," said Joachim. "Come along, boys."

His men trailed after him, carrying the boxes of

gifts. Sean and Ilaloa stayed within the boat, partly to guard it and partly because Joachim didn't fancy what might happen if Hadji Petroff's eye fell on the girl. Rhythmic footfalls beat on stone as the guard tramped in the rear. A gorgeously dressed trumpeter blew a flourish when they came to the castle gates.

And I think the ships stand too much on ceremony! reflected Joachim.

But it was inevitable. The ex-Nomads had taken over a barbaric system; it followed with the ruthless logic of history that they would themselves be barbarized.

Every human male was a high noble, and every Erulani—in theory—a slave. Modern weapons were only permitted to the overlords; the natives remained in the early Iron Age. Tribute was exacted from a swollen empire to support the masters in luxury. On the surface, it looked as if the Hadjis and the Mountain Men had a good thing.

But, Joachim's thoughts continued, they were themselves captives of their own creation. The court seethed with intrigue and corruption. No strong man could rest; he must always be watching for betrayal from his savagely ambitious underlings or murder from his wary superiors. Human speech and dress and dreams were being lost, as one by one the victors took over the patterns of their slaves. A verse went through the Peregrine's memory. *What shall it profit a man if he gaineth the whole world and loseth his own soul?*

They went through looming vaulted halls until they reached the audience chamber. It was a monstrous place, the roof lost in a dusk of sheer height, the narrow windows throwing bloody lances of sunlight onto the thick-piled rugs. The room shouted with gold, jewels, banners and tapestries; the walls were lined with rigid native guards, and a swarm of slaves prostrated themselves before Kaukasu's enthroned nobles. Trumpets blew again above a thunder of kettledrums.

Joachim and his men kowtowed ceremonially before the Arkulan. This was a middle-aged man, stiff in his robes, the crowned head erect with arrogance. But he greeted them well—more hospitably than some of his barons, who gave the Nomads ugly glances. *Uh-huh. They've got business under way that the chief doesn't know about, and it involves their not wanting visitors.*

Chairs were brought for the guests. Joachim distributed his gifts and sat down, smoking and gossiping with the Arkulan. As wine was drunk, the company relaxed, and there was no difficulty about getting the king's permission for such crewmen as wished to go sight-seeing.

"But I'll try to entertain you here," said Petroff. "It's been a long time since we had a ship drop in. Why aren't you coming to trade?"

"We have other business, Your Majesty," said Joachim.

"Ah, so? Looking for new territories?

"I wouldn't," said Thorkild. "By now, you should know the Great Cross doesn't have enough civilization to make exploration worth while."

"Oh, I don't know," responded Joachim. "What're you building those new ships for if not to do some starfaring for yourselves?"

"I'm having that done," said another noble, Hadji Kogama, "since I have the slaves and the machinery. But I only take them to Sura—you know the planet?"

"N-no. Too many planets for a man to remember."

"It's a long and not very interesting story," said Kogama, "but they're a backward system out Canopus way who've been visited a few times by Galactic Survey and would like a space fleet. An agent of mine was on Thunderhouse a few years back to make some purchases, and happened to meet one of theirs who was looking for a contractor to build them ships. I arranged to do it. The ships are flown to Sura and paid for in goods. Naturally, the natives don't know where their contractor lives, but they don't care, either."

"I see." *Like hell I do! Since when did an Eru-lani noble turn manufacturer—or bother explaining himself in such detail?*

"But what are you here after?" persisted Thorkild.

Joachim invented a planet. It had good trading possibilities, but the social structure was an elaborate master-slave system with an unbelievable ceremony-fetish. He wanted to get some pointers from Kaukasu as to how the natives should be handled.

"It's a long way to come just for information," said Petroff.

"Oh, not actually, Your Majesty," said Joachim. "We've found us a world not very far from here—satellite of a J-planet—with some pretty rich ore lodes. Since we were going there anyway, it wasn't much off our track to stop by Erulan."

"Where is this system?" asked Thorkild.

Joachim looked pained. "Now really," he said, "you don't expect me to tell you that, do you?"

Petroff chuckled. "No, I reckon not."

A banquet was given after sunset. When enough liquor had disappeared, the affair got as wild as a Nomad Mutiny. Joachim was sorry to miss it, but he thought it advisable to swallow a soberpill in advance and merely play drunk. His shipmates didn't act, but secrecy toward outsiders was a conditioned reflex in every proper crewman. He himself let slip a tantalizing hint or two in the right direction, and noticed Thorkild's eyes. The fish was nibbling.

When he finally steered a wavering course to his bedroom, he found that the Arkulan had hospitably provided him with a servant.

The girl didn't rank high in the harem, but she knew some gossip and Joachim bribed it out of her. It didn't *prove* that Thorkild and Kogama, among others, were conspiring against the Arkulan; but it was enough for his purposes.

He wandered about the castle the next day, asking questions that fitted his ostensible reason for being there, and wasn't surprised when a slave handed him a note requesting his attendance on Thorkild. He followed the native along a warren of corridors and up a ramp into one of the towers. There was a chamber just below the roof, its windows open to a frosty air and a dizzying downward view. The place was austerely furnished, more like an office than a noble's reception room. Thorkild sat behind a desk, his body wrapped in furs, his shaven head bent over some papers.

"Sit down, Peregrine," he invited curtly, not looking up.

Joachim found a chair, crossed his legs, and got out his pipe.

Finally the long, lean face turned to him. "Have you learned what you came here for?" asked the baron.

"Oh, I've gotten a few useful ideas," said Joachim.

"Let's not feint." Thorkild's countenance was immobile and unreadable. "This room is spy-proofed. We can talk plainly: What did you mean last night when you said the Great Cross had some very interesting possibilities? And when you said it was a pity Hadji Kogama was building ships for Sura, when a really juicy market lay right to hand?"

"Well," said Joachim, "I have a low mind. Things occur to me. Like the possibility that Kogama wasn't selling his ships at all, but just stockpiling them somewhere until he has enough of a fleet to take over this business."

"He isn't doing that. I know."

"Because you're both figuring to run Erulan?"

"We aren't traitors." Thorkild's voice was flat.

"Mmmmmm—no, I never said that. Only His

Majesty might misinterpret certain information. Such as—" Joachim mentioned a suborned vizier and a captain of household troops to whom promises had been made.

"If you start meddling in things that are none of your concern," flashed Thorkild, "I might forget you're a guest."

"If you do, lad, you'll be the first fatality. And if I don't come back, the *Peregrine* will start bombarding." Then, with a smile: "But let's not fight, Ed. We're old friends, and I know this isn't my business. As a matter of fact, I wanted to pass the word to you."

"What word?"

"Palace scuttlebutt. Maybe it means something, maybe it doesn't."

"How could you learn secrets I can't get?"

"I'm a stranger. The women find me interesting— really, that purdah you keep 'em in must get awful boring. They know I'll be gone tomorrow, and meanwhile I give 'em some nice presents. Why shouldn't they talk to me? And why shouldn't they intrigue in the first place?"

Thorkild tugged nervously at his queue. Joachim could almost read the thoughts inside that narrow skull. There was no chance for a noble to torture secrets out of the royal concubines. "What have you learned?" he asked finally.

"Well—" Joachim looked at the ceiling. "I've always thought of you as my friend, Ed. I gave you some pretty good things yesterday."

They argued over the bribe till Joachim had recouped a fair percentage of his earlier outlay. Then he said, untruthfully—but it was based on a shrewd guess—"Kogama has harem and royal guard contacts you may not know about. Word circulates. There's a rumor that you and several others are associated with Kogama in building this fleet. Only the ships are staying right here."

Thorkild's face was utterly masklike. To Joachim, that was as good an indication as any. He fed the noble a concoction of hints and whispers suggesting that Kogama had plans for his own allies, when their mutual scheme had gone through. *It might even be correct, at that!*

There was a silence when the narrative was finished. Thorkild sat resting his chin in one hand, the fingers of the other drumming on the desk top.

Joachim waited a moment, then leaned forward confidentially. "I'd like to make a guess, Ed," he murmured. "I think there's another civilization in this volume of space. I think they're hiding from man, Cosmos knows why. But you're building ships for them, you and your clique. The—strangers—are paying you well, I imagine in gold, so that you can build up an organization. The present Arkulan's a pretty smart boy. He's arranged things so it'd be hard to overthrow him, but you think you can do it with that new wealth. Am I right?"

"If you were, what would you do with the knowledge?"

"I don't know. It might be sort of interesting to those aliens. May be money in it. Or if they're hostile to us, the ships ought to know about it." His eyes lifted and held the other man's. "I'd like to ask you one thing, though, Ed. If a powerful otherling empire grows up all around Erulan, what good is the throne here to you?"

"They aren't otherlings, or natives." Thorkild's tones were strained. "They're human."

Human!

"They're a strange sort. Talk Basic with the weirdest accent, don't wear clothes, don't—I don't know. They have the ways of natives, but they're human, I'll swear."

"What do they want?" asked the Peregrine.

"Ships. They contacted us about five years ago. Yes,

they pay in metal, and I gather they're from some-where in the Cross. But that's a very big region, Joachim. Maybe it's foolish of us to deal with them, but you don't get ahead except by taking chances."

"No," agreed Joachim. "No, you don't."

CHAPTER X

It was near evening of the first day that an Erulani brought a scribbled note from Joachim out to the spaceboat. *"All right to go prowling in town, but don't go too far. We may have to leave in a hurry."* Sean stood for a moment in the airlock, straining his eyes to read in the last dull light. The wind was low and cold; beneath the castle, roofs and towers were black against the sky.

Ilaloa sat up on one elbow as he entered the bunkroom. "It's too late to go out now," he said. "We'll do it tomorrow morning. Is that all right?"

She nodded.

"I know you don't like being penned here," he said. "I'm sorry."

"It is nothing. I was gone in thoughts, Sean."

He stood regarding her. His eyes followed the gentle curve of her body to the face, and rested. "You wish you were back on Rendezvous, don't you?"

She smiled, and then suddenly she laughed. It was like a tinkling of bells. "Poor silly Sean. You think too much." He drew her against him and she pressed close. His mouth brushed the fragrance of her hair and closed the parted lips below his.

Well—she's right. I worry too much, and it gets me nowhere.

Gently, he disengaged himself. "How about some solid fuel?"

She nodded and moved lightly to the boat's gravity shaft. "This falling up is fun," she called. "You have so many toys."

"Toys?" he echoed. But she was already gone, floating along the upward beam toward the galley near the bows.

The next morning, he donned Nomad folk dress but added a heavy tunic. He had to wait for Ilaloa to finish her shower. She was always taking long baths aboard ship, as if to wash off some hidden uncleanliness.

"Put on some thick clothes, dear," he advised, feeling a warm husband sense within him.

She wrinkled her nose. "Do I have to?"

"If you don't want to freeze out there, yes. What's wrong with dressing, anyway?"

"It is the—shut-away from sun and rain and all the many winds," she answered. "There is a dead skin around and it is another darkness. You are locked from life, Sean." But she did clothe herself and danced eagerly before him to the airlock.

The morning was chill and misted; wet flagstones gleamed underfoot as they went toward the outer gates. They walked under mountainous towers and down the hill into the city.

It was already awake, and its noise grew loud as they entered the streets—shrill clamor of voices, thump of hoofs, groaning wheels and clashing iron. The smells were there, too. Sean snorted and glanced down at Ilaloa. But she didn't seem to mind; she was looking around with a wide-eyed wonder he hadn't seen in her before.

The streets were narrow and cobbled, slippery with muck, twisting fantastically between the high walls of peak-roofed houses. Doors were heavy and brass-bound, windows no more than narrow slits; overhanging balconies shut out the sky. Flimsy wooden booths lined the façades, each with its wares on display— pottery, clothing, tools, weapons, rugs, food, wine, all the poor needs and luxuries of the planet cried by their raucous merchants. Here and there a temple stood, minareted and grotesquely ornamented with the blood-smeared effigies of gods.

The crowd swirled about Sean and Ilaloa, trying hard not to jostle the sacred human figures but sometimes pushed against them. It was the kind of spectacle which is only romantic at long range. Sean thought he could feel the violence that boiled around him.

Ilaloa tugged at his sleeve and he stooped to hear her under the din. "Do you know this city, Sean?"

"Not very well," he admitted. "I can show you a few sights if—" He hesitated. "If you want to."

"Oh yes!"

A trumpet brayed up ahead, and the Erulani sprang to the walls. Sean pulled Ilaloa with him, aware of what was coming. A squad of guardsmen galloped past, armored and helmeted, mud sheeting from the hoofs. Their bugler had a lash that he swung about him. There was a human in their midst, the chief, dressed even as they.

A woman screamed in the wake of the troop. Before the crowd had filled the street again, Sean saw that she was bent over a small furry shape. Her child had not been fast enough.

His throat was so tight that it hurt him. "This way, Ilaloa," he said. "Back this way."

"There was death," said Ilaloa quietly.

"Yes," he replied. "That's the way Erulan is."

They entered another thoroughfare. There was a procession of slaves coming, chained neck to neck. Their feet bled as they walked. A couple of soldiers urged them along with whips, but they didn't look up.

Sean regarded Ilaloa again. She stood watching the slaves go by, but somehow the compassion in her face didn't go deep.

A gallows was in the market square on which the street opened. Three bodies swung aloft. Beneath them, a gallantly clad Erulani was thrumming a small harp. It was a happy tune.

Ilaloa's fingers tightened around his. "You are with grief, Sean."

"It's this damned, bloody planet," he answered. "It's all so unnecessary!"

She looked steadily at him, and her voice was serious. "You have been long shut away from life," she said. "You have forgotten the sweetness of rain and summer nights. There is a hollowness in your breast, Sean."

"What has that got to do with this?"

"This is life around us," she said. "You have forgotten how it can be hot and dark and cruel. You burn your dead in fire and forget that flesh molders into earth. The land should be strong with your bones and blossom where you died. You would have it forever day, not remembering night and storm. You live with ghosts and dreams in your own darkness. That is wrong, Sean."

"But *this—!*"

"Oh, it is hard and angry here, but it lives in the now. Are you afraid of the riving and screaming in childbirth? Do you fear to remember the hunter by moonlight, how she strikes down life to feed her young? Do you know the lust of killing and ruling?"

"You d-don't think that's right, do you?"

"No. But it *is*. Oh, Sean, you cannot love life till you are life, all of it, not as it should be, but as it is, laughter and grief, cruelty and kindness, beyond yourself— No, you do not understand."

They walked on. After a moment, she said gently, "Oh, the real can be made better. There is no need for this endless strife and suffering. But it is still more—right—than that which is in the city Stellamont."

"You mean," he asked, "that reason is wrong? That instinct—"

She laughed, though it had a wistful tone. "You are kind, but your kindness is so far away." Suddenly she almost cried aloud. "Oh, Sean, if we could have children—"

He drew her close to him, forgetting the cat-stares around, and kissed her. Somehow, he felt lightened. They had tried to know each other, and even the failure was a kind of victory.

After lunch, the thoroughfares emptied as city folk retired for a siesta. They wandered into a labyrinth of crooked streets and blind alleys and were lost. That wasn't serious; they need only go in the general direction of the castle to spot it from some open plaza.

Sean peered up a street, a narrow tunnel under crazily leaning houses, wondering if it might lead somewhere. "Shall we try this?"

There was no reply. He hadn't expected it; Ilaloa left half his questions hanging. But when he turned around, he was shocked.

He had seen love in her face, merriment, alarm, grief, loneliness, disgust, timidity, and the blankness of withdrawal. But he had never before seen her really frightened.

"'Lo—what's wrong?" he whispered it, and his gun seemed to slide of itself from the holster.

Her eyes sought his, strickenly. One hand covered her opened mouth as if to fend off a shriek. *"Amuriho,"* she gasped. *"Hualalani amuriho."*

He drew her behind him, against the wall, and faced out into the street. It was empty.

"A thought. A thought from—no, Sean!"

He didn't look at her. His eyes hunted up and down the road where nothing stirred. "X," he said.

"It was not of man and not of Erulan," she breathed shakingly. "It was cruel and a hollow night filled with stars. And cold, cold!"

"Where?"

"Near this place. Behind some wall."

"We're getting out of here!"

"Again—there it is again!" She clawed at his body, thrusting close. Her face was buried against him and he felt her shiver.

"C-can you read the mind?" he stammered.

"Darkness," she gulped. "Darkness and emptiness, full of stars, a picture of stars like a sickle around a shining field."

The gun butt was slippery in his hand. "Can they sense us?"

"I do not know." The whisper was raw, there in the bloody twilight. "It thinks of stars beyond stars, but always that picture of a sickle reaping shiningness. There is scorn and mastery in it, like steel and—" Her voice trailed off.

"It is gone again now," she said in a small and childlike tone. "I cannot feel it any more."

He broke into a trot, holding her wrist with one hand and the gun with the other. "Joachim's hunch was right," he said between his teeth. "Now we've got to get off this planet!"

CHAPTER XI

No one could accuse the ships of bearing a particularly intellectual society; still, reading was one way
to pass the long times of voyage. The *Peregrine*, like
her sisters, had a fair-sized library. It was a long
double-tiered room in the outer ring, near the waist
of the ship and not far off the park. Trevelyan had
spent a good deal of time there on the journey from
Nerthus.

He wandered in now. It was quiet, almost deserted
save for the dozing attendant and a couple of old men
reading at a table. The walls were lined with shelves
holding micro-books from civilized planets: references,
philosophies, poetry, fiction, *belles-lettres*, an incredible
jackdaw's nest of anything and everything. But there
were also large-sized folios, written by the natives of
a hundred worlds or by the Nomads themselves. It
was the compendious history of the ships which he
took down and opened.

It began with the memoirs of Thorkild Erling, first captain of the Nomads. The bare facts were known to every educated person in the Union by now: how the first *Traveler*, an emigrant ship in the early days of interstellar voyaging, blundered into a trepidation vortex—then a totally unsuspected phenomenon, and even now little understood—and was thrown some two thousand light-years off her course. The hyperdrive engines of that day had needed a good ten years simply to get back into regions where the constellations looked halfway familiar; and after that, the vessel had ranged about for another decade, hopelessly searching. They found an untenanted E-planet, Harbor, and built their colony, and most of them were glad to forget that wild hunt through the deeps of forever. But a few couldn't; so in the end, they took the *Traveler* and went out once more.

That much was history. Now, reading Thorkild's words, Trevelyan caught something of the glamour which had been in those first years. But dreams change. By the very fact of realization, an ideal ceases to be such. There was a note of disappointment in Thorkild's later writings; his new society was evolving into something other than what he had imagined. *That's humanity again, never really able to follow out the logic of its own wishes.*

Trevelyan paged rapidly through the volume, looking for hints on the evolution of Nomad economy. A spaceship can be made a closed ecology, and the Nomad vessels did maintain their own food plants— hydroponics, yeast-bacteria synthesis of protein foods and vitamins—as well as doing a lot of their own repair, maintenance, and construction work. Cut adrift, they could last indefinitely. But it was easier and more rewarding to exploit the planets, as traders and entrepreneurs.

It was not all trade—sometimes they might work a mine or other industry for a while; and robbery, though frowned on, was not unknown. From whatever they gained, they took what was needed and used the rest for barter or sale.

Such enterprises were always carried out by individuals or groups of individuals, once the captain had made whatever preliminary arrangements were necessary. A small tax was enough to support the various public facilities and undertakings.

The society was democratic, though only adult men had the franchise. Matters of general Nomad policy were settled at rendezvous, the Captains' Council being empowered to make certain decisions while others were referred to the crews. Within a ship, the assembled men discussed and voted on whatever issues the captain couldn't handle as routine, and all the Nomads seemed quite passionately political-minded. The captain had broad powers and, if he used it right, an even broader influence—the fact that Joachim could take the *Peregrine* scouting this way, on his own decision, spoke for itself. If—

Trevelyan glanced up with a sudden consciousness and felt his pulse quicken. Nicki had just come in.

She had a book under one arm, which she replaced on its shelf. Turning, she smiled at him. "Where've you been the last few days? I've hardly seen you."

"Around," he said vaguely. "Anything new?"

She shook her head, and the light slid across its dark yellow tresses. "I'm weaving now," she told him. "Ferenczi Mei-Ling—Karl's wife, you know—wants a new rug, and she can pay for it." The broad forehead drew into a scowl. "Nothing new ever happens."

"I should think your whole Nomad life was founded on the idea of having something new always happening," he said.

"Oh, we jump from one planet to another still crazier, but what does it mean?"

"Life," he reproved with a smile, "has no extrinsic purpose or meaning; it's just another phenomenon of the physical universe, it simply *is*. And that's also true of any society. What you're angry about is that you can't find a purpose for yourself."

Her eyes were smoky-blue, meeting his. "There you go again!" she flared. "Can't you look at anything or do anything at all without it as a—a specific case of a general law?"

As a matter of fact, thought Trevelyan, *no.*

Aloud, he said mildly, "I have my fun. I like a glass of beer as well as the next man. Speaking of which, will you join me in a gulp?"

"You're not answering me," she accused him. "It's always the same. Women can't think! Leave them with the kitchen and the kids. I'm getting sick of it!"

"I'm a Solarian," he reminded her. "We'd be the last to have ideas of male superiority."

"Sol—" For an instant her expression softened, the long soot-black lashes dropped and she breathed the word with a caress. Then, scornfully: "What has Sol to offer? What are you doing there but trying smugly to run the universe according to a bunch of—of equations? A theory!"

"Any culture is based on a theory," he said. "Ours simply happens to be explicitly formulated."

"There are times when I hate you," she said, and her fists clenched.

"I'm not trying to talk down to you," he snapped. "If I wanted to tell you a soothing fairy tale, you'd never know I was doing it. But don't spit on what you can't understand!"

She countered his gaze steadily and then, amazingly, smiled. "All right, I surrender," she laughed. "Let's go for that beer, shall we?"

And I thought I was a good psychologist! Trevelyan reflected wildly.

A siren whooped. Nicki stiffened, listening to the blasts.

"What's that?" he asked.

"Signal," she answered tightly. "Battle stations alert. All hands stand by for hyperdrive."

"This close to the planet?"

"It may be urgent." She ran over to the library Eye.

There were many such televisor screens aboard— each apartment had one, as well as public places. They would be tuned to any of the scanners throughout the ship, strategically mounted to give a view of all points where something of general interest might happen. Nicki dialed swiftly past scenes from the airlocks. The Nomad readers crouched by her and Trevelyan looked over their shoulders.

Minutes stumbled by before the flickering screen steadied on one image. Trevelyan recognized the egress from one of the boathouses. Joachim was just emerging, and his face was grim.

His words roared out of the ship's loudspeakers. "Attention, all Peregrines! This is the captain. We're getting out of here on gravity drive at once. You hear me, engine room? Full gravity drive north from the ecliptic at once. Stand by to go into hyper if necessary." The voice relaxed a little. "No, I don't *think* we're being chased or that they're angry with us on Erulan, but you can't tell. We've picked up some information that could be worth a lot of lives, and we're going where it's safe to know things."

Trevelyan felt the deck quiver, ever so faintly, with the forward surge. Gravitic acceleration being uniform on all objects, he experienced no pressure, but he imagined they were running skyward at a good fifty G's.

Joachim's voice jarred him. "Will Trevelyan Micah please report to me on the bridge at once? I'll need some help on this."

Nicki thrust past the men. "What can it be?"

"That's what I'm going to find out," said Trevelyan.

"Then I'll come, too."

❖   ❖   ❖

Joachim stood by the astrogational computer, letting Ferenczi direct the ship. Sean was on hand, his thin features twisted. But it was to Ilaloa that Trevelyan's eyes went. She sat in the astrogator's chair, crouched over the desk, and he could see how tension bent her form into a bow.

"What's the matter?" he asked.

"I'm not sure yet—" Joachim looked at Nicki, who stood above Ilaloa with one hand laid on the Lorinyan's head. "What're you doing here?"

Nicki lifted her face and stamped one foot. "Any objections?"

"Well, no, I reckon not. Maybe you can calm down the girl. She's had a pretty bad fright." He relayed in curt words what had been learned on Erulan: humans of strange habits secretly buying spaceships, and Ilaloa's reception of a thought no mind should have had to endure. "They broke in on me, she and Sean, just when I was thinking of leaving," he finished. "That settled it. 'Lo's a good girl, though. She didn't break down till we were safe."

Trevelyan regarded the two women. Ilaloa was weeping on Nicki's breast now, sobs tearing at her.

"A really alien thought?" inquired the Terrestrial. "But if she can't read our minds, how could she read this?"

"Wave-patterns vary." Sean's answer was harsh. "This chanced to be one more like her own than man's is. But the content of it was—other."

"Micah, what do you make of this?" asked Joachim.

"Well—assuming it wasn't a mistake or something— hm." Trevelyan rubbed his chin. "Humans in the one case, aliens in the other. Could they be operating independently, maybe unaware of each other?"

"Well," said Joachim dubiously, "I reckon they could, but it just doesn't seem very believable."

"Maybe not. I have an idea, though—" Trevelyan saw that Ilaloa was sitting up. She trembled still, but the tears weren't running. He noticed that weeping didn't disfigure her as it does a human.

"Go easy on her," said Nicki quietly.

"I will." Trevelyan went over and sat on the desk, swinging his legs. The Lorinyan's violet eyes met his with a forlorn kind of steadiness. "Ilaloa," he asked, "do you want to talk about this?"

"No," she said. "But I will do so, since it is necessary."

"Good girl!" Trevelyan smiled. Looking on the warmth of his face, Nicki wondered how much of it was acting. "Just describe to me what the thought in Kaukasu was like. How did it feel? Did it say anything?"

"If you have never felt thought, I have no words."

"Oh, I have. It comes all at once, doesn't it? A main thread, but there are all sorts of little sidelines and overtones, hints, whispers, glimpses. And the whole thing is never the same; it's always changing. Is that right?"

She nodded. "As well as words can put it, that is right."

"Very well, then, Ilaloa. As nearly as you can, will you tell me what this thought you sensed was like?"

She stared before her, and the slim fingers gripped the chair arms until the knuckles stood white. "It was all at once," she whispered. "It came, pulsing, as if something lay under a pool and moved up, and then sank back into dark."

A shiver went across her. Sean started forward, but Joachim pushed him back. "It was of power, and scorn, and hugeness," she told them. "A hand gripping a universe, like iron. But slow, patient, watchful. And there was a shiningness against sky-black, a field of light, stars all around. They curved like a sickle to reap the field. And there was one star brighter than all, high and cold, and there was another shining coil which was so far away that the farness made me want to scream and—" She shook her head. "No," she breathed shakily. "No more."

"I see." Trevelyan clasped his hands and leaned forward, elbows on knees. "Do you think you could draw a picture of those stars?"

"A—picture? Why—"

"I'd like to put you under hypnosis, Ilaloa," he said. "That's just a sleep. I want total recall. You won't know it. And by that means I can take the fear from you."

She looked down, then up again, and her mouth quivered. "Yes," she said. "You may do that. I want to help you."

The hypnotism didn't take long. Ilaloa went under fast. Sean winced at the violence of her re-enactment, but the peace that followed was worth it. Trevelyan gave her a pencil and she sketched a star-field with swift assurance, adding the forms of nebulae and a section of Milky Way. The Coordinator took the paper and brought her out of the trance. She smiled sleepily, got up, and came into Sean's arms.

"It should be all right," said Trevelyan. "I think I removed the associated panic. It was due to sheer strangeness, not to personal menace." Then he turned away, and his features hardened with thought.

"What've we got?" asked Joachim.

"Well," said Trevelyan, "apparently these X beings think on a varying band and wave-form; Ilaloa caught only such fragments as were similar to her race's pattern. The fact may tell us something about the thinker—I'm not sure yet. What's more important is this star picture. It represents another region of space—presumably the home sky of X."

"Ummm, that's obvious." Joachim considered the drawing. "We've got a damn good clue, then. Let's see. The shiningness is a bright gaseous nebula, of course, and the remote spiral is probably the Andromeda galaxy. That very bright star could only be Canopus, if you're in the Cross region, and here's the same dent in the Milky Way you can see from here." He gestured to a view-screen overhead, blackness and the ghostly bridge of stars.

"In short," said Trevelyan with a note of triumph, "We've got a pretty good idea of where the enemy lives."

"Uh-huh. I think more can be done with this. Hey, Manuel!"

The young astrogator looked up. Joachim folded the drawing into a paper airplane and shot it over to him. "Find me this part of space as accurately as you can," directed the captain. "Use all our star tables and computers if you have to, but identify it within a centimeter of its life."

CHAPTER XII

Time was lost.

Within the ship, there was always light, cool glow in the halls and public rooms, someone walking by on an errand or sitting and waiting in patience. Darkness came only when switches were turned in the homes.

Outside, a night of stars, enormous and eternal.

There was no time. Clocks rounded a weary cycle, telling off the meaningless hours and days, but for man there was only waking and sleeping, eating, working, idling, waiting. The old dreamed of what had been and the young of what was to be, but the now was forever.

A few incidents were sharp in Trevelyan's memory. There were some of the talks he had with Nomads, Joachim before all, tales of faring in the cold Galactic splendor. There were his trips with Nicki, prowling the labyrinthine corridors of the ship.

There was the time a dark young man with unhappy eyes, Abbey Roberto, had searched out the Coordinator and warned him that Ilaloa was a witch. Trevelyan remembered Sean's account of Roberto having overheard something about telepathy. There *had* been mutterings and sidelong glances when Ilaloa passed by. And the mounting tension aboard ship as they plunged into mystery could unsettle stabler minds than these.

At least the *Peregrine* had a fairly definite goal now. The point in space from which the sky should look as Ilaloa's vision said could be identified within a few tens of light-years. At full cruising speed, it lay about six weeks' journey from Erulan.

A month passed. It could have been a week or a century, but the clocks said it was a month.

They were in the park, four of them together talking and wanting companionship. Nicki sat crossed-legged beside Trevelyan, linking an arm with his. Opposite them was Sean, Ilaloa leaning against his side.

The park was the largest division of the ship from cargo space and, after the hyper-engines, the most impressive. It filled ninety degrees of hull curvature on the outermost deck, and its length reached a hundred and twenty meters from the bows. But that was necessary.

In the day of great cities, men had been caged in the stony, glassy mountains of their creation, and it was not strange that so many had retreated into madness. What then of humanity locked in a shell of metal and raw energy, between the stars? They could not have endured it without some relief, grass cool and damp underfoot, the rustle of leaves and ripple of flowing water.

This was the place of assembly, the captain speaking to men who stood on the wide green lawn in front of him. But just now there were only some children playing ball there. Otherwise the park was a place of trees, the trees of Earth, and of hedges, flower beds, fountains, winding paths and secret bowers.

Trevelyan and his party were in one of the bowers, leaning against the dwarf trees hemming it in. An oak spread above them, its branches dripping with heavy grapevines; and rosebushes and willows made a little grotto of the place.

A viewscreen opened on the outside. It sat vertically, like a window, and its metal outlines were drowned in ivy. Space loomed frightfully there, framed in a gentleness of leaves, ablaze with the diamond points of stars, falling outward to the uttermost ends of the universe. Ilaloa sat on the farther side of Sean, not looking at the screen.

They were talking of civilization. Always Nicki drew Trevelyan out, asking him about his home, and he was not loath to respond. He wanted the Nomads to understand what was going on.

"In some ways," he declared, "we're in a position like that of Earthbound man in, say, the sixteenth through early nineteenth centuries. That was a time when any part of the world was accessible, but the voyages were long and difficult and communications lagged. Transmission of information—the ideas, discoveries, developments of both home and colonies— was slow. Coordination was virtually impossible—oh, they did influence each other, but only in part. It wasn't even appreciated how foreign the colonies were becoming. North America was not England; the whole ethos became something else. If they had had radio then, even without better ships, Earth's history would have taken a fantastically different course.

"Well, what have we today? A dozen or more highly civilized races, scattering themselves over this part of the Galaxy, intercourse limited to spaceships that may need weeks to get from one sun to the next—and nothing else. Not even the strong economic ties which did, after all, bind Europe to its colonies. Cross-purposes are breeding which are someday going to clash—they've already done so in several cases, and it's meant annihilation."

"Hmm—yeah." Sean ran a hand through his unruly hair. The other arm was about Ilaloa, whose eyes were somber, and he saw that she was tensed as if waiting for something.

Nicki nodded toward the Lorinyan girl. "'Lo is right," she said. "You do think too damn much, Micah, and you're too lonesome up there in your own head." She gestured at the view-screen.

"Look out there, Micah. That's *our* universe. We belong here. Forget your damned science for a while. Reach out and take the Galaxy in your hands!"

"A big Galaxy," he murmured.

"D'you think the Nomads don't know how big it is?" she cried. "You think we haven't spent our lives out here, seeing worlds beyond worlds and always new suns beyond those? The stars don't know we exist, and when we're dead they'll go on as they always did, as if we'd never been. But still we belong, Micah! We're one atom in the universe, but at least we're that much!"

She stopped, and a slow flush crept up her cheekbones. "I'm really mouthy today," she said. "Blame it on 'Lo. That way of talk she has is catching."

He smiled, wordlessly.

"But I would not say such things," whispered Ilaloa. "Your belongingness is not mine. Micah feels himself part of a pattern, a not-real, something like a thought in his head. And you of the ship think of fire and metal and that hollowness out there; to you life is just a stirring in dead matter. Oh, no!" She buried her face against Sean's shoulder.

"And what do you think, then?" asked Trevelyan. "What is most real to you?"

She looked up again. "Life," she said. "Life that

is in all space and time, the forces—no, the *is* and
becomes that shapes itself. It—" She stopped help-
lessly. "You have not the words. You try to understand life, as if you could be outside it. But you
cannot. It is not to be understood but to be known.
Felt, and you not locked in a house of bone but
part of it—like a river, and you are a wave which
rises and will sink back again, but the river flows
on."

Sean stroked her hair. "You say some funny things,
sweetheart," he murmured. His lips brushed the
smooth pale cheek.

"Bergson," said Trevelyan.

"Hm?" Nicki raised her brows.

"A philosopher of Earth, 'way back when. He had
ideas which sound much like Ilaloa's. But I doubt if
he carried them out the way she could. Someday,"
he added thoughtfully, "I'd like to ask you about your
people, Ilaloa. I've been so busy studying the ship
that I've neglected you, but I think you could teach
me something."

"I will try." Her voice was almost inaudible.

"Micah," began Nicki slowly, "are we Nomads so
very different from your Union?"

He nodded. "More than you imagine."

"I mean—oh, we live differently, yes, but we're still
human beings, from Sol to Galaxy's edge. And do we
really think so otherwise?"

"Of course. We're all flesh and blood. What are
you getting at?"

"The way you talked before, I thought you thought
we'd become some kind of poison-breathing monsters.
I was wondering, though, how you and I—our people,
that is—could ever get along."

"Strife isn't necessary," he answered dully. "But as
long as the two cultures exist, there can't be any real
union. We live for things that are too different. Just
remember what happened to some of those you

adopted, or to Nomads who tried to settle down in a colony."

"I thought that was what you'd say." Slowly, Nicki withdrew her hand from his. He didn't move.

Sean stirred clumsily, "I think I'll stroll around the park," he said. "Come along with me, 'Lo, will you?"

They had risen, he and the Lorinyan girl, when they felt a tremor pulse briefly through them, a sudden nauseating twist.

"What the hell—!" Nicki sprang to her feet.

"The gravity-field generators—" began Sean.

Another surge came, shaking them. Their eyes blurred, and a huge windy sigh went through the leaves overhead. Voices lifted in shouts. Someone cursed.

"X!" gasped Sean. "They're attacking us!"

Trevelyan was erect now, standing behind Nicki and gripping her arms. "No," he answered. "A ship in hyperdrive *can't* be assaulted. It—"

Ilaloa screamed.

Looking in her direction, Trevelyan saw the stars waver in the view screen. There was a sheet of fire and the screen went dead. Smoke curled acridly from it.

Another wave and another, tossing them to the floor. Metal groaned. Trevelyan saw an oak branch snapped off and hurled across the shivering room. He scrambled back to a swaying stance. Nicki stumbled against him and his arms closed around her.

Lightning flared, a blue-white hell of electric discharge from wall to wall. After it came the thunder, booming and echoing within the hull like a great gong. The floor heaved underfoot. The light went out and there was lurid darkness torn by crackling arcs. The ship rang.

Through the tumult, Trevelyan heard the amplified voice as a distant cry: *"Micah! Trevelyan Micah, can you hear me? This is Joachim. Come up to the bridge and give me some help!"*

Lightning speared across the dark and the voice blanked out. A siren was hooting emergency stations, crazily, unnecessarily. A body crashed into Trevelyan and brought him again to the floor.

"Vortex!" he shouted. "We've hit a trepidation vortex!"

CHAPTER XIII

Trepidation Vortex: *A large traveling force-field of uncertain origin and nature, manifested as a gravitational turbulence with gyromagnetic and electric side-effects. The name derives from the fact that the differential equations describing conditions on the fringes are similar to those for a vortex in hydrodynamics, as well as from the popular association with a maelstrom. These vortices are responsible for a number of phenomena, including trepidation of planets and other small bodies. The fluctuating forces they exert on spaceships, as well as the irregularities they introduce into hyperdrive fields, have violent consequences, the vessel often being destroyed or hurled far off course; doubtless the vortices are responsible for most otherwise inexplicable disappearances of ships. The best theory of the trepidation vortex is due to Ramachandra and proposes that local concentrations of nascent mass—*

Dictionary definitions! Was the lexicographer ever in such a storm?

Lightning sheeted through the room and thunder banged in its wake. By its glare Sean saw an uprooted tree falling, and rolled to escape it. The branches flayed off his shirt.

"Ilaloa!" he cried. "Ilaloa!"

He felt her in his arms and held her close, straining against the floor. It toned with a giant vibration through flesh and skull and brain. By another electric flash he saw Trevelyan grope across the park, Nicki clinging to his hand. A woman cried out. Then the reverberance of metal drowned human voices.

Induced currents— His body felt the heat under him, and he smelled the grass as it began to char. They couldn't stay here! The floor rocked, falling dizzily away and then rising to smash at his ribs. Shifting gravitation— "Come on, 'Lo, come on," he groaned.

They lurched up, clutching for each other. The darkness was a chaos of echoes, booming and banging, shriek, whistle, crack and crash. From some forgotten corner of his mind a memory was spewed up. You couldn't have an electric field inside a hollow charged conductor. The lightning discharges had been between non-conductors, trees, and these were down now. But there would be fire!

A heave and pitch sent him staggering. Broken twigs knifed his skin. He climbed erect again, leaning on Ilaloa—somehow she had kept her feet. They crawled over the tree.

Light was dimly reborn, blue fireballs created in the air and drifting on its winds. He saw Ilaloa's face etched against the dark. She wasn't frightened now, but he couldn't read her expression.

A lightning ball swooped past, like a small sun. He felt a tingle in his nerves and every hair stood up by itself. Beyond the dull radiance was a howling night.

Someone blundered into him. He looked on a boy's distorted face. *"Have you seen my sister?"*

The voice was dim under the endless metallic roar. Hands clutched at his shoulders. *"Where's Janie?"*

"Come with us—" Ilaloa reached for the boy. He was suddenly gone, whirled away. Sean saw pain in her face, then the murk closed in again.

Gravitation tilted horribly. He went to his knees, sliding down a curve of hot steel. He fetched up brutally against a wall. Ilaloa was still with him, arm locked in arm.

Another globe of ball lightning hovered by. He saw a man gasping toward them. His face was hollow with terror and he drooled from an open mouth.

"Abbey! Abbey Roberto!" Sean shouted through the sundering roar of metal, hardly knowing he did.

The man stumbled closer. There was a knife in his hand, and Ilaloa gasped. Abbey snarled, swinging the blade at her.

"Witch! Damned murdering witch, you did this!" Ilaloa grabbed for his knife wrist. He struck at her with the free hand, a buffet that sent her to her knees.

Sean's world reddened. He stepped above Ilaloa's crouching form, driving a knee into Abbey's stomach. The other man choked and thrust at him. Sean caught the descending arm in his hands, and twisted the knife loose. Abbey clawed for his eyes. Sean stabbed him.

The lightning ball exploded, thunder and fury and a rain of fire. Its glare was livid over the trembling, staggering walls. Sean crouched with Ilaloa, holding her close and waiting.

The restless forces had thrown Trevelyan across the room, to skid along toning metal and strike a fallen tree. He came out of it in a minute, focusing blurred vision on the riven ship. Nicki was holding his head, frantically. Gathering himself, he willed the pain out of his consciousness.

"Come on," he said. The iron roar trampled his words underfoot. "Come on, let's go."

She helped him up and they made a slow way through skirling, ringing murk. By the brief glare of spinning fireballs they saw a wreck of tangled branches, splintered trunks, and tumbled bodies. Now and again they passed an injured human, but there weren't many in sight. The Nomads were meeting this well, thought Trevelyan; they were going to emergency posts without stopping for panic.

The end of the park was ahead now. Nicki lurched, and he caught her, pulling her to him. For a moment they stood face to face in raving gloom. Then a fireball blew up, flaring the incandescence of hell across the ruins, and he saw her limned against night, eyes on his and lips parted, hair tossing in the wind.

Thunder followed, a doomsday bank and roar. He kissed her.

It lasted for a long while. Then they drew apart, staring at each other without real understanding, and ran on toward the bridge.

There was a flash suspended over the astrogation desk, a well of radiance and all the rest an enormous moving dark. Joachim's battered face was sliding shadow and dim highlights. His roar lifted above the sundering echoes: "There you are! What in Cosmos' name can we do?"

For just an instant, Trevelyan recalled that something in the processes in a vortex had been known to Sol for almost a hundred years. But the frontier wanderers, to whom that knowledge could be life, had never heard of it. "Let me see your instruments," he shouted.

Outside was utter black, the viewscreens dead, but the ship's meters still registered. Needles flickered insanely across dial faces. Gravitational and electric potentials, gradients, magnetism, gyration, frequencies and amplitudes—he took it in at a single hurling glance, and his trained subconscious computed.

"We're still on the fringes," he cried. "But we've got to get clear. Components of the vibration have the ship's resonant frequencies. They'll shake us apart, atom by atom!"

Steel groaned under his voice.

"If we get the ship as a whole in phase with the major space-pulsations— Can you signal the engine room yet?"

Joachim nodded.

"All right. Pulse the hyperdrive, sinusoid—here, I'll give you the figures." He scribbled on a page of the log. Joachim tore it out and punched the keys of the emergency telewriter.

The ship howled! The floor fell away beneath Trevelyan; he was floating free, falling and falling endlessly through darkness. Then a titan's hand grabbed him and threw him at the wall. He twisted in mid-air, drilled reasonless reflex, and landed on his feet. Wave after wave beat through the ship. The floor buckled. He heard the snapping of girders.

He shouted for Nicki, stumbling up and reaching into a night that shuddered. Metal belled and gonged around him. "Nicki! Nicki!"

Thunder bawled through the ship. He heard the hoof-beats of ruin galloping across the desk. The clangorous war cry filled his universe.

And died!

Slowly, slowly, the vibrant metal shrilled into silence. He stood listening to that waning voice and wondered if this were death. He seemed to be afloat in endless space and time. He groped into thick night, not sure whether he was blind or not, and heard the cries of men about him.

"Nicki!" he sobbed.

"We're free." Joachim's voice came quiet, resonant, from far away. "We're free of the storm."

The hyperdrive went off. Joachim must have signaled for that. They hung in normal state, open space. The burned-out viewscreens functioned as ordinary ports, and Trevelyan saw the stars.

By the hazy sheen of the Milky Way, river of suns spilling across infinity, he saw Nicki. Remembered words came to him, as if someone else were speaking into the great silence. *"Hast thou commanded the morning since thy days; and caused the dayspring to know his place? . . ."*

Joachim stared out at heaven. "Where are we?" he asked.

"The constellations don't look any different! No, wait, they do a little." Ferenczi was at another port, his body black against the Milky Way. "That ridge shape wasn't there before."

Joachim pointed to the lurid brilliance of Canopus. "We're still in the general region," he said. "But vortices have been known to throw ships—any distance."

"There's a sun pretty close to us. Look over here."

Joachim went to where young Petroff Manuel stood, legs spread wide as he stared down into the port under him. Yes, a nearby star, a reddish one maybe only light-hours off. Its luster hurt his eyes.

He blinked, looking away from it to the soothing gloom of the bridge. Gravitationally overhead, a port glittered with stars. He glanced at it and grew stiff.

"Thunder and fury!" he breathed. "Lads, come over here. We've arrived!"

They followed him with their eyes and saw the configuration in the sky. A filamented web of light sprawled in the sickle-shaped curve of a dozen bright stars. "The nebula!" shouted Joachim. "The storm threw us to where we were going!"

Ferenczi's teeth gleamed in his shadowy face.

Joachim turned from the frosty nimbus and his voice snapped. "Work to do, lads."

He saw Trevelyan and Nicki by one of the ports. They were looking at each other, eyes into eyes, hands clasped. Briefly, Joachim smiled. Life went on. Whatever happened, life went on.

"All right, break it up over there," he called. "Save it for later."

"We will!" There was a sob of laughter in Nicki's voice.

Slowly, Trevelyan turned and walked over to the captain. Nicki followed, brushing back her tangled hair with hands that trembled a little. Joachim was already on the intercom. Some parts of the ship's communications system were out, but he was able to call most stations. The answers came shakily, not fully believing in salvation.

"All right," Joachim faced back to his officers. "We're banged up, but we seem to be in running order. Karl, take charge up here, and if anyone calls asking for orders, you give 'em. Meanwhile, straighten up this mess a bit. Find out where we are, as nearly as you can, and study that red sun. I'm going on a little tour of inspection. Want to come, Micah?"

"Yes, of course. Not much I can do here."

"You did enough, lad. If it hadn't been for you, this boat'd be split right down the middle."

"Well—" Trevelyan's bruised lips managed a smile. "Coordinators do come in handy."

Joachim looked archly at Nicki. "Make nice pets too, huh?"

She didn't answer. She was wiping the blood from a cut in Trevelyan's face.

They went down the companionway. It had been twisted into an S, and its lower end had torn loose from the deck plates. Beyond the hall, their wide-angled flashlights touched on havoc. The park was a heap of windowed trees, shattered fountains, and blackened grass. A thin haze of smoke hung in the unmoving air.

"Ventilators dead hereabouts," noted Joachim. "That'll rate high on the fix-it list."

They walked the length of the park. A man lay sprawled against a dwarf oak, eyes bulging sightlessly and neck awry. Beyond, there was a woman with a broken leg, but already someone was tending her. It was quiet here, little sound or motion.

"Your people rally well," said Joachim, shrugging. Then: "Hullo, somebody seems unhappy."

He led the way, pushing through a torn hedge into what had been an arbor. Ilaloa was crouched there, shuddering with sorrow. Sean sat by. Near them was a dead man with a knife in him.

Joachim bent to look at the corpse. "Abbey Roberto," he murmured.

"He tried to kill Ilaloa," said Sean, tonelessly.

"Hmm, yeah, I reckon he had some funny ideas. But so do ships' courts. However" —Joachim pulled out the knife—"Roberto must have got his when he stumbled onto a jagged edge of something." He wiped the knife clean and returned it to Abbey's sheath.

"Thanks," said Sean.

"Forget it, lad. We've got troubles enough as is."

They rounded the ship, looking in everywhere and gathering a picture of the damage. Casualties were fairly light—a few dead, a score or so seriously injured, the rest only superficially hurt. There was a tremendous wreckage of the more fragile equipment, but nothing irreparable; and the essential structure of the ship was intact. Joachim left a trail of organized working parties.

"We should be able to get under way again in a few hours," he summed up, "but it'll take longer to get us back in fighting shape. We'll have to find a place where we can hide out for a while to complete repairs."

"It doesn't have to be a planet, does it?" asked Trevelyan.

"Well, just about. If nothing else, I'd like to get some excess mass for the converter—we're low on it, and you know how hungry a ship in hyperdrive is. And there might be demands from our weapons, too. Pick up a few tons of something, maybe a couple of meteors. Then our food plant is banged up, too. We can live off preserved stuff if we must, but green vegetables from an E-planet would help morale until we get our own tanks producing again. And we need to recalibrate our instruments, too. I'll bet the storm raised merry hell with 'em. That calls for observations taken inside a planetary system. And—"

"Never mind, I see your point. Go to it. Nicki and I'll lend a hand here."

"Sure, lad. See you." Joachim stumped off toward the bridge. The lighting had been restored by now, and his stocky shape looked oddly alone as it dwindled down the metal length of hall.

Nicki turned back to Trevelyan. "It's not possible," she said softly.

"What isn't?"

"That I could be so happy."

He smiled and kissed her, taking his time about it. He thought briefly of Diane, back on Earth, and hoped she wouldn't be lonely long.

The ship had run into a vortex—why? Such things did happen, of course, but ... Did X have his home behind a screen of storm? No, that couldn't be. A vortex traveled at high speed; it was completely improbable that X's sun should have precisely the velocity of this turbulence.

Could the thinker in Kaukasu have deliberately given Ilaloa a pattern? Following the most direct route to the sector revealed would indeed have led the *Peregrine* into the storm.

He turned the data over to his subconscious for

whatever it could do with them, and gave himself to the manual labor of repair. The Nomads were shaken by their experience, but were recovering.

There were several hours' rest yet, though. Trevelyan saw Nicki to her door but didn't enter; then he returned to his own room and threw himself into bed.

He awoke when the siren wailed its signal and men grew rigid at their posts.

"Hoo-oo-oo . . . hoo-hoo . . . hoo-oo-oo . . . hoo-oo-oo . . . hoo-hoo-hoo—Stand by! All hands stand by battle stations! Strange spaceship detected where no spaceship has any business being!"

CHAPTER XIV

Standing on the bridge, where Joachim had hastily summoned him, Trevelyan looked out to a great sweep of stars and a single planet. The sun was a ruddy disc; with the glare filtered out by the restored viewscreens, he could see the dark whirlpools of spots across its photosphere. Like most giant stars, it had a big family of planets.

It was a J-planet, though, a colossus more massive even than Jupiter, its atmosphere a hell's broth of hydrogen, methane, ammonia, and less well-known compounds. It was a beautiful sight, hanging there in space, a flattened globe of soft amber radiance, belted with greens and blues and dusky browns, one red spot like a pool of blood. The man discerned three moons close enough to show perceptible crescents.

"It doesn't make sense!" Joachim stared at the flickering meters which told of a spaceship nearby.

At this range, the neutrinos given off by its engines were detectable, and there was the "wake" of gravity fluctuations by the drive, and even the faint pull of its own mass. The *Peregrine*'s maltreated instruments might be somewhat inaccurate, but there could be no mistaking their message.

"It doesn't make sense!" Joachim repeated. "We know there's nobody here with atomic power."

"X," said Trevelyan. "Suppose they have a patrol vessel in each system of their empire—or at least in many systems within the volume they regard as their own. By mounting detectors in suitable orbits around this star, they would automatically know of our arrival. So their ship could run at high acceleration to intercept us."

"Yeah, yeah, I suppose." Joachim lit a clay pipe and drew heavily on it. "And we're in no condition to fight. Should we clear out as of now?"

"Well, we came here to study the Great Cross beings."

"Uh-huh. We can always go into hyperspace. All right, let's wait."

The *Peregrine* went into free fall, curving slowly down toward the J-planet. The bridge was still. Only the muted purr of engines had voice—warmed up, waiting. Down the length of the ship, men stood by guns and missile racks. Armed boats hovered in space a few meters from the vessel. Sean would be piloting one of them, Trevelyan thought.

The communications man looked up from his set. "I've tried the whole band," he said. "Not a whisper of a signal. Shall I call them?"

"No," said Joachim. "They know we're here."

He took a restless turn about the bridge and came back to give Trevelyan a defiant glance. "Your Union exists for peace," he said. "What if we have to fight these otherlings?"

The Coordinator's green eyes were steady and flat.

"If we are attacked without provocation, we can fight as much as necessary to save our lives. But we have to find out *why* we are assaulted. Their reasons may be completely valid in terms of their own thinking."

"And my epitaph will be: *'Here lies a law-abiding citizen!'*"

Petroff Manuel's shout ripped the quiet. "I can see 'em now!"

They hurried to his screen and peered out at darkness. There was a tiny point of reflected red light moving swiftly across the stars. It grew even as they watched. Joachim turned the screen to full magnification, and the image of a spaceship was before them.

It had the elongated shape necessary to any hyperdrive ship, where field generators must be mounted fore and aft. But it was no vessel of man's building. The cylinder was beveled into flat planes; the stern bulged, and the nose held a spear-shaped mast of some kind. Its metal was a coppery alloy, flaming ruddy in the harsh sunlight, and they could see that the hull was patched and pitted—*old*.

Trevelyan sucked a hissing breath through his teeth. Joachim gave him a long stare. "You know that design?"

"Tiunra."

"Huh?"

"I've seen pictures of their ships."

"The same otherlings who lost boats out here in the Cross, four hundred years ago—"

"X is Tiunran?" murmured Ferenczi.

"It isn't logical," replied Trevelyan shakily. "The Tiunrans were explorers and scientists. They were neither physically nor culturally fitted for conquest. And when a technology has advanced to the point of interstellar drive, it doesn't *need* an empire."

"X," said Joachim, "has one." The ship was drawing closer, matching velocities as it approached. He stepped down the magnification.

"Maybe!" snapped the Coordinator. "We don't know yet."

The stranger was only a hundred kilometers or so from the *Peregrine* by now, visible to the naked eye as a blink of light. In the magnifying screens it was a grotesque spindle in the sky. Joachim's stubby fingers punched signals to his crew on the communications board.

A meter jumped and an alarm buzzed. Electronic computers flashed orders to the robot pilots. Joachim read the signals. "That's a self-guiding missile on its way," he said. "No parley, no warning, no nothing— just a fission warhead tossed at us. You still want to play peacemaker with 'em, Cordy?"

Trevelyan didn't reply. He was staring out at the ship, wondering what crew it had. They could be anything; there was no telling. And there were so few who could see past ugliness, strangeness, hostility, to the ultimate kinship of life. *Stranger, enemy, kill it!*

Light glared soundlessly in space. The *Peregrine*'s computers had intercepted the missile with one of their own. Another followed it, to be snatched up by a gravity beam and hurled back at the sender. And now the *Peregrine* threw her own barrage, swift gleams and hellish fury exploding short of the target.

Constellations swung insanely across the viewscreens as the *Peregrine* dodged a patterned flight of shells. The crew didn't feel it; the internal gravity generators automatically compensated for acceleration. But the crew watched dials, fed the guns and missile racks, tending a robot's brain as it fought for them. Flesh and blood and the human mind were too slow and weak for this battle.

Strange combat, thought Trevelyan. It was a flickering shadow play of stars and bursting light, a chess game played by machines while men stood watching. The only sound was the irregular hum of the gravity-drive engines and the faint *whoosh-whoosh-whoosh* of ventilators.

No—wait. He heard another noise, a creak and groan in the girders of the hull. Overtaxed by the storm, not yet inspected and repaired, the structure was giving before the stress of swinging that huge mass through the maze of thrust, feint, parry, and dodge.

And Ferenczi's bearded hatchet face was grim as he looked up from the computer indicators. "We're lagging," he said. "Our detectors and calculators aren't fast and accurate enough. Before long, one of those shells or missiles is going to hit us."

"I thought so." Joachim sprang to the communications board and grabbed the radio mike. "All boats return! All boats back to the ship!"

This was the danger point. The little spacecraft had to come back, enter the boathouses to be under the drive field's action. And as they dropped in, the *Peregrine* had to ease the violence of her maneuvers lest she hurl them through her own outer shell. All those instants, the enemy might—

Joachim studied the detector dials. "They're easing up. Not throwing as much at us. *Why?*"

Trevelyan looked out to the stranger. "Maybe," he said softly, "they don't want to annihilate us."

"Huh?" Joachim's expression was almost comical. "But what—"

"They didn't assail us with more than we could handle. They're going slow now, just when any determined commander would be tossing all he had at us. Are we simply being warned off?"

A buzz cut across his voice. "Everybody in," said Joachim. He threw over the engine-room signal switch. "So long, friend."

This close to star and planet, the hyperdrive built up with distressing irregularity. Trevelyan hung onto a table top, fighting his stomach. It was over in minutes and the red sun was dwindling astern. Space glittered chill around them.

Joachim wiped his face. It was wet. "I wouldn't want to go through that again?"

Ferenczi's tones fell dry. "We've taken astronomical data on this whole region. There's a Sol-type star about ten light-years from here."

"If the others are there, too—" began Petroff.

Joachim shrugged. "We have to go somewhere. All right, Karl, give me a course for that sun."

"The aliens, if they are the same as X, know we favor GO dwarf stars," said Trevelyan. "Has it occurred to you, Hal, that we're being herded?"

Joachim regarded him strangely. "It's a thought," he said slowly. "But we haven't much choice in the matter, have we?"

Trevelyan left the bridge and returned to his room. Bathed and freshly clothed, he went in search of Nicki. He found her waiting at the door of her apartment. For a moment he stood looking at her; then she came to him and he drew her close.

After a long time she sighed and opened her eyes. "Let's go to one of the boathouses," she said. "Only place we can have some privacy. The park's full of working parties. But I'm off duty just now."

He glanced toward the apartment, but she gestured him away. "Sean and 'Lo are in there," she told him. "He was out in his boat, you know, gunning missiles, and it doesn't have the computers or the power to escape one. I thought 'Lo would go to pieces."

They went down the corridor. Her fingers tightened convulsively about his. "I thought we were all done for," she said with sudden harshness. "I knew we were all done for," she said with sudden harshness. "I knew we couldn't stand off a real attack, and you were on the bridge and I couldn't be there—"

"It's all over. Nobody was hurt."

"If you were killed," she said, "I'd steal a ship and go hunting for the killer till I found him."

"You'd do better to help correct the conditions that led to my being killed."

"You're too civilized," she said bitterly.

The ancient war, he thought, the immemorial struggle of intelligence to master itself. Nicki could never stay on Earth. As if reading his mind, she said slowly, "If we ever get clear of this, we're going to have to make some decisions."

"Yes."

"There is a chance you would stay with the ship?" she asked wistfully. "Be adopted?"

"I don't know. I wasn't brought up for that. To me, life is more than starjumping and trading. I can't escape myself."

"But you wander a lot on your jobs," she said. "I could go along. Don't you ever need an—assistant?"

"When I do, I get one, another Coordinator, most likely an otherling. But—we'll see, Nicki."

They went down a companionway, through the lower level and into one of the boathouses. There wasn't much room between the boat and the surrounding fliers, but they were alone, standing in metal and looking out a viewscreen at the stars.

She turned on him fiercely. "You're wiser than I am. You know better what will come of this. Only I'm not going to set you free. Not ever."

"If you went from the ship with me," he asked, "wouldn't you ever miss it?"

She paused. "Yes. They're stupid and narrow and mean here, sometimes, but they're my people. I'd do it, though, and never be sorry."

"No," he agreed. "You're not one to back down on a decision."

He looked out at the steely light of stars. "We'll wait and see."

✧   ✧   ✧

The *Peregrine* went on across space. Her crew worked hard, repairing, restoring—preparing for whatever might lie at journey's end. Joachim drove them ruthlessly, less to get the job done than to take their minds off danger.

Near the end of the third day, they went out of hyperdrive and accelerated inward. The instruments peered and murmured, and clicked forth a picture of the system. Eight worlds were detected. One of them circled its primary at a distance of slightly over one astronomical unit, and the ship moved toward it, matching velocities as she neared. Telescopes, spectroscopes, and gravitometers strained ahead during the hours of flight.

There was no sign of atomic energy; and as the *Peregrine* took up an orbit around her destination, there was no other ship. The crew gathered at the viewers for a look at the planet.

It was Earthlike to many points of classification. It was a serene and lovely sight as they approached; against the naked blaze of the stars, it was a sign for peace.

Joachim directed an orbit some thousand kilometers up, using gravity drive to remain above a chosen spot. "It looks pretty," he said. "We'll send down a boatful of scouts. I think Ilaloa should go with them. That telepathy or whatever-it-is of hers may pick up something. Then Sean will have to go, too. And you, Micah; you're trained to spot aliens."

"I'm quite willing," said the Coordinator, "but if I go, you'll have to tie up Nicki to keep her aboard."

"That wouldn't do any good unless we could gag her, too. All right, take her along."

CHAPTER XV

Landing on a planet of this sort was a stylized procedure which Trevelyan watched with interest. Nomad doctrine closely paralleled that for a Survey vessel; but the equipment used was not so elaborate and some items of sheer ritual had crept in.

Two fliers went ahead, each bearing two men, plunging down from the sky at reckless velocity. The region chosen was an island about a thousand kilometers long and three hundred wide, a place of hills and forests and broad river valleys. The fliers cruised just above the treetops for a good half hour, men peering with eyes and instruments. There was no sign of habitation, no metal, no building, no agriculture. Geosonic probes revealed that the ground was firm thick soil over normal bedrock and water tables. No outsize animals, or even large herds, were spotted. It was safe to land.

The boat followed more slowly, settling to the

ground with a crew of twenty, and the fliers dropped
to rest on either side of her. Men stood by the guns,
but that seemed a meaningless gesture. The landscape
beyond the ports was utterly peaceful.

"In the name of Cosmos, sanctuary," said the boat's
captain, Kogama Iwao, formally. "All right, boys, hop
to it."

Ten spacesuited men clashed down their helmets
and moved to the airlock. The inner door shut on
them and a high whine signaled the sterilizing radia-
tions and supersonics which filled the chamber while
the outer door was open.

A sunbeam touched Ilaloa's hair with molten silver. "It is free and light out there," she said. "Why
do you hide from it in dead steel?"

"It looks nice," agreed Nicki, "but you can't tell.
There might be germs, molds—a hundred kinds of
death. Those leaves might be poisonous even to touch.
We're not afraid of hungry monsters, 'Lo. It's easy
enough to handle them. But sickness that gets inside
you—"

"But there is no danger," said the Lorinyan.
Bewilderment still overrode her voice. "This is the
home of peace."

"We'll find that out," said Kogama brusquely.
"What's the word on the atmosphere, Phil?"

Levy glanced at the dials of his molecular analyzer,
which had sucked in an air sample. "No poison gases
in any quantity, except of course the usual tinge of
ozone," he replied. "A few bacteria and spores, naturally. I'll tell you about them in a minute."

The analyzer buzzed to itself, scanned the organic
structure of the microscopic life it had trapped. A cell
of such-and-such nature must feed on a fairly definite range of tissues in a certain manner, and give
off predictable by-products. One by one, the specimens were tabulated until the verdict stood: nothing
airborne that was harmful to man.

By that time, the armored gang was back, carrying samples of soil, plants, water, and even a couple of insects. They were made aseptic in the airlock before entering. The prophylaxis was too brief to affect anything below the surface of their specimens, and Levy's crew got to work with practiced skill.

Analyses disclosed Earth-type life, similar down to most of the enzymes, hormones, and vitamins; nothing to cause disease in man. Marooned humans could live here indefinitely.

Kogama chuckled at the final word and rubbed his hands. "All's well," he said. "We can go out and relax, I suppose."

"You're aware, of course, that you haven't taken a fair sample of this planet's life forms?" asked Trevelyan.

"Oh, no doubt there are things which can hurt us— venomous plants, for instance. But nothing we can't handle, I'm sure."

Trevelyan nodded. "What's your next line of study?"

"Sending parties out to hike around. Let's see—" Kogama looked out the western port. "Say five hours to sunset. That's time enough to get a pretty good notion of the layout here. Want to go, Micah?"

"Of course."

"A few'll have to stay in the boats, just in case. Might as well be me in that group. I'm lazy." Kogama belied his yawn by snapping a string of orders. Sixteen people were organized into four parties, each assigned to walk in a definite direction and come back before sunset by another route. Sketch maps made from the air were provided, to be filled in by the hikers as well as possible, and samples of anything unusual were to be brought back for study.

Trevelyan leagued himself with Sean, Nicki, and Ilaloa to make one group. The three humans wore coveralls, boots, skin-tight gloves, wrist radios, guns and canteens and medic kits at waist. Ilaloa had flatly refused to wear extra clothing.

"Let her have her way," said Kogama. "If something poisons her, it'll be a handy way for us to learn what's dangerous."

"There is no danger," insisted Ilaloa. She sprang from the airlock to the grass and stood almost shuddering with ecstasy. Slowly, she lifted her hands and closed eyes to the sun.

Nicki regarded the slim white form with a touch of envy. "Wish I had her nerve—or foolishness," she said. Then, looking about her and drawing a deep slow breath: "It's beautiful. It's as beautiful as Rendezvous, and I never thought there could be two such planets."

Trevelyan had to agree with her; a man could make his home here.

As he went toward the forest, Trevelyan became aware of its noises. They were like Earth's in their myriad small whispers, but he missed the songs of grasshopper and meadowlark. Even the wind in the leaves had a different sound.

Ilaloa danced before her companions, laughing aloud, wild with the sudden joy of release. Like a wood nymph, thought Trevelyan—and any moment Pan might come piping from the brush.

The four went up the hill slope, guiding themselves by a gyrocompass powered from the boat.

"It could be a park," said Nicki, after a long silence.

Trevelyan blinked in surprise. Something about the landscape had been haunting him; now something chilled him. "Who," he asked slowly, "is the caretaker?"

"Why"—Nicki's eyes regarded him with puzzlement—"nobody. It was just something I said."

"It *could* happen this way," he answered flatly, "but life is usually a struggle for place. This looks—landscaped!"

"But that's silly, Micah. Nobody lives here. Not even X would make a park of a whole world which he didn't inhabit."

Trevelyan looked ahead of him. Ilaloa was standing by a tree whose branches were heavy with dusk-colored fruit. Sean tried to stop her as she plucked one, but she laughed and bit into it.

"That's pretty careless," said Trevelyan. Nicki, arm in arm with him, felt his muscles grow rigid.

Sean was still protesting as the two approached. Ilaloa held the fruit to him. "It is good," she said, "There is sunlight in it."

"But—"

"Try it, my dearest." Her voice softened. "Would I give you that in which there was harm?"

"No. No, you wouldn't. All right, then." Sean accepted the gift and tasted. A slow expression of delight crossed his thin features.

"It's delicious!" he called to his companions. "Try some."

"No thanks," said Trevelyan. "Leave unanalyzed stuff alone. Even if it doesn't hit you right away, it might have slow-working effects."

They came out in an open meadow. Trevelyan shot an animal, a small quadruped. Its green color proved to be due to algae living in its fur.

"Hey!" yelled Sean. "Hey, look over here!"

Trevelyan followed him to the tree on the pasture's edge. It was a graceful thing, not unlike a poplar, swaying and whispering in the wind. But the leaves had prominent veins and—

And they would glow in the dark, Trevelyan knew. This was one of the species reported by Survey, the same life-forms impossibly scattered over half a dozen worlds. And the pieces of the puzzle fell together.

"It's a torch tree!" exclaimed Sean. "A torch tree just like on Rendezvous—"

"X," whispered Nicki. "X has been on our planet, too." Her hand stole to her gun.

Their wrist radios shattered stillness with a jagged urgency: "Attention, all parties! Attention! This is Kogama at the boat. Natives approaching!"

Trevelyan lifted his eyes to Ilaloa. He did not see victory on her face. It was more like a sudden grief. "Yes," she said.

"They're humanoid all the way down the line." Kogama's voice rattled above the talking forest. "White skins, bluish-white hair, males, beardless—all naked and weaponless, coming slowly out of the woods— *No!*" It was almost a scream. "They can't be! Attention, all parties, attention! These are—"

Kogama's voice faded in a gasp, and then there was silence.

Trevelyan's hand rested on the butt of his gun, but he didn't draw. "What was done, Ilaloa?" he asked, very quietly.

"A sleep gas blown down the wind." Her voice was small and toneless. "They are not hurt, only sleeping."

"*Ilaloa*—" Sean started forward, his gun half out. "*Ilaloa*—"

The natives stood before them, a few meters away on the edge of the meadow. *They must have trailed us without our knowing,* thought Trevelyan. He looked them up and down, the superb naked forms of half a dozen men, white as marble statues come to life. Their silver hair streamed in the wind, past the cleanly chiseled faces of Hellenic gods, tossing over broad shoulders. One of them carried a thing like a big gray egg, a few metallic insect forms hovering about it.

"Stand back!" Sean had his gun free now, pointed shakingly at the strangers. His cry was animal. "Back or I'll shoot!"

A slow smile curved the lips of the men. The one with the egg spoke in human Basic, accented but fluent, like music from his throat: "If I tell the dwellers in this nest to sting you to death, they will do so. Or if I drop the nest, they will. Put down your weapon and listen."

Nicki raised an arrogant head. "We'll fill you with holes first."

"You do not understand." Ilaloa stepped in front of the humans. "Your kind is sundered from life, and bears within it the fear of death and the longing for death. We have neither. Throw down your guns."

Trevelyan sighed. At this moment, he felt only a colossal weariness. "Go ahead, do it," he ordered. "Our getting killed wouldn't help matters any, nor do we know how many more of—these—there are watching us. Put down your weapons, Sean, Nicki." He dropped his own into the grass.

The stranger who bore the egg of death nodded. "That is well."

CHAPTER XVI

Oddly, it was on Ilaloa that Trevelyan's gaze rested. The pride had fallen from her like a dropped cloak, and she took a step toward Sean with her hands held out to him.

The Nomad turned, making a sound like a strangled sob. He went to Nicki as if she were his mother, and she held him close. Ilaloa stood for a small moment watching them. Then she slipped into the forest and was lost.

She still has that intuition of the right thing to do, thought Trevelyan. *Now isn't the time for her.*

Slowly, he faced around to the tall being who had spoken. That one was carefully setting the gray nest into a tree crotch. His hands free, the captor smiled again. It made his face a warm dazzle. "Welcome."

Trevelyan folded his arms and stood regarding the other from expressionless eyes. "That's a curious thing to say to us."

"But it is true," insisted the alien gently. "You are guests here. It is not a euphemism. We are genuinely glad to see you."

"Would you be glad to see us go?" asked Trevelyan wryly.

"Not immediately, no. We should like to give you some understanding of us first." The handsome head lowered. "May I perform the introduction? This planet we call Loaluani, and we are the Alori. That word is not quite equivalent to your 'human,' but you can assume for the present that it is. I am designated— named Esperero."

Trevelyan gave the names of his party, adding, "We are from the Nomad ship *Peregrine*—"

"Yes. That much we know already."

"But Ilaloa didn't say— Are you telepaths?"

"Not in the sense you mean. But we were expecting the *Peregrine*."

"What are your intentions toward us?"

"Peaceful. We—a few of us who know the art— will take our boat back to the ship. The crew will not suspect anything, having received no radio alarm, and being too high for telescopic observation of what happened. Once in the boathouse, we shall release the sleep gas, which will be quickly borne through the ventilators. All the Nomads will be taken down here in the boats. But no one will be harmed.

"Do you wish to come with us? Our party is going toward that section of the island where we feel you will be most comfortable. Your fellows will be landed there."

"Yes—yes, of course."

Nicki flashed Trevelyan a crooked grin. She walked a little behind him, one hand on Sean's shoulder. The Nomad moved like a blind man. Trevelyan stayed beside Esperero, and the other Alori flowed on either side. *Flowed*—there was no word for the rippling grace of their movements, soundless under sun-dappled shadows. The forest closed in around them.

"Ask whatever you like," said Esperero. "You are here to learn."

"How did you arrange for us to come? How did you know?"

"As regards Lorinya, or Rendezvous as you call it," said Esperero, "we had colonized it for about fifty years when the Nomads came, and we watched and studied them for a long while. Their language was already known to some of us, and we had means of spying on them even when none of the Alori were present." As Trevelyan lifted his brows, the alien said only, "The forest told our people."

After a moment, he went on: "Four years ago, Captain Joachim was heard to mention his suspicions of this part of space to others. It was logical that he would sooner or later investigate it, and we determined to get an agent aboard his ship. Ilaloa was chosen and trained. When the *Peregrine* came back this year, it was not hard for her, using the empathic faculties of our people, to find someone who would take her along. I do not know yet just what she did to influence your journey—"

"I can tell you that." Trevelyan related what had happened in Kaukasu. "Obviously there was no thinker behind the walls. She's a superb actress."

"Yes. Ilaloa gave you a star-configuration such that your most direct route from the planet to here would run you into the storm."

"M-hm. And I suppose she'd been given post-hypnotic blocks so that she responded as desired even under hypnotism?"

"Did you try that? Yes, of course, they would have guarded her in any way possible."

"Except against the storm itself," said Trevelyan grimly. "That nearly annihilated us."

"If so," said Esperero, "we would at least have removed one potential enemy."

There was an unhumanness in his tone. It was not cynical indifference, it was something else—a sense of destiny? An acceptance?

"However, you did survive," continued the Alorian. "Our idea was to drive you to a colony so that we might capture you, as we have done. There were half a dozen equally probable colonies, and each of them has been ready for your arrival. I happen to have been the one whom you—picked, shall we say?" His smile was impish, and Trevelyan couldn't help a once-sided grin.

"I should have known," he said ruefully. "If I'd thought to investigate Ilaloa at all, I would have seen the truth."

"You are not a Nomad, are you?"

"No. The Nomads didn't stop to check the facts or reason the thing through, and I had too much else on my mind. But if I'd known that the Lorinyans were supposed to be mere savages . . . !

"Ilaloa spoke nearly perfect Basic, with an unusual vocabulary even for a human. She knew obsolete words like 'sickle,' which she could only have found in literary references—and she didn't read much, if at all, on the trip. And when we tried to argue each other's philosophies out, she often had very sophisticated remarks. I assumed that she came from a rather high culture which had had a good deal to do with the Nomads."

"That was true enough," said Esperero.

"Yes, but to the Nomads the Lorinyans were primitives. They— Never mind." Trevelyan sighed. Every time you thought you had reality expressed in a system you stumbled against a new facet. The sane man must be always distrustful of his own beliefs.

"You will not be harmed," said Esperero.

The hills rolled away under their striding feet,

woods and shadows and the slowly declining sun. Trevelyan saw animal life everywhere, climbing up the trees, crawling over the ground, rising heavenward on glorious wings. He heard a song which was all whistles and trills, happy lilt in a bower of blossoms. The Alori bent their heads to listen, and one of them whistled back, up and down the same scale. The bird replied differently. It was almost as if they spoke together.

They passed a large mammal, like a graceful blue-furred antelope, one horn spiraling from the poised head. It watched them out of calm eyes. Didn't the Alori hunt at all?

Nicki spoke behind Trevelyan. "Micah, we Nomads should have realized that the Lorinyans weren't native to Rendezvous. Every other backboned animal there has six limbs."

Trevelyan turned back to Esperero. "Where did you come from originally?"

"Alori. It is a planet not far from here, as astronomical distances go. But it is very unlike your Earth. That is why our civilization has developed such a different basis from yours that—" Esperero paused.

"That one must destroy the other?" finished Trevelyan softly.

"Yes, I believe so. But that need not mean physical destruction of the beings who have the culture."

"You're not going to meddle with *my* mind!" Nicki snapped.

Esperero smiled. "No one will try to force you to anything. We ask only that you see for yourselves."

"In what ways are you so different?" asked Trevelyan.

"That will take a long time to explain," said Esperero. "Let us say that your civilization has a mechanical basis and ours a biological. Or that you seek to master things, where we wish only to live as a part of them."

"Let the differences go for now," Trevelyan said.

"If you don't go in for inventiveness—the mechanical kind, anyway—how did you get off your home planet?"

"There was a ship that landed, long ago, an exploring vessel from Tiunra, with strange, furry little beings in it—"

"Yes, I know."

"The Alori are a unified culture. They evolved as one, whereas your kind did not. That is again a reflection of the gulf between us. Our people had already climbed the mountain peaks that reached above Alori's shielding clouds. They had seen the stars and, by methods different from yours, had learned something about them. They made the Tiunrans prisoner and decided that they must defend themselves."

"The Tiunrans hadn't hurt you, had they?" asked Sean.

"No. But—you must wait, must see more of our life before you can understand. . . . The Alori took the ship and went out among the stars. Many of them lost their minds to that strangeness and had to be taken back for healing. But the rest went on. They encountered other Tiunran ships—they captured three.

"No more Tiunran ships came here, but it was realized that many races would be starfaring and some inevitably come to us. And the very fact of their building spacecraft meant they would be of the same alien stamp. We began colonizing habitable planets throughout this region. There were not many like Alori, which is an unusual type, but we found beauty in worlds like this, too. We spread the life we knew between the stars, so that the universe was no longer quite so cold."

Esperero paused. The sun was getting low; this planet had about a twenty-hour day. "I think," he said, "that we will camp soon. We could easily go on through the night, but you will wish to rest."

"Go on with your history," urged Trevelyan.

"Oh, yes." A shadow crossed the graven face. "As you like. We found, in our explorations, that we were almost unique. You can understand that that increased our uneasiness for the future. We colonized all untenanted worlds habitable to us, bringing Alorian life-forms and modifying the native ecology as much as necessary. A few other planets—" He hesitated.

"Yes?" Trevelyan's voice held ruthlessness.

"We exterminated the natives. It was gently done. They hardly knew it was happening, but it was carried through. We needed the worlds and the natives could not be made to co-operate."

"And you say man is dangerous!"

"I never accused you of being unmerciful." Esperero shook his head. "Perhaps later you will understand how it is."

Trevelyan's will surged out to clamp on his feelings. Man's history had been violent. If he respected intelligent life today, it was because he had learned by fire and sword and tyrant's gibbet that he must.

"All right," said the Solarian. "Continue."

"At present, we have colonized about fifty planets," went on Esperero. "It is not a large domain, though it covers a considerable volume of space by virtue of our planets being widely scattered. And we cannot build machines ourselves. That would destroy the very thing we seek to preserve.

"We watched the Union grow. I need not tell you in detail how we studied it. Among so many races, it was easy to pose as members of yet another. I myself have spent years wandering about your territories, investigating them in every aspect. We have seen your gradual expansion toward us and known that sooner or later you would discover our existence. Against that day we have prepared. We have seized spaceships which took orbits unawares about our planets, thus adding to our fleet. In Erulan, we buy ships outright."

"The man there," said Trevelyan slowly, "told us that humans bought the ships for gold. He was sure they were humans."

"Yes. Other races have joined with us and taken on our life. Among them have been crews, and descendants of crews, from those spaceships we took."

"And you expect *us* to—" Nicki's whisper held a note of terror.

"You will not be forced," said Esperero.

They came out on the brow of a hill and looked across deep dales to the horizon. The sun was setting in a rush of color.

"Let us rest," said Esperero.

His followers moved quietly to their few tasks. Some of them disappeared into the woods, to return presently bearing fruits and nuts and berries and less identifiable plants. Others broke off gourds, which proved to be hollow, and large soft leaves.

Trevelyan fingered one of the gourds curiously. It was perfect for its use—a line of cleavage made it easy to open; a spike on the bottom could be driven into the ground. There was even a handle. "Do these grow naturally?"

Esperero chuckled. "Yes, but we first taught them to do so."

"How about shelter?"

"We will not need it. We do have tree dwellings, but we can sleep outside. Would you really rather lock yourself in with your own sweat and breathing?"

"N-no, I suppose not. If it isn't raining."

"Rain is clean. But you will understand later."

Twilight deepened to a silky blue. The Alori sat in a grave circle. One of them said a few words, and the others responded. There was a ritual in it, as in everything they did—even the handing out of the food was somehow a ceremony.

Trevelyan sat by Nicki, smiling. A milk-filled nut which was its own goblet was given him, and he touched it to hers. "Your health, darling."

"You may eat and drink without fear," Esperero told him. "There is no fear on this planet—no poison, no hungry beasts, no hidden death of germs. Here is the end of all strife."

Trevelyan tasted of what was offered him. It was delicious, a dozen new and subtle flavors, textures that his teeth liked, nourishment coursing along his veins. Nicki joined him with equal fervor.

Sean stood leaning against a tree, looking over the moon-flooded valley. He felt hollow inside, as if nothing were altogether real.

Ilaloa came to him. He saw her white in the moonlight, and she slipped up till he could have touched her. He didn't look at her, but kept his eyes on the valley. Here and there in its darkness the torch trees were like spears of radiance.

"Sean," she said.

"Go away," he replied.

"Sean, may I talk to you?"

"No," he said. "Begone, I tell you."

"I did what I had to, Sean. These are my people. But I wanted to say that I love you."

"I'd like to break your back," he said.

"If you wish that, Sean, then do it."

"No. You're not worth the trouble."

She shook her head. "I cannot quite understand it. I do not think any other of the Alori has ever felt the way I do. But we love each other, you and I."

He wanted to deny it, but words seemed futile mouthings.

"I will wait, Sean," she said. "I will always be waiting."

CHAPTER XVII

The Nomads had been taken to a valley on the island's northwestern coast, surrounded by hills and opening on the sea. When Trevelyan's band got there, the initial confusion was over. Fifteen hundred people had settled down to a dazed waiting for whatever came next.

Joachim met the new arrivals on the valley's edge. "Been waiting for you. One of the natives told me you'd be coming down this trail."

"How did they know that?" asked Nicki. Esperero's men had left them a few kilometers back, pointing out the route for them to follow.

"I don't know," shrugged Joachim. "Telepathy?"

"No," answered Trevelyan. "Incredible as it seems, I'm beginning to think that the forest here forms a communications network."

"The original grapevine telegraph, huh? Well, let it go. We had a little trouble to start with, but those

boys can handle themselves." Joachim clicked his
tongue admiringly. "Their judo starts where ours
leaves off. No harm done, though, and the crew's
pretty well quieted down now."

"You've been given living quarters?"

"Yeah. Such of the natives as know Basic told us
they'd evacuated this bunch of tree houses for our
benefit. They said they wanted to be friends, even
if they couldn't let us go back to bring down the
human race on 'em. Since then, nobody's been
around. Tactful." Joachim looked keenly at Sean. "If
I was you, lad, I wouldn't show myself either for a
few days."

"I understand," said Sean.

"They'll realize it wasn't your fault, and cool off,
after a while, but I came to warn you. I know of a
couple of trees away from the main village where you
can stay." The captain turned to the Coordinator. "You
got any ideas as to just what we're supposed to do?"

"Settle down. Learn more about the setup before
attempting anything."

"Uh-huh. Snatched my ship right out from under
me! Transplanted me like a vegetable! It's enough to
drive a man from drink."

Trevelyan studied the Alori houses with more than
casual interest. They were reminiscent of the naturally hollow trees in which the Nerthusian aborigines dwelt, but incomparably farther advanced. Each
bole contained a smoothly cylindrical room that was
a good seven meters across, light and airy; the wood
hard and beautifully grained. There were windows
which could be closed by transparent flaps of tissue
that were part of the tree; a similar, heavier curtain
served for a door. The floor was carpeted with a
mosslike growth whose springiness held a living
warmth.

A couple of extruded shelves formed table space;
there was no other furniture, but the floor made a

restful bed. Vines tendriled about the trunk looped inside with a riot of flowers, among which hung bladders that glowed after dark with cool yellow light. These could be "turned off" by drawing their own loose husks about them. From one wall a hollow, inward-growing branch yielded clear water when squeezed, a natural drain below taking the run-off. Next to the tree grew a bush whose waxy fruits were an excellent soap surrogate; the other needs of the body could be taken care of in the boundless forest.

Trevelyan moved into an isolated tree, Sean and Nicki taking its neighbors. His own tastes not being elaborate, he didn't miss the ordinary appurtenances of human life.

The village, he found, was actually an extensive settlement, comprising some five hundred units—more than enough for the Peregrines, especially when one could live just as well outdoors. The dew took a little habituation; thereafter, even the trees seemed cramped and stuffy.

Pets had also been taken from the ship. It was strange to see a terrier barking at a rainbow-winged insect, or sleeping in the shade of a half-meter broad flower. Soon after the humans' arrival, some of the Alori returned with a courteous offer to bring whatever else was desired from the *Peregrine*—now in free orbit just above the atmosphere. Joachim got a list of wants from his people, mostly tools. It seemed to amuse the Alori, but they brought the things. Joachim listed his own whiskey, tobacco, and a few pipes at the top.

The Nomads began to relax. It was evident by now that no harm was intended by their captors, who were apparently content to leave them to their own devices.

Trevelyan met several of the Alori often. He used to walk into the forest, alone or with Nicki. When he felt like talking to one of the—natives—it wasn't usually long before somebody showed up. Esperero seemed to be his special mentor.

"What plans do you have for us?" asked the Coordinator.

Esperero smiled. "I have said we will not coerce you—directly. But you are a restless folk. Most of you will soon begin longing for open space again."

"So—?"

"So I anticipate spasmodic activity among you. Handicrafts will resume, for one thing. The forest offers many possibilities to the creative mind, and our people will give advice when needed. That will help break down the unfriendliness toward us."

"Some of those projects you may not like," said Nicki.

"I know. For example, men will begin to think of hunting. They will make bows and other weapons. But they will find that the animal life has disappeared. In like manner, their other unsuitable ambitions will be frustrated."

"And if they turn against you?" asked Trevelyan.

"They will know better than to try organizing a war party against a whole planet. But Nomad culture, like any other, is the product of an environment and its necessities. Here the physical environment, open space, is gone. The planet will absorb them.

"They won't become Alori. This generation, and even the next and the next, will not be fully absorbed. But, one by one, as they are ready, they will go spaceward again—for us." Esperero nodded wisely. "It has been thus with our other spacefaring guests."

Theirs was a long-range plan, Trevelyan knew, but the Alori had patience to spare. And what was the form of their restraining influences? Every culture must have some. Modern Solarian society tried to inculcate a pattern of habits and reactions in the individual—a morality and a world-view. Technically, his was a guilt culture. The Nomads, with their emphasis on personal honor and prestige, wealth, and conspicuous consumption had a shame culture. And the Alori?

The realization grew in him that Alori culture was a planet-wide symbiosis. Belonging within an organic whole was their fundamental motivation—a modified fear culture.

Esperero's prophecy was good. Handicrafts were being practiced again among the marooned Nomads. The loom and anvil and potter's wheel began to appear.

Trevelyan met him one day, and the Alorian asked if he would like to attend a festival.

"Certainly," said the Coordinator. "When?"

Esperero shrugged. "When everyone has come. Shall we go?"

It was as simple as that. Trevelyan, however, ducked back to invite Nicki and Sean. The man refused bitterly, but Nicki came gladly enough.

They traveled south, the humans and a few Alori, moving leisurely over hills and valleys. It rained most of one day, but nobody cared. Toward the end of the second day they came to the place of festival.

It was in a small cup-shaped dale, and the trees about the central meadow were of kinds Trevelyan had not seen before. A hundred or so Alori were already gathered. They moved softly about, friend greeting friend with grave ceremony; everything was part of one harmonious ritual. Trevelyan was made welcome, and found opportunities to exercise his knowledge of the language. Nicki, with no particular linguistic ability, remained still; but she smiled. She had grown strangely serene in the past month.

Both moons would be full tonight. As the blue dusk deepened, the man and the woman joined the seated Alori around the meadow. For a while there was silence.

A single note lifted and hung on the air. Trevelyan started, looking for the source. The note rose, swelling

triumphantly, and others joined it, weaving in and out
on a scale unknown to him but strangely pleasing.
He knew with surprise, and then with calmness, that
it was the forest which sang.

Night closed over the turning planet. The pale
bridge of the Milky Way arched across a vault of clear
darkness. The moons climbed swiftly, turning the
ground into a silver-and-shadow dream, and the first
dew caught their light in tiny glitters like fallen
planets.

Music rose higher. It was the voice of the forest,
windy roar of branches, crystal pouring of water, bird
song, beast cry, underneath it a great steady pulse like
a living heart. Now the dancers came, whirling out
of shadow into the unreal moonlight, soaring as if they
had wings. In and out, back and forth, and the glowing fireballs were with them, birds with luminous
feathers darted between their flying white forms, and
the music sang of springtime.

Now it was summer, growth and strength, a giant
rush of rain; clouds burst apart, sunlight speared
through, it blazed across an endlessness of ocean. Land
raised green from the sea, surf white against its cliffs,
trees lifting heavenward and striving their roots into
the planet. An animal roared, shaking his horns in
might and splendor. The dance leaped into fury.

It became slower, stately, the passion of laden
boughs and the land turning gold for harvest. The
death of summer lay in hazy distances and cool nights.
Far overhead, a wedge of birds flew southward, and
their cry was a lonely song for wanderers.

Trevelyan wondered what the music was to the
Alori. To him it was Earth, the sweeping years and
final sinking back against the strong ones of the world.
But he was human; he held Nicki close.

Winter. The dancers scattered like blowing leaves;
moonlight fell on chill emptiness, and the music
keener with hungry winds. Cold gripped the planet,

daylight like steel, night of bitter stars, hissing snow and the southward-grinding glaciers. Aurora shimmered weirdly over the face of heaven. One dancer came forth and stood for an instant as if in despair. Then she stamped her foot, once, twice, and began to dance the end of all things. Trevelyan saw that it was Ilaloa.

She danced slowly at first, groping as if through mists and flying snow. The music lifted again, sharp and savage; she danced faster, fleeing, cowering, the flutter of broken wings, hunger and ruin, cold and death and oblivion. She danced with a wildness and a hopelessness that numbed him to watch. The music was like the crash of glaciers trampling mountains underfoot, spilling across broad plains and proud forests. It was like winter gone mad, wind and snow, night and storm, calving icebergs in the north and whelping hurricanes in the south. The world groaned under its weight.

The storm died. Slowly, the dancer moved away, slow as life fading from creation. When she was gone, there was only the heavy dead thunder of the ice and sea, mourning wind and the sun smoldering to ash. It was over.

And yet there was fulfillment in it. Life had been, had struggled, and died. Reality *was*—no man needed more.

When silence and moonlight came back, the Alori did not stir. They sat for a long while without moving or speaking. Then, one by one, they rose and disappeared into the shadows. The festival was over.

Nicki's face was white under the moons. They were sinking. Trevelyan saw with dim surprise. Had it only been one night?

When they got back to the Nomad camp, Joachim said the marriage service over them. Afterward there was a feast and merrymaking, but Trevelyan and Nicki didn't stay long.

CHAPTER XVIII

They wandered from the settlement, two of them
alone, and ranged about the island. There was no
hurry. When they found a place they liked especially
well—a sandy cove, a hidden glen, the lonely heights
of a mountain—they stayed until a vague restlessness
blew them on.

Trevelyan wanted to learn more about the Alori
civilization. But to know it, he had to contemplate
it.

Often they encountered Alori in the woods, or
stumbled onto one of their villages. They were always
made welcome and their questions were freely answered.
As he became more adept in the language, he took to
thinking in it, for no speech in his civilization could
fully handle the new concepts.

In so far as Alori culture could be compared to any
human society at all, it was Apollonian—restrained,
moderate, everything balance and order and

adjustment. It had little use for the aggressive individual; nevertheless, each individual was fully developed, very much himself, free to choose his own endeavor within the pattern.

It was not a perfect society, even by its own standards. Utopia is a self-contradictory dream. There was sorrow here, as elsewhere in the universe; but grief was a part of living.

Nor was the Great Cross domain a place of mindless contentment. In its own way, it was as scientific a culture as Sol's. But the underlying theoretical foundation was altogether alien. The Alorian mind did not analyze into factors; it saw the entire problem as one unified whole. When the question itself was incomplete, a man would say he had not taken all the relevant data into consideration; an Alorian would say the organization did not feel (look? seem? There is no equivalent word in Basic) right.

On the other hand, the Alori were fumble-fingered when it came to the simplest compound machines. The most intelligent of them could not understand an ordinary radio transceiver, and they were astronauts entirely by rule of thumb. They had only the vaguest notion of the atom, none at all of the nucleus. General field theory was so alien to them as to be repellent.

More and more Trevelyan realized what an implacable hostility this people had—not to being within his civilization, but to the civilization itself.

"If they don't think they can stand competition," he said once, "their own philosophy ought to tell them that their way of life is unfit and should go under. But they *can* take it if they have to. They have knowledge we would pay anything for. And there wouldn't even be competition in the normal sense, not when every planetary system is or can easily be made completely self-sufficient."

"I don't know," answered Nicki. "Does it matter very much?"

He looked sharply down at her. "Yes," he said at last. "It does."

They were standing on the southern coast, atop a rocky headland. Before them lay the sea; a fresh damp wind blew in under the high sky, tossing Nicki's dark yellow hair.

"It's almost as if they were fanatics, like the militant religions of the statist tyrannies of old days on Earth," he said.

"So one way of life gives place to another," said Nicki. "Is that worth killing about?"

"It's more than that. War corrupts as much as power. When I told you once there was no reason for interstellar empire, I ignored one possibility because I didn't think it existed any more. Empires are a defense. If someone attacked for ideological reasons, the planets assaulted would need a tight organization to fight back."

"But would they—the Union—have to fight? Wouldn't it be easier to give in?"

"It's not a question of whether they would *have* to fight or not. The fact is that they would. A society tends to be self-maintaining, especially against outside pressure." Trevelyan laid a hand on his wife's shoulder. "This doesn't sound like you, darling. You used to be a regular fire-breathing dragon."

"I wasn't happy then," she said. "But this—it's so quiet and beautiful, Micah. It—" Her voice trailed off.

"Don't you want to go starjumping again?"

"Oh, yes. Someday. But why not for the Alori?"

"Because when the last comes to the last, Nicki, we're humans. Man has always been a fighter. We can take what is good for us, but it must be on our own terms."

"You've got an answer for everything, haven't you?"

He grinned. Nicki was still a spirited wench.

Later he made open inquiries of the Alori, and fitted their polite but unyielding answers into the pattern he was assembling in his own mind. They saw they universe as an organic whole in which everything *must* belong. Division was madness.

The mechanical civilization of the Union was abhorrent to them.

In spite of that, they could have left the Union alone; but its drive was outward, and they lay in its path. Their knowledge was beyond price to Man; he would want to *know*.

And contact would be deadly for them. Intercourse would modify both cultures, but the Alori could not stand change.

"I can understand it," said Nicki softly. "Suppose somebody caught me, Micah, and used one of those personality machines on me so I wouldn't love you any more. I'd know that when they were finished, it would be all right. You wouldn't mean anything to me then. But I'd fight every step of the way. I'd be gouging eyes and kicking low and screaming my throat out."

He kissed her, there in the rustling darkness of the forest.

The suggestion that the Union would be sympathetic and willing to isolate the Great Cross met with only a courteous skepticism. And Trevelyan had to admit that was justified. Such an isolation would only be a temporary expedient. Sooner or later, on one pretext or another, there would be contact. By that time, the Union would be too strong to cope with. The Alori meant to act now; they had already been acting for some time.

If they won an absolute victory, the prospect was bearable. The dreadful thing was the chance of their trying and losing. Then there would be two civilizations plunged down toward night.

And Trevelyan admitted to a prejudice in favor of his own society. His race had created something unique, and he didn't want it to go for naught.

He didn't hate the Alori; more and more he came to love them. If their achievement died, a light would go out in the universe. Their wholeness-principle was something which had never been properly formulated in Union logic. It should be possible to make integrators which would not fit isolated data together but consider a local complex—society and its needs, physical environment, known scientific laws—in its entirety. Alori science, with the knowledge it had of the nervous system, would indicate ways to build such computers.

He sat with Nicki on a small skerry to which they had swum. You could never be sure how much the forest heard.

"We have to escape," he said. "We must warn the Union of what's brewing here, and tell it that the answer to its biggest question is waiting."

"What will happen then?" Her words were low, hardly audible in the ripping wind.

"The Alori will accept a *fait accompli*," he answered. "They'll give in and make the best of it. It's not as if we came to enslave them."

"We haven't the right," she whispered.

"What are they planning for us?"

"Oh, I know—but do two wrongs make a right?"

"No," he said. "But this isn't a matter of ethics. We're going to stay free—and that's that." His gaze was challenging. "Don't you ever want to go out to the stars again? Not on a mission, not with a purpose, but because it's your own life, and you do as you choose with it?"

She lowered her eyes. A bird winged overhead. It was native to the planet, not yet brought into the symbiosis; it was hunting for something to kill.

"The world is as it is," he said. "We've got to live with that—not with the world as we think it should be."

She nodded, very slowly.

CHAPTER XIX

Where the valley opened on the sea, there was a wide beach sloping from high grass-grown dunes to the steady wash of the tides. Joachim's party found themselves a place to sit and made a crescent, facing inward toward the captain. He stood up, a burly, hairy man darkened by the sun, and fumbled a cold pipe in his hands. Slowly, he scanned the ring of faces and bronzed bodies.

There were some twenty-five Nomads present, besides himself and Trevelyan. The Coordinator sat next to the skipper, one arm about Nicki's waist. She leaned close to him and her look was unhappy. The rest were strained with expectation. Sean was here, plunged into the gloom that had been his since he arrived on Loaluani.

Joachim cleared his throat. "All right," he said. "I think we can talk freely. No big fat trees to crawl up on us and eavesdrop. This one has been sort of sounding people out, and got the impression that all of you here are pretty much of a mind. Then Micah came back and built a fire under me, so I called this picnic. I think all of you got the idea." He paused, meeting their eyes. "I want to get out of here," he said then. "Anybody want to come along?"

They stirred, and words muttered between them, an oath snapped out, fists clenched. "It's not too bad a life," went on Joachim, "but it's got its drawbacks. I reckon they're different for each of you."

"It's plain enough," said Petroff Dushan. "I want to go starjumping. This planet is—dull!"

"Yeh," growled Ortega. "Just a park. Every morning I check my skin to see if moss ain't started growing."

"Remember Hralfar?" asked Petroff Manuel wistfully. "There was snow. You could feel the cold, like the air was liquid. You wanted to run and shout, and you could hear sounds for kilometers around, it was that quiet."

"Give me a city," said Levy. "Bars and bright lights, noise, a wench and maybe a good fight. If I could sit in the Half Moon on Thunderhouse again, by the Grand Canal—!"

"A place with some spice to it," said MacTeague. "The flying city on Aesgil IV, and the war between the birds and the centauroids. Some place *new!*"

"Once we're converted to this Alori life," said Joachim, "they'll let us spacefare—for them."

"Yeah. But we never will be, and you know it," said Kogama. "And who ever heard of a Nomad traveling for somebody else? We go where we please."

"All right, all right," said Joachim. "I know how you all feel."

Thorkild Elof compressed his mouth bleakly. "We'll end up marrying within our own ship," he said. "I've already noticed boys and girls going together, because there's no one else. It's obscene."

"Are they going to make Alori of us?" cried

Ferenczi. "It's been done to the others. The old *Roamer, Tramp, Tzigani, Soldier of Fortune*—they aren't any more! Their crews aren't Nomads."

"Yeah," Joachim nodded. His face tightened. "They took *my* ship and *my* crew. They've got to be paid back for that."

"Just a minute," interposed Trevelyan. "I've explained—"

"Oh, sure, sure. Let the Cordys handle the Alori. I only want to get loose again." Joachim turned his pipe over and over in stubby fingers. "I've burned up all my tobacco and killed all my bottles. The Alori don't drink or smoke."

"It's all very well to talk," said Elof impatiently. "But we're down here and the *Peregrine* is up there. What can we do about it?"

"Things." Joachim sat down, crossing his legs. "I've gotten you people together so I could be sure you were with me." He sucked hard on the empty pipe. "Look, this one's been asking around among the Alori. They're very frank and polite, you've got to admit that. They know I don't like being here, but they also know I can't jump into space by my own legs—so they answer my questions.

"Well, the *Peregrine* is the only star ship around, for parsecs. Her boats were flown to a small island about twenty kilometers northwest of here. The Alori don't need 'em, so they're just sitting there. Some kind of guard is mounted—plants or animals or something that won't let a human land without an Alorian's say-so."

"Wait a minute!" exclaimed Petroff Dushan. "You don't mean we should snatch us an Alorian and make him—"

"Wouldn't work," said Ferenczi. "These natives just aren't afraid to die. Anyway, I don't think we could capture one without all the damned woods knowing it and bringing the whole island down on our necks."

"Please," said Joachim. "My idea isn't that crude." His gaze turned on Sean, and he went on quietly: "Ilaloa's been around a little."

The young man's face flushed. He spat.

"Now don't be so hard on the poor lass," said Joachim. "She only did her duty. This one saw her a couple of times flitting around, and has never seen anybody so woebegone. We got to talking and she kind of poured out her troubles. She loves you, Sean."

"Huh!" It was a savage grunt.

"No, no, it's a fact. She belongs with Alori, but she loves you, and knows you're about as unhappy as you can get. And I think she's been a bit—corrupted by us, too. A few drops of Nomad have gotten into her blood. Poor kid."

"Well, what am I expected to do?" snapped Sean.

"Go to her. Take her to a place where you can't be overheard and ask her to arrange our escape."

Sean shook his head unbelievingly. "She wouldn't."

"Well, there's no harm in trying, is there? Her only alternative is to take some kind of psychological treatment to get you out of her mind, and she doesn't want to do that."

"I understand," murmured Nicki.

"B-but she'll know I'm lying!" protested Sean.

"*Will* you be lying? You'll say you still care for her and want to take her away if she'll help. I think that'll be the truth."

Sean sat still for a long while. "Do you think so?"

Joachim nodded. After a moment he added slowly, "You might bear this in mind, too. If we do get away, this whole business will have worked out very well. A menace will be converted to a profitable enterprise. I think people will feel pretty kindly toward 'Lo."

"Well—I—"

"On your way, lad."

Sean stood up. He was shaking, ever so faintly. He

turned and walked stiff-legged from the gathering. Nobody looked after him.

There was silence, wind and surf and the high crying of the birds.

Ferenczi said, "It'll only be us here who make the break, eh?"

"Yeah. A bigger bunch would be risky. We can take the ship back to Nerthus. Hard work and short rations, but we can do it."

"I was thinking about the others. They'll be hostages here."

"I asked 'Lo about that, and what she said bore out my own hunch. The Alori don't do things without a purpose. They won't mistreat our people when they've already lost the game." Joachim got to his feet, stretching. "Any more questions? If not, the meeting's adjourned until we know better where we stand. Avoid the natives, all of you. They'll sense your excitement. Let's get up a snappy game of volleyball to calm us down."

Trevelyan stood with his arm about Nicki, looking over the beach. A few hundred meters off, Joachim's ball game got under way.

"What are you thinking of, Micah?"

He smiled, "You," he said. "And your people."

"What of us?"

"You know the Service doesn't like the Nomads. They're a disrupting influence on an already unstable civilization. But I'm beginning to think that a healthy culture needs such a devil."

"Are we so bad, we starjumpers?"

"No, you aren't that either. You aren't necessarily cruel to anyone. You have brought as much good as evil to the planets you visited, I think."

His lips brushed her hair, and he caught the faint wild fragrance of it. "I'll have to report back home," he said, "and you'd like to visit Sol anyway. But after that—Nicki, I'm not sure yet, but I think I'll turn Nomad myself."

"Micah!—Oh, my dearest!" She held him desperately close.

"Peregrine Trevelyan," he murmured, as his mind raced on. This was his answer. The integrators would have to give a final verdict, but he believed he had found the way. Pure Nomad? No—but with his abilities, he would eventually become a power among the ships and influence what they did. And other Coordinators would be adopted, too.

They would give Nomad life a direction and a restraint it lacked and needed, quietly, without disrupting its spirit.

Sean walked down the beach until he was alone between the forest and the sea. He climbed a dune, and stood looking out over the huge sweep of loneliness. Grass grew thin and harsh here, cutting at his bare legs. He shaded his eyes with one hand, looking at the shoreward march of grass where it blended into meadow and woods.

She came to him, walking timidly out of the forest. A few hundred meters away she paused, tensed for flight as if he had a gun. He stood watching her, his hands hanging empty. She ran.

He held her close to him, murmuring wordlessly, stroking the wind-whipped hair and the fine blue-veined skin, and let her weep herself out. Only then did he kiss her with an overwhelming gentleness. "Ilaloa," he whispered. "I love you, Ilaloa."

Her eyes were blind and wild, staring up at him. "You cannot remain here? You must go?"

"We must go," he said.

She looked away. "These are my people."

"It's not as if they would be harmed," he told her. "I have my people too. And they're yours as well."

"I could be treated. I could be healed of you."

He let her go. "Then do it," he said bitterly.

"No." her lips were parted wide, as if she couldn't

breathe. "No, that would be against life, too. I cannot."

"Is your life so much better than ours that it has to destroy us?" he asked.

"No." She laced her fingers together, twisting them around each other. "I think you are right, Sean. This is a dark and empty world—universe—we have to find what warmth we can."

She straightened and faced him. Suddenly her tones were clear. "I will help you if I am able."

CHAPTER XX

Two nights later a gale blew from the southeast, out of the sea and over the island and out to the water again. Trevelyan heard it whistle as if it were calling him. He looked at Nicki, and she was very close and dear in the warm yellow light of his home.

She smiled, and it struck him with a hideous chill that she might be killed in the escape. But she would not hear other than that she should be with him.

The tree was snug, a hearthfire in an endless hooting dark. Seated on the mossy floor, he felt the slight tremble of it under the thrust of wind. Nicki started as the door curtain was pulled aside and flapped thunderously in the blast. Joachim stood there, fully clothed, his mantle drawn hard about his bearlike form. There was a recklessness in his eyes which they had never seen before.

"All set, folks," he said. "Come on to the beach.

I'm passing the word." He nodded and was gone again; the darkness gulped him down.

Slowly, Nicki stood up. A tremble ran over her, and the blue eyes were haunted. She smiled, stroking one hand along the smooth wall of their home. Then, shaking her head so the tawny locks flew: "All right, Micah, let's go."

Rising with her, he stepped over to the shelf on which their belongings lay dustily forgotten.

"Before we go," he said, turning to Nicki, and kissing her.

When he stepped out, holding Nicki's hand, the blackness was like a rush of great waters. He heard the trees shouting; the wind snarled in their branches and they answered with a gallows groan.

They stumbled to the beach. When they came out on the shore, the wind was a blow in the face. Briefly, the ragged clouds tore open to show a half-moon flying between far pale stars.

Most of Joachim's party was already assembled, standing there waiting. The moonlight glistened frostily on the blades of knives and the heads of hunting spears, forged during the long days here.

They were standing in a damp gully where the river crossed the strand. A boat lay there, brought down from the woods by Ilaloa. Trevelyan reached out and touched the hull with a feeling of awe.

The boat was long and narrow, with a single mast— fore-and-aft sail and a jib, dark green—and a rudder and a small cabin. But she was a living tree, fed by sea minerals and earth laid in the bottom.

He saw Ilaloa, seated near the tiller. She was holding Sean close to her, as if she were already drowning. "Everybody's here, I reckon." Joachim's voice was almost lost in the wind. "We'd better get going. I'm not so sure the Alori haven't some notion of this caper."

The boat had to be taken past the surf. Trevelyan splashed in the shallow river between grunting, cursing Nomads he could barely see. The hull was cold and slippery under his hands.

He felt the keel grate on a sandbar at the river mouth. Now—heave! Over the bar and into the surf! It rose swiftly as he waded out. The offshore wind flattened it, but he felt a vicious undertow yank at his legs.

"Cram 'er through!" roared Joachim. "Cram 'er through!"

Trevelyan hurled his muscles against the solidity of hull. His feet groped for a hold, lost it; he clung to the gunwale and then a giant's hand scooped him up. Water exploded over his head. A million thunders banged in his skull. They were in the real surf now!

The boat staggered. Trevelyan held on with fingers that seemed ready to rip from their sockets. A buffet sent him choking away, lungs aflame. He gasped, kicking with his feet, driving the boat outward.

She lay in pitching sea. A hand caught Trevelyan's hair, and the swift bright pain of it stabbed his mind back into him. He splashed against the heaving gunwale, gripped the rail, and pulled himself over. Turning, he stooped to help the next one.

The moon broke out again and he looked on an immensity of tumbled waters. To windward the land was a bulking shadow, black against moon-limned clouds. Inboard was a jammed mass of faces. He could barely hear the voices over the screeching wind and thunderous waves. Joachim stood upright, legs planted far apart, stooped over as he counted.

"One missing." He rose, peering into the dark swirl over the side. "MacTeague Alan gone. He was a good lad."

Slowly, he turned to face Ilaloa at the tiller. His hand lifted and swung down again. She nodded, a fey figure under the moon, and spoke to Sean. He and a couple of others fought the sails up.

The boat leaped! Her mast, which had been swinging crazily against the sky, heeled over so that Trevelyan thought she must capsize. The boom reached far out, almost at right angles to the lean hull, and the living ropes hummed. Water slanted icy-white from the bows, the wake coiled in shattered flame behind her, and she ran!

Trevelyan gasped, shaking his drenched head with wonder. "We made it," he breathed. He didn't quite dare believe it yet. "We made it."

Nicki hugged him, wordlessly. They crawled over their fellows, into the bows where they could see ahead. Spindrift stung their faces, but they looked over the sea and were glad.

The clouds were breaking up and the halfmoon, as big as Luna at the full, was dazzlingly brilliant. But it was straight ahead, to the northwest, that Trevelyan and Nicki stared. There lay the boats and the way home.

Joachim crept up to the bows, saw the two sitting there, and smiled. Turning, he made his way back sternward, checking on his people. No casualties so far, except poor Alan. Joachim wondered how he was going to tell it to the boy's father.

When he came to the stern, he saw Sean and Ilaloa helping each other steer. It was hard to figure how the girl kept her bearings without a compass, but she was doing it. The shore was already lost to sight; they were walled in ringing, sundering darkness. The tiller threshed, fighting like a live animal. Sean and Ilaloa were on either side of it, shoulder against shoulder, hands interlocked on the rod. The man had a strained look, but the captain had seldom seen such inward happiness.

He approached closer, hanging onto the rail with one hand and bending near so they could hear him call. "How's it going?" The wind yelled around his words.

"Pretty good," answered Sean. "We should raise the island soon. We could see it now if this were daylight."

Joachim leaned on the pitching bulwark, and looked own the length of the vessel. Strange that she wasn't shipping water—no, the water came inboard and was soaked up, blotted away; a fine rain sprang from the boat's sides, back down into the sea. She did her own bailing, too.

He looked over the sea as if he stood on a mountain. Overhead was a sky of flickering candle-stars and cloud streamers; under and around him the swooping, trampling, shouting sea, everywhere the wind. It might have been across light-years that he saw the hazy form of the other boat.

He gripped Ilaloa's shoulder so that she cried out. Slowly, he pointed, and she and Sean followed the line of his arm.

She stood for a bare second, not moving. He had seen a man once with a bullet in his heart, not yet aware that he was dead, standing just that way.

Joachim leaned over to shout in Ilaloa's ear: "Would anyone else be sailing on a night like this?"

She shook her head.

"Well," he said between his teeth, "hang on to your heads, lads, we're going to make a run for it."

As they mounted another crest, he saw the island. It was hard to gauge distances, but that sheer loom of rock couldn't be far now. Peering into the blast, he made out the other vessel. It closed the gap rapidly, quartering in from portside stern. No windjammer, this; the Alori had sent a real longboat after them. It was big and high stemmed, no mast, and it was drawn by something that swam. He could only see the great white curve of a back rising from the waves, the thresh of its tail and now and again a monster fluke.

Canst thou draw out Leviathan with a hook? . . . Will he make a covenant with thee?

Ilaloa said something to Sean, who nodded and gestured to Joachim. A few rags of words came to the captain's ears: "—take rudder—reef—" he came around and closed hands on the kicking bar. Sean groped to the boom lines. The island was very close now, standing in a white flame of surf. They had to go around it, no doubt, tack—in this weather?

The sail slatted and banged, and the boat yawed, coming around on another tack. It was clumsy handling—Ilaloa could have done better, but she had inexperienced help. They lost most of their forward speed. The Alori vessel drew closer; it might only be a few hundred meters away now. Joachim saw the tall forms of her crew standing in the bows. He had a notion one of them was Esperero, but he couldn't be sure.

The island was a mountain before them. Joachim saw the surf that geysered under its cliffs and felt his heart stumble. The Alori boat pulled in, almost even with them now, though a good fifty meters lay between. Joachim looked at the sea-beast's back and the tail that ripped the water.

No—not yet, by heaven! The sailboat sprang forward. Surf was just ahead of her now; he felt her lurch with its shock. A wave rushed in over the bow, thundering along the length of the hull, and then the keel slammed against a reef.

Ilaloa pointed wildly over the side. *Jump! Jump!* He stared for a dumb instant. The living sail tore across, and rigging snapped like rotten twine. He eased himself overboard.

There was bottom a meter down. This must be shallows. And, he thought with sudden glee, the sea monster couldn't swim in here!

Trevelyan and Nicki joined him, standing in water that clawed at them and broke over their heads. A

woman fell, going under. Trevelyan grasped her arms,
helping her. Nicki took her by the dress, and they
splashed slowly to shore.

Ilaloa stood there, Sean beside her, at the head of
a trail winding up the cliff face. She gestured back
those who would have climbed it. The crew stood
waiting, jammed together.

Trevelyan looked past the smoking surf, out to sea.
The Alorian boat was drawing up alongside the reef,
where it shelved abruptly off. They were here and
the spacecraft only meters away . . .

He caught his emotions. Ilaloa hadn't given up yet,
at least. And here came Joachim, splashing and grunting out of the ocean—that meant everybody was off
the boat.

He saw that the Nomads were moving, and fell into
their shadowy line. Nicki, behind him, held tight to
his belt. Ilaloa must be taking them up now, past the
island's guardians. But the Alori—

He looked down, but it was into a well of blackness. The Alori would be after them, yes—but in this
wind, their gases and probably their stinging insects
were useless. It would be hand-to-hand, down there
at the end of the line, as Joachim and a few others
fought a savage rear-guard action. Trevelyan cursed,
wanting to go down and help, but the trail was too
narrow, too slippery.

They came up on the heights of the island. It was
overgrown with brush and wind-gnarled trees, vague
in the shaking dark. But he saw thorns on flexible
vines, coiled about the trunks, and thought he glimpsed
eyes. He didn't know just what kind of watchers they
were, but Ilaloa had commanded them to stay their
attack.

Running, slipping on wet rock and crashing into
half-seen boughs, he went with the Nomads through
that abatis of woods. It was a short, gasping dash, and
at its end the trees opened and he saw the boats.

They stood clustered as if ready to leap, spearheads poised at infinity, moonlight icy-gray on their sides. Sean was already at one of them, groping after the switch in the landing braces. He yanked it down. Under the screech of wind, Trevelyan heard the motor start up, whining. The airlock opened and the gangway ladder came down and it was nightmarishly slow.

Swinging about, Trevelyan saw the last of the Nomads burst into the clearing, Joachim bringing up the rear. They ran for the ladder as if all hell were at their heels. One by one swiftly but with some degree of order, they scampered up into the boat. He sent Sean, Ilaloa and Nicki up, and waited.

The Alori spilled out into the meadow, running hard. Joachim motioned Trevelyan up, then followed him, facing backwards. Esperero—he recognized that handsome face now—climbed in pursuit, his fellows behind him.

The captain paused near the airlock, lifting one booted foot. He had to shout to be heard, but there was an immense calm in him: "Any closer, lad, and you get your teeth bashed in."

Esperero paused. There was a sudden strangeness in the answer—pity? sorrow? "Why do you flee thus? We would not harm you. We would be your friends."

"That," said Joachim, "is just the trouble, I think."

Esperero nodded, slowly. A crooked grin twisted his face. "You have a gesture, you humans," he said. "May I shake your hand?"

"Hm?" Joachim braced himself. It might be a trick, only it was hard to see what could be gained by capturing him alone. "All right. Sure." Joachim reached down. Esperero's hand was small and supple, with a warm strength, in his own clasp.

"Goodbye, my friend," said the Alorian.

He released Joachim and descended the ladder. The Nomad stared after him, then shrugged and went on up. Trevelyan pushed a button and the ladder was drawn in as the outer door whined shut. The wind's noise dimmed and silence came down like a falling moon. He locked the motor; the boat could only be opened from the inside now.

Ilaloa was standing there, too, wet and cold in the bleak white light. Her eyes were wide with a reborn fear. "Quickly," she said. "Be off, fast. There are other boats, and they can be flown too. And they have guns!"

Joachim sprang to the nearest viewscreen, but he would see only darkness and flying clouds. He threw the intercom switch. "Emergency stations! Battle stations! And take off!"

It wasn't a normally organized crew, but the men all had some training. Boots clanged on metal as they ran for action posts. There were guns and missile tubes in the gliding fins and just above the gravity drive cones, and one heavy cannon in the nose. Joachim stayed at the centrally located airlock; Trevelyan whirled and went up the gravity shaft to the bows. Ilaloa didn't follow him, though Sean was pilot. She remained with the captain, drawing herself into a corner as if she wanted to be invisible.

Trevelyan glimpsed Nicki in one of the bunk-rooms as he fell upward, and hailed her. She answered with a wave. She was helping care for one of the women, hurt in the shipwreck land-fall. Emerging in the bow chamber, he saw Sean in the pilot chair, looking out the forward viewscreen as his fingers danced across studs and switches. The Nomad's tousled hair turned with laughter toward him. "Good man, Micah! Can you handle one of those big friends?"

"Yes, sure. But get us off the ground, Sean!" Trevelyan jumped into the gun-tender's seat. The Long John was automatically loaded and fired, but it took two men to direct the robots. Petroff Dushan was the other one; his dripping, flame-colored beard brushed the gleaming control panel. Kogama Iwao was in the co-pilot's chair, and Ferenczi sat in the background.

"I'll get her off in good time," Sean said.

It was strange, thought Trevelyan, that utter happiness should make a man so reckless of death.

The boat trembled. Sean took her up so smoothly that for an instant Trevelyan didn't realize they were headed skyward. Skyward, outward, starward—the words were a song within him.

They didn't have figures for the *Peregrine's* orbit, but she wouldn't be hard to find and board. And after that—

"They're firing, Sean," said Kogama.

Sean looked at the detector dials. The craft lurched a bit from a near miss, exploded her own counterfire. "Yeah," he said. "And—oh, oh!" He spoke into the intercom. "Pilot to captain. They're taking another of the boats after us. Neutrino emission."

"Just let me focus my screen," answered Joachim. "Uh-huh. I see it now. Brethren, this is not a good thing."

Sean reached out and worked the dials of his own auxiliary screen until it showed the ground below. That was a huge circle, falling away as they climbed for heaven. The moonlight picked out steel below them, rising.

"Can we give 'em the slip?" asked Ferenczi.

"No," said Sean. "They're coming too fast. We'd better swing around so we can use our heavy stuff."

Joachim's voice rattled over the intercom: "Captain to crew. Captain to crew. Looks like a fight. Strap in."

The boat didn't have internal gravity fields, except for the shaft. Trevelyan buckled the webbing about himself and looked out into a night of rushing wind. His hands moved along the polished deadlines of the Long John's controls. *I had hoped we could get away without this,* he thought.

His head swooped as Sean brought the boat around. They slanted over the planet's surface, seeking to use the advantage of height. The other boat climbed steeply toward them. Trevelyan saw flame as the intercepted shells blew up. Once a shrapnel burst struck the hull near the bows, and it rang like a great gong.

"His piloting stinks," said Sean. "This'll be easy."

"Do we have to do it?" Surprisingly, it was Ferenczi who said that. "Can't we just outrun him?"

"And be gunned down from behind? If that lunatic doesn't know when he's beaten, he'll have to be shown." The hardness died in Sean's voice and he bit his lip. "But I hate to do this!"

Esperero, thought Trevelyan grayly, *is my friend.* For a moment the philosophy of a lifetime buckled. *How long will we have to accept the world as it is? How long will we have to stand by with empty hands and see injustice done?*

The Nomad boat dived close, swooping on her enemy like a hawk. The Alorian pilot tried to evade them, swerving clumsily aside. Sean passed within meters of the other, and everything his boat had cut loose as he rushed by. Fire lanced over the sky and the Alorian boat went down in a hot rain of metal.

It wasn't right! They shouldn't have died that way!

The Nomads turned upward again; Trevelyan saw that they had crossed the edge of night. The sun was low in the east, shadows long across a forest world that glittered with dew.

"We're away." Suddenly Sean threw back his head and laughed. "We're away and free again!"

Trevelyan heard a shout over the intercom— Joachim's bull roar, broken in the middle. After it came a great howling of wind.

"What the hell—?" Sean bent over his mike. "What's wrong, Skipper?"

The wind hooted. There was a cold draft up the gravity tube. "I'll go," said Trevelyan. His voice seemed as if it came from outside himself. "I'll go find out what it is."

Trevelyan threw off the safety webbing, and ran across the deck, two steps to the shaft and then down the beam like a dead leaf falling in England's October. He heard Joachim over the loudspeakers: "It's all right. Just a little accident. Captain to crew, remain at battle posts."

Trevelyan emerged in the airlock vestibule. The outer door was open to a sky that seemed infinitely blue. Joachim stood by the chamber with his clothes whipping about a stooped form. The battered homely face turned to him, fighting to keep itself steady. Joachim was crying. He didn't know how; he wept so heavily and awkwardly that it was as if it would shake his body apart. "How'll I tell him, Micah? How'll I tell the lad?"

"She jumped?"

"I was busy at the screen, watching. I saw the boat blow up, and stood there for a minute after. Then I hard the airlock motor start. The door was open a little bit, and Ilaloa stood there. I ran to grab her, but the door opened just enough more for her to go out."

Joachim shook his head. "But how am I going to tell Sean?"

Trevelyan didn't answer. He thought of Ilaloa, falling through the sky down to her forest, and wondered what she had been thinking of in that time. He thumbed the switch, and the door closed.

Trevelyan Micah straightened himself and laid a hand on Joachim's shoulder. "It's all right," he said. "There's more to Sean than you know. But let's not tell him just yet."

The sky darkened around them and the stars came forth.